# *The Best* Victorian Ghost Stories

———

— ANNOTATED AND ILLUSTRATED —
*Tales of Murder, Mystery,*
*Horror and Hauntings*

———

*Edited, Annotated, and Illustrated By*

M. GRANT KELLERMEYER, M.A.

◌

— SECOND EDITION –

EXPAND YOUR SUPERNATURAL FICTION
COLLECTION
*By Acquiring These*
— ANNOTATED AND ILLUSTRATED EDITIONS —

WWW.OLDSTYLETALES.COM

## WEIRD FICTION/HORROR BY:
Algernon Blackwood
Robert W. Chambers
F. Marion Crawford
William Hope Hodgson
Arthur Machen
Guy de Maupassant
Fitz-James O'Brien
Edgar Allan Poe
Ambrose Bierce
H. G. Wells

## CLASSIC GHOST STORIES BY:
Charles Dickens
Sir Arthur Conan Doyle
W. W. Jacobs
Henry James
J. Sheridan Le Fanu
E. Nesbit
Robert Louis Stevenson
Bram Stoker
E. T. A. Hoffmann
Washington Irving

## CLASSIC GOTHIC NOVELS:
Dracula
Frankenstein
The Phantom of the Opera
Dr. Jekyll and Mr. Hyde
The Turn of the Screw
The Invisible Man
The Picture of Dorian Gray

## FIRESIDE HORROR SERIES:
Ghost Stories for Christmas Eve
Victorian Ghost Stories
Supernatural Cats
Demons and the Devil
Mummies and Curses
Pirates and Ghost Ships
Werewolves

## OLDSTYLE TALES

*This edition published 2013 by*
OLDSTYLE TALES PRESS
2424 N. Anthony Blvd
Fort Wayne, Indiana
46805–3604

*For more information, or to request permission
to reprint selections or illustrations from
this book, write to the Editor at*
oldstyletales@gmail.com

NOTES, INTRODUCTIONS, AND ILLUSTRATIONS
COPYRIGHT © 2013 BY MICHAEL GRANT KELLERMEYER

Readers who are interested in further titles from
Oldstyle Tales Press are invited to visit our website at

— WWW.OLDSTYLETALES.COM —

# — TABLE *of* CONTENTS —

# CONCERNING WHAT
## YOU ARE ABOUT TO READ

IF YOU DECIDE TO READ THIS BOOK, you will be confronted with a selection of stories that do not necessarily match the average Victorian ghost story: many of these are darker, more psychologically-invigorated, cynical, and disturbing than the typical Victorian ghost tale. They are, in fact, quite atypical and quite exquisite compared with the more popular sentimental, moralistic fare that graced Christmas and Hallow-mass periodicals of the mid to late nineteenth century. "Schalken the Painter" details the rapacious demon buying the soul of a young woman from her uncle. "The Signal-Man" was written after Charles Dickens was nearly killed in a train crash that took dozens of lives and left him shocked and disturbed until his death soon after. The chilling horrors of "The Kit-Bag," "Lost Hearts," and "The Top Attic" all foretell the gruesome, neo-Gothic, weird horror of H.P. Lovecraft's Cthulhu mythos, with their innocent protagonists and demonical antagonists – hardly "A Christmas Carol." "Man-Sized in Marble" and the "Mystery of the Semi-Detached" – both by Edith Nesbit – are cynical and haunting stories of good people receiving unwarranted horrors, "The Red Room" is a morose study in the shapeless psychology of terror, and "Some Strange Disturbances" is a clear precursor to more popular but perhaps less nuanced stories by H.P. Lovecraft ("The Rats in the Walls") and Bram Stoker ("The Judge's House"). "The Old Nurse's Story" is a grimly Gothic narrative of one child being lured to death by the ghost of another, while "Nothing But the Truth" and "Behold, it was a Dream!" – Rhoda Broughton at her best – are sophisticated far beyond their decade (the 1870s) in their sense of psychological realism and genuine horror. Having read dozens upon dozens of anthologized supernatural tales from this era, I have selected these few to represent the exemplar (rather than the standard) of Victorian ghost fiction.

   A word or two on what you will read: the Victorian era spans Queen Victoria's reign of 1837 to 1901. I extend beyond that, justifiably, to track the progress of the Gothic short story from the sinking of HMS *Birkenhead* (the origin of "women and children first" – a moment of genuine nobility of spirit) to the sinking of RMS *Titanic* (where the selfsame creed was proven deadly and ineffectual, and the ideals of the Victorians foundered), spanning 1852-1912. I am beginning in the midst of Victoria's reign and leaving off at the culmination of the Edwardian period where the Victorian story saw a sudden reformation after the moral uncertainty caused by the mythic loss of *Titanic* and the savagery of the First World War and the Spanish Flu. In a later edition I will specifically examine the ghost fiction of the Long Edwardian Era (1895 – 1921), but I reap from several technically Edwardian stories to show the depths of psychological complexity and philosophical cynicism that the gothic story developed to from the bawdy machismo and moral certainty of 1852.

## WHAT YOU SHOULD KNOW
## BEFORE READING THESE STORIES

THE VICTORIAN AGE WAS AN EPOCH of severe social and industrial transition for the countries of Europe and their colonial objectives. The United Kingdom – the country whose literary stockpiles are the focus of this collection – is perhaps best remembered during this stage of human events
(which bore its monarch's name) for ushering in the industrial revolution, for its jingoistic and often bloody foreign policies, and for its stringent observance of moral, sexual, and gender-related self-regulations. Perhaps it is because of this unshakable exterior of personal restriction and national hubris that the generations succeeding the Victorians have been most enraptured with the diseased, fungal underbelly of their glorious society. Jack the Ripper's gruesome spree in the whore-impregnated streets of East London, the moral ineptitude of grime-lacquered children being exploited for cheap and replaceable labor in Dickensian mill towns and mine shafts, and the slew of rumored sexual indulgences haunting the Royal family and the upper echelons of British society (from the Oscar Wilde trial to Cleveland Street scandal) are the events which most stringently retain the public interest and grace the screens of Hollywood and household

televisions with lurid embellishments and milquetoast understatements alike.

The Victorian gothic has been its longest-lasting legacy in print as well; Sherlock Holmes' fog-bloated London, Jane Eyre's nocturnal terrors, Scrooge's ghoulish encounters, and the mystique of Heathcliffe's diabolical parentage represent a larger portion of our collective twenty-first century imagination than do the bourgeois sentimentality in which the era sought its legacy. Today Conan Doyle is further renowned than Tennyson, and Jack the Ripper is astronomically more well-known than General Gordon or Dr. Livingston. In our collective unconscious the Victorian era is a whitewashed tomb; its well-manicured exterior cloaks a vault of noxious corpses and bloated secrets straining against a yielding membrane of delusion.

ဆ

The Victorian era saw an explosion in innovation not only for steel and rifling, but also in the short ghost story. An anthology covering the supernatural literature of the Georgian era (1714 – 1830) would yield up voluminous (literally) gothic novels with bleeding statues, animated suits of armor, and owl-infested graveyards – the camp that fuelled the B horror movies of the 1960s with their campy material. On a smaller scale, only existential essays and poems (Thomas Gray's churchyard "Elegy" comes most to mind), but nary a short anthologizable story. The genre had not yet seen its dawning day. But it soon came with the help of one crossbreed of elements: steam. With steam power came the advent of river cutters and locomotives, and with these (and the subsequent suburbanization of the new capitalist aristocracy) came the new dawn of the work commute. Commuters and train-travelers needed entertainment to make the time go by, but the time went by much too quickly to read Mr Dickens' latest novel in bulk. Periodicals rapidly capitalized from the need printing either short stories for a forty minute digestion, or novels in serial form to be returned to each week in a much more manageable format.

Almost as soon as the short story arrived in the laps of middle-classed men across the European world, the horror story arrived with it. Washington Irving's "The Spectre Bridegroom," "Rip Van

10

Winkle," and "The Legend of Sleepy Hollow" ushered in a venue for such gloom-infatuated minds as Poe and Hawthorne to ignite their readership with a taste for the morbid and macabre. In the United Kingdom, where emotion was reserved for the imperial battlefields and sexuality denied in the obviously fetishized British ideal of womanhood, ghost stories provided an outlet whereby the unspeakable could be spoken, the unbelievable believed, and the unredeemable redeemed. Ghost stories subverted societal conventions by the very nature of their supernatural unconventionality: villains who would in the real world go unchallenged (e.g. Scrooge) – and heroes – who would in the real world go unnoticed (e.g. Hester Prynne) – are given their just desserts through otherworldly intervention.

ℭ

Typical practitioners of the ghost story were often ineffectual writers whose sappy moral parables and cliché-riddled, agonizingly predictable plots have faded forever into history – and rightfully so. It has long been a literary truism that the hardest story to write is a good ghost story, and the Gothic drudgery that populated Victorian magazines proved this belief with ridiculous stories that could cause the modern reader to audibly groan. But there were masters of the craft. J. Sheridan Le Fanu was in the first rank, a writer whose grasp of irony, visceral horror, and philosophical tact allowed him to craft the century's best supernatural tales, ripe with nuance and genuine horror – both psychological and physical. His niece Rhoda Broughton inherited his taste for the macabre, and was fostered by the era's most famous writer of English ghost stories, Charles Dickens, who – though a splendid hand at the weird and chilling – ranks behind Le Fanu and his peers, Algernon Blackwood, M. R. James, and E. Nesbit, all of whom ushered the Edwardian ghost story into existence with their harsh spiritual philosophies and thrilling grasp of dramatic tension and mental terror. Nearly all popular authors of the era contributed to the genre, which the British public adored and British publishers craved. Dickens, Arthur Conan Doyle, H.G. Wells, Rudyard Kipling, Thomas Hardy, Oscar Wilde, and Robert Louis Stevenson – all of whom are more remembered for their literary fiction, adventure, dramas, science fiction, or detective fiction – continue to be admired by supernaturalists for their ghost stories and weird fiction. While some writers were specialists in speculative and supernatural literature (such as Le Fanu, Stoker, and M. R. James, a writer need not be a connoisseur to get a ghost story published, and an established author had very little trouble marketing a tale that bore their name and the titillating subtitle, "A Ghost Story."

While men like James and Le Fanu unquestionably excelled at their crafts, the ghost story was largely a female craft, and many of the genre's most gifted masters were in fact mistresses: Mrs Oliphant, Mrs Henry Wood, Mary E. Braddon, Broughton, Mrs Gaskell, Mary Louisa Molesworth, Mrs J.H. Riddell, Amelia B. Edwards, and Nesbit dominated the literature (E.F. Bleiler counts Riddell, Broughton, and Edwards as the only Victorians to threaten Le Fanu's supremacy – while I would count half-a-dozen others in that group, I certainly agree with his high opinion of their literary prowess). The best stories of these women convey a high level of emotional and psychological depth, often grounded in real-life anxieties that fail to resound quite so noticeably in the works of their male counterparts. Ghost stories were subversive by nature, allowing hidden realities to manifest in the face of public denial and avoidance, and women readily swarmed to the genre as a means of expressing unpopular anxieties about class, gender, sex, patriarchy, nationalism, religion, philosophy, society, war, crime, suicide, morality, and family life. American women of the age shared their British sisters' desire to address these issues which – in literary fiction – would have created a scandal (think *Lady Audley's Secret* or *The Awakening*), but were accepted as socially palatable when presented as supernatural: Edith Wharton (I would argue) tackled abortion, adultery, and spousal abuse in "The Lady's Maid's Bell," Mary E. Wilkins Freeman addressed dysfunctional families in "The Shadows on the Wall," and Charlotte Perkins Gilman's one-hit-wonder, "The Yellow Wallpaper" is a psychological horror story of the first degree that stands alongside *The Awakening* and *Pygmalion* as a staple of feminist literature. Women often wrote to support their families, or themselves, and female supernatural fiction is redolent with themes of social anxiety, financial insecurity, abuse of power by authority figures, and a mistrust of the sacred cows of Victorian society.

While not included in this volume, I would earnestly recommend to you the works of **Mrs Henry Wood** ("Reality or Delusion?"), **Mrs J.H. Riddell** ("A Terrible Vengeance," "Nut Bush Farm"), and **Mary Louisa Molesworth** ("The Story of a Rippling Train"). Amongst the male writers whom we have not represented, I would turn your attention to **Wilkie Collins** ("A Terribly Strange Bed," "The Haunted Hotel," " Miss Jeromette and the Clergyman"), **Barry Pain** ("The Four-Fingered Hand"), and **Bernard Capes** ("An Eddy on the Floor," "The Thing in the Forest"). Bram Stoker, Rudyard Kipling, and R.L. Stevenson should, of course, also be considered.

℘

Michael Cox and R.A. Gilbert tackle the nature of the Victorian ghost in their Oxford anthology; unlike the fleeting and aimless apparitions that (supposed) eyewitnesses to spirit manifestations report, the phantoms "of
Victorian fiction ... hardly ever lacked motivation ... they revealed secrets, avenged wrongs, reenacted ancient tragedies, in some cases proffered help and comfort to the living, or bore witness to the workings of divine providence. Most disquieting of all, they could pursue blameless living victims with a relentless and unfathomable malignity" (xv-xvi). Ghost stories were particularly useful to an age of transition where the feudal past still existed in the landscape and memories of the industrial present.

It was an era where progress was so visceral but the popular sense was that despite their steam, rails, telegraphs, and couture – in spite of all their supposed advancement – the violence and injustice of agrarian Britain still heated their blood and lingered threateningly in the air around them like a watchful miasma. They were not so far removed from days of torture, rape, regicides, and massacres – a silent understanding which would be excited into public acknowledgment when the Ripper flourished in London's gin-sopped red light district. Ghost stories offered an entertaining medium to address the inexpugnable stains of previous generations by acknowledging the omnipresence of the past and by paying homage to its power over the present: "In personal terms, ghosts were obvious, though still potent,

13

images of the lost past – past sins, past promises, past attachments, past regrets – and could be used to confront, and exorcise, the demons of guilt and fear" (viii). And the ghosts of the Victorians' past have indeed voyaged beyond their confines into the future of the twenty-first century.

The gothic tale has proved one of the most memorable and endurable from the canon of Victorian literature. *Jane Eyre, Wuthering Heights, A Christmas Carol, Dracula, Dr. Jekyll and Mr. Hyde, The Hound of the Baskervilles,* and *The Picture of Dorian Gray* have far exceeded the works of contemporary favorites William Makepeace Thackeray, William Ernest Henley, and Rudyard Kipling in enduring popularity. They feed a realization in our own society 150 years later that civilization is for some a delusion and for some a pretense; regardless of how we manage or restrict our passions and impulses, fervor with bubble up and under the lid. This may present itself in the despairing paroxysm of fear, the brutal outburst of murder, or the sublime confection of moving art. Collected here for your enjoyment and meditation are samplings of all three.

*M. Grant Kellermeyer*
*Madison, Indiana, Christmas Eve 2013*

*WRITING on Christmastime, a season that he (partnering with Washington Irving and Prince Albert) largely revitalized in the English-speaking world, Charles Dickens apportioned roughly a third of his Yuletide essay, "The Christmas Tree," to a survey of English ghost lore, tropes, summaries, and exemplars. While the literary ghost story is the only remnant of Victorian supernatural fiction that this volume concerns itself with, we happily open the scene with a glimpse into the parlor of a typical middle-classed parlor on a night in November or December. The fire is red and low, and the company has decided to spend the night rather than risk the nocturnal drive through the blizzard. While wassail and Indian tea are passed around, a favorite uncle settles into his favorite wingback chair. He lights his pipe with a cinder from the hearth, and while the children pool at his feet and the adults settle into the shadows, you will hear some of these tales issue from his mustachioed lips...*

---

CHRISTMAS GHOST STORIES
EXCERPTED *from the* ESSAY "THE CHRISTMAS TREE"
{1850}
*Charles Dickens*

THERE IS PROBABLY A SMELL OF ROASTED CHESTNUTS and other good comfortable things all the time, for we are telling Winter Stories — Ghost Stories, or more shame for us — round the Christmas fire; and we have never stirred, except to draw a little nearer to it. But, no matter for that. We came to the house, and it is an old house, full of great chimneys where wood is burnt on ancient dogs upon the hearth, and grim portraits (some of them with grim legends, too) lower distrustfully from the oaken panels of the walls. We are a middle-aged nobleman, and we make a generous supper with our host and hostess and their guests — it being Christmas-time, and the old house full of company — and then we go to bed. Our room is a very old room. It is hung with tapestry. We don't like the portrait of a cavalier in green, over the fireplace. There are great black beams in the ceiling, and there is a great black bedstead, supported at the foot by two great black figures, who

15

seem to have come off a couple of tombs in the old baronial[1] church in the park[2], for our particular accommodation. But, we are not a superstitious nobleman, and we don't mind. Well! we dismiss our servant, lock the door, and sit before the fire in our dressing-gown, musing about a great many things. At length we go to bed. Well! we can't sleep. We toss and tumble, and can't sleep. The embers on the hearth burn fitfully and make the room look ghostly. We can't help peeping out over the counterpane, at the two black figures and the cavalier[3] — that wicked- looking cavalier — in green. In the flickering light they seem to advance and retire: which, though we are not by any means a superstitious nobleman, is not agreeable. Well! we get nervous — more and more nervous. We say "This is very foolish, but we can't stand this; we'll pretend to be ill, and knock up[4] somebody." Well! we are just going to do it, when the locked door opens, and there comes in a young woman, deadly pale, and with long fair hair, who glides to the fire, and sits down in the chair we have left there, wringing her hands. Then, we notice that her clothes are wet. Our tongue cleaves to the roof of our mouth, and we can't speak; but, we observe her accurately. Her clothes are wet; her long hair is dabbled with moist mud; she is dressed in the fashion of two hundred years ago; and she has at her girdle a bunch of rusty keys. Well! there she sits, and we can't even faint, we are in such a state about it.   Presently she gets up, and tries all the locks in the room with the rusty keys, which won't fit one of them; then, she fixes her eyes on the portrait of the cavalier in green, and says, in a low, terrible voice, "The stags know it!"   After that, she wrings her hands again, passes the bedside, and goes out at the door. We hurry on our dressing-gown, seize our pistols (we always travel with pistols), and are following, when we find the door locked. We turn the key, look out

---

[1] Being a church on the grounds of a baronet's lands or estate
[2] Sprawling rural territory used for hunting and riding by the proprietor
[3] A member of the aristocracy who sided with King Charles I during the English Civil War. While romanticized by various generations of Englishmen – especially the Victorians – the cavaliers were associated with debauchery, moral decay, and aristocratic excess by the  working and middle classes who tended to have Parliamentarian sympathies
[4] Waken – literally knock on a sleeping chamber door

into the dark gallery; no one there. We wander away, and try to find our servant. Can't be done. We pace the gallery till daybreak; then return to our deserted room, fall asleep, and are awakened by our servant (nothing ever haunts him) and the shining sun. Well! we make a wretched breakfast, and all the company say we look queer. After breakfast, we go over the house with our host, and then we take him to the portrait of the cavalier in green, and then it all comes out. He was false to a young housekeeper once attached to that family, and famous for her beauty, who drowned herself in a pond, and whose body was discovered, after a long time, because the stags refused to drink of the water. Since which, it has been whispered that she traverses the house at midnight (but goes especially to that room where the cavalier in green was wont to sleep), trying the old locks with the rusty keys. Well! we tell our host of what we have seen, and a shade comes over his features, and he begs it may be hushed up; and so it is. But, it's all true; and we said so, before we died (we are dead now) to many responsible people.

There is no end to the old houses, with resounding galleries, and dismal state-bedchambers, and haunted wings shut up for many years, through which we may ramble, with an agreeable creeping[1] up our back, and encounter any number of ghosts, but (it is worthy of remark perhaps) reducible to a very few general types and classes; for, ghosts have little originality, and "walk" in a beaten track. Thus, it comes to pass, that a certain room in a certain old hall, where a certain bad lord, baronet, knight, or gentleman, shot himself, has certain planks in the floor from which the blood WILL NOT be taken out. You may scrape and scrape, as the present owner has done, or plane and plane, as his father did, or scrub and scrub, as his grandfather did, or burn and burn with strong acids, as his great- grandfather did, but, there the blood will still be — no redder and no paler — no more and no less — always just the same. Thus, in such another house there is a haunted door, that never will keep open; or another door that never will keep shut, or a haunted sound of a spinning-wheel, or a hammer, or a footstep, or a

---

[1] As M. R. James termed it, "a pleasing terror" – that shiver of delight that continues to proliferate the consumption of horror stories and horror movies

cry, or a sigh, or a horse's tramp, or the rattling of a chain. Or else, there is a turret-clock, which, at the midnight hour, strikes thirteen when the head of the family is going to die; or a shadowy, immovable black carriage which at such a time is always seen by somebody, waiting near the great gates in the stable-yard. Or thus, it came to pass how Lady Mary went to pay a visit at a large wild house in the Scottish Highlands, and, being fatigued with her long journey, retired to bed early, and innocently said, next morning, at the breakfast-table, "How odd, to have so late a party last night, in this remote place, and not to tell me of it, before I went to bed!" Then, every one asked Lady Mary what she meant? Then, Lady Mary replied, "Why, all night long, the carriages were driving round and round the terrace, underneath my window[1]!" Then, the owner of the house turned pale, and so did his Lady, and Charles Macdoodle of Macdoodle signed to Lady Mary to say no more, and every one was silent. After breakfast, Charles Macdoodle told Lady Mary that it was a tradition in the family that those rumbling carriages on the terrace betokened death. And so it proved, for, two months afterwards, the Lady of the mansion died. And Lady Mary, who was a Maid of Honour at Court, often told this story to the old Queen Charlotte[2]; by this token that the old King always said, "Eh, eh? What, what? Ghosts, ghosts? No such thing, no such thing!" And never left off saying so, until he went to bed.

Or, a friend of somebody's whom most of us know, when he was a young man at college, had a particular friend, with whom he made the compact that, if it were possible for the Spirit to return to this earth after its separation from the body, he of the twain who first died, should reappear to the other. In course of time, this compact was forgotten by our friend; the two young men having progressed in life, and taken diverging paths that were wide asunder. But, one night, many years afterwards, our friend being in the North of England, and staying for the night in an inn, on the Yorkshire Moors, happened to look out of bed; and there, in the moonlight, leaning on a bureau near

---

[1] The plot of Mary E. Braddon's "At Creighton Abbey" is derived from such a legend
[2] Charlotte of Mecklinburg-Strelitz (1744 – 1818), consort of King George III of Great Britain

the window, steadfastly regarding him, saw his old college friend! The appearance being solemnly addressed, replied, in a kind of whisper, but very audibly, "Do not come near me. I am dead. I am here to redeem my promise. I come from another world, but may not disclose its secrets!" Then, the whole form becoming paler, melted, as it were, into the moonlight, and faded away.

Or, there was the daughter of the first occupier of the picturesque Elizabethan house, so famous in our neighbourhood. You have heard about her? No! Why, SHE went out one summer evening at twilight, when she was a beautiful girl, just seventeen years of age, to gather flowers in the garden; and presently came running, terrified, into the hall to her father, saying, "Oh, dear father, I have met myself!" He took her in his arms, and told her it was fancy, but she said, "Oh no! I met myself in the broad walk, and I was pale and gathering withered flowers, and I turned my head, and held them up!" And, that night, she died; and a picture of her story was begun, though never finished, and they say it is somewhere in the house to this day, with its face to the wall.

Or, the uncle of my brother's wife was riding home on horseback, one mellow evening at sunset, when, in a green lane close to his own house, he saw a man standing before him, in the very centre of a narrow way. "Why does that man in the cloak stand there!" he thought. "Does he want me to ride over him?" But the figure never moved. He felt a strange sensation at seeing it so still, but slackened his trot and rode forward. When he was so close to it, as almost to touch it with his stirrup, his horse shied, and the figure glided up the bank, in a curious, unearthly manner — backward, and without seeming to use its feet — and was gone. The uncle of my brother's wife, exclaiming, "Good Heaven! It's my cousin Harry, from Bombay!" put spurs to his horse, which was suddenly in a profuse sweat, and, wondering at such strange behaviour, dashed round to the front of his house. There, he saw the same figure, just passing in at the long French window of the drawing-room, opening on the ground. He threw his bridle to a servant, and hastened in after it. His sister was sitting there, alone. "Alice, where's my cousin Harry?" "Your cousin Harry, John?" "Yes. From Bombay[1]. I

---

[1] Modern-day Mumbai, India, then a British colony

met him in the lane just now, and saw him enter here, this instant." Not a creature had been seen by any one; and in that hour and minute, as it afterwards appeared, this cousin died in India.

Or, it was a certain sensible old maiden lady, who died at ninety-nine, and retained her faculties to the last, who really did see the Orphan Boy; a story which has often been incorrectly told, but, of which the real truth is this — because it is, in fact, a story belonging to our family — and she was a connexion of our family. When she was about forty years of age, and still an uncommonly fine woman (her lover died young, which was the reason why she never married, though she had many offers), she went to stay at a place in Kent[1], which her brother, an Indian-Merchant, had newly bought. There was a story that this place had once been held in trust by the guardian of a young boy; who was himself the next heir, and who killed the young boy by harsh and cruel treatment. She knew nothing of that. It has been said that there was a Cage in her bedroom in which the guardian used to put the boy. There was no such thing. There was only a closet. She went to bed, made no alarm whatever in the night, and in the morning said composedly to her maid when she came in, "Who is the pretty forlorn-looking child who has been peeping out of that closet all night?" The maid replied by giving a loud scream, and instantly decamping[2]. She was surprised; but she was a woman of remarkable strength of mind, and she dressed herself and went downstairs, and closeted herself with her brother. "Now, Walter," she said, "I have been disturbed all night by a pretty, forlorn-looking boy, who has been constantly peeping out of that closet in my room, which I can't open. This is some trick." "I am afraid not, Charlotte," said he, "for it is the legend of the house. It is the Orphan Boy. What did he do?" "He opened the door softly," said she, "and peeped out. Sometimes, he came a step or two into the room. Then, I called to him, to encourage him, and he shrunk, and shuddered, and crept in again, and shut the door." "The closet has no communication[3], Charlotte," said her brother, "with any other part of the house, and it's nailed up." This was undeniably true, and it took two

---

[1] Pastoral county in southeastern England

[2] Quitting and running away without notice

[3] That is to say, has no outlet to any other hallway or room

carpenters a whole forenoon to get it open, for examination. Then, she was satisfied that she had seen the Orphan Boy. But, the wild and terrible part of the story is, that he was also seen by three of her brother's sons, in succession, who all died young. On the occasion of each child being taken ill, he came home in a heat, twelve hours before, and said, Oh, Mamma, he had been playing under a particular oak-tree, in a certain meadow, with a strange boy — a pretty, forlorn-looking boy, who was very timid, and made signs! From fatal experience, the parents came to know that this was the Orphan Boy, and that the course of that child whom he chose for his little playmate was surely run.

Legion[1] is the name of the German castles, where we sit up alone to wait for the Spectre — where we are shown into a room, made comparatively cheerful for our reception — where we glance round at the shadows, thrown on the blank walls by the crackling fire — where we feel very lonely when the village innkeeper and his pretty daughter have retired, after laying down a fresh store of wood upon the hearth, and setting forth on the small table such supper-cheer as a cold roast capon, bread, grapes, and a flask of old Rhine wine — where the reverberating doors close on their retreat, one after another, like so many peals of sullen thunder — and where, about the small hours of the night, we come into the knowledge of divers supernatural mysteries. Legion is the name of the haunted German students, in whose society we draw yet nearer to the fire, while the schoolboy in the corner opens his eyes wide and round, and flies off the footstool he has chosen for his seat, when the door accidentally blows open. Vast is the crop of such fruit, shining on our Christmas Tree; in blossom, almost at the very top; ripening all down the boughs!

---

*DICKENS, who almost single-handedly revived the tradition of old fashioned Christmases (as opposed to the virtually secular bank holiday it had become after the Puritan Revolution) was himself inspired by the Christmas stories of another ghost story writer, the godfather of*

---

[1] Thousands – literally 3,000 to 6,000

American literature, Washington Irving. His depiction of old fashioned English Christmases in The Sketch Book of Geoffrey Crayon, Gent. (the same collection that contained "The Legend of Sleepy Hollow" and "Rip Van Winkle") and Bracebridge Hall charmed the young Dickens – an Irving devotee – and was incorporated into the imagery and rhetoric of A Christmas Carol. Irving also adored the ghost story – though he often lampooned it. In the beginning of Tales of a Traveler (much of which is the 19th century version of the Scary Movie franchize), a lover of English ghost lore rhapsodizes about the tropes of the literature. In his beaming catalog we can detect the inspiration for Dickens loving homage above:

" By my soul but I should not be surprised if some of those good-looking gentlefolks that hang along the walls [in picture frames] should walk about the rooms of this stormy night; or if I should find the ghost of one of these long-waisted ladies turning into my bed in mistake for her grave in the church-yard... Oh, I should like it of all things... Some dark oaken room, with ugly, wo-begone portraits that are dismally at one, and about which the housekeeper has a power of delightful stories of love and murder. And then a dim lamp, a table with a rusty sword across it, and a spectre all in white to draw aside one's curtains at midnight..."

*THE Victorian Era was ostensibly one of confidence: confidence in queen and country, in God and duty, in science and virtue. But beneath the solid wainscoting crawled many rats. H.G. Wells, who wrote a half-dozen splendid ghost stories, knew that the genre had potential to expose the vulnerability of British social and philosophical vulnerability, and in "The Red Room," he does so with chilling skill. This story is not horrifying, but it is terrifying, if somewhat understated. The ghosts that lurk in our nightmares are not rattling chains or wrapped in billowing shrouds; they are chaos, meaninglessness, and the futility of human aspirations. We begin with a story that rejects the very foundations of Victorian society, which saw itself as a bringer of light to a world in darkness. Wells doubts the ability of that light to keep the beast at bay.*

---

# THE RED ROOM
## OR, THE GHOST OF FEAR
### {1894}
### *H. G. Wells*

"IT'S YOUR OWN CHOOSING[1]," said the man with the withered arm[2] once more. I heard the faint sound of a stick and a shambling step on the flags in the

passage outside. The door creaked on its hinges as a second old man entered, more bent, more wrinkled, more aged even than the first. He supported himself by the help of a crutch, his eyes were covered by a

---

[1] Choice and free will feature prominently in horror fiction because it summons doubts about human agency, engages anxieties about fate, and develops dramatic tension and irony

[2] Disused, mangled, or defective limbs are often used in literature to symbolize one of two things: moral corruption (e.g. *Richard III*) or moral distinction (e.g. *To Kill a Mockingbird*). The ambiguity in this man's malformed arm is telling: is he trustworthy or malicious?

shade[1], and his lower lip, half averted, hung pale and pink from his decaying yellow teeth. He made straight for an armchair on the opposite side of the table, sat down clumsily, and began to cough. The man with the withered hand gave the newcomer a short glance of positive dislike[2]; the old woman took no notice of his arrival, but remained with her eyes fixed steadily on the fire.

"I said—it's your own choosing," said the man with the withered hand, when the coughing had ceased for a while.

"It's my own choosing," I answered[3].

The man with the shade became aware of my presence for the first time, and threw his head back for a moment, and sidewise, to see me. I caught a momentary glimpse of his eyes, small and bright and inflamed. Then he began to cough and splutter again.

"Why don't you drink?" said the man with the withered arm, pushing the beer toward him. The man with the shade poured out a glassful with a shaking hand, that splashed half as much again on the deal table. A monstrous shadow of him crouched upon the wall, and mocked his action as he poured and drank. I must confess I had scarcely expected these grotesque custodians[4]. There is, to my mind, something inhuman in senility, something crouching and atavistic[5]; the human qualities seem to drop from old people insensibly day by day. The three of them made me feel uncomfortable with their gaunt silences, their bent carriage, their evident unfriendliness to me and to one another. And that night,

---

[1] A visor made of green felt, celluloid, or horn, worn by the visually impaired to protect the eyes from unintended sun damage

[2] The atmosphere in the house is already tense with human drama and emotional pettiness

[3] As if signing a document, he takes ownership of his will and responsibility for his fate

[4] Calling to mind the warped guardians of the mythological Hades and Dante's *Inferno*

[5] Primeval, a leftover from evolution. The "custodians" symbolize mankind's underdeveloped, primitive nature. As the narrator prepares to enter the room of Fear, he must first cross paths with these reminders of his own inborn spiritual pettiness, corruption, and dysfunction

perhaps, I was in the mood for uncomfortable impressions. I resolved to get away from their vague fore-shadowings of the evil things upstairs[1].

"If," said I, "you will show me to this haunted room of yours, I will make myself comfortable there."

The old man with the cough jerked his head back so suddenly that it startled me, and shot another glance of his red eyes at me from out of the darkness under the shade, but no one answered me. I waited a minute, glancing from one to the other. The old woman stared like a dead body, glaring into the fire with lack-lustre eyes.

"If," I said, a little louder, "if you will show me to this haunted room of yours, I will relieve you from the task of entertaining me."

"There's a candle on the slab outside the door," said the man with the withered hand, looking at my feet as he addressed me. "But if you go to the Red Room[2] to-night—"

"This night of all nights!" said the old woman,
softly. "—You go alone."

"Very well," I answered, shortly, "and which way do I go?"

"You go along the passage for a bit," said he, nodding his head on his shoulder at the door, "until you come to a spiral staircase; and on the second landing is a door covered with green baize[3]. Go through that, and down the long corridor to the end, and the Red Room is on your left up the steps."

"Have I got that right?" I said, and repeated his directions. He corrected me in one particular.

"And you are really going?" said the man with the shade, looking at me again for the third time with that queer, unnatural tilting of the face.

"This night of all nights!" whispered the old woman.

"It is what I came for," I said, and moved toward the door. As I did so, the old man with the shade rose and staggered round the table, so as to be closer to the others and to the fire. At the door I turned and looked at them, and saw they were all close together, dark against the firelight,

---

[1] Indeed, they are the visible reflections of the invisible things he will ultimately face

[2] A name redolent with Gothic intrigue, mystery, and horror – a pastiche more than anything

[3] Felt

staring at me over their shoulders, with an intent expression on their ancient faces.

"Good-night," I said, setting the door open.

"It's your own choosing," said the man with the withered arm.

I left the door wide open until the candle was well alight, and then I shut them in, and walked down the chilly, echoing passage.

I must confess that the oddness of these three old pensioners[1] in whose charge her ladyship had left the castle[2], and the deep-toned, old-fashioned furniture of the housekeeper's room, in which they foregathered, had affected me curiously in spite of my effort to keep myself at a matter-of-fact phase. They seemed to belong to another age[3], an older age, an age when things spiritual were indeed to be feared, when common sense was uncommon, an age when omens and witches were credible, and ghosts beyond denying. Their very existence, thought I, is spectral; the cut of their clothing, fashions born in dead brains; the ornaments and conveniences in the room about them even are ghostly — the thoughts of vanished men, which still haunt rather than participate in the world of to-day. And the passage I was in, long and shadowy, with a film of moisture glistening on the wall, was as gaunt and cold as a thing that is dead and rigid. But with an effort I sent such thoughts to the right-about[4]. The long, drafty subterranean passage was chilly and dusty, and my candle flared and made the shadows cower and quiver. The echoes rang up and down the spiral staircase, and a shadow came sweeping up after me, and another fled before me into the darkness overhead. I came to the wide landing and stopped there for a moment listening to a rustling that I fancied I heard creeping behind me, and then, satisfied of

---

[1] Retirees who have been allotted a sum of money and a lodging, most likely due to dutiful careers as faithful family servants. They are essentially biding their time between retirement and death – another acerbic parallel to general humanity

[2] The unseen owner of the place, a noblewoman, likely owns several properties, leaving them in the care of custodians during her absences

[3] The terms atavistic, primordial, primitive, and unevolved apply to these spectral geriatrics

[4] "Right, about face!" – a military command to turn and leave; he sent them away

the absolute silence, pushed open the unwilling baize-covered door and stood in the silent corridor.

The effect was scarcely what I expected, for the moonlight, coming in by the great window on the grand staircase, picked out everything in vivid black shadow or reticulated[1] silvery illumination. Everything seemed in its proper position; the house might have been deserted on the yesterday instead of twelve months ago. There were candles in the sockets of the sconces[2], and whatever dust had gathered on the carpets or upon the polished flooring was distributed so evenly as to be invisible in my candlelight. A waiting stillness was over everything. I was about to advance, and stopped abruptly. A bronze group[3] stood upon the landing hidden from me by a corner of the wall; but its shadow fell with marvelous distinctness upon the white paneling, and gave me the impression of someone crouching to waylay me. The thing jumped upon my attention suddenly. I stood rigid for half a moment, perhaps. Then, with my hand in the pocket that held the revolver[4], I advanced, only to discover a Ganymede and Eagle[5], glistening in the moonlight. That incident for a time restored my nerve, and

a dim porcelain Chinaman on a buhl[6] table, whose head rocked as I passed, scarcely startled me.

The door of the Red Room and the steps up to it were in a shadowy corner. I moved my candle from side to side in order to see clearly the nature of the recess in which I stood, before opening the door. Here it was, thought I, that my predecessor was found, and the memory of that story gave me a sudden twinge of apprehension. I glanced over my

---

[1] Arranged precisely in purposeful patterns; designed

[2] Wall mountings for candles, flambeaux, or light bulbs

[3] Statuary made up of multiple figures

[4] Compare this to the plot of Broughton's "Nothing But the Truth," and the subsequent mythology of 50 Berkeley Square (in many versions, the hapless ghost hunter is armed with a revolver in case the ghost is a prankster)

[5] In Roman mythology, Ganymede was a beautiful Trojan prince, whom Jupiter lustfully abducted in the form of an eagle. A symbol of homoerotic passion, he also symbolizes the encounter of humanity with the supernatural: just as Ganymede was swept up by Jupiter, the narrator is entering the realm of the uncanny and unnatural

[6] Furniture decorated in brass and tortoiseshell

shoulder at the black Ganymede in the moonlight, and opened the door of the Red Room rather hastily, with my face half turned to the pallid silence of the corridor.

I entered, closed the door behind me at once, turned the key I found in the lock within, and stood with the candle held aloft surveying the scene of my vigil, the great Red Room of Lorraine Castle, in which the young Duke had died; or rather in which he had begun his dying, for he had opened the door and fallen headlong down the steps I had just ascended[1]. That had been the end of his vigil, of his gallant attempt to conquer the ghostly tradition of the place, and never, I thought, had apoplexy[2] better served the ends of superstition. There were other and older stories that clung to the room, back to the half-incredible beginning of it all, the tale of a timid wife and the tragic end that came to her husband's jest of frightening her. And looking round that huge shadowy room with its black window bays, its recesses and alcoves, its dusty brown-red hangings[3] and dark gigantic furniture, one could well understand the legends that had sprouted in its black corners, its germinating[4] darknesses. My candle was a little tongue of light in the vastness of the chamber; its rays failed to pierce to the opposite end of the room, and left an ocean of dull red mystery and suggestion, sentinel shadows and watching darknesses beyond its island of light. And the stillness of desolation brooded over it all.

I must confess some impalpable quality of that ancient room disturbed me. I tried to fight the feeling down. I resolved to make a systematic examination of the place, and so, by leaving nothing to the imagination, dispel the fanciful suggestions of the obscurity before they obtained a hold upon me. After satisfying myself of the fastening of the door, I began to walk round the room, peering round each article of furniture, tucking up the valances[5] of the bed and opening its curtains

---

[1] An almost certain reference to the story of 50 Berkeley Square
[2] An often fatal stroke caused by brain hemorrhage resulting in grotesque spasms
[3] Tapestries
[4] The darkness is characterized as alive, growing, and not yet arrived at its full potential
[5] Overhanging linen lining which covers the gap between the bed and floor

wide. In one place there was a distinct echo to my footsteps, the noises I made seemed so little that
they enhanced rather than broke the silence of the place. I pulled up the blinds and examined the fastenings of the several windows. Attracted by the fall of a particle of dust, I leaned forward and looked up the blackness of the wide chimney. Then, trying to preserve my scientific attitude of mind[1], I walked round and began tapping the oak paneling for any secret opening, but I desisted before reaching the alcove[2]. I saw my face in a mirror—white.

There were two big mirrors in the room, each with a pair of sconces bearing candles, and on the mantelshelf, too, were candles in china candle-sticks. All these I lit one after the other. The fire was laid—an unexpected consideration from the old housekeeper—and I lit it, to keep down any disposition to shiver[3], and when it was burning well I stood round with my back to it and regarded the room again. I had pulled up a chintz[4]-covered armchair and a table to form a kind of barricade before me. On this lay my revolver, ready to hand. My precise examination had done me a little good, but I still found the remoter darkness of the place and its perfect stillness too stimulating for the imagination. The echoing of the stir and crackling of the fire was no sort of comfort to me. The shadow in the alcove at the end of the room began to display that indefinable quality of a presence, that odd suggestion of a lurking living thing that comes so easily in silence and solitude. And to reassure myself, I walked with a candle into it and satisfied myself that there was nothing tangible there. I stood that candle upon the floor of the alcove and left it in that position.

By this time I was in a state of considerable nervous tension, although to my reason there was no adequate cause for my condition. My mind, however, was perfectly clear. I postulated quite unreservedly that nothing supernatural could happen, and to pass the time I began

---

[1] Unlike the "atavistic," under-evolved custodians, the narrator prides himself in his progressive, rationalistic materialism

[2] A recess in a wall, often used for storage, displays, or sitting

[3] "Disposition?" He claims to be shivering because of a physical propensity, although we understandably may question the cause

[4] Glazed, calico print – evocative of the 18th century

stringing some rhymes together, Ingoldsby[1] fashion, concerning the original legend of the place. A few I spoke aloud, but the echoes were not pleasant for the same reason I also abandoned, after a time, a conversation with myself upon the impossibility of ghosts and haunting. My mind reverted to the three old and distorted people downstairs, and I tried to keep it upon that topic.

The sombre reds and grays of the room troubled me; even with its seven candles the place was merely dim. The light in the alcove flaring in a draft, and the fire flickering, kept the shadows and penumbra[2] perpetually shifting and stirring in a noiseless flighty dance. Casting about for a remedy, I recalled the wax candles I had seen in the corridor, and, with a slight effort, carrying a candle and leaving the door open, I walked out into the moonlight, and presently returned with as many as ten. These I put in the various knick-knacks of china with which the room was sparsely adorned, and lit and placed them where the shadows had lain deepest, some on the floor, some in the window recesses, arranging and rearranging them until at last my seventeen candles were so placed that not an inch of the room but had the direct light of at least one of them[3]. It occurred to me that when the ghost came I could warn him not to trip over them. The room was now quite brightly illuminated. There was something very cheering and reassuring in these little silent streaming flames, and to notice their steady diminution of length offered

---

[1] *The Ingoldsby Legends* were a wildly popular collection of fairy tales, myths, and ghost stories set into writing by English cleric Richard Harris Barham in 1837

[2] The indeterminately hazy part of a shadow that is not entirely shadow; the area between complete darkness and complete light. It serves to underscore the narrator's tenuous position between confidence and terror, the quantifiable and the unknowable

[3] The candles symbolize wisdom, human agency, intellect, and rational assurance. So long as the narrator can light-away the darkness, he is assured of its materiality. Likewise, so long as a man can make excuses for or explain away existential anxieties, he is impervious to their influence... this, however, Wells wants us to see, is just as dependable as the narrator's faint candles keeping the darkness at bay

me an occupation and gave me a reassuring sense of the passage of time.

Even with that, however, the brooding expectation of the vigil weighed heavily enough upon me. I stood watching the minute hand of my watch creep towards midnight.

Then something happened in the alcove. I did not see the candle go out, I simply turned and saw that the darkness was there, as one might start and see the unexpected presence of a stranger[1]. The black shadow had sprung back to its place. "By Jove[2]," said I aloud, recovering from my surprise, "that draft's a strong one;" and taking the matchbox from the table, I walked across the room in a leisurely manner to relight the corner again. My first match would not strike[3], and as I succeeded with the second, something seemed to blink on the wall before me. I turned my head involuntarily and saw that the two candles on the little table by the fireplace were extinguished. I rose at once to my feet.

"Odd," I said. "Did I do that myself in a flash of absent-mindedness?"

I walked back, relit one, and as I did so I saw the candle in the right sconce of one of the mirrors wink and go right out, and almost immediately its companion followed it. The flames vanished as if the wick had been suddenly nipped between a finger and thumb, leaving the wick neither glowing nor smoking[4], but black. While I stood gaping the candle at the foot of the bed went out, and the shadows seemed to take another step toward me.

"This won't do!" said I, and first one and then another candle on the mantelshelf followed.

"What's up?" I cried, with a queer high note getting into my voice somehow. At that the candle on the corner of the wardrobe went out, and the one I had relit in the alcove followed.

"Steady on!" I said, "those candles are wanted," speaking with a half-hysterical facetiousness[5], and scratching away at a match the while, "for

---

[1] The "stranger" is Fear, which has arrived
[2] Incidentally the Anglicized name for Jupiter – the supernatural force which carried off Ganymede
[3] Human agency begins to show its weaknesses – it is not dependable in the least
[4] No symptom of human industry is left behind; it is black and soulless
[5] Sarcasm; flighty, foolish language

the mantel candlesticks." My hands trembled so much that twice I missed the rough paper of the matchbox. As the mantel emerged from darkness again, two candles in the remoter end of the room were eclipsed. But with the same match I also relit the larger mirror candles, and those on the floor near the doorway, so that for the moment I seemed to gain on the extinctions. But then in a noiseless volley there vanished four lights at once in different corners of the room, and I struck another match in quivering haste, and stood hesitating whither to take it.

As I stood undecided, an invisible hand seemed to sweep out the two candles on the table. With a cry of terror I dashed at the alcove, then into the corner and then into the window, relighting three as two more vanished by the fireplace, and then, perceiving a better way, I dropped matches on the iron-bound deedbox[1] in the corner, and caught up the bedroom candlestick. With this I avoided the delay of striking matches, but for all that the steady process of extinction went on, and the shadows I feared and fought against returned, and crept in upon me, first a step gained on this side of me, then on that. I was now almost frantic with the horror of the coming darkness, and my self-possession deserted me. I leaped panting from candle to candle in a vain struggle against that remorseless advance.

I bruised myself in the thigh against the table, I sent a chair headlong, I stumbled and fell and whisked the cloth from the table in my fall. My candle rolled away from me and I snatched another as I rose. Abruptly this was blown out as I swung it off the table by the wind of my sudden movement, and immediately the two remaining candles followed. But there was light still in the room, a red light that streamed across the ceiling and staved off the shadows from me. The fire! Of course I could still thrust my candle between the bars and relight it.

I turned to where the flames were still dancing between the glowing coals and splashing red reflections upon the furniture; made two steps toward the grate, and incontinently[2] the flames dwindled and vanished, the glow vanished, the reflections rushed together and disappeared, and

---

[1] An iron chest sized between a shoebox and microwave, used to store important documents
[2] Immediately, without restrain, delay, or candor

as I thrust the candle between the bars darkness closed upon me like the shutting of an eye, wrapped about me in a stifling embrace, sealed my vision, and crushed the last vestiges of self-possession from my brain. And it was not only palpable darkness, but intolerable terror. The candle fell from my hands. I flung out my arms in a vain effort to thrust that ponderous blackness away from me, and lifting up my voice, screamed with all my might, once, twice, thrice. Then I think I must have staggered to my feet. I know I thought suddenly of the moonlit corridor[1], and with my head bowed and my arms over my face, made a stumbling run for the door.

But I had forgotten the exact position of the door, and I struck myself heavily against the corner of the bed. I staggered back, turned, and was either struck or struck myself against some other bulky furnishing. I have a vague memory of battering myself thus to and fro in the darkness, of a heavy blow at last upon my forehead, of a horrible sensation of falling that lasted an age, of my last frantic effort to keep my footing, and then I remember no more.

I opened my eyes in daylight. My head was roughly bandaged, and the man with the withered hand was watching my face. I looked about me trying to remember what had happened, and for a space I could not recollect. I rolled my eyes into the corner and saw the old woman, no longer abstracted, no longer terrible[2], pouring out some drops of medicine from a little blue phial[3] into a glass. "Where am I?" I said. "I seem to remember you, and yet I cannot remember who you are."

They told me then, and I heard of the haunted Red Room as one who bears a tale. "We found you at dawn," said he, "and there was blood on your forehead and lips."

---

[1] Desperately craving light – read: existential assurance – he surges into the notably dangerous hallway with its stairs, statues, and furniture

[2] The primordial pensioneers have lost their hideousness because they are no longer opponents to the narrator's material worldview, but fellow victims, conscious of a universe beset with chaos, hostile to humanity, and impermeable to human industry

[3] Blue glass was typically used for pharmaceuticals – possibly a pain killer or relaxant

I wondered that I had ever disliked him[1]. The three of them in the daylight seemed commonplace old folk enough. The man with the green shade had his head bent as one who sleeps.

It was very slowly I recovered the memory of my experience. "You believe now," said the old man with the withered hand, "that the room is haunted?" He spoke no longer as one who greets an intruder, but as one who condoles with a friend.

"Yes," said I, "the room is haunted."

"And you have seen it. And we who have been here all our lives have never set eyes upon it. Because we have never dared. Tell us, is it truly the old earl who—"

"No," said I, "it is not."

"I told you so," said the old lady, with the glass in her hand. "It is his poor young countess who was frightened—"

"It is not," I said. "There is neither ghost of earl nor ghost of countess in that room; there is no ghost there at all, but worse, far worse, something impalpable[2]—"

"Well?" they said.

"The worst of all the things that haunt poor mortal men," said I; "and that is, in all its nakedness—'Fear!' Fear that will not have light nor sound, that will not bear with reason[3], that deafens and darkens and overwhelms. It followed me through the corridor, it fought against me in the room—"

I stopped abruptly. There was an interval of silence. My hand went up

---

[1] Literally, the disfigurement is now shown for what it is: symbolic of the burden he bears as one who is aware of the untamable nature of the Universe; his arm is withered and useless just as human understanding, will, and industry are withered and useless

[2] In a virtually Lovecraftian understanding of his nocturnal adversary, the narrator dispels Gothic tropes, forms, and expectations which – compared to his analysis – would be far more comforting and bearable. No, indeed, he did not find the ghosts of human souls, but the spirit of a malicious cosmos which plays with human hubris as a cat plays with a plucky mouse

[3] It resists and repels human rationality, intellect, and comprehension, working entirely outside of the sphere of mankind's knowledge and capabilities

to my bandages. "The candles went out one after another, and I fled—"

Then the man with the shade lifted his face sideways to see me and spoke.

"That is it," said he. "I knew that was it. A Power of Darkness[1]. To put such a curse upon a home[2]! It lurks there always. You can feel it even in the daytime, even of a bright summer's day, in the hangings, in the curtains, keeping behind you however you face about. In the dusk it creeps in the corridor and follows you, so that you dare not turn. It is even as you say. Fear itself is in that room. Black Fear.... And there it will be... so long as this house of sin endures[3]."

---

*"THE Red Room" is a study in terror. Horror is the nauseating sense of repulsion and fear caused by a gruesome sight; terror is the grueling anxiety caused by anticipation of horror. Terror, Wells implies, is the heart of fear. It is not the graphic revelation, but the blind vulnerability that promotes our deepest human insecurities. When the narrator is interrogated by the pensioners after his recovery, he disappoints their thirst for a tangible, measurable horror (the old earl, the young countess...) and subsequently subverts the expectations of Victorian readers who were used to melodrama. Instead, and far more existentially disturbing, the answer is terror: naked, indefinable, boundless, shapeless chaos – animal vulnerability in its most potent manifestations. Even in "the daytime, even of a bright summer's day," the old man observes –*

---

[1] Not to say "Satanic" or even supernatural, but the literal power of Darkness – of uncertainty, of nonexistence, of chaos, the vacuum of existence

[2] "Upon a home" – the "home" Wells is symbolically referring to is humankind; our minds, intellects, and spirits have been cursed with false pride and inevitable devestation

[3] Once again, the "house of sin" is humanity. So long as men live, the brutal power of uncertainty and Fear will stalk their nightmares

*even when we are secure and comforted by denial – we "can feel it": the heavy weight of naked terror – of death and insecurity, of the purposelessness of human existence in an illimitable and hostile cosmos – stalks our hearts. The "Red Room" in question is the universe that mankind inhabits, a universe that – in spite of all of our science and learning, and in spite of all our self-discipline and intellectual pride – reviles our intrusion and strikes back at our ambitions. The conclusion of Wells' story, in which he finds companionship and solace in the company of the primeval geriatrics – relics of a time of folklore and superstition – suggest the cynical cosmicism that H. P. Lovecraft would later hone:*

*"The most merciful thing in the world, I think, is the inability of the human mind to correlate all its contents. We live on a placid island of ignorance in the midst of black seas of infinity, and it was not meant that we should voyage far. The sciences, each straining in its own direction, have hitherto harmed us little; but some day the piecing together of dissociated knowledge will open up such terrifying vistas of reality, and of our frightful position therein, that we shall either go mad from the revelation or flee from the light into the peace and safety of a new dark age."*

*ALTHOUGH Wells could not be outdone in spaceless existential panic, this collection of letters between two affluent women is a century before its time in the chilling realism that causes it to throb with relatability: who hasn't secretly boasted of their relationship with a close friend, been hurt when well-intended advice is rejected, or felt annoyed by a sick child? It isn't until the jarring, emotional conclusion that events swerve into the unnatural – when Jane Austen morphs into Mary Shelley. They could be emails between your mom and her elderly aunt, or phone conversations between your girlfriend and her sister. That's what makes the last pages so disquieting. Broughton often sought to locate the dread lurking in the domestic – the secret anxieties, repressions, and rage stuffed into the dark spaces in the minds and hearts of British society women. Externally, all was well-kempt, proper, and acceptable, but under the floorboards of even the most wholesome home, corpses may lie rotting.*

---

## THE TRUTH, THE WHOLE TRUTH,
## AND NOTHING BUT THE TRUTH
## {1868}
### *Rhoda Broughton*

MRS DE WYNT TO MRS MONTRESOR.
18, Eccleston Square[1], May 5th.

MY DEAREST CECILIA, Talk of the friendships of Orestes and Pylades[2], of Julie and Claire[3], what are they to ours? Did Pylades ever

---

[1] Located in Belgravia, one of the poshest neighborhoods in London

[2] Orestes and Pylades were famous friends, cousins, and (according to some accounts) homosexual lovers in Greek mythology, contemporaneous with the Trojan War

[3] "Julie and Claire" are likely meant to refer to a pair of friends known by Mrs. De Wynt and Mrs. Montresor – a demonstration of Broughton's stunning commitment to creating a realistic climate by including two names

go ventre à terre[1], half over London on a day more broiling than any but an âme damnée[2] could even imagine, in order that Orestes might be comfortably housed for the season?

Did Claire ever hold sweet converse with from fifty to one hundred house agents, in order that Julie might have three windows to her drawing-room and a pretty portière[3]? You see I am determined not to be done out of my full meed[4] of gratitude.

Well, my friend, I had no idea till yesterday how closely we were packed in this great smoky beehive, as tightly as herrings in a barrel. Don't be frightened, however. By dint of squeezing and crowding, we have managed to make room for two more herrings in our barrel, and those two are yourself and your other self, i.e. your husband. Let me begin at the beginning. After having looked over, I verily believe, every undesirable residence in West London[5]; after having seen nothing intermediate between what was suited to the means of a duke, and what was suited to the needs of a chimney-sweep; after having felt bed-ticking, and explored kitchen-ranges till my brain reeled under my accumulated experience, I arrived at about half-past five yesterday afternoon at 32,--Street, May Fair[6].

'Failure No. 253, I don't doubt,' I said to myself, as I toiled up the steps with my soul athirst for afternoon tea, and feeling as ill-tempered as you please. So much for my spirit of prophecy.

---

which are never referred to twice: an inside reference between the two correspondents
[1] French: at a great speed; literally "belly-to-the-ground"
[2] Henchman or lackey, colloquially, but in this context a demon – a "damned soul" literally
[3] Heavy curtain hung across a doorway
[4] Merited gift
[5] Wealthy end of the capital demarcating the fashionable neighborhoods west of Charing Cross
[6] May Fair is a posh neighborhood in Westminister, central London, famed for its wealth, prestige, and some of the highest priced rents in the world. This is a four minute walk from 50 Berkeley Square, a purportedly haunted house which received its most famous ghost tradition from *this* story, which was mistaken by many for nonfiction

Fate, I have noticed, is often fond of contradicting us flat, and giving the lie to our little predictions. Once inside, I thought I had got into a small compartment of Heaven by mistake.

Fresh as a daisy, clean as a cherry, bright as a seraph's[1] face, it is all these, and a hundred more, only that my limited stock of similes[2] is exhausted. Two drawing-rooms[3] as pretty as ever woman crammed with people she did not care two straws about; white curtains with rose-coloured ones underneath, festooned in the sweetest way; marvellously, immorally becoming, my dear, as I ascertained entirely for your benefit, in the mirrors, of which there are about a dozen and a half; Persian mats, easy chairs, and lounges suited to every possible physical conformation, from the Apollo Belvedere to Miss Biffin[4]; and a thousand of the important little trivialities that make up the sum of a woman's life: peacock fans, Japanese screens, naked boys and décolletée[5] shepherdesses; not to speak of a family of china pugs, with blue ribbons round their necks, which ought of themselves to have added fifty pounds a year to the rent. Apropos[6], I asked, in fear and trembling, what the rent might be--'Three hundred pounds a year[7]. A feather would have knocked me down. I could hardly believe my ears, and made the woman repeat it several times, that there might be no mistake. To this hour it is a mystery to me.

With that suspiciousness which is so characteristic of you, you will

---

[1] Angel

[2] Figure of speech used to draw comparisons

[3] From the term *withdrawing* room – a long chamber used for entertaining guests

[4] Apollo Belvedere is a Classical Greek statue of the selfsame god standing in the act of shooting a fatal arrow at his victim; Miss [Sarah] Biffin (1786-1860) was a girl born without limbs, hands, or feet, made famous for her fantastic miniature portraits drawn with her mouth. By conjuring these beautiful subjects with grim and macabre backgrounds, Broughton is undoubtedly foreshadowing the wonderful house's grotesque nature.

[5] With low-cut necklines

[6] Fitting to the situation; naturally

[7] $28,000 in 2013 USD – an enormous amount for a middle-classed family, but a pittance for a thriving member of the Victorian aristocracy

immediately begin to hint that there must be some terrible unaccountable smell, or some odious inexplicable noise haunting the reception-rooms. Nothing of the kind, the woman assured me, and she did not look as if she were telling stories. You will next suggest – remembering the rose-coloured curtains – that its last occupant was a member of the demimonde[1]. Wrong again. Its last occupant was an elderly and unexceptionable Indian officer, without a liver[2], and with a most lawful wife. They did not stay long, it is true, but then, as the housekeeper told me, he was a deplorable old hypochondriac[3], who never could bear to stay a fortnight in any one place. So lay aside that scepticism, which is your besetting sin, and give unfeigned thanks to St Brigitta, or St Gengulpha, or St Catherine of Siena, or whoever is your tutelar saint[4], for having provided you with a palace at the cost of a hovel, and for having sent you such an invaluable friend as

Your attached ELIZABETH DE WYNT.

P.S.--I am so sorry I shall not be in town to witness your first raptures, but dear Artie looks so pale and thin and tall after the whooping-cough, that I am sending him off at once to the sea[5], and as I cannot bear the child out of my sight, I am going into banishment likewise.

MRS MONTRESOR TO MRS DE WYNT.
32,--Street, May Fair, May 14th.

Dearest Bessy, Why did not dear little Artie defer his whooping-cough convalescence till August? It is very odd, to me, the perverse way in which children always fix upon the most inconvenient times and

---

[1] Literally, the underworld – a society of decadent hedonists who lived lavishly

[2] That is to say, not a drinking man

[3] A chronically nervous person filled with anxiety and restlessness

[4] A guardian saint. Those listed are patron saints of generosity and charity

[5] Resorts in southern and eastern English coastal towns were popular retreats for city-dwellers whose health suffered in the tarry, coal-dusted air and revived in the fresh sea air

seasons for their diseases. Here we are installed in our Paradise, and have searched high and low, in every hole and corner, for the serpent, without succeeding in catching a glimpse of his spotted tail. Most things in this world are disappointing, but 32,--Street, May Fair, is not. The mystery of the rent is still a mystery. I have been for my first ride in the Row[1] this morning; my horse was a little fidgety; I am half afraid that my nerve is not what it was. I saw heaps of people I knew. Do you recollect Florence Watson? What a wealth of red hair she had last year! Well, that same wealth is black as the raven's wing this year[2]! I wonder how people can make such walking impositions of themselves, don't you? Adela comes to us next week; I am so glad. It is dull driving by oneself of an afternoon; and I always think that one young woman alone in a brougham[3], or with only a dog beside her, does not look good. We sent round our cards a fortnight before we came up, and have been already deluged[4] with callers. Considering that we have been two years exiled from civilised life, and that London memories are not generally of the longest, we shall do pretty well, I think. Ralph Gordon came to see me on Sunday; he is in the — the Hussars[5] now. He has grown up such a dear fellow, and so good-looking! Just my style, large and fair and whiskerless! Most men nowadays make themselves as like monkeys, or Scotch terriers, as they possibly can[6]. I intend to be quite a mother to him. Dresses are gored to as indecent an extent as ever; short skirts are rampant. I am sorry; I hate them. They make tall women look

---

[1] Rotten Row, a horse track in Hyde Park, a fashionable place for wealthy Londoners to socialize

[2] Gossiping about hair dye... Broughton masterfully creates a realistic portrait of two society chums – a superficial veneer which will ultimate collapse at the intrusion of the supernatural

[3] Pronounced "broom" – a light, closed carriage

[4] Overwhelmed

[5] Hussars were members of elegantly-dressed light cavalry units renowned for their skill, prestige, romantic image, and indefatigable courage. His background as a brave and physically fit soldier will be an important element of the story's climax

[6] Another casual comment on society matters that makes the narrative believable and realistic

lank, and short ones insignificant. A knock! Peace is a word that might as well be expunged from one's London dictionary.

Yours affectionately, CECILIA MONTRESOR.


MRS DE WYNT TO MRS MONTRESOR.
The Lord Warden, Dover, May 18th.

Dearest Cecilia, You will perceive that I am about to devote only one small sheet of note-paper to you. This is from no dearth[1] of time, Heaven knows! time is a drug in the market here, but from a total dearth of ideas. Any ideas that I ever have, come to me from without, from external objects; I am not clever enough to generate any within myself. My life here is not an eminently suggestive one. It is spent digging with a wooden spade, and eating prawns. Those are my employments at least; my relaxation is going down to the Pier, to see the Calais boat come in[2]. When one is miserable oneself, it is decidedly consolatory to see someone more miserable still; and wretched and bored, and reluctant vegetable as I am, I am not sea-sick. I always feel my spirits rise after having seen that peevish[3], draggled procession of blue, green and yellow fellow-Christians file past me. There is a wind here always, in comparison of which the wind that behaved so violently to the corners of Job's house was a mere zephyr[4]. There are heights to climb which require more daring perseverance than ever Wolfe

---

[1] Shortage, lack
[2] A small ferry boat that carried travelers across the narrow Strait of Dover between southeast England and Calais, France
[3] Irritable, crabby
[4] A very, very telling reference. In the biblical book of Job, a violent wind dashed his home to pieces, killing his children who were holding a raucous party. Job was a tremendously prosperous and wealthy man whose life was transformed into abject misery by the interference of Satan. Likewise, the two friends are about to find their carefree life of luxury threatened by supernatural assault. A zephyr is a bright, invigorating breeze

displayed, with his paltry heights of Abraham[1]. There are glaring white houses, glaring white roads, glaring white cliffs. If any one knew how unpatriotically I detest the chalk-cliffs of Albion[2]! Having grumbled through my two little pages--I have actually been reduced to writing very large in order to fill even them--I will send off my dreary little billet. How I wish I could get into the envelope myself too, and whirl up with it to dear, beautiful, filthy London. Not more heavily could Madame de Staël have sighed for Paris from among the shades of Coppet[3].

Your disconsolate, BESSY.

MRS MONTRESOR TO MRS DE WYNT.
32,--Street, May Fair, May 27th.

Oh, my dearest Bessy, how I wish we were out of this dreadful, dreadful house! Please don't think me very ungrateful for saying this, after your taking such pains to provide us with a Heaven upon earth, as you thought. What has happened could, of course, have been neither foretold, nor guarded against, by any human being. About ten days ago, Benson (my maid) came to me with a very long face, and said, 'If you please, 'm, did you know that this house was haunted?' I was so startled: you know what a coward I am. I said, 'Good Heavens! No! is it?' 'Well, 'm, I'm pretty nigh sure it is,' she said, and the expression of her countenance was about as lively as an undertaker's; and then she told me that cook had been that morning to order groceries from a shop in the neighbourhood, and on her giving the man the direction

---

[1] General James Wolfe (1727-1759) famously scaled the intimidating cliffs beneath Quebec to fight the battle of the Plains of Abraham at which, just as the battle was won, he was killed. Further foreshadowing.

[2] That is, England

[3] Germaine se Stael (1766-1816) was a French-speaking Swiss author whose chateau in Coppet, Switzerland was the site of one of her salons, Paris being the site of another. During the French Revolution she was essentially exiled from Paris and spent her time in Coppet longing to be reunited with her beloved Parisian salon

where to send the things to, he had said, with a very peculiar smile, 'No. 32,--Street, eh? h'm? I wonder how long you'll stand it; last lot held out just a fortnight.' He looked so odd that she asked him what he meant, but he only said, 'Oh! nothing! only that parties never do stay long at 32. He had known parties go in one day, and out the next, and during the last four years he had never known any remain over the month.

Feeling a good deal alarmed by this information, she naturally inquired the reason; but he declined to give it, saying that if she had not found it out for herself, she had much better leave it alone, as it would only frighten her out of her wits; and on her insisting and urging him, she could only extract from him, that the house had such a villainously bad name[1], that the owners were glad to let it for a mere song[2]. You know how firmly I believe in apparitions, and what an unutterable fear I have of them: anything material, tangible, that I can lay hold of--anything of the same fibre, blood, and bone as myself, I could, I think, confront bravely enough; but the mere thought of being brought face to face with the 'bodiless dead[3]', makes my brain unsteady.

The moment Henry came in, I ran to him, and told him; but he pooh-poohed the whole story, laughed at me, and asked whether we should turn out of the prettiest house in London, at the very height of the season, because a grocer said it had a bad name. Most good things that had ever been in the world had had a bad name in their day; and, moreover, the man had probably a motive for taking away the house's character, some friend for whom he coveted the charming situation and the low rent. He derided my 'babyish fears', as he called them, to such an extent that I felt half ashamed, and yet not quite comfortable either; and then came the usual rush of London engagements, during which one has no time to think of anything but how to speak, and act, and look for the moment then present. Adela was to arrive yesterday, and in the morning our weekly hamper of flowers, fruit, and vegetables

---

[1] Bad reputation

[2] An almost unreasonably low amount of cash

[3] A reference to Coleridge's brooding, Gothic poem of vampirism and seduction, "Christabel"

arrived from home. I always dress the flower vases myself, servants are so tasteless; and as I was arranging them, it occurred to me--you know Adela's passion for flowers--to carry up one particular cornucopia of roses and mignonette[1] and set it on her toilet-table[2], as a pleasant surprise for her.

As I came downstairs, I had seen the housemaid--a fresh, round-faced country girl--go into the room, which was being prepared for Adela, with a pair of sheets that had been airing over her arm. I went upstairs very slowly, as my cornucopia was full of water, and I was afraid of spilling some. I turned the handle of the bedroom-door and entered, keeping my eyes fixed on my flowers, to see how they bore the transit, and whether any of them had fallen out. Suddenly a sort of shiver passed over me; and feeling frightened--I did not know why--I looked up quickly. The girl was standing by the bed, leaning forward a little with her hands clenched in each other, rigid, every nerve tense; her eyes, wide open, starting out of her head, and a look of unutterable stony horror in them; her cheeks and mouth not pale, but livid[3] as those of one that died awhile ago in mortal pain[4]. As I looked at her, her lips moved a little, and an awful hoarse voice, not like hers in the least, said, 'Oh! my God, I have seen it!' and then she fell down suddenly, like a log, with a heavy noise. Hearing the noise, loudly audible all through the thin walls and floors of a London house, Benson came running in, and between us we managed to lift her on to the bed, and tried to bring her to herself by rubbing her feet and hands, and holding strong salts[5] to her nostrils. And all the while we kept glancing over our shoulders, in a vague cold terror of seeing some awful,

---

[1] A fragrant, spiky, green herb

[2] Essentially a vanity in the form of a bedstand; a spot to wash one's face and apply makeup

[3] Leadish in hue – bluish-grey

[4] Suggests that indeed, while she may be alive, some part of her essentially being has died; she is no longer the "fresh, round-faced country girl" who went into that cursed room

[5] Smelling salts were made of ammonium carbonate, which was produced by distilling the horns of red deer, hence the alternative name "spirit of hartshorn"

shapeless apparition. Two long hours she lay in a state of utter unconsciousness.

Meanwhile Harry, who had been down to his club[1], returned. At the end of two hours we succeeded in bringing her back to sensation and life, but only to make the awful discovery that she was raving mad[2]. She became so violent that it required all the combined strength of Harry and Phillips (our butler) to hold her down in the bed. Of course, we sent off instantly for a doctor, who on her growing a little calmer towards evening, removed her in a cab to his own house. He has just been here to tell me that she is now pretty quiet, not from any return to sanity, but from sheer exhaustion. We are, of course, utterly in the dark as to what she saw, and her ravings are far too disconnected and unintelligible to afford us the slightest clue[3]. I feel so completely shattered and upset by this awful occurrence, that you will excuse me, dear, I'm sure, if I write incoherently. One thing I need hardly tell you, and that is, that no earthly consideration would induce me to allow Adela to occupy that terrible room. I shudder and run by quickly as I pass the door.

Yours, in great agitation, CECILIA.

------------------------------------------------

[1] Social fraternities such as this were seen as escapes for men from their wives and children. Depending upon the social rank of the members, clubs could range from intellectual salons where men shared research and literature over sherry, to elitist societies where captains of industry, peers, and aristocrats gathered to hob-nob

[2] One of the most famous elements of the 50 Berkeley Square myth is the sudden madness of a maid brought on when preparing a room in broad daylight. In some cases she dies, but in none does she regain her sensibility; the encounter with the Thing has left her changed indelibly

[3] The genius and beauty of this apparition is that no one is capable of describing it; it is formless, without a identity which could aid in understanding its motives, background, weaknesses, or intentions. All who encounter it are rendered either mad or dead before they can elaborate their fears and elucidate the situation

MRS DE WYNT TO MRS MONTRESOR.
The Lord Warden[1], Dover, May 28th.

Dearest Cecilia, Yours just come[2]; how very dreadful! But I am still unconvinced as to house being in fault. You know I feel a sort of godmother to it, and responsible for its good behaviour. Don't you think that what the girl had might have been a fit[3]? Why not? I myself have a cousin who is subject to seizures of the kind, and immediately on being attacked his whole body becomes rigid, his eyes glassy and staring, his complexion livid, exactly as in the case you describe. Or, if not a fit, are you sure that she has not been subject to fits of madness? Please be sure and ascertain whether there is not insanity in her family. It is so common nowadays, and so much on the increase, that nothing is more likely[4]. You know my utter disbelief in ghosts. I am convinced that most of them, if run to earth, would turn out about as genuine as the famed Cock Lane one[5]. But even allowing the possibility, nay, the actual unquestioned existence of ghosts in the abstract, is it likely that there should be anything to be seen so horribly fear-inspiring, as to send a perfectly sane person in one instant raving mad, which you, after three weeks' residence in the house, have never caught a glimpse of? According to your hypothesis, your whole household ought, by this time, to be stark staring mad. Let me implore you not to give way to a panic which may, possibly, probably prove utterly groundless. Oh, how I wish I were with you, to make you listen to reason!

Artie ought to be the best prop ever woman's old age was furnished

---

[1] A hotel where Mrs. De Wynt is staying with her convalescing son
[2] "Your[ last letter has] just come"
[3] A bout of epilepsy – it would have to be unprecedentedly severe to turn a sane girl mad
[4] Exposure to industrial chemicals, materials, and compounds such as mercury, lead, and asbestos was certainly responsible for an uptick of insanity amongst Britain's working class
[5] A reference to a hoaxed haunting that swept London in 1762. The "Cock Lane Ghost" turned out to be a father forcing his daughter to fake visions of a former tenant's dead, ostensibly poisoned wife, in order to exact revenge for unfulfilled debts.

with, to indemnify[1] me for all he and his whooping-cough have made me suffer. Write immediately, please, and tell me how the poor patient progresses. Oh, had I the wings of a dove! I shall be on wires[2] till I hear again.

Yours, BESSY.


MRS MONTRESOR TO MRS DE WYNT.
No. 5, Bolton Street, Piccadilly, June 12th.

Dearest Bessy, You will see that we have left that terrible, hateful, fatal house. How I wish we had escaped from it sooner! Oh, my dear Bessy, I shall never be the same woman again if I live to be a hundred. Let me try to be coherent, and to tell you connectedly what has happened. And first, as to the housemaid, she has been removed to a lunatic asylum, where she remains in much the same state. She has had several lucid intervals, and during them has been closely, pressingly questioned as to what it was she saw; but she has maintained an absolute, hopeless silence, and only shudders, moans, and hides her face in her hands when the subject is broached. Three days ago I went to see her, and on my return was sitting resting in the drawing-room, before going to dress for dinner, talking to Adela about my visit, when Ralph Gordon walked in. He has always been walking in the last ten days, and Adela has always flushed up[3] and looked very happy, poor little cat, whenever he made his appearance. He looked very handsome, dear fellow, just come in from the park; seemed in tremendous spirits,

---

[1] Protect

[2] "On pins and needles" – left in great suspense

[3] Blushed, beamed. We may, with little difficulty, look at this as a codified means of describing sexual arousal in Victorian literature. To become flushed in the face is to experience blood flow in other areas of the body. Gordon's masculine sexuality places him in a role of dominance and power, capable of attracting, placating, chiding, and impressing the women who adore him

50

and was as sceptical as even you could be, as to the ghostly origin of Sarah's seizure. 'Let me come here tonight and sleep in that room; do, Mrs Montresor[1],' he said, looking very eager and excited. 'With the gas lit and a poker, I'll engage to exorcise every demon that shows his ugly nose; even if I should find---Seven white ghostisses Sifting on seven white postisses[2].' 'You don't mean really?' I asked, incredulously. 'Don't I? that's all,' he answered emphatically.

'I should like nothing better. Well, is it a bargain?' Adela turned quite pale. 'Oh, don't,' she said, hurriedly, 'please, don't! why should you run such a risk? How do you know that you might not be sent mad too?' He laughed very heartily, and coloured[3] a little with pleasure at seeing the interest she took in his safety. 'Never fear,' he said, 'it would take more than a whole squadron of departed ones, with the old gentleman[4] at their head, to send me crazy.' He was so eager, so persistent, so thoroughly in earnest, that I yielded at last, though with a certain strong reluctance, to his entreaties. Adela's blue eyes filled with tears, and she walked away hastily to the conservatory, and stood picking bits of heliotrope[5] to hide them.

Nevertheless, Ralph got his own way; it was so difficult to refuse him anything[6]. We gave up all our engagements for the

---

[1] The most famous element of the 50 Berkeley Square myth rides on the appearance of a cocksure nobleman who takes a bet to spend the night in the haunted room, only to…

[2] A child's rhyme, demonstrating Gordon's gloating nonchalance. Other editors have struggled to find the source; in the 1861 novel by Charlotte Mary Yonge (1823 – 1901), *Hopes and Fears*, I discovered a variant (the number is changed to three) which refers to it as an "old Sussex rhyme" – "There were three ghostisses / Sitting on three postisses / Eating of three crustisses"

[3] Blushing – the attraction is mutual, and the life-affirming arousal is mutual – soon to be quashed

[4] A humorous, belittling term for Satan – a flippant remark that further illustrates Gordon's hubris

[5] Lacy purple flowers

[6] Without being sophomoric or perverse, it is not unreasonable to suggest a sexual atmosphere about this observation: Gordon is a virile, commanding

evening, and he did the same with his. At about ten o'clock he arrived, accompanied by a friend and brother officer, Captain Burton, who was anxious to see the result of the experiment. 'Let me go up at once, he said, looking very happy and animated. 'I don't know when I have felt in such good tune; a new sensation is a luxury not to be had every day of one's life; turn the gas up as high as it will go; provide a good stout poker, and leave the issue to Providence and me.' We did as he bid. 'It's all ready now,' Henry said, coming downstairs after having obeyed his orders; 'the room is nearly as light as day. Well, good luck to you, old fellow!' 'Good-bye, Miss Bruce,' Ralph said, going over to Adela, and taking her hand with a look, half laughing, half sentimental-- 'Fare thee well, and if for ever then for ever, fare thee well, that is my last dying speech and confession[1]. Now mind,' he went on, standing by the table, and addressing us all; 'if I ring once, don't come. I may be flurried, and lay hold of the bell without thinking; if I ring twice, come.' Then he went, jumping up the stairs three steps at a time, and humming a tune[2]. As for us, we sat in different attitudes of expectation and listening about the drawing-room. At first we tried to talk a little, but it would not do; our whole souls seemed to have passed into our ears. The clock's ticking sounded as loud as a great church bell close to one's ear. Addy lay on the sofa, with her dear little white face hidden in the cushions. So we sat for exactly an hour; but it seemed like two years, and just as the clock began to strike eleven, a sharp ting, ting, ting, rang clear and shrill through the

---

figure of masculine authority whose combination of manly confidence, boyish bravado, and childish impetuusness cause him to be the hero in the eyes of the women he encounters, elevated to the status of demigod

[1] From Byron's "Fare Thee Well" (1816). The sentiment is not without tremendous foreboding

[2] His waggish confidence and determination to impress are absolutely adolescent; while he may be a show off, he is nothing if not gushing with vitality and life

house. 'Let us go,' said Addy, starting up and running to the door. 'Let us go,' I cried too, following her. But Captain Burton stood in the way, and intercepted our progress. 'No,' he said, decisively, 'you must not go; remember Gordon told us distinctly, if he rang once not to come. I know the sort of fellow he is, and that nothing would annoy him more than having his directions disregarded[1].'

'Oh, nonsense!' Addy cried passionately, 'he would never have rung if he had not seen something dreadful; do, do let us go!' she ended, clasping her hands. But she was overruled, and we all went back to our seats. Ten minutes more of suspense, next door to unendurable[2]; I felt a lump in my throat, a gasping for breath;--ten minutes on the clock, but a thousand centuries on our hearts. Then again, loud, sudden, violent, the bell rang! We made a simultaneous rush to the door. I don't think we were one second flying upstairs. Addy was first. Almost simultaneously she and I burst into the room. There he was, standing in the middle of the floor, rigid, petrified, with that same look--that look that is burnt into my heart in letters of fire[3]-- of awful, unspeakable, stony fear on his brave young face. For one instant he stood thus; then stretching out his arms stiffly before him, he groaned in a terrible, husky voice, 'Oh, my God! I have seen it!' and fell down

---

[1] The story showcases the vulnerability of even assertive, jingoistic Victorian masculinity to the forces beyond human control, leaving the women utterly exposed by the loss of this presumed male security. Ironically, the women's intuitive move to rescue Gordon is impeded by further machismo in the form of Captain Burton's blind obedience. Not unlike Tennyson's "Charge of the Light Brigade," (1854) wherein whole droves of brave Hussars are splintered to pieces by grapeshot during an ill-designed assault on an enemy battery, famously caused by the unwillingness of British officers to question their superiors' sometimes ill-planned orders

[2] Admittedly a weak point: although we do not know what caused him to ring the first time, surely he would have left the room in the interim rather than wait ten whole minutes to ring again. Of course, this fails to factor Gordon's unwavering self-pride and hubris

[3] A reference to the Hand of God which wrote a fiery message of doom for the Babylonian Empire during a wild feast given by the king. Detailed in Daniel Chapter 5, it is the source of the phrase "the writing on the wall"

dead. Yes, dead. Not in a swoon or in a fit, but dead[1]. Vainly we tried to bring back the life to that strong young heart; it will never come back again till that day when the earth and the sea give up the dead that are therein[2]. I cannot see the page for the tears that are blinding me; he was such a dear fellow! I can't write any more today[3].

Your broken-hearted CECILIA.

THIS IS A TRUE STORY[4].

---

[1] Not only has It sent a girl to a lunacy asylum, It has killed a rambunctious man in the very prime of his youth. The women, who looked to their brave men for protection, assurance, and dependability are left adrift in a universe where even the men are weak victims of its merciless power. Rich, young, brave, popular – none of these traits ensure protection from the blind cosmos

[2] A phrase from the Common Book of Prayer – used at funerals

[3] Writing has been her means of expression – using witty banter laced with French and literary references has provided her an opportunity to be heard and understood. Now that mechanism is incapable of recovering her emotional trauma

[4] While the phrase is anticlimactic, ironically exposing the fourth wall that may have been momentarily forgotten, it does in fact shed light on an issue of Victorian gender roles: the story is true in the sense that women in Victorian society learned that manly pride, the mortar that was said to hold the empire together, was not invulnerable to cruel fate, and that women – especially those born to high society – who depend upon their men as faultless superheroes, will be shocked and horrified by the chilling truth: even in a patriarchal society where men monopolize power and wealth and dictate the fates of the nations from Parliaments and battlefields, no one is immune to disaster and cosmic comeuppance – not even a brave, high-society hussar

*ANOTHER study in terror, Broughton's epistolary sketch is far more interested in psychology than melodramatics. What and why are far less important than how – namely, how the characters respond to the presence of a socially-destabilizing infestation. This story could just as easily have been written about cholera or a house fire, because its victims – ranging from a lower-class female servant to an aristocratic male hussar – are struck down without warning or opportunity for self-defense. Cecilia's worldview of protection and privilege is devastated by the May Fair phantom's rampage – blind to class distinctions, and stripped of mercy. The strong, dependable men of affluence and distinction (whom she and Bessy sexually idolize) are no more capable of staving off death than the illiterate girls who empty their shit pots. The leering Specter of Death, Broughton warns, takes us unawares, regardless of our resistance, evasion, or denial. It is the terror of its devastating menace rather than the horror of its ubiquitous form. As befits the niece of J. S. Le Fanu, Broughton's grasp of terror is enormous and overwhelming.*

*THE typical ghost story in Victorian Britain followed this formula: a misdeed is done, often secretly, and the truth is not exposed until a supernatural agency intervenes – either to assist a third party in uncovering the wrongdoing, or in personally tormenting the malefactor. The following, then, is (unlike most of our tales) a typical Victorian ghost story in plot. But in execution, it is excellent. Writing in an aggressive present tense, Braddon generates a slow-burning terror that exponentially increases after the tale's tragic midpoint. Several masters of the ghost story appear to have been entranced by her plot of emotional neglect and supernatural comeuppance: Algernon Blackwood modelled two stories after it – "The Tryst" (which follows a cavalier fiancée who goes abroad and returns years later for the woman he assumed would be waiting for him) and "The Dance of Death" (which closely follows Braddon's chilling dance hall climax) – Mrs J. H. Riddell used it as the basis for one of her finest stories – a violently erotic tale of murder and class disparity called "A Terrible Vengance" – and M. R. James' flesh-prickling "Martin's Close" is so similar in nature that it is better to let you read this story without further comment.*

---

## THE COLD EMBRACE
### {1860}
#### *Mary Elizabeth Braddon*

HE WAS AN ARTIST[1]--such things as happened to him happen sometimes to artists.

He was a German[2]--such things as happened to him happen

---

[1] Artistic temperments are often depicted as more congruous and conducive to the whims of nature, and are therefore more susceptible to the *supernatural*

[2] Oftentimes, in English literature, Germany, Germans, and German-speaking peoples, are portrayed as having a propensity for the Gothic, the weird, and the wonderful (e.g., Poe's "Ligeia," Irving's "The ... German Student," Mary Shelley's *Frankenstein*)

sometimes to Germans.

He was young, handsome, studious, enthusiastic, metaphysical[1], reckless, unbelieving, heartless.

And being young, handsome and eloquent, he was beloved.

He was an orphan, under the guardianship of his dead father's brother, his uncle Wilhelm, in whose house he had been brought up from a little child; and she who loved him was his cousin--his cousin Gertrude, whom he swore he loved in return.

Did he love her? Yes, when he first swore it. It soon wore out, this passionate love; how threadbare and wretched a sentiment it became at last in the selfish heart of the student! But in its golden dawn, when he was only nineteen, and had just returned from his apprenticeship to a great painter at Antwerp[2], and they wandered together in the most romantic outskirts of the city at rosy sunset, by holy moonlight, or bright and joyous morning, how beautiful a dream!

They keep[3] it a secret from Wilhelm, as he has the father's ambition of a wealthy suitor for his only child--a cold and dreary vision beside the lover's dream.

So they are betrothed; and standing side by side when the dying sun and the pale rising moon[4] divide the heavens, he puts the betrothal ring upon her finger, the white and taper finger whose slender shape he knows so well. This ring is a peculiar one, a massive golden serpent, its

---

[1] Intrigued by the supernatural world and existential, theological, and scientific philosophies

[2] A major European center of finance, culture, and diplomacy located in Belgium

[3] Henceforth we are in present tense – generating a sense of anticipation and anxiety

[4] Dual natures meeting in the midst of their natural circuits: like the rising moon and setting sun which meet at dusk when the world is neither light nor dark, these two lovers are on different paths – one to life and fulfillment, the other to death and despair – yet they commune at a moment in their shared lives when their trajectories are unapparent in the dusky years of early youth

tail in its mouth, the symbol of eternity[1]; it had been his mother's, and he would know it amongst a thousand. If he were to become blind tomorrow, he could select it from amongst a thousand by the touch alone.

He places it on her finger, and they swear to be true to each other for ever and ever--through trouble and danger--sorrow and change--in wealth or poverty. Her father must needs be won to consent to their union by and by, for they were now betrothed, and death alone could part them.

But the young student, the scoffer at revelation, yet the enthusiastic adorer of the mystical[2], asks:

"Can death part us? I would return to you from the grave, Gertrude. My soul would come back to be near my love. And you--you, if you died before me--the cold earth would not hold you from me; if you loved me, you would return, and again these fair arms would be clasped round my neck as they are now."

But she told him, with a holier light in her deep-blue eyes than had ever shone in his--she told him that the dead who die at peace with God are happy in heaven, and cannot return to the troubled earth; and that it is only the suicide--the lost wretch on whom sorrowful angels shut the door of Paradise--whose unholy spirit haunts the footsteps of the living.

The first year of their betrothal is passed, and she is alone, for he has gone to Italy, on a commission for some rich man, to copy Raphaels, Titians, Guidos[3], in a gallery at Florence. He has gone to win fame, perhaps; but it is not the less bitter--he is gone!

Of course her father misses his young nephew, who has been as a son to him; and he thinks his daughter's sadness no more than a cousin should feel for a cousin's absence.

In the meantime, the weeks and months pass. The lover writes--often

---

[1] A prominent motif of this story is the perpetuity of sin and guilt, and of love and desire. Regardless of how dearly a person may wish to forget their lowest moments or to bury their darkest anxieties, the memories – more importantly, the ramifications – will prove stubborn

[2] He is academically intrigued with the spiritual, yet is a practicing skeptic, failing to respect the import of his mystical language

[3] Great artists of the late Renaissance

at first, then seldom--at last, not at all.

How many excuses she invents for him! How many times she goes to the distant little post-office, to which he is to address his letters! How many times she hopes, only to be disappointed! How many times she despairs, only to hope again!

But real despair comes at last, and will not be put off any more. The rich suitor appears on the scene, and her father is determined. She is to marry at once. The wedding-day is fixed--the fifteenth of June.

The date seems to burn into her brain.

The date, written in fire, dances for ever before her eyes.

The date, shrieked by the Furies[1], sounds continually in her ears.

But there is time yet--it is the middle of May--there is time for a letter to reach him at Florence; there is time for him to come to Brunswick[2], to take her away and marry her, in spite of her father--in spite of the whole world.

But the days and the weeks fly by, and he does not write--he does not come. This is indeed despair which usurps her heart, and will not be put away.

It is the fourteenth of June. For the last time she goes to the little post-office; for the last time she asked the old question, and they give her for the last time the dreary answer, "No; no letter."

For the last time--for tomorrow is the day appointed for the bridal. Her father will hear no entreaties; her rich suitor will not listen to her prayers. They will not be put off a day--an hour; to-night alone is hers--this night, which she may employ as she will.

She takes another path than that which leads home; she hurries through some by-streets of the city, out on to a lonely bridge, where he and she had stood so often in the sunset, watching the rose-coloured

---

[1] Goddesses of vengeance in Greek literature -- "those who beneath the earth punish whosoever has sworn a false oath." Our German artist is certainly vulnerable to their rage

[2] Braunschweig – a large city located in the north central German plains, in Lower Saxony

light glow, fade, and die upon the river[1].

&#8371;

He returns from Florence. He had received her letter. That letter, blotted with tears, entreating, despairing--he had received it, but he loved her no longer. A young Florentine, who has sat to him for a model[2], had bewitched his fancy--that fancy which with him stood in place of a heart--and Gertrude had been half-forgotten. If she had a rich suitor, good; let her marry him; better for her, better far for himself. He had no wish to fetter himself with a wife. Had he not his art always?--his eternal bride, his unchanging mistress[3].

Thus he thought it wiser to delay his journey to Brunswick, so that he should arrive when the wedding was over--arrive in time to salute[4] the bride.

And the vows--the mystical fancies--the belief in his return, even after death, to the embrace of his beloved? O, gone out of his life; melted away for ever, those foolish dreams of his boyhood.

So on the fifteenth of June he enters Brunswick, by that very bridge on which she stood, the stars[5] looking down on her, the night before. He strolls across the bridge and down by the water's edge, a great rough dog at his heels, and the smoke from his short meerschaum-pipe[6] curling in blue wreaths fantastically in the pure morning air. He has his sketch-book under his arm, and attracted now and then by some object that catches his artist's eye, stops to draw: a few weeds and pebbles on the

---

[1] Symbolized by the warm, life affirming, generous sun (her lover is the cold, funereal, reclusive moon), Gertrude follows its arch, sinking into the river and into night

[2] A level of implied coarseness is involved here: she is likely a nude model – an occupation taken up by crude, lower classed women, and girls with notorious morals

[3] What is art and what reality? Reality, it appears, has become art, and art reality: his poetic vow will not be taken figuratively, and his desire for an eternal mistress will be delivered by a source formerly flesh and blood

[4] Toast

[5] Symbolic of God – the divine, spiritual purity and integrity

[6] A large, deep vase-like ivory pipe

61

river's brink--a crag on the opposite shore--a group of pollard willows in the distance. When he has done, he admires his drawing, shuts his sketch-book, empties the ashes from his pipe, refills from his tobacco-pouch, sings the refrain of a gay drinking-song, calls to his dog, smokes again, and walks on. Suddenly he opens his sketch-book again; this time that which attracts him is a group of figures: but what is it?

It is not a funeral, for there are no mourners.

It is not a funeral, but a corpse lying on a rude bier[1], covered with an old sail, carried between two bearers.

It is not a funeral, for the bearers are fishermen--fishermen in their everyday garb.

About a hundred yards from him they rest their burden on a bank--one stands at the head of the bier, the other throws himself down at the foot of it[2].

And thus they form the perfect group; he walks back two or three paces, selects his point of sight, and begins to sketch a hurried outline. He has finished it before they move; he hears their voices, though he cannot hear their words, and wonders what they can be talking of. Presently he walks on and joins them.

"You have a corpse there, my friends?" he says.

"Yes; a corpse washed ashore an hour ago."

"Drowned?"

"Yes, drowned. A young girl, very handsome."

"Suicides are always handsome[3]," says the painter; and then he stands

---

[1] Platform or riser meant to elevate a coffin for viewing

[2] Postures of respect, reverence – even worship

[3] A popular – if macabre – motif in Romantic culture was the beauty of the female suicide (stereotypically a drowning victim). Like the female victim of tuberculosis (another popular romantic motif), the girlish suicide was preserved in her beauty by the form of her death. Most famous was L'Inconnue de la Seine – the unknown girl from the Seine – a (supposed) suicide victim whose (supposed) death mask became a worldwide sensation. The beautiful female face was the envy of European women, who began to style their hair and arrange their makeup in similar manners due to the wry, ironic beauty, said to compare nicely with the crooked smile and ambiguous emotions of the Mona Lisa

for a little while idly smoking and meditating, looking at the sharp outline of the corpse and the stiff folds of the rough canvas covering.

Life is such a golden holiday for him--young, ambitious, clever--that it seems as though sorrow and death could have no part in his destiny[1].

At last he says that, as this poor suicide is so handsome, he should like to make a sketch of her.

He gives the fishermen some money, and they offer to remove the sailcloth that covers her features.

No; he will do it himself. He lifts the rough, coarse, wet canvas from her face. What face?

The face that shone on the dreams of his foolish boyhood; the face which once was the light of his uncle's home. His cousin Gertrude--his betrothed!

He sees, as in one glance, while he draws one breath, the rigid features--the marble arms--the hands crossed on the cold bosom; and, on the third finger of the left hand, the ring which had been his mother's--the golden serpent; the ring which, if he were to become blind, he could select from a thousand others by the touch alone.

But he is a genius[2] and a metaphysician--grief, true grief, is not for such as he. His first thought is flight--flight anywhere out of that accursed city--anywhere far from the brink of that hideous river--anywhere away from remorse--anywhere to forget.

೫೦

He is miles on the road that leads away from Brunswick before he knows that he has walked a step.

It is only when his dog lies down panting at his feet that he feels how exhausted he is himself, and sits down upon a bank to rest. How the landscape spins round and round before his dazzled eyes, while his morning's sketch of the two fishermen and the canvas-covered bier glares redly at him out of the twilight.

---

[1] He is immersed in art – eternality and limitless beauty – but is doomed to be drawn out of his reverie into lethal reality due to this selfsame fixation with incorruptible perfection
[2] An inspired visionary

63

At last, after sitting a long time by the roadside, idly playing with his dog, idly smoking, idly lounging, looking as any idle, light-hearted travelling student might look, yet all the while acting over that morning's scene in his burning brain a hundred times a minute; at last he grows a little more composed, and tries presently to think of himself as he is, apart from his cousin's suicide. Apart from that, he was no worse off than he was yesterday. His genius was not gone; the money he had earned at Florence still lined his pocket-book; he was his own master, free to go whither he would.

And while he sits on the roadside, trying to separate himself from the scene of that morning--trying to put away the image of the corpse covered with the damp canvas sail--trying to think of what he should do next, where he should go, to be farthest away from Brunswick and remorse, the old diligence[1] coming rumbling and jingling along. He remembers it; it goes from Brunswick to Aix-la-Chapelle[2].

He whistles to the dog, shouts to the postillion[3] to stop, and springs into the *coupé*.

During the whole evening, through the long night, though he does not once close his eyes, he never speaks a word; but when morning dawns, and the other passengers awake and begin to talk to each other, he joins in the conversation. He tells them that he is an artist, that he is going to Cologne[4] and to Antwerp to copy Rubenses, and the great picture by Quentin Matsys, in the museum. He remembered afterwards that he talked and laughed boisterously, and that when he was talking and laughing loudest, a passenger, older and graver than the rest, opened the window near him, and told him to put his head out. He remembered the fresh air blowing in his face, the singing of the birds in his ears, and the flat fields and roadside reeling before his eyes. He remembered this, and then falling in a lifeless heap on the floor of the diligence.

It is a fever that keeps him for six long weeks on a bed at a hotel in Aix-la-Chapelle.

---

[1] A sturdy coach (so named because of its reliable time table)

[2] Aachen – a spa town in west central Germany, in North-Rhein Westphalia

[3] Horseman directing the progress of a team of horses from the back of one of the leaders

[4] A major city in west central Germany

He gets well, and, accompanied by his dog, starts on foot for Cologne. By this time he is his former self once more. Again the blue smoke from his short meerschaum curls upwards in the morning air--again he sings some old university drinking song--again stops here and there, meditating and sketching.

He is happy, and has forgotten his cousin--and so on to Cologne. It is by the great cathedral he is standing, with his dog at his side. It is night, the bells have just chimed the hour, and the clocks are striking eleven; the moonlight shines full upon the magnificent pile, over which the artist's eye wanders, absorbed in the beauty of form.

He is not thinking of his drowned cousin, for he has forgotten her and is happy.

Suddenly some one, something from behind him, puts two cold arms round his neck, and clasps its hands on his breast.

And yet there is no one behind him, for on the flags[1] bathed in the broad moonlight there are only two shadows, his own and his dog's. He turns quickly round--there is no one--nothing to be seen in the broad square but himself and his dog; and though he feels, he cannot see the cold arms clasped round his neck.

It is not ghostly, this embrace, for it is palpable to the touch[2]--it cannot be real, for it is invisible[3].

He tries to throw off the cold caress. He clasps the hands in his own to tear them asunder, and to cast them off his neck. He can feel the long delicate fingers cold and wet beneath his touch, and on the third finger of the left hand he can feel the ring which was his mother's--the golden serpent--the ring which he has always said he would know among a thousand by the touch alone. He knows it now!

His dead cousin's cold arms are round his neck--his dead cousin's wet hands are clasped upon his breast. He asks himself if he is mad. "Up,

---

[1] Flagstones – pavement

[2] A grisly touch that transcends typical Victorian sensibilities

[3] As in twilight when light and dark become indistinctly intertwined – when the sun and moon cross paths and their domains become blurred – the laws separating the natural and the supernatural become indistinct and crosshatched. The invisible is palpable, and reality (the reassuring shadows on the flags) becomes unreliable

Leo!" he shouts. "Up, up, boy!" and the Newfoundland leaps to his shoulders--the dog's paws are on the dead hands, and the animal utters a terrific howl, and springs away from his master.

The student stands in the moonlight[1], the dead arms around his neck, and the dog at a little distance moaning piteously.

Presently a watchman, alarmed by the howling of the dog, comes into the square to see what is wrong.

In a breath the cold arms are gone.

He takes the watchman home to the hotel with him and gives him money; in his gratitude he could have given the man half his little fortune.

Will it ever come to him again, this embrace of the dead?

He tries never to be alone[2]; he makes a hundred acquaintances, and shares the chamber of another student. He starts up if he is left by himself in the public room of the inn where he is staying, and runs into the street. People notice his strange actions, and begin to think that he is mad.

But, in spite of all, he is alone once more; for one night the public room being empty for a moment, when on some idle pretence he strolls into the street, the street is empty too, and for the second time he feels the cold arms round his neck, and for the second time, when he calls his dog, the animal shrinks away from him with a piteous howl.

After this he leaves Cologne, still travelling on foot--of necessity now, for his money is getting low. He joins travelling hawkers, he walks side by side with labourers, he talks to every foot-passenger he falls in with, and tries from morning till night to get company on the road.

At night he sleeps by the fire in the kitchen of the inn at which he stops; but do what he will, he is often alone, and it is now a common thing for him to feel the cold arms around his neck[3].

---

[1] The domain of death, isolation, and vulnerability

[2] Gertrude, it may be recalled, killed herself because of her abandonment – her loneliness and isolation. It is tremendously fitting that her vengeful spirit preys upon her faithless beloved when he is alone and isolated

[3] It bears mentioning that there is a queasy intimacy about this embrace – not about the trunk as in a hug, but about the neck as in a passionate kiss. Libidinal and erotic, it offers him the life-affirming romance he had stood to

Many months have passed since his cousin's death--autumn, winter, early spring. His money is nearly gone, his health is utterly broken, he is the shadow of his former self, and he is getting near to Paris. He will reach that city at the time of the Carnival[1]. To this he looks forward. In Paris, in Carnival time, he need never, surely, be alone, never feel that deadly caress; he may even recover his lost gaiety, his lost health, once more resume his profession, once more earn fame and money by his art.

How hard he tries to get over the distance that divides him from Paris, while day by day he grows weaker, and his step slower and more heavy!

But there is an end at last; the long dreary roads are passed. This is Paris, which he enters for the first time--Paris, of which he has dreamed so much--Paris, whose million voices are to exorcise his phantom.

To him to-night Paris seems one vast chaos of lights, music, and confusion--lights which dance before his eyes and will not be still--music that rings in his
ears and deafens him--confusion which makes his head whirl round and round.

But, in spite of all, he finds the opera-house, where there is a masked ball. He has enough money left to buy a ticket of admission, and to hire a domino[2] to throw over his shabby dress. It seems only a moment after his entering the gates of Paris that he is in the very midst of all the wild gaiety of the opera-house ball.

No more darkness, no more loneliness, but a mad crowd, shouting and dancing, and a lovely Débardeuse[3] hanging on his arm.

---

attain – the eternal mistress – but in a macabre perversion, he is attached to a rotting, clammy corpse-bride. This also implies the disturbing proximity of her dead, waterlogged face to his own

[1] Mardi Gras – a major religious holiday in Catholic countries and neighborhoods, where the final day before Lent (a forty day season of self-denial and penance) is spent in debauchery

[2] Dark, loose cloak and a domino mask (popularized by the Lone Ranger, it is small and black)

[3] Literally a dockworker or stevedore – a woman disguised as such, wearing pants. The costume was popular amongst the Bohemians and artists, who celebrated the dockworkers – whose livelihood came from busting up rafts

The boisterous gaiety he feels surely is his old light-heartedness come back. He hears the people round him talking of the outrageous conduct of some drunken student, and it is to him they point when they say this--to him, who has not moistened his lips since yesterday at noon, for even now he will not drink; though his lips are parched, and his throat burning, he cannot drink. His voice is thick and hoarse, and his utterance indistinct; but still this must be his old light-heartedness come back that makes him so wildly gay.

The little Débardeuse is wearied out--her arm rests on his shoulder heavier than lead--the other dancers one by one drop off.

The lights in the chandeliers one by one die out.

The decorations look pale and shadowy in that dim light which is neither night nor day[1].

A faint glimmer from the dying lamps, a pale streak of cold grey light from the new-born day, creeping in through half-opened shutters.

And by this light the bright-eyed Débardeuse fades sadly. He looks her in the face. How the brightness of her eyes dies out! Again he looks her in the face. How white that face has grown! Again--and now it is the shadow of a face alone that looks in his.

Again--and they are gone--the bright eyes, the face, the shadow of the face. He is alone; alone in that vast saloon.

Alone, and, in the terrible silence, he hears the echoes of his own footsteps in that dismal dance which has no music.

No music but the beating of his breast. The the cold arms are round his neck--they whirl him round, they will not be flung off, or cast away; he can no more escape from their icy grasp than he can escape from death. He looks behind him--there is nothing but himself in the great empty *salle*; but he can feel--cold, deathlike, but O, how palpable!--the long slender fingers, and the ring which was his mother's.

He tries to shout, but he has no power in his burning throat. The silence of the place is only broken by the echoes of his own footsteps in

---

and driftwood from the Seine to sell as firewood – as earthy, genuine characters, unlike the nobles, capitalists, and aristocrats they loathed

[1] Twilight returns, recalling the oppositional natures of the lover and her beloved, the uncertainty of life or death, and the blurring of the natural and the supernatural

the dance from which he cannot extricate himself. Who says he has no partner? The cold hands are clasped on his breast, and now he does not shun their caress. No! One more polka, if he drops down dead.

The lights are all out, and, half an hour after, the *gendarmes*[1] come in with a lantern to see that the house is empty; they are followed by a great dog that they have found seated howling on the steps of the theatre. Near the principal entrance they stumble over--

The body of a student, who has died from want of food, exhaustion, and the breaking of a blood-vessel[2].

---

[1] Police – literally, "gentlemen-at-arms" (French)
[2] While consumption and weakened hearts are both deaths symbolic of a pure and affected spirit, strokes often symbolize the lethal torment of a guilty conscience

*EDGAR Allan Poe often followed the doomed relationships of emotionally complex women, and the insensitive geniuses who saw them as a fixed, artistic ideal. These men hoped to divorce the spirit (beauty, poise, affection) from the body (needs, mortality, subjectivity) by objectifying their lovers and ignoring or denying their emotional and physical dynamism. In this story, which closely follows Poe's model (cf. "The Oval Portrait," "Ligeia," "Morella," "Berenice") ponders another favorite theme of America's master of philosophical horror: the tenuous balance between the physical and the psychical – mind and mater, spirit and self. The German artist exalts the spirit, but denies the body – he lavishes on his lover's ideal form, but neglects her shifting needs as a living person. He approaches the world as if it were all art and no reality, and it is telling that he dies from "want of food, exhaustion, and the breaking of a blood-vessel" – by mistreating his own physical and mental needs, he forfeits life for pretense, and becomes another victim of his one-dimensional view of people. Careless, insensitive, and emotionally stunted, he serves as a warning to men who imagine that negligence of a lover is a small matter. Women are dynamic and complex, she warns, and while the ramifications of a jilt may not be swift in coming, a neglectful lover should always beware the consequences of his abuses: the man who spurns a tender kiss may find himself drawn into an un-relinquishing embrace.*

*ELIZABETH Gaskell – like Broughton and Oliphant – wrote ghost stories with a critical (and notably feminist) perspective of British society. Her fiction explored the unstable nature (and looming doom) of a culture that failed to question the abuses of privilege: industrialists and aristocrats, males and English nationals. Her tales explored the instability of class-based prejudice and the anxieties of socially-vulnerable victims ("Lois the Witch," set during the Salem Trials, is a fine standout). This ghost story is a masterful standout among the dramatic and dull; it is a story about a child – nothing new to Victorians who couldn't get enough of children in dire straits. But this child is not the ward of an omniscient third-person Charles Dickens: she is the responsibility of a teenage girl desperate to preserve her from disaster. No dashing gentleman is here to sally forth; the only other characters are – like Wells' tenants – ancient and infirm. It is a story about absolute vulnerability, and about the accumulative psychological torture that can be suffered throughout a lifetime after a single act of hate.*

---

## THE OLD NURSE'S STORY
{1852}
### *Elizabeth Gaskell*

YOU KNOW, MY DEARS, that your mother was an orphan, and an only child; and I dare say you have heard that your grandfather was a clergyman up in Westmoreland[1], where I come from. I was just a girl in the village school, when, one day, your grandmother came in to ask the mistress if there was any scholar there who would do for a nurse-maid[2]; and mighty proud I was, I can tell ye, when the mistress called me up, and spoke to my being a good girl at my needle[3], and a steady, honest

---

[1] Historical region in northwest England – in southern Cumbria – near the Scottish border
[2] Female servant and attendant for an infant or toddler
[3] Needlework was to a young girl's education what Latin and grammar was to a boy's: the foundation upon which every other lesson was laid. Boys were then taught basic mathematics (sometimes followed by trigonometry,

72

girl, and one whose parents were very respectable, though they might be poor. I thought I should like nothing better than to serve the pretty young lady, who was blushing as deep as I was[1], as she spoke of the coming baby, and what I should have to do with it. However, I see you don't care so much for this part of my story, as for what you think is to come, so I'll tell you at once. I was engaged and settled at the parsonage before Miss Rosamond[2] (that was the baby, who is now your mother) was born. To be sure, I had little enough to do with her when she came, for she was never out of her mother's arms, and slept by her all night long; and proud enough was I sometimes when missis trusted her to me. There never was such a baby before or since, though you've all of you been fine enough in your turns; but for sweet, winning ways, you've none of you come up to your mother. She took after her mother, who was a real lady born; a Miss Furnivall, a grand-daughter of Lord Furnivall's, in Northumberland[3]. I believe she had neither brother nor sister, and had been brought up in my lord's family till she had married your grandfather, who was just a curate[4], son to a shopkeeper in Carlisle[5]— but a clever, fine gentleman as ever was—and one who was a right-down hard worker in his parish, which was very wide, and scattered all abroad

---

algebra, and geometry), history (English, European, and Antiquity), modern languages (French, German, or Italian), and rhetoric. Girls were taught art, sometimes music, sometimes French, domestic tasks, etiquette, and manners

[1] Indicative of humility, modesty – the kind of gentility of spirit which the Furnivalls lack

[2] A name which means "rose of the world," which implies the pure but exposed, vulnerable nature of this little heroine, who represents the last hope of her family, and is surrounded by thistles, thorns, and the encroaching frost that threatens to smother her

[3] Northumberland – the northernmost English county – shares the Scottish border with Cumbria, and is renowned for its dreary wastes, stormy coast, and romantic, wild country

[4] Cleric, pastor

[5] Known as "the Border City," located in Cumbria, just south of the Scottish boundary

over the Westmoreland Fells[1]. When your mother, little Miss Rosamond, was about four or five years old, both her parents died in a fortnight— one after the other. Ah! that was a sad time. My pretty young mistress and me was looking for another baby, when my master came home from one of his long rides, wet and tired, and took the fever he died of; and then she never held up her head again, but just lived to see her dead baby[2], and have it laid on her breast, before she sighed away her life. My mistress had asked me, on her death-bed, never to leave Miss Rosamond; but if she had never spoken a word, I would have gone with the little child to the end of the world.

The next thing, and before we had well stilled our sobs, the executors and guardians came to settle the affairs. They were my poor young mistress's own cousin, Lord Furnivall, and Mr. Esthwaite, my master's brother, a shopkeeper in Manchester; not so well-to-do then as he was afterwards, and with a large family rising about him. Well! I don't know if it were their settling, or because of a letter my mistress wrote on her death-bed to her cousin, my lord; but somehow it was settled that Miss Rosamond and me were to go to Furnivall Manor House, in Northumberland; and my lord spoke as if it had been her mother's wish that she should live with his family, and as if he had no objections, for that one or two more or less could make no difference in so grand a household. So, though that was not the way in which I should have wished the coming of my bright and pretty pet to have been looked at— who was like a sunbeam in any family, be it never so grand—I was well pleased that all the folks in the Dale[3] should stare and admire, when they heard I was going to be young lady's maid[4] at my Lord Furnivall's at Furnivall Manor.

---

[1] High hills or low mountains, typically bleak and barren

[2] A stillbirth often symbolizes a lost hope, a squelched ambition, or a stifled future. Amidst this disastrous time in her family's history, Rosamond is their only hope, ambition, and future left

[3] The low country – the town, the places where the common people dwelled

[4] One of the highest, most reputable stations a maid could attain – to be a lady's maid was to be accepted into the confidence of the nobility, and made the envy of kitchen and cleaning staff

But I made a mistake in thinking we were to go and live where my lord did. It turned out that the family had left Furnivall Manor House fifty years or more. I could not bear that my poor young mistress had ever been there, though she had been brought up in the family; and I was sorry for that, for I should have liked Miss Rosamond's youth to have passed where her mother's had been.

My lord's gentleman[1], from whom I asked as many questions as I durst[2], said that the Manor House was at the foot of the Cumberland Fells, and a very grand place; that an old Miss Furnivall, a great-aunt of my lord's, lived there, with only a few servants; but that it was a very healthy place[3], and my lord had thought that it would suit Miss Rosamond very well for a few years, and that her being there might perhaps amuse his old aunt.

I was bidden by my lord to have Miss Rosamond's things ready by a certain day. He was a stern, proud man, as they say all the Lords Furnivall were; and he never spoke a word more than was necessary. Folk did say he had loved my young mistress; but that, because she knew that his father would object, she would never listen to him, and married Mr. Esthwaite; but I don't know. He never married, at any rate. But he never took much notice of Miss Rosamond; which I thought he might have done if he had cared for her dead mother. He sent his gentleman with us to the Manor House, telling him to join him at Newcastle that same evening; so there was no great length of time for him to make us known to all the strangers before he, too, shook us off; and we were left, two lonely young things (I was not eighteen) in the great old Manor House. It seems like yesterday that we drove there. We had left our own dear parsonage very early, and we had both cried as if our hearts would break, though we were travelling in my lord's carriage, which I thought so much of once. And now it was long past noon on a September day, and we stopped to change horses for the last time at a little smoky town, all full

---

[1] Valet – the male equivalent of a lady's maid: a nobleman's personal servant and attendant

[2] Dared – in the domestic hierarchy, a nobleman's valet is superior to a lady's maid

[3] One with fresh, clean air (as opposed to a bogland, marsh, or swamp with foul, malarial air)

of colliers and miners[1]. Miss Rosamond had fallen asleep, but Mr. Henry told me to waken her, that she might see the park[2] and the Manor House as we drove up. I thought it rather a pity; but I did what he bade me, for fear he should complain of me to my lord. We had left all signs of a town, or even a village, and were then inside the gates of a large wild park— not like the parks here in the south, but with rocks, and the noise of running water, and gnarled thorn-trees, and old oaks, all white and peeled with age[3].

The road went up about two miles, and then we saw a great and stately house, with many trees close around it, so close that in some places their branches dragged against the walls when the wind blew, and some hung broken down; for no one seemed to take much charge of the place—to lop the wood, or to keep the moss-covered carriage-way in order. Only in front of the house all was clear. The great oval drive was without a weed; and neither tree nor creeper[4] was allowed to grow over the long, many-windowed front; at both sides of which a wing projected[5], which were each the ends of other side fronts; for the house, although it was so desolate, was even grander than I expected. Behind it rose the Fells, which seemed unenclosed and bare enough; and on the left hand of the house, as you stood facing it, was a little, old-fashioned flower-garden, as I found out afterwards. A door opened out upon it from the west front; it had been scooped out of the thick, dark wood for some old Lady Furnivall; but the branches of the great forest-trees had grown and overshadowed it again, and there were very few flowers that would live

---

[1] Gaskell was a famous social critic, and many of her stories and novels call attention to the abuses (both social and environmental) of the industrial age, which rocked northern England and southern Scotland: the former being dominated by coal mining, and the later by paper making, which left the air sooty and the rivers polluted, respectively

[2] A contained mixture of woodland and pastureland set aside for a noble family's usage (hunting, riding, fishing, etc.), and typically set in front of the manor

[3] Suggestive of the Furnivalls' character – warped, forbidding, aged, and ponderous

[4] Ivy, vertically climbing plants which grow on walls and trunks

[5] A classic layout for a Georgian manorhouse

there at that time[1].

When we drove up to the great front entrance, and went into the hall, I thought we should be lost—it was so large, and vast, and grand. There was a chandelier all of bronze, hung down from the middle of the ceiling; and I had never seen one before, and looked at it all in amaze. Then, at one end of the hall, was a great fireplace, as large as the sides of the houses in my country, with massy andirons and dogs[2] to hold the wood; and by it were heavy, old-fashioned sofas. At the opposite end of the hall, to the left as you went in—on the western side—was an organ built into the wall, and so large that it filled up the best part of that end[3]. Beyond it, on the same side, was a door; and opposite, on each side of the fireplace, were also doors leading to the east front; but those I never went through as long as I stayed in the house, so I can't tell you what lay beyond.

℅

The afternoon was closing in, and the hall, which had no fire lighted in it, looked dark and gloomy; but we did not stay there a moment. The old servant, who had opened the door for us, bowed to Mr. Henry, and took us in through the door at the further side of the great organ, and led us through several smaller halls and passages into the west drawing-room, where he said that Miss Furnivall was sitting. Poor little Miss

---

[1] Much like Rosamond's name implies, this garden suggests that pure, virtuous inclinations are under assault in this household. From a Freudian perspective, the plotted flower garden represents the ideals of the Super-Ego – intentional, good behavior – and the shadowy, aggressive forest with its randomized landscape suggests the Id – impulsive, selfish behavior. Suggestive of spiritual/moral danger, but *also* of a real physical threat to the vulnerable girl

[2] Apparatuses used to stoke and clean the fireplace, and to contain the stored firewood

[3] Most famously in *Phantom of the Opera*, and Mary Braddon's "The Haunted Organist of Hurly-Burly," organs have been used as Gothic props in horror literature. Known for their gloomy, powerful sound, their associations with religious ceremonies (the spiritual realm), and the often old-fashioned (even in the 1850s), billowing music made for them, they are well-suited to the genre

Rosamond held very tight to me, as if she were scared and lost in that great place[1]; and as for myself, I was not much better. The west drawing-room was very cheerful-looking, with a warm fire in it, and plenty of good, comfortable furniture about. Miss Furnivall was an old lady not far from eighty, I should think, but I do not know. She was thin and tall, and had a face as full of fine wrinkles as if they had been drawn all over it with a needle's point. Her eyes were very watchful, to make up, I suppose, for her being so deaf as to be obliged to use a trumpet[2]. Sitting with her, working at the same great piece of tapestry, was Mrs. Stark, her maid and companion, and almost as old as she was. She had lived with Miss Furnivall ever since they both were young, and now she seemed more like a friend than a servant; she looked so cold, and grey, and stony, as if she had never loved or cared for any one; and I don't suppose she did care for any one, except her mistress; and, owing to the great deafness of the latter, Mrs. Stark treated her very much as if she were a child. Mr. Henry gave some message from my lord, and then he bowed good-bye to us all—taking no notice of my sweet little Miss Rosamond's outstretched hand—and left us standing there, being looked at by the two old ladies through their spectacles.

I was right glad when they rung for the old footman[3] who had shown us in at first, and told him to take us to our rooms. So we went out of that great drawing-room, and into another sitting-room, and out of that, and then up a great flight of stairs, and along a broad gallery—which was something like a library, having books all down one side, and windows and writing-tables all down the other—till we came to our rooms, which I was not sorry to hear were just over the kitchens; for I began to think I should be lost in that wilderness of a house. There was an old nursery, that had been used for all the little lords and ladies long ago, with a pleasant fire burning in the grate, and the kettle boiling on the hob, and tea-things spread out on the table; and out of that room was the night-

---

[1] A telling detail – as if the hostile atmosphere threatens to absorb or consume her
[2] A fluted brass cone held to the ear of hearing impaired persons to funnel in sound
[3] A male servant who waits on guests, serves at the dinner table, and acts as a messenger

nursery, with a little crib for Miss Rosamond close to my bed. And old James called up Dorothy, his wife, to bid us welcome; and both he and she were so hospitable and kind, that by-and-by Miss Rosamond and me felt quite at home; and by the time tea was over, she was sitting on Dorothy's knee, and chattering away as fast as her little tongue could go. I soon found out that Dorothy was from Westmoreland, and that bound her and me together, as it were; and I would never wish to meet with kinder people than were old James and his wife. James had lived pretty nearly all his life in my lord's family, and thought there was no one so grand as they. He even looked down a little on his wife; because, till he had married her, she had never lived in any but a farmer's household. But he was very fond of her, as well he might be. They had one servant under them, to do all the rough work. Agnes they called her; and she and me, and James and Dorothy, with Miss Furnivall and Mrs. Stark, made up the family; always remembering my sweet little Miss Rosamond! I used to wonder what they had done before she came, they thought so much of her now. Kitchen and drawing-room, it was all the same. The hard, sad Miss Furnivall, and the cold Mrs. Stark, looked pleased when she came fluttering in like a bird, playing and pranking hither and thither, with a continual murmur, and pretty prattle of gladness. I am sure, they were sorry many a time when she flitted away into the kitchen, though they were too proud to ask her to stay with them, and were a little surprised at her taste; though to be sure, as Mrs. Stark said, it was not to be wondered at, remembering what stock her father had come of. The great, old rambling house was a famous[1] place for little Miss Rosamond. She made expeditions all over it, with me at her heels: all, except the east wing, which was never opened, and whither we never thought of going. But in the western and northern part was many a pleasant room; full of things that were curiosities to us, though they might not have been to people who had seen more. The windows were darkened by the sweeping boughs of the trees, and the ivy which had overgrown them; but, in the green gloom[2], we could manage to see old

---

[1] Beloved, well-used

[2] The aggressive vegetation – symbolic of a haunted, diseased psyche – discolors the light coming through the windows (read: truth, ease of mind, spiritual peace) and casts their lives in suggestive shadows and darkness

china jars and carved ivory boxes, and great heavy books, and, above all, the old pictures!

Once, I remember, my darling would have Dorothy go with us to tell us who they all were; for they were all portraits of some of my lord's family, though Dorothy could not tell us the names of every one. We had gone through most of the rooms, when we came to the old state drawing-room over the hall, and there was a picture of Miss Furnivall; or, as she was called in those days, Miss Grace, for she was the younger sister. Such a beauty she must have been! but with such a set, proud look, and such scorn looking out of her handsome eyes, with her eyebrows just a little raised, as if she wondered how anyone could have the impertinence to look at her, and her lip curled at us, as we stood there gazing. She had a dress on, the like of which I had never seen before, but it was all the fashion when she was young: a hat of some soft white stuff like beaver, pulled a little over her brows, and a beautiful plume of feathers sweeping round it on one side; and her gown of blue satin was open in front to a quilted white stomacher. "Well, to be sure!" said I, when I had gazed my fill. "Flesh is grass', they do say; but who would have thought that Miss Furnivall had been such an out-and-out beauty, to see her now?"

"Yes," said Dorothy. "Folks change sadly. But if what my master's father used to say was true, Miss Furnivall, the elder sister, was handsomer than Miss Grace. Her picture is here somewhere; but, if I show it you, you must never let on, even to James, that you have seen it Can the little lady hold her tongue, think you?" asked she.

I was not so sure, for she was such a little sweet, bold, open-spoken child, so I set her to hide herself; and then I helped Dorothy to turn a great picture, that leaned with its face towards the wall, and was not hung up as the others were. To be sure, it beat Miss Grace for beauty; and I think, for scornful pride, too, though in that matter it might be hard to choose. I could have looked at it an hour but Dorothy seemed half frightened at having shown it to me, and hurried it back again, and bade me run and find Miss Rosamond, for that there were some ugly

---

[1] That is to say, the beautiful age and die just as readily and easily as grass grows and is cut

places[1] about the house, where she should like ill for the child to go. I was a brave, high-spirited girl, and thought little of what the old woman said, for I liked hide-and-seek as well as any child in the parish; so off I ran to find my little one.

As winter drew on, and the days grew shorter, I was sometimes almost certain that I heard a noise as if some one was playing on the great organ in the hall. I did not hear it every evening; but, certainly, I did very often, usually when I was sitting with Miss Rosamond, after I had put her to bed, and keeping quite still and silent in the bedroom. Then I used to hear it booming and swelling away in the distance. The first night, when I went down to my supper, I asked Dorothy who had been playing music, and James said very shortly that I was a gowk to take the wind soughing[2] among the trees for music; but I saw Dorothy look at him very fearfully, and Bessy, the kitchen-maid, said something beneath her breath, and went quite white. I saw they did not like my question, so I held my peace till I was with Dorothy alone, when I knew I could get a good deal out of her. So, the next day, I watched my time, and I coaxed and asked her who it was that played the organ; for I knew that it was the organ and not the wind well enough, for all I had kept silence before James. But Dorothy had had her lesson, I'll warrant, and never a word could I get from her. So then I tried Bessy, though I had always held my head rather above her, as I was evened to James and Dorothy, and she was little better than their servant so she said I must never, never tell; and if ever told, I was never to say she had told me; but it was a very strange noise, and she had heard it many a time, but most of all on winter nights, and before storms; and folks did say it was the old lord playing on the great organ in the hall, just as he used to do when he was alive; but who the old lord was, or why he played, and why he played on stormy winter evenings in particular, she either could not or would not tell me. Well! I told you I had a brave heart; and I thought it was rather pleasant to have that grand music rolling about the house, let who would be the player; for now it rose above the great

---

[1] Ugly is a suggestive yet ambiguous word. In the context of the time, it would be understood that the term did not mean unattractive, but rather dangerous, disreputable, or unpleasant

[2] Moaning, howling, sighing

gusts of wind, and wailed and triumphed just like a living creature, and then it fell to a softness most complete, only it was always music, and tunes, so it was nonsense to call it the wind. I thought at first, that it might be Miss Furnivall who played, unknown to Bessy; but one day, when I was in the hall by myself, I opened the organ and peeped all about it and around it, as I had done to the organ in Crosthwaite Church once before, and I saw it was all broken and destroyed inside, though it looked so brave and fine; and then, though it was noon-day, my flesh began to creep a little, and I shut it up, and run away pretty quickly to my own bright nursery; and I did not like hearing the music for some time after that, any more than James and Dorothy did. All this time Miss Rosamond was making herself more and more beloved. The old ladies liked her to dine with them at their early dinner James stood behind Miss Furnivall's chair, and I behind Miss Rosamond's all in state; and, after dinner, she would play about in a corner of the great drawing-room as still as any mouse, while Miss Furnivall slept, and I had my dinner in the kitchen. But she was glad enough to come to me in the nursery afterwards; for, as she said Miss Furnivall was so sad, and Mrs. Stark so dull; but she and were merry enough; and, by-and-by, I got not to care for that weird rolling music, which did one no harm, if we did not know where it came from.

$\wp$

That winter was very cold. In the middle of October the frosts began, and lasted many, many weeks. I remember one day, at dinner, Miss Furnivall lifted up her sad, heavy eyes, and said to Mrs. Stark, "I am afraid we shall have a terrible winter," in a strange kind of meaning way. But Mrs. Stark pretended not to hear, and talked very loud of something else. My little lady and I did not care for the frost; not we! As long as it was dry, we climbed up the steep brows behind the house, and went up on the Fells which were bleak and bare enough, and there we ran races in the fresh, sharp air; and once we came down by a new path, that took us past the two old gnarled holly-trees, which grew about half-way down by the east side of the house.

But the days grew shorter and shorter, and the old lord, if it was he, played away, more and more stormily and sadly, on the great organ.

One Sunday afternoon—it must have been towards the end of November—I asked Dorothy to take charge of little missy when she came out of the drawing-room, after Miss Furnivall had had her nap; for it was too cold to take her with me to church, and yet I wanted to go, and Dorothy was glad enough to promise and was so fond of the child, that all seemed well; and Bessy and I set off very briskly, though the sky hung heavy and black over the white earth, as if the night had never fully gone away, and the air, though still, was very biting[1].

"We shall have a fall of snow," said Bessy to me. And sure enough, even while we were in church, it came down thick, in great large flakes—so thick, it almost darkened the windows. It had stopped snowing before we came out, but it lay soft, thick, and deep beneath our feet, as we tramped home. Before we got to the hall, the moon rose, and I think it was lighter then—what with the moon, and what with the white dazzling snow—than it had been when we went to church, between two and three o'clock. I have not told you that Miss Furnivall and Mrs. Stark never went to church; they used to read the prayers together, in their quiet, gloomy way; they seemed to feel the Sunday very long without their tapestry-work to be busy at. So when I went to Dorothy in the kitchen, to fetch Miss Rosamond and take her upstairs with me, I did not much wonder when the old woman told me that the ladies had kept the child with them, and that she had never come to the kitchen, as I had bidden her, when she was tired of behaving pretty in the drawing-room. So I took off my things and went to find her, and bring her to her supper in the nursery. But when I went into the best drawing-room, there sat the two old ladies, very still and quiet, dropping out a word now and then, but looking as if nothing so bright and merry as Miss Rosamond had ever been near them. Still I thought she might be hiding from me; it was one of her pretty ways—and that she had persuaded them to look as if they knew nothing about her; so I went softly peeping under this sofa and behind that chair, making believe I was sadly frightened at not finding her.

---

[1] The contrast between the soft, glowing landscape and the harsh, fierce sky suggests the conflict between genuine purity and subconscious evil. The omnipresence of night implies the lingering influence of repressed evils, past wickedness, and hidden motives

"What's the matter, Hester?" said Mrs. Stark sharply. I don't know if Miss Furnivall had seen me for, as I told you, she was very deaf, and she sat quite still, idly staring into the fire, with her hopeless face. "I'm only looking for my little Rosy Posy," replied I, still thinking that the child was there, and near me, though I could not see her.

"Miss Rosamond is not here," said Mrs. Stark. "She went away, more than an hour ago, to find Dorothy." And she, too, turned and went on looking into the fire.

My heart sank at this, and I began to wish I had never left my darling. I went back to Dorothy and told her. James was gone out for the day, but she, and me, and Bessy took lights, and went up into the nursery first; and then we roamed over the great, large house, calling and entreating Miss Rosamond to come out of her hiding-place, and not frighten us to death in that way. But there was no answer; no sound.

"Oh!" said I, at last, "can she have got into the east wing and hidden there?"

But Dorothy said it was not possible, for that she herself had never been in there; that the doors were always locked, and my lord's steward[1] had the keys, she believed; at any rate, neither she nor James had ever seen them: so I said I would go back, and see if, after all, she was not hidden in the drawing-room, unknown to the old ladies; and if I found her there, I said, I would whip her well for the fright she had given me; but I never meant to do it. Well, I went back to the west drawing-room, and I told Mrs. Stark we could not find her anywhere, and asked for leave to look all about the furniture there, for I thought now that she might have fallen asleep in some warm, hidden corner; but no! we looked— Miss Furnivall got up and looked, trembling all over—and she was nowhere there; then we set off again, every one in the house, and looked in all the places we had searched before, but we could not find her. Miss Furnivall shivered and shook so much that Mrs. Stark took her back into the warm drawing-room; but not before they had made me promise to bring her to them when she was found. Well-a-day! I began to think she never would be found, when I bethought me to look into the great front court, all covered with snow. I was upstairs when I looked out; but, it was

---

[1] Servant charged with maintaining the kitchen and the upkeep of the manor

such clear moonlight, I could see, quite plain, two little footprints, which might be traced from the hall-door and round the corner of the east wing. I don't know how I got down, but I tugged open the great stiff hall-door, and, throwing the skirt of my gown over my head for a cloak, I ran out. I turned the east corner, and there a black shadow fell on the snow but when I came again into the moonlight, there were the little footmarks going up—up to the Fells. It was bitter cold; so cold, that the air almost took the skin off my face as I ran; but I ran on, crying to think how my poor little darling must be perished and frightened. I was within sight of the holly-trees, when I saw a shepherd[1] coming down the hill, bearing something in his arms wrapped in his maud[2]. He shouted to me, and asked me if I had lost a bairn[3]; and, when I could not speak for crying, he bore towards me, and I saw my wee bairnie, lying still, and white, and stiff in his arms, as if she had been dead. He told me he had been up the Fells to gather in his sheep, before the deep cold of night came on, and that under the holly-trees (black marks on the hill-side, where no other bush was for miles around) he had found my little lady— my lamb—my queen—my darling—stiff and cold in the terrible sleep which is frost-begotten. Oh! the joy and the tears of having her in my arms once again I for I would not let him carry her; but took her, maud and all, into my own arms, and held her near my own warm neck and heart, and felt the life stealing slowly back again into her little gentle limbs[4]. But

---

[1] There is wry suitability in the nature of Rosamond's savior: a shepherd – one whose task in life is the guardianship of sheep – has recovered Hester's "little lamb." The lonesome herder conjures another famous rescuer: Christ, the "Good Shepherd." A fitting ally against the ghosts

[2] A large, loose cloak of grey plaid worn by shepherds in and near Scotland

[3] Pronounced *behrn* – a child (Scots)

[4] The manor's ancient Lady and her devilish maid are cold, aloof, unemotional, and despondent. Hester and Rosamond serves as foils to their emotional iciness, and Hester's desire for proximity to, and communion with her charge – desires motivated by love and affection – are similar foils to the curse on the Furnivall house. By pulling the cold body against her warm one, and pouring life and heat into it, Hester both physically and spiritually restores the warmth of affectionate life in the face of the chill of isolated death

she was still insensible when we reached the hall, and I had no breath for speech. We went in by the kitchen-door.

"Bring the warming-pan,"[1] said I; and I carried her upstairs, and began undressing her by the nursery fire, which Bessy had kept up. I called my little lammie[2] all the sweet and playful names I could think of—even while my eyes were blinded by my tears; and at last, oh! at length she opened her large blue eyes. Then I put her into her warm bed, and sent Dorothy down to tell Miss Furnivall that all was well; and I made up my mind to sit by my darling's bedside the live-long night. She fell away into a soft sleep as soon as her pretty head had touched the pillow, and I watched by her till morning light; when she wakened up bright and clear—or so I thought at first—and, my dears, so I think now.

℘

She said, that she had fancied that she should like to go to Dorothy, for that both the old ladies were asleep, and it was very dull in the drawing-room; and that, as she was going through the west lobby, she saw the snow through the high window falling—falling—soft and steady; but she wanted to see it lying pretty and white on the ground; so she made her way into the great hall: and then, going to the window, she saw it bright and soft upon the drive; but while she stood there, she saw a little girl, not so old as she was, "but so pretty," said my darling; "and this little girl beckoned to me to come out; and oh, she was so pretty and so sweet, I could not choose but go." And then this other little girl had taken her by the hand[3], and side by side the two had gone round the east

---

[1] An enclosed brass pan filled with smoldering coals which was slid between sheets before sleeping to warm the bed – a primitive electric blanket

[2] Baby lamb

[3] It is chilling that the shining lure which tempted Rosamond to a death by hypothermia was a pretty playmate, a girl just barely younger than her. Children often feature in ghost stories (most famously in Henry James' *Turn of the Screw*), typically as potential victims to inherit the punishments earned by adults in the past. Such metaphors imply the crucial nature of addressing and rectifying wrongdoings before their seep into the culture and pollute future generations. For a child to be haunted by a child only makes the irony more beastly

corner.

"Now you are a naughty little girl, and telling stories," said I. "What would your good mamma, that is in heaven, and never told a story in her life, say to her little Rosamond, if she heard her—and I dare say she does— telling stories!"

"Indeed, Hester," sobbed out my child, "I'm telling you true. Indeed I am."

"Don't tell me!" said I, very stern. "I tracked you by your foot-marks through the snow; there were only yours to be seen: and if you had had a little girl to go hand-in-hand with you up the hill, don't you think the footprints would have gone along with yours?"

"I can't help it, dear, dear Hester," said she, crying, "if they did not; I never looked at her feet, but she held my hand fast and tight in her little one, and it was very, very cold. She took me up the Fell-path, up to the holly-trees; and there I saw a lady weeping and crying; but when she saw me, she hushed her weeping, and smiled very proud and grand, and took me on her knee, and began to lull me to sleep, and that's all, Hester—but that is true; and my dear mamma knows it is," said she, crying. So I thought the child was in a fever, and pretended to believe her[1], as she went over her story—over and over again, and always the same. At last Dorothy knocked at the door with Miss Rosamond's breakfast; and she told me the old ladies were down in the eating parlour, and that they wanted to speak to me. They had both been into the night-nursery the evening before, but it was after Miss Rosamond was asleep; so they had only looked at her—not asked me any questions.

"I shall catch it,"[2] thought I to myself, as I went along the north gallery. "And yet," I thought, taking courage, "it was in their charge I left her; and it's they that's to blame for letting her steal away unknown and unwatched." So I went in boldly, and told my story. I told it all to Miss Furnivall, shouting it close to her ear; but when I came to the mention of the other little girl out in the snow, coaxing and tempting her out, and wiling her up to the grand and beautiful lady by the holly-tree, she threw her arms up—her old and withered arms—and cried aloud, "Oh! Heaven forgive! Have mercy!"

---

[1] Compare to Mrs Oliphant's similarly themed "The Open Door"

[2] *Boy am I ever going to get it; the shit is going to hit the fan*

Mrs. Stark took hold of her; roughly enough, I thought; but she was past Mrs. Stark's management, and spoke to me, in a kind of wild warning and authority.

"Hester! keep her from that child! It will lure her to her death! That evil child! Tell her it is a wicked, naughty child." Then, Mrs. Stark hurried me out of the room; where, indeed, I was glad enough to go; but Miss Furnivall kept shrieking out, "Oh, have mercy! Wilt Thou never forgive! It is many a long year ago"—

I was very uneasy in my mind after that. I durst never leave Miss Rosamond,
night or day, for fear lest she might slip off again, after some fancy or other; and all the more, because I thought I could make out that Miss Furnivall was crazy, from their odd ways about her; and I was afraid lest something of the same kind (which might be in the family, you know) hung over my darling. And the great frost never ceased all this time; and, whenever it was a more stormy night than usual, between the gusts, and through the wind we heard the old lord playing on the great organ. But, old lord, or not, wherever Miss Rosamond went, there I followed; for my love for her, pretty, helpless orphan, was stronger than my fear for the grand and terrible sound. Besides, it rested with me to keep her cheerful and merry, as beseemed her age. So we played together, and wandered together, here and there, and everywhere; for I never dared to lose sight of her again in that large and rambling house. And so it happened, that one afternoon, not long before Christmas-day[1], we were playing together on the billiard-table in the great hall (not that we knew the right way of playing, but she liked to roll the smooth ivory balls with her pretty hands, and I liked to do whatever she did); and, by-and-by, without our noticing it, it grew dusk indoors, though it was still light in the open air[2], and I was thinking of taking her back into the nursery, when, all of a sudden, she cried out—

_____

[1] Traditionally associated with telling ghost tales, and often their setting
[2] The darkness is starting to become associated *within* the house itself – not just the region or even the property – as the supernatural powers outside threaten to shed light on the family's sins. Just as the phantom girl stands outside, wanting admission, so too the light hovers outside

"Look, Hester! look! there is my poor little girl out in the snow!"

I turned towards the long narrow windows, and there, sure enough, I saw a little girl, less than my Miss Rosamond—dressed all unfit to be out-of-doors such a bitter night—crying, and beating against the window panes, as if she wanted to be let in. She seemed to sob and wail, till Miss Rosamond could bear it no longer, and was flying to the door to open it, when, all of a sudden, and close upon us, the great organ pealed out so loud and thundering, it fairly made me tremble; and all the more, when I remembered me that, even in the stillness of that dead-cold weather, I had heard no sound of little battering hands upon the window-glass, although the phantom child had seemed to put forth all its force; and, although I had seen it wail and cry, no faintest touch of sound had fallen upon my ears. Whether I remembered all this at the very moment, I do not know; the great organ sound had so stunned me into terror; but this I know, I caught up Miss Rosamond before she got the hall-door opened, and clutched her, and carried her away, kicking and screaming, into the large, bright kitchen, where Dorothy and Agnes were busy with their mince-pies.

"What is the matter with my sweet one?" cried Dorothy, as I bore in Miss Rosamond, who was sobbing as if her heart would break.

"She won't let me open the door for my little girl to come in; and she'll die if she is out on the Fells all night. Cruel, naughty Hester," she said, slapping me[1]; but she might have struck harder, for I had seen a look of ghastly terror on Dorothy's face, which made my very blood run cold.

"Shut the back-kitchen door fast, and bolt it well," said she to Agues. She said no more; she gave me raisins and almonds[2] to quiet Miss Rosamond; but she sobbed about the little girl in the snow, and would not touch any of the good things. I was thankful when she cried herself to sleep in bed. Then I stole down to the kitchen, and told Dorothy I had made up my mind. I would carry my darling back to my father's house in

---

[1] The previously loving and playful Rosamond is now – at the invocation of "[her] little girl" – spiteful and sullen, even disrespectful to the point of violence. Whatever these ghosts bring with them is accompanied by a spirit of divisiveness, selfishness, and bitter spite

[2] Treats (both healthy and tasty) on par with modern candy and chocolate in the eyes of a child

Applethwaite[1]; where, if we lived humbly, we lived at peace. I said I had been frightened enough with the old lord's organ-playing; but now that I had seen for myself this little moaning child, all decked out as no child in the neighbourhood could be[2], beating and battering to get in, yet always without any sound or noise— with the dark wound[3] on its right shoulder; and that Miss Rosamond had known it again for the phantom that had nearly lured her to death (which Dorothy knew was true); I would stand it no longer.

I saw Dorothy change colour once or twice. When I had done, she told me she did not think I could take Miss Rosamond with me, for that she was my lord's ward, and I had no right over her; and she asked me would I leave the child that I was so fond of just for sounds and sights that could do me no harm; and that they had all had to get used to in their turns[4]? I was all in a hot, trembling passion; and I said it was very well for her to talk, that knew what these sights and noises betokened[5], and that had, perhaps, had something to do with the spectre child while it was alive. And I taunted her so, that she told me all she knew at last; and then I

---

[1] A village among foothills in the center of Cumbria (today the population still is less than 300)

[2] Both due to the outdated fashion of her early Georgian attire, and to the fact that no child would be permitted outside in such a state of undress, or indeed, be able to survive the walk to the manor without succumbing

[3] This brutal hematoma – a bruise or blood spot – suddenly detracts from the cherubic image that Rosamond had previously summoned: no longer a sweet, lovely child, the phantom – further described as evil and wicked – is now revealed to suffer a marring disfigurement. Wounds to the body typically symbolize wounds to the soul, spirit, or identity. This child – otherwise lovely we can be sure – is blotted with a deep, recognizable stain, one left in a past age which continues to discolor the distant present

[4] The collective avoidance of the staff and family – their refusal to confront the specters and openly accept and resolve the meaning of their appearances – is what prevents them from disappearing. While Dorothy suggests that Hester simply learn to ignore and live with the problem, the young maid refuses to deny the very genuine (and very dangerous) reality

[5] Meant, suggested. *What*, she is asking, *is going on in this house? What went on in this house?*

wished I had never been told, for it only made me more afraid than ever.

She said she had heard the tale from old neighbours that were alive when she was first married; when folks used to come to the hall sometimes, before it had got such a bad name on the country side: it might not be true, or it might, what she had been told.

ℇↄ

The old lord was Miss Furnivall's father—Miss Grace, as Dorothy called her, for Miss Maude was the elder, and Miss Furnivall by lights. The old lord was eaten up with pride. Such a proud man was never seen or heard of; and his daughters were like him. No one was good enough to wed them, although they had choice enough; for they were the great beauties of their day, as I had seen by their portraits, where they hung in the state drawing-room. But, as the old saying is, "Pride will have a fall;" and these two haughty beauties fell in love with the same man, and he no better than a foreign musician[1], whom their father had down from London to play music with him at the Manor House. For, above all things, next to his pride, the old lord loved music[2]. He could play on nearly every instrument that ever was heard of; and it was a strange thing it did not soften him; but he was a fierce, dour[3] old man, and had broken his poor wife's heart with his cruelty, they said. He was mad after music, and would pay any money for it. So he got this foreigner to come; who made such beautiful music, that they said the very birds on the trees stopped their singing to listen. And, by degrees, this foreign gentleman got such a hold over the old lord, that nothing would serve him but that he must come every year; and it was he that had the great organ brought from Holland, and built up in the hall, where it stood now. He taught the old lord to play on it; but many and many a time, when Lord Furnivall

---

[1] While it may seem small and petty, for an English noblewoman to marry *either* a foreigner *or* a musician was equally as distasteful, but to marry both would have been a sizable scandal

[2] They are, therefore, interrelated, and the continuation of the lord's music-playing is symbolic of the continuance of his pride – the original germ which caused *all* of the problems at Furnivall

[3] Sour, stern, unpleasant

was thinking of nothing but his fine organ, and his finer music[1], the dark foreigner was walking abroad in the woods, with one of the young ladies: now Miss Maude, and then Miss Grace.

Miss Maude won the day and carried off the prize, such as it was; and he and she were married, all unknown to any one; and, before he made his next yearly visit, she had been confined of a little girl at a farm-house on the Moors, while her father and Miss Grace thought she was away at Doncaster Races[2]. But though she was a wife and a mother, she was not a bit softened, but as haughty and as passionate as ever; and perhaps more so, for she was jealous of Miss Grace, to whom her foreign husband paid a deal of court—by way of blinding her—as he told his wife. But Miss Grace triumphed over Miss Maude, and Miss Maude grew fiercer and fiercer, both with her husband and with her sister; and the former—who could easily shake off what was disagreeable, and hide himself in foreign countries—went away a month before his usual time that summer, and half-threatened that he would never come back again. Meanwhile, the little girl was left at the farm-house, and her mother used to have her horse saddled and gallop wildly over the hills to see her once every week, at the very least; for where she loved she loved, and where she hated she hated[3]. And the old lord went on playing—playing on his organ; and the servants thought the sweet music he made had soothed down his awful temper, of which (Dorothy said) some terrible tales could be told. He grew infirm too, and had to walk with a crutch; and his son—that was the present Lord Furnivall's father—was with the army in America[4], and the other son at sea; so Miss Maude had it pretty much her own way, and she and Miss Grace grew colder and bitterer to each other every day; till at last they hardly ever spoke, except when the

---

[1] Distracted by pride, he neglected his family and allowed them to be abused by a rake who knew to use vanity to capture the old man's attention. And thus the organ plays on and on

[2] A high society event

[3] Hatred appears to literally dwell in the manor house – away from it, love can survive

[4] Dating this portion of the story to some period between 1754 and 1783. The "American War" referenced in British literature is almost always the War of Independence, however, so we may assume that the date be refined to some point between 1775 and 1783

old lord was by. The foreign musician came again the next summer, but it was for the last time; for they led him such a life with their jealousy and their passions, that he grew weary, and went away, and never was heard of again[1]. And Miss Maude, who had always meant to have her marriage acknowledged when her father should be dead, was left now a deserted wife, whom nobody knew to have been married, with a child that she dared not own, although she loved it to distraction; living with a father whom she feared, and a sister whom she hated. When the next summer passed over, and the dark foreigner never came, both Miss Maude and Miss Grace grew gloomy and sad; they had a haggard look about them, though they looked handsome as ever. But, by-and-by, Miss Maude brightened; for her father grew more and more infirm, and more than ever carried away by his music, and she and Miss Grace lived almost entirely apart, having separate rooms, the one on the west side, Miss Maude on the east—those very rooms which were now shut up. So she thought she might have her little girl with her, and no one need ever know except those who dared not speak about it, and were bound to believe that it was, as she said, a cottager's[2] child she had taken a fancy to[3]. All this, Dorothy said, was pretty well known; but what came afterwards no one knew, except Miss Grace and Mrs. Stark, who was even then her maid, and much more of a friend to her than ever her sister had been. But the servants supposed, from words that were dropped, that Miss Maude had triumphed over Miss Grace, and told her that all the time the dark foreigner had been mocking her with pretended love—he was her own husband. The colour left Miss Grace's cheek and lips that very day for ever, and she was heard to say many a time that sooner or later she would have her revenge; and Mrs. Stark was for ever spying about the east rooms.

---

[1] Jealousy and passion were the behaviors which first attracted his attention – and his disgrace – and later drove him away – exacerbating and compounding the disgrace; the family's ghosts are those of petty vanity and spite, and it was haunted before any of them died

[2] Tenant on the family land – a poor farmer

[3] This rouse is not as stupid as it appears: nobles were known to occasionally develop pet-like affections for poor children, sometimes bringing orphans home as sources of entertainment, as one would a clever monkey or stray dog

One fearful night, just after the New Year had come in, when the snow was lying thick and deep; and the flakes were still falling—fast enough to blind any one who might be out and abroad—there was a great and violent noise heard, and the old lord's voice above all, cursing and swearing awfully, and the cries of a little child, and the proud defiance of a fierce woman, and the sound of a blow, and a dead stillness, and moans and wailings, dying away on the hill-side! Then the old lord summoned all his servants, and told them, with terrible oaths, and words more terrible, that his daughter had disgraced herself, and that he had turned her out of doors—her, and her child—and that if ever they gave her help, or food, or shelter, he prayed that they might never enter heaven. And, all the while, Miss Grace stood by him, white and still as any stone; and, when he had ended, she heaved a great sigh, as much as to say her work was done, and her end was accomplished. But the old lord never touched his organ again, and died within the year[1]; and no wonder ! for, on the morrow of that wild and fearful night, the shepherds, coming down the Fell side, found Miss Maude sitting, all crazy and smiling, under the holly-trees, nursing a dead child[2], with a terrible mark on its right shoulder. "But that was not what killed it," said Dorothy: "it was the frost and the cold. Every wild creature was in its hole, and every beast in its fold, while the child and its mother were turned out to wander on the Fells! And now you know all! And I wonder if you are less frightened now?"

I was more frightened than ever; but I said I was not. I wished Miss Rosamond and myself well out of that dreadful house for ever; but I would not leave her, and I dared not take her away. But oh, how I watched her, and guarded her! We bolted the doors, and shut the window-shutters fast, an hour or more before dark, rather than leave

---

[1] Finally aware of his deception – that he was made a fool by the musician, and that his musical monomania was the instrument of his disgrace – the old lord's pride is finally broken, and while the organ music haunts the house (just as do the ramifications of his pride), the pride living in his spirit has expired, and so has the music that symbolized it

[2] What better metaphor could be found for parental abuse, emotional neglect, and the impossibility of changing the past than a stupefied mother vainly trying to nurse a dead baby with her frozen breast? Tragically poetic

them open five minutes too late. But my little lady still heard the weird[1] child crying and mourning; and not all we could do or say could keep her from wanting to go to her, and let her in from the cruel wind and snow. All this time I kept away from Miss Furnivall and Mrs. Stark, as much as ever I could; for I feared them—I knew no good could be about them, with their grey, hard faces, and their dreamy eyes, looking back into the ghastly years that were gone. But, even in my fear, I had a kind of pity for Miss Furnivall, at least. Those gone down to the pit[2] can hardly have a more hopeless look than that which was ever on her face. At last I even got so sorry for her—who never said a word but what was quite forced from her—that I prayed for her; and I taught Miss Rosamond to pray for one who had done a deadly sin; but often, when she came to those words, she would listen, and start up from her knees, and say, "I hear my little girl plaining and crying, very sad—oh, let her in, or she will die[3]!"

§

One night—just after New Year's Day had come at last, and the long winter had taken a turn, as I hoped—I heard the west drawing-room bell ring three times, which was the signal for me. I would not leave Miss Rosamond alone, for all she was asleep—for the old lord had been playing wilder than ever—and I feared lest my darling should waken to hear the spectre child; see her I knew she could not. I had fastened the windows too well for that. So I took her out of her bed, and wrapped her up in such outer clothes as were most handy, and carried her down to the drawing-room, where the old ladies sat at their tapestry-work as usual. They looked up when I came in, and Mrs. Stark asked, quite astounded, "Why did I bring Miss Rosamond there, out of her warm bed?" I had begun to whisper, "Because I was afraid of her being

---

[1] Ghostly, witchlike, spooky

[2] Hell – Miss Grace is tormented by her guilt, caught in a living hell

[3] Restitution must be had before the ghosts will depart: "Let her in!" – openly acknowledge the sins that were committed, don't merely hope to pray them away – "or she will die!" – and who, might we venture to ask, is the "she" here? Ostensibly the (already dead) girl in the snow, possibly the guilt-laden old woman, but Rosamond may be unknowingly foretelling her own fate – that is, if the sins of the past are not absolved and cleansed from the cursed house

tempted out while I was away, by the wild child in the snow," when she stopped me short (with a glance at Miss Furnivall), and said Miss Furnivall wanted me to undo some work she had done wrong[1], and which neither of them could see to unpick. So I laid my pretty dear on the sofa, and sat down on a stool by them, and hardened my heart against them, as I heard the wind rising and howling.

Miss Rosamond slept on sound, for all the wind blew so; and Miss Furnivall said never a word, nor looked round when the gusts shook the windows. All at once she started up to her full height, and put up one hand, as if to bid us listen.

"I hear voices!" said she. "I hear terrible screams—I hear my father's voice!"

Just at that moment my darling wakened with a sudden start: "My little girl is crying, oh, how she is crying!" and she tried to get up and go to her, but she got her feet entangled in the blanket, and I caught her up; for my flesh had begun to creep at these noises, which they heard while we could catch no sound. In a minute or two the noises came, and gathered fast, and filled our ears; we, too, heard voices and screams, and no longer heard the winter's wind that raged abroad. Mrs. Stark looked at me, and I at her, but we dared not speak. Suddenly Miss Furnivall, went towards the door, out into the ante-room[2], through the west lobby, and opened the door into the great hall. Mrs. Stark followed, and I durst not be left, though my heart almost stopped beating for fear. I wrapped my darling tight in my arms, and went out with them. In the hall the screams were louder than ever; they seemed to come from the east wing—nearer and nearer—close on the other side of the locked-up doors—close behind them. Then I noticed that the great bronze chandelier seemed all alight, though the hall was dim, and that a fire was blazing in the vast hearth-place, though it gave no heat; and I shuddered up with terror, and folded my darling closer to me. But as I did so the east door shook, and she, suddenly struggling to get free from me, cried, "Hester! I must go. My little girl is there I hear her; she is coming! Hester, I must go!"

I held her tight with all my strength; with a set will, I held her. If I had

---

[1] Needlework – recall Hester's prowess "at the needle"
[2] Entryway or lobby that leads up to a larger room

died, my hands would have grasped her still, I was so resolved in my mind. Miss Furnivall stood listening, and paid no regard to my darling, who had got down to the ground, and whom I, upon my knees now, was holding with both my arms clasped round her neck; she still striving and crying to get free.

All at once, the east door gave way with a thundering crash, as if torn open in a violent passion[1], and there came into that broad and mysterious light, the figure of a tall old man, with grey hair and gleaming eyes. He drove before him, with many a relentless gesture of abhorrence, a stern and beautiful woman, with a little child clinging to her dress.

"O Hester! Hester!" cried Miss Rosamond; "it's the lady! The lady below the holly-trees; and my little girl is with her. Hester! Hester! let me go to her; they are drawing me to them. I feel them—I feel them. I must go!"

Again she was almost convulsed by her efforts to get away; but I held her tighter and tighter, till I feared I should do her a hurt[2]; but rather that than let her go towards those terrible phantoms. They passed along towards the great hall-door, where the winds howled and ravened for their prey; but before they reached that, the lady turned; and I could see that she defied the old man with a fierce and proud defiance; but then she quailed[3]—and then she threw up her arms wildly and piteously to save her child—her little child—from a blow from his uplifted crutch.

And Miss Rosamond was torn as by a power stronger than mine, and writhed in my arms, and sobbed (for by this time the poor darling was growing faint).

"They want me to go with them on to the Fells—they are drawing me

---

[1] Symbolically, the memories, anxieties, fears, and crimes long denied (or repressed or avoided) by being locked away in the unconscious (read: the East Wing) have been broken free by the resurging force of the passions and bitterness that caused them in the first place

[2] This prefigures the death of Miles in James' "Turn of the Screw," wherein – during the climactic appearance of the ghosts – the governess embraces her little charge, until (as some interpret it) she inadvertently smothers him or crushes him to death

[3] Showed fear or apprehension, relinquished her pride – unlike her father, she shunned her inborn pride in the defense of her child

to them[1]. Oh, my little girl! I would come, but cruel, wicked Hester holds me very tight." But when she saw the uplifted crutch, she swooned away, and I thanked God for it. Just at this moment—when the tall old man, his hair streaming as in the blast of a furnace[2], was going to strike the little shrinking child—Miss Furnivall, the old woman by my side, cried out, "O father! father! Spare the little innocent child[3]!" But just then I saw—we all saw— another phantom shape itself, and grow clear out of the blue and misty light that filled the hall; we had not seen her till now, for it was another lady who stood by the old man, with a look of relentless hate and triumphant scorn. That figure was very beautiful to look upon, with a soft, white hat drawn down over the proud brows, and a red and curling lip. It was dressed in an open robe of blue satin. I had seen that figure before. It was the likeness of Miss Furnivall in her youth; and the terrible phantoms moved on, regardless of old Miss Furnivall's wild entreaty—and the uplifted crutch fell on the right shoulder of the little child[4], and the younger sister looked on, stony, and deadly serene. But at that moment, the dim lights, and the fire that gave no heat, went out of themselves, and Miss Furnivall lay at our feet stricken down by the

---

[1] The little ghost acts as a doppelgänger to Rosamond – a suggestive double. Just as one generation (represented by the child) was stripped of its future and innocence and security by the crimes of adults, so to can the generations of the future be abused and decimated by those same, lingering sins, until they are absolved and rectified. Until Miss Furnivall confesses her crimes and pleads in her sister's defense, Rosamond is vulnerable to destruction by the same forces of pride, spite, and revenge that drew her supernatural double into oblivion

[2] Suggests hell – whether or not this is the source of the heat, the family is in a sense damned – damned to repeat this sinful tableau until it is rectified

[3] Finally, she speaks out in defense of her sister and niece – too late for them, not for Rosamond

[4] The shoulder was certainly dislocated, the bones likely broken, the collarbone, ribs, and shoulder blade likely broken or fractured, and the muscles and tendons torn – make no mistake, while not as sexy as a pistol shot or saber cut, this wound is far more than a plain bruise: the girl would be horribly brutalized and traumatized by such an assault

palsy[1]—death-stricken.

Yes! She was carried to her bed that night never to rise again. She lay with her face to the wall, muttering low, but muttering always: "Alas! alas! what is done in youth can never be undone in age! What is done in youth can never be undone in age[2]!"

---

*THE end is abrupt – almost jarring – and it jostles the expectations we held for the characters. Who, in fact, is the real focus of the story? We are secure in the old nurse's fate and the fate of her young charge, whose children she is addressing. It is the withered Miss Grace, whose dying words fade the story out, who takes center stage at the end of the drama. It is her past wickedness (and the collective psychological avoidance and denial of the residents and staff) that threatens an innocent generation, steeping the manor in moral impotence and spiritual vulnerability , nearly luring Rosamund into a frosty demise. Guilt and denial haunt Miss Grace and everyone in her proximity. Gaskell adds her story to the mythology of the Victorians, who were well-aware that the imperial sins they incurred (and collectively tried to deny), could haunt the present generation and lure their grandchildren into world wars, economic recessions, colonial insurrections, and wide class disparity. A family that quietly enabled the old squire's negligence and abuses cannot expect to escape the ramifications of his selfish violence, just as a nation that turns a blind eye to the maltreatment of class and empire cannot pray to avoid the angry echoes of the past. "Be generous and slow to anger, young ones," the old nurse warns, "right your wrongs and behave with calm compassion, because the ugly repercussions of impulses and abuses may be impossible to fend off before they cause cataclysm."*

---

[1] This fatal seizure is identified as palsy, or epilepsy

[2] Our moral is clean and precisely stated: despite her best attempts to deny or avoid her guilt, the sins committed in Miss Furnivall's youth are not erased by ignoring their ramifications. This is what (I believe) she means when she insanely gibbers her dying refrain: it is not a mere moral, but a confession – "I can't change the past by ignoring it; I can't change the past by ignoring it; I can't change the past by ignoring it..."

*EDITH Nesbit mastered the late Victorian supernatural tale, and this very short sketch – almost flash fiction – is an underappreciated jewel of her work. Her stories featured calamity reaching out of the invisible world, afflicting completely innocent persons. Most Victorian tales of this genre – the clairvoyant dream – result in prevention and avoidance (Riddell's "Forewarned, Forearmed" is a fine example). While the vision is partially avoided, it proves fateful, challenging Victorians' optimism and trust in the power of will and industry. Like "The Red Room," it offers a glimpse into a misanthropic and incomprehensible cosmos – hostile and cruelly indifferent to the efforts of human diligence. This report is called "The Mystery of the Semi-Detached," and it is no misnomer (the only more accurate title, perhaps, would be "The Awful Thing He Saw in the Semi-Detached"), because unanswered questions and unoffered explanation fuel the heat of the revulsion this sketch engenders. Grim, cynical, and inexplicable, the vision of the semi-detached is perhaps more atrocious to the unwitting, helpless seer than to its slaughtered victim.*

---

## THE MYSTERY OF THE SEMI-DETACHED
### {1893}
### *Edith Nesbitt*

HE WAS WAITING FOR HER, he had been waiting an hour and a half in a dusty suburban lane, with a row of big elms on one side and some eligible building sites on the other – and far away to the south-west the twinkling yellow lights of the Crystal Palace[1]. It was not quite like a country lane, for it had a pavement and lamp-posts, but it was not a bad place for a meeting[2] all the same: and farther up, towards the cemetery, it was really quite rural, and almost pretty, especially in

---

[1] Massive cast iron and plate glass structure built in Hyde Park, London, to house the Great Exhibition of 1851. It was (appropriately) 1,851 feet long and 128 feet high

[2] By "meeting" he means a tryst. The nature of this meeting – combined with the family's disapproval, and with his later familiarity with her bedroom – suggest a sexual encounter

twilight. But twilight had long deepened into the night, and still he waited. He loved her, and he was engaged to be married to her, with the

complete disapproval of every reasonable person who had been consulted[1]. And this half-clandestine meeting was tonight to take the place of the grudgingly

sanctioned weekly interview[2] –because a certain rich uncle was visiting at her house, and her mother was not the woman to acknowledge to a moneyed uncle, who might "go off" any day, a match so deeply ineligible as hers with him[3].

So he waited for her, and the chill of an unusually severe May evening entered into his bones[4].

The policeman passed him with a surly response to his "Good night". The bicyclists went by him like grey ghosts with foghorns; and it was nearly ten o'clock, and she had not come[5].

He shrugged his shoulders and turned towards his lodgings. His road led him by her house—desirable, commodious, semi-detached[6]—and he walked slowly as he neared it. She might, even now, be coming out. But

---

[1] Stubborn, proud, and resistant to external advice, the couple who feature in this tale are universally disapproved of. This might be due to a difference in social rank or in personality, character, or disposition, but subtle clues throughout the piece imply that the libertine nature of their "meetings" have caused a moral scandal

[2] The couple pay court to each  other only once a week due to the disapproval of the families

[3] The concern here is that the wealthy uncle who may die at any moment would disinherit his niece if he was made aware of the pairing

[4] It is important to note the emotional backdrop that Nesbit has woven: before encountering the horror, the protagonist's personal life is fraught with uncertainty, whisperings, and danger

[5] Once again, ten o'clock is a very late hour for a respectable, unmarried couple to be rendezvousing – the meeting is almost certainly not of a reputable nature

[6] That is to say, a duplex; two identical houses built alongside one another sharing a party wall and a floor plan Chic, modern, and fashionable for a young woman of society

she was not There was no sign of movement about the house, no sign of life, no lights even in the windows. And her people were not early people. He paused by the gate, wondering.

Then he noticed that the front door was open-wide open-and the street lamp shone a little way into the dark hall. There was something about all this that did not please him—that scared him a little, indeed. The house had a gloomy and deserted air. It was obviously impossible that it harboured a rich uncle. The old man must have left early. In which case—

He walked up the path of patent glazed tiles, and listened. No sign of life. He passed into the hall. There was no light anywhere. Where was everybody, and why was the front door open? There was no one in the drawing room, the dining room and the study (nine feet by seven) were equally blank. Everyone was out, evidently. But the unpleasant sense that he was, perhaps, not the first casual visitor to walk through that open door impelled him to look through the house before he went away and closed it after him. So he went upstairs, and at the door of the first bedroom he came to he struck a wax match, as he had done in the sitting rooms[1]. Even as he did so he felt that he was not alone. And he was prepared to see something but for what he saw he was not prepared. For what he saw lay on the bed, in a white loose

---

[1] The scandalous nature of the protagonist and his fiancée's relationship is apparent in their friends' responses, but it is heavily implied by his intrusion into the bedroom – an act of familiarity that would have been perceived as indecent and crass. The Freudian implications of his disquieting sense that he was "not the first casual visitor to walk through [the] open door" of her apartment and his subsequent suspicious intrusion into the bedroom may speak to the loose sexual nature of their relationship, and the anxieties of a man who is undaunted by entering into an erotic relationship with a woman, but desperately resents any previous dalliances with past lovers. Has anyone else entered this room?

gown—and it was his sweetheart, and its[1] throat was cut from ear to ear[2]. He doesn't know what happened then, nor how he got downstairs and into the street; but he got out somehow, and the policeman found him in a fit, under the lamp-post at the corner of the street. He couldn't speak when they picked him up, and he passed the night in the police cells, because the policeman had seen plenty of drunken men before, but never one in a fit[3].

The next morning he was better, though still very white and shaky. But the tale he told the magistrate[4] was convincing, and they sent a couple of constables with him to her house.

There was no crowd about it as he had fancied there would be, and the blinds were not down[5].

He held on to the door-post for support...

"She's all right, you see," said the constable, who had found him under the lamp. "I told you you was drunk, but you would know best."

When he was alone with her he told her—not all—for that would not bear telling—but how he had come into the commodious[6] semi-detached, and how he had found the door open and the lights out, and that he had been into that long back room facing the stairs, and had seen something—in even trying to hint at which he turned sick and

---

[1] Laid suggestively across a bed, dressed in what appears to be a revealing, negligee-like garment, with her throat viciously mangled, the figure is comfortably codified as a victim of rape. Considering the suspected nature of his relationship with his fiancée, the protagonist almost certainly feels a soup of emotions on seeing her sexually-receptive body violated: outrage, sorrow, and agony, yes, but also jealousy, suspicion, and lust

[2] The rapacious imagery is self-incriminating. The protagonist will be the first suspect, will have no alibi, and will have had excellent opportunity, but beyond these simply logistical issues, psychologically he must question his ability to perform such an act

[3] Agitated to the point of wild spasms and convulsions

[4] He has been taken to jail as a suspected drunk, but successfully appeals his case

[5] A traditional practice during mourning done to keep the family's trauma private

[6] Comfortable, inviting

broke down and had to have brandy given him.

"But, my dearest," she said, "I dare say the house was dark, for we were all at the Crystal Palace with my uncle, and no doubt the door was open, for the maids will run out if they're left. But you could not have been in that room, because I locked it when I came away, and the key was in my pocket. I dressed in a hurry and I left all my odds and ends lying about."

"I know," he said; "I saw a green scarf on a chair, and some long brown gloves, and a lot of hairpins and ribbons, and a prayerbook, and a lace handkerchief on the dressing table. Why, I even noticed the almanack on the mantelpiece—21 October. At least it couldn't be that, because this is May. And yet it was. Your almanack is at 21 October, isn't it?"

"No, of course it isn't," she said, smiling rather anxiously; "but all the other things were just as you say. You must have had a dream, or a vision, or something[1]."

He was a very ordinary, commonplace, City young man, and he didn't believe in visions, but he never rested day or night till he got his sweetheart and her mother away from that commodious semi-detached, and settled them in a quiet distant suburb[2]. In the course of the removal he incidentally married her, and the mother went on living with them[3].

His nerves must have been a good bit shaken, because he was very queer for a long time, and was always enquiring if anyone had taken the

---

[1] Considering that the articles on the dressing table were all hers, the vision certainly suggests that the disaster would have befallen her had not her fiancée been supernaturally alerted. The mangled woman on the bed was not meant to be anyone other than her – without the interference of fate – and the implications suggest that the future killer may indeed have been our protagonist (inspired by who knows what – jealousy, anxiety, lust) had he continued courting her in that place

[2] The theme of the corrupting influence of the city versus the purifying spirit of the country runs throughout this brief piece – in the beginning he is comforted by the almost "rural" scenery of Hyde Park while the Crystal Palace gleams coldly in the background

[3] A life of "semi-clandestine" courtship – including, I suspect, sexual exploration – has been traded for a settled, domestic life with a respectable marriage and a settled mother-in-law

desirable semi-detached; and when an old stockbroker with a family took it, he went the length of calling on the old gentleman and imploring him by all that he held dear, not to live in that fatal house.

"Why?" said the stockbroker, not unnaturally.

And then he got so vague and confused, between trying to tell why and trying not to tell why, that the stockbroker showed him out, and thanked his God he was not such a fool as to allow a lunatic to stand in the way of his taking that really remarkably cheap[1] and desirable semi-detached residence.

Now the curious and quite inexplicable part of this story is that when she came down to breakfast on the morning of the 22 October she found him looking like death, with the morning paper in his hand. He caught hers—he couldn't speak, and pointed to the paper. And there she read that on the night of the 21st a young lady, the stockbroker's daughter, had been found, with her throat cut from ear to ear, on the bed in the long back bedroom facing the stairs of that desirable semi-detached[2].

---

[1] Recall "Nothing But the Truth" – could the low price of the Semi-Detached be due to the fact that some influence inhabits it, which causes tragedies to occur there?

[2] With no report of a burglary or of stolen items (as may explain a person's murder in their sleep), with no suggestion of a family-wide massacre (as may befall a rich and important man), and no mention of a loud brawl between lovers (as may befall a young woman whose throat is cut), the implication is that the girl was slain while sleeping in bed, and that the crime extends beyond murder to rape. By whom is unimportant to Nesbit – the antagonist is the spirit that inhabits the house, and it may be possessing any of a variety of faceless, motiveless agents

*A brief sketch in horror (terror takes the back seat in this nightmarish episode), Nesbit's story begins with an emotional atmosphere in an unlikely setting. Bourgeois, posh, and refined, the neighborhood is nonetheless crawling with unease. The policeman's brusque salute, the fog-polluted avenues, and the protagonist's brooding mind introduce us to an impressionistic landscape of doom. Little time passes before the young man casually enters the gaping door and stumbles on the gore-drenched vision. The mechanics of the vision are never explained: who was the murderer, why did the vision appear to the young fellow, and why was the butchery and inevitability? Nesbit is not concerned with explaining the supernatural engineering to her story, but with the emotional trauma of the young man and the cruel unflappability of fate. Powerless to prevent the murder – one with definite overtones of sexual violence – he is deflated from a reckless playboy to a shaken phantom of his former self. Formerly engaged in a sexually scandalous relationship (familiar with his lover's bedroom and resistant to the "complete disapproval of every reasonable person who had been consulted") the protagonist is shocked into adopting a safe and settled lifestyle of cautious marriage. The power of a single episode of horror to utterly transform a man's spirit is the heart of Nesbit's cynical meditation.*

*NONE of the Victorian supernaturalists rivaled the complex and visceral horror of J. S. Le Fanu. M. R. James adored him, Bram Stoker plagiarized him[1], and Henry James counted himself amongst the Irishman's devotees. The cause of his celebrity was his departure from Victorian conventions of fright, the psychological complexity, moral ambiguity, and dedication to realism of his fiction. Presaging the two Jameses – and even Lovecraft, who (unfairly, I hold) disliked him – Le Fanu populated his universe with relentlessly violent supernatural avengers, victorious villains, hellish torment of innocent victims, and grisly monstrosities stalking a literary genre chiefly populated by visually unimpressive ghosts. In "Aungier Street," Le Fanu revisits a theme raised by Gaskell and others: the sins of the past do not go to the grave with their malefactors – they may linger in the cultural atmosphere for centuries before being exorcised... or overwhelmed by more direful crimes. The ghost that taunts the tenets of Aungier Street does not seek justice or hope to right a wrong; he is a truly nasty villain if ever one lumbered down the attic stairs.*

---

## AN ACCOUNT OF SOME STRANGE OCCURRENCES IN AUNGIER STREET
### {1853}
#### *Joseph Sheridan Le Fanu*

IT IS NOT WORTH TELLING, this story of mine—at least, not worth writing. Told, indeed, as I have sometimes been called upon to tell it, to a circle of intelligent and eager faces, lighted up by a good after-dinner fire on a winter's evening, with a cold wind rising and wailing outside, and all snug and cosy within, it has gone off – though I say it, who should not – indifferent well. But it is a venture to do as you would have me. Pen, ink, and paper are cold vehicles for the marvellous, and a "reader" decidedly a more critical animal than a

---

[1] It is well known that Carmilla inspired Dracula, but "Aungier Street" was practically redressed like a stolen car to make Stoker's most famous ghost story, "The Judge's House"

"listener"[1]. If, however, you can induce your friends to read it after nightfall, and when the fireside talk has run for a while on thrilling tales of shapeless terror; in short, if you will secure me the *mollia tempora fandi*[2], I will go to my work, and say my say, with better heart. Well, then, these conditions presupposed, I shall waste no more words, but tell you simply how it all happened.

My cousin (Tom Ludlow) and I studied medicine together. I think he would have succeeded, had he stuck to the profession; but he preferred the Church, poor fellow, and died early, a sacrifice to contagion, contracted in the noble discharge of his duties[3]. For my present purpose, I say enough of his character when I mention that he was of a sedate but frank and cheerful nature; very exact in his observance of truth, and not by any means like myself—of an excitable or nervous temperament.

My Uncle Ludlow—Tom's father—while we were attending lectures, purchased three or four old houses in Aungier Street[4], one of which was unoccupied. *He* resided in the country, and Tom proposed that we should take up our abode in the untenanted house, so long as it should continue unlet; a move which would accomplish the double end of settling us nearer alike to our lecture-rooms and to our amusements, and of relieving us from the weekly charge of rent for our lodgings.

Our furniture was very scant—our whole equipage remarkably modest and primitive; and, in short, our arrangements pretty nearly

---

[1] Le Fanu's narrator modestly argues that *writing* a ghost story is harder than *telling* one because there is a closer bond and sympathy between speakers and listeners than that between writers and readers (who, he suggests, are more critical and prone to disbelief). If you truly want to have your blood curdled, he asserts, you should hear him tell rather than read the story. This entire introduction is tremendously evocative of the self-deprecating style of Charles Dickens

[2] Latin: the favorable time for speaking, or – as Ambrose Bierce would have put it – the suitable surroundings

[3] While tending to the sick in his parish, he caught the illness and died

[4] A real street situated in the old neighborhood of Dublin City South, near St. Patrick's Cathedral, a few blocks south of the River Liffey

as simple as those of a bivouac[1]. Our new plan was, therefore, executed almost as soon as conceived. The front drawing-room was our sitting-room. I had the bedroom over it, and Tom the back bedroom on the same floor, which nothing could have induced me to occupy.

The house, to begin with, was a very old one. It had been, I believe, newly fronted[2] about fifty years before; but with this exception, it had nothing modern about it. The agent who bought it and looked into the titles for my uncle, told me that it was sold, along with much other forfeited property, at Chichester House, I think, in 1702; and had belonged to Sir Thomas Hacket, who was Lord Mayor of Dublin in James II's time[3]. How old it was *then*, I can't say; but, at all events, it had seen years and changes enough to have contracted all that mysterious and saddened air, at once exciting and depressing, which belongs to most old mansions.

There had been very little done in the way of modernising details; and, perhaps, it was better so; for there was something queer and by-gone in the very walls and ceilings—in the shape of doors and windows—in the odd diagonal site of the chimney-pieces—in the beams and ponderous cornices—not to mention the singular solidity of all the woodwork, from the banisters to the window-frames, which hopelessly defied disguise, and would have emphatically proclaimed their antiquity through any conceivable amount of modern finery and varnish.

An effort had, indeed, been made, to the extent of papering the drawing-rooms; but, somehow the paper looked raw and out of keeping; and the old woman, who kept a little dirt-pie of a shop in the lane, and whose daughter—a girl[4] of two and fifty—was our solitary handmaid, coming in at sunrise, and chastely receding again as soon as she had made all ready for tea in our state apartment;—this woman, I say, remembered it, when old Judge Horrocks (who, having earned the

---

[1] Campsite
[2] Updated in exterior appearance
[3] Serving from 1687 to 1688, during the final year of King James II's reign, Hackett was known for his abuses of the Irish people
[4] Servant

reputation of a particularly "hanging judge,"[1] ended by hanging himself, as the coroner's jury found, under an impulse of "temporary insanity," with a child's skipping-rope, over the massive old banisters) resided there, entertaining good company, with fine venison and rare old port. In those halcyon[2] days, the drawing-rooms were hung with gilded leather, and, I dare say, cut a good figure, for they were really spacious rooms.

The bedrooms were wainscoted, but the front one was not gloomy; and in it the cosiness of antiquity quite overcame its sombre associations. But the back bedroom, with its two queerly-placed melancholy windows, staring vacantly at the foot of the bed, and with the shadowy recess to be found in most old houses in Dublin, like a large ghostly closet[3], which, from congeniality of temperament, had amalgamated with the bedchamber, and dissolved the partition. At night-time, this "alcove"—as our "maid" was wont to call it—had, in my eyes, a specially sinister and suggestive character. Tom's distant and solitary candle glimmered vainly into its darkness. *There* it was always over-looking him—always itself impenetrable. But this was only part of the effect. The whole room was, I can't tell how, repulsive to me. There was, I suppose, in its proportions and features, a latent discord—a certain mysterious and indescribable relation, which jarred indistinctly upon some secret sense of the fitting and the safe, and raised indefinable suspicions and apprehensions of the imagination. On the whole, as I began by saying, nothing could have induced me to pass a

---

[1] A judge known for the severity of their sentences, their lack of mercy, and their delight in punishment, which include a liberal application of capital punishment, hence the name. Sir George Jeffreys – "The Hanging Judge" – is most likely the prototype for this story (as he is for Bram Stoker's rip-off – for such it is – "The Judge's House"). An infamously callous and prolific justice during the regin of James II, he is best known for his (reportedly) loose morals and vulgarity, his relentless persecution of opponents to the Jacobite throne, a reviled loyalty to Jacobite policies and sympathies, and for hanging some 500 defendants in one day following the anti-Jacobite Monmouth Rebellion in 1685, an event known as "the Bloody Assizes"
[2] Untroubled, carefree
[3] In this case, a small, intimate room outside of and leading to a bedroom

night alone in it.

I had never pretended to conceal from poor Tom my superstitious weakness; and he, on the other hand, most unaffectedly ridiculed my tremors. The sceptic was, however, destined to receive a lesson, as you shall hear.

80

We had not been very long in occupation of our respective dormitories, when I began to complain of uneasy nights and disturbed sleep. I was, I suppose, the more impatient under this annoyance, as I was usually a sound sleeper, and by no means prone to nightmares. It was now, however, my destiny, instead of enjoying my customary repose, every night to "sup full of horrors."[1] After a preliminary course of disagreeable and frightful dreams, my troubles took a definite form, and the same vision, without an appreciable variation in a single detail, visited me at least (on an average) every second night in the week.

Now, this dream, nightmare, or infernal illusion[2]—which you please—of which I was the miserable sport, was on this wise:—

I saw, or thought I saw, with the most abominable distinctness, although at the time in profound darkness, every article of furniture and accidental arrangement of the chamber in which I lay. This, as you know, is incidental to ordinary nightmare. Well, while in this clairvoyant condition, which seemed but the lighting up of the theatre in which was to be exhibited the monotonous tableau of horror[3], which made my nights insupportable, my attention invariably became, I know not why, fixed upon the windows opposite the foot of my bed; and, uniformly with the same effect, a sense of dreadful anticipation always took slow but sure possession of me. I became somehow conscious of a sort of horrid but undefined preparation going forward in some unknown quarter, and by some unknown agency, for my torment; and,

---

[1] This quote from *Macbeth* (V.v.14), a play steeped in supernaturalism, witchcraft, and angry ghosts, begins to pound the drum of warning, albeit softly: "something wicked this way comes"

[2] Trick from Satan

[3] M. R. James, a delighted fan of Le Fanu, would use this imagery in his "Haunted Doll's House"

after an interval, which always seemed to me of the same length, a picture suddenly flew up to the window, where it remained fixed, as if by an electrical attraction, and my discipline of horror then commenced, to last perhaps for hours. The picture thus mysteriously glued to the window-panes, was the portrait of an old man, in a crimson flowered silk dressing-gown, the folds of which I could now describe, with a countenance embodying a strange mixture of intellect, sensuality, and power, but withal sinister and full of malignant omen[1]. His nose was hooked, like the beak of a vulture; his eyes large, grey, and prominent, and lighted up with a more than mortal cruelty and coldness. These features were surmounted by a crimson velvet cap, the hair that peeped from under which was white with age, while the eyebrows retained their original

blackness. Well I remember every line, hue, and shadow of that stony countenance, and well I may! The gaze of this hellish visage was fixed upon me, and mine returned it with the inexplicable fascination of nightmare, for what appeared to me to be hours of agony. At last—"*The cock he crew, away then flew*" the fiend who had enslaved me through the awful watches of the night; and, harassed and nervous, I rose to the duties of the day.

I had—I can't say exactly why, but it may have been from the exquisite anguish and profound impressions of unearthly horror, with

---

[1] Horrocks – whose lustful character would later be fleshed out in Le Fanu's thematic prequel, "Mr Justice Harbottle" – is an invasive, uncomfortably casual, satyr-like personality. Le Fanu loved to make his ghosts comfortable in the company of their victims. Horrocks is not – like Stoker's judge – draped in his robes of office: he lives among his haunt, comfortably plush in a satin robe, his bare head (an extreme liberty of manners during an era where a gentleman never went outside without his wig) cozily cradled in a velvet cap. Later, his flabby bare feet will flop on the hard wood flooring, announcing the presence of someone who is not an intruder, but someone who actively lives and relaxes in the same quarters where he so casually appears. He is not annoyed by the lodgers or made uncomfortable by their presence; to the contrary – he is unnervingly at home in the house, and his casual manner is nauseatingly sinister

which this strange phantasmagoria[1] was associated—an insurmountable antipathy to describing the exact nature of my nightly troubles to my friend and comrade. Generally, however, I told him that I was haunted by abominable dreams; and, true to the imputed materialism of medicine[2], we put our heads together to dispel my horrors, not by exorcism, but by a tonic[3].

I will do this tonic justice, and frankly admit that the accursed portrait began to intermit its visits under its influence. What of that? Was this singular apparition—as full of character as of terror—therefore the creature of my fancy, or the invention of my poor stomach? Was it, in short, *subjective* (to borrow the technical slang of the day) and not the palpable aggression and intrusion of an external agent[4]? That, good friend, as we will both admit, by no means follows. The evil spirit, who enthralled my senses in the shape of that portrait, may have been just as near me, just as energetic, just as malignant, though I saw him not. What means the whole moral code of revealed religion regarding the due keeping of our own bodies, soberness,

---

[1] A complex, multifaceted supernatural vision

[2] As students of medicine, the two are inclined towards a material cure for what they assume to be a material (that is to say, a biological or neurological) ailment

[3] A mixture of drugs commonly dissolved in alcohol. There is a distinct possibility that cocaine or opium (laudanum) might be involved in this tonic, since it was most likely a tonic for the nerves. The Victorians continued to prescribe laudanum, cocaine, and morphine liberally for anxiety or insomnia, although the addictive side effects were well known and documented

[4] Le Fanu's ghosts are rarely, if ever, light, vaporous shades; they are intruders upon the material world, tremendously physical, often murderous or rapacious, and always chillingly realistic. They are not shining fogs or willowy visions, but ugly, pock-marked men, dark and surly faces, lustful-looking cavaliers with hideous birthmarks, and half-decapitated gentlemen pacing in their sensuous dressing gowns. He demands that we recognize that overlap between the immaterial and the material, that the two realms can merge and beg the question: which is more real, the haunted or the haunter?

temperance, etc.? Here is an obvious connexion between the material and the invisible; the healthy tone of the system, and its unimpaired energy, may, for aught we can tell, guard us against influences which would otherwise render life itself terrific[1]. The mesmerist and the electro-biologist[2] will fail upon an average with nine patients out of ten—so may the evil spirit. Special conditions of the corporeal system are indispensable to the production of certain spiritual phenomena. The operation succeeds sometimes—sometimes fails—that is all.

I found afterwards that my would-be sceptical companion had his troubles too. But of these I knew nothing yet. One night, for a wonder, I was sleeping soundly, when I was roused by a step on the lobby outside my room, followed by the loud clang of what turned out to be a large brass
candlestick, flung with all his force by poor Tom Ludlow over the banisters, and rattling with a rebound down the second flight of stairs; and almost concurrently with this, Tom burst open my door, and bounced into my room backwards, in a state of extraordinary agitation.

I had jumped out of bed and clutched him by the arm before I had any distinct idea of my own whereabouts. There we were—in our shirts[3]— standing before the open door—staring through the great old banister opposite, at the lobby window, through which the sickly light of a clouded moon was gleaming.

"What's the matter, Tom? What's the matter with you? What the devil's the matter with you, Tom?" I demanded, shaking him with nervous impatience.

He took a long breath before he answered me, and then it was not very coherently.

"It's nothing, nothing at all—did I speak?—what did I say?—where's the candle, Richard? It's dark; I—I had a candle!"

---

[1] Good health and high energy, he argues, may prevent us from noticing the strange disturbances of our own lives; perhaps the fears and sensations experienced during physical weakness are brushes with a reality that we are too distracted to notice during peak condition

[2] Both are pseudo-scientists interested in studying the phenomenon of "animal magnetism" – second sight, heightened intuition, and unconscious affinities or aversions

[3] Night shirts

"Yes, dark enough," I said; "but what's the matter?—what *is* it?—why don't you speak, Tom?—have you lost your wits?—what is the matter?"

"The matter?—oh, it is all over. It must have been a dream—nothing at all but a dream—don't you think so? It could not be anything more than a dream."

"Of *course*," said I, feeling uncommonly nervous, "it *was* a dream."

"I thought," he said, "there was a man in my room, and—and I jumped out of bed; and—and—where's the candle?"

"In your room, most likely," I said, "shall I go and bring it?"

"No; stay here—don't go; it's no matter—don't, I tell you; it was all a dream. Bolt the door, Dick; I'll stay here with you—I feel nervous. So, Dick, like a good fellow, light your candle and open the window—I am in
a *shocking state*."

I did as he asked me, and robing himself like Granuaile[1] in one of my blankets, he seated himself close beside my bed.

Everybody knows how contagious is fear of all sorts, but more especially that particular kind of fear under which poor Tom was at that moment labouring. I would not have heard, nor I believe would he have recapitulated, just at that moment, for half the world, the details of the hideous vision which had so unmanned him.

"Don't mind telling me anything about your nonsensical dream, Tom," said I, affecting contempt, really in a panic; "let us talk about something else; but it is quite plain that this dirty old house disagrees with us both, and hang me if I stay here any longer, to be pestered with indigestion and— and—bad nights, so we may as well look out for lodgings—don't you think so?—at once."

Tom agreed, and, after an interval, said—

"I have been thinking, Richard, that it is a long time since I saw my father, and I have made up my mind to go down to-morrow and return in a day or two, and you can take rooms for us in the meantime."

I fancied that this resolution, obviously the result of the vision which had so profoundly scared him, would probably vanish next morning

---

[1] An Irish folkheroine – Grace O'Malley – a female pirate who famously negotiated Anglo-Irish diplomatic relations with Queen Elizabeth I

with the damps and shadows of night. But I was mistaken. Off went Tom at peep of day to the country, having agreed that so soon as I had secured suitable lodgings, I was to recall him by letter from his visit to my Uncle Ludlow.

ဆ

Now, anxious as I was to change my quarters, it so happened, owing to a series of petty procrastinations and accidents, that nearly a week elapsed before my bargain was made and my letter of recall on the wing to Tom; and, in the meantime, a trifling adventure or two had occurred to your humble servant, which, absurd as they now appear, diminished by distance, did certainly at the time serve to whet my appetite for change considerably.

A night or two after the departure of my comrade, I was sitting by my bedroom fire, the door locked, and the ingredients of a tumbler of hot whisky-punch[1] upon the crazy spider-table[2]; for, as the best mode of keeping the

> "Black spirits and
> white, Blue spirits and
> grey,"[3]

with which I was environed, at bay, I had adopted the practice recommended by the wisdom of my ancestors, and "kept my spirits up by pouring spirits down."[4] I had thrown aside my volume of Anatomy,

---

[1] A typically recipe called for a sugar loaf to be dissolved in boiling water, after which sliced lemons and quantities of Irish whiskey were added – essentially a modern whiskey sour

[2] A table built with six or more legs arching from a base in the center, resembling a spider

[3] A misquote from *Macbeth* (IV.i) "Black Spirits and White: Red Spirits and Gray / Mingle, Mingle, Mingle, you mingle that may" – Le Fanu fuses humor with horror (much like his devotee, M. R. James) by making a pun on spirits (liquor) while evincing the witches' song from *Macbeth*, wherein the witch queen conjures the various elements of the spirit world to invade the realm of the mortals

[4] From "The Way to Keep Your Spirits Up," a Scots New Year's drinking song: "'Tis New Year's day; I wonder why / Some people look sae glum? / As if

118

and was treating myself by way of a tonic, preparatory to my punch and bed, to half-a-dozen pages of the *Spectator*,[1] when I heard a step on the flight of stairs descending from the attics. It was two o'clock, and the streets were as

silent as a church-yard[2]—the sounds were, therefore, perfectly distinct. There was a slow, heavy tread, characterised by the emphasis and deliberation of age, descending by the narrow staircase from above; and, what made the sound more singular, it was plain that the feet which produced it were perfectly bare[3], measuring the descent with something between a pound and a flop, very ugly to hear[4].

I knew quite well that my attendant had gone away many hours before, and that nobody but myself had any business in the house. It was quite plain also that the person who was coming downstairs had no intention whatever of concealing his movements[5]; but, on the contrary, appeared disposed to make even more noise, and proceed more deliberately, than was at all necessary. When the step reached the foot of the stairs outside my room, it seemed to stop; and I expected every

---

John Anderson had nocht / Of brandy, gin, and rum; / Or Nicol whisky, if inclin'd – / The very best in town. / If you would keep your spirits up, / Then pour the spirits down"

[1] A weekly British conservative magazine, still in publication, available since July 1828. In 1852, -- the year before this story was published – Le Fanu lost the election for Tory MP of County Carlow due to his criticisms of government "indifference … to the Irish famine"

[2] Connotations of being surrounded by death and the dead

[3] A burglar does not tread with bare feet – someone entirely at home and comfortable with their station, someone unafraid to let their presence be known, someone so casually informal and laid-back that they don't even bother to put on slippers or socks, let alone shoes. It is nerve-wracking to imagine hearing the tread of bare feet flopping on your floor when you know yourself to be alone

[4] A disgustingly visceral description – Le Fanu makes certain to highlight the unsightly, unsexy physicality of this physically-threatening spirit

[5] The worst thing about this ghost's characterization is his self-satisfied sense of shamelessness and unapologetic, unmated, un-muffled brashness of its presence

moment to see my door open spontaneously, and give admission to the original of my detested portrait. I was, however, relieved in a few seconds by hearing the descent renewed, just in the same manner, upon the staircase leading down to the drawing-rooms, and thence, after another pause, down the next flight, and so on to the hall, whence I heard no more.

Now, by the time the sound had ceased, I was wound up, as they say, to a very unpleasant pitch of excitement. I listened, but there was not a stir. I screwed up my courage to a decisive experiment—opened my door, and in a stentorian[1] voice bawled over the banisters, "Who's there?" There was no answer, but the ringing of my own voice through the empty old house,—no renewal of the movement; nothing, in short, to give my unpleasant sensations a definite direction. There is, I think, something most disagreeably disenchanting in the sound of one's own voice under such circumstances, exerted in solitude and in vain[2]. It redoubled my sense of isolation, and my misgivings increased on perceiving that the door, which I certainly thought I had left open, was closed behind me; in a vague alarm, lest my retreat should be cut off, I got again into my room as quickly as I could, where I remained in a state of imaginary blockade, and very uncomfortable indeed, till morning.

Next night brought no return of my barefooted fellow-lodger; but the night following, being in my bed, and in the dark—somewhere, I suppose, about the same hour as before, I distinctly heard the old fellow again descending from the garrets[3].

This time I had had my punch, and the *morale* of the garrison[4] was consequently excellent. I jumped out of bed, clutched the poker as I passed the expiring fire, and in a moment was upon the lobby. The sound had ceased by this time—the dark and chill were discouraging; and, guess my horror, when I saw, or thought I saw, a black monster,

---

[1] Deep, loud and booming
[2] Suggestive of a universe that ignores the appeals of the individual souls – an indifferent, if not entirely malignant cosmos that mocks and stifles the human spirit in crisis
[3] Upstairs attics
[4] A military unit charged with holding and defending a city or fort

whether in the shape of a man or a bear I could not say, standing, with its back to the wall, on the lobby, facing me, with a pair of great greenish eyes shining dimly out. Now, I must be frank, and confess that the cupboard which displayed our plates and cups stood just there, though at the moment I did not recollect it. At the same time I must honestly say, that making every allowance for an excited imagination, I never could satisfy myself that I was made the dupe of my own fancy in this matter; for this apparition, after one or two shiftings of shape, as if in the act of incipient[1] transformation, began, as it seemed on second thoughts, to advance upon me in its original form. From an instinct of terror rather than of courage, I hurled the poker, with all my force, at its head; and to the music of a horrid crash made my way into my room, and double-locked the door. Then, in a minute more, I heard the horrid bare feet walk down the stairs, till the sound ceased in the hall, as on the former occasion.

If the apparition of the night before was an ocular delusion of my fancy sporting with the dark outlines of our cupboard, and if its horrid eyes were nothing but a pair of inverted teacups, I had, at all events, the satisfaction of having launched the poker with admirable effect, and in true "fancy" phrase, "knocked its two daylights into one," as the commingled fragments of my tea-service testified. I did my best to gather comfort and courage from these evidences; but it would not do. And then what could I say of those horrid bare feet, and the regular tramp, tramp, tramp, which measured the distance of the entire staircase through the solitude of my haunted dwelling, and at an hour when no good influence was stirring? Confound it!—the whole affair was abominable. I was out of spirits[2], and dreaded the approach of night.

It came, ushered ominously in with a thunder-storm and dull torrents of depressing rain. Earlier than usual the streets grew silent; and by twelve o'clock nothing but the comfortless pattering of the rain was to be heard.

I made myself as snug as I could. I lighted *two* candles instead of

---

[1] Beginning stages, embryonic stages
[2] A pun – courage as well as whiskey

one. I forswore bed, and held myself in readiness for a sally[1], candle in hand; for, *coute qui cout*[2], I was resolved to *see* the being, if visible at all, who
troubled the nightly stillness of my mansion. I was fidgety and nervous and, tried in vain to interest myself with my books. I walked up and down my room, whistling in turn martial and hilarious music, and listening ever and anon for the dreaded noise. I sate down and stared at the square label on the solemn and reserved-looking black bottle, until FLANAGAN & CO.'S BEST OLD MALT WHISKY[3] grew into a sort of subdued accompaniment to all the fantastic and horrible speculations which chased one another through my brain.

Silence, meanwhile, grew more silent, and darkness darker. I listened in vain for the rumble of a vehicle, or the dull clamour of a distant row[4]. There was nothing but the sound of a rising wind, which had succeeded the thunder-storm that had travelled over the Dublin mountains quite out of hearing. In the middle of this great city I began to feel myself alone with nature, and Heaven knows what beside. My courage was ebbing. Punch, however, which makes beasts of so many, made a man of me again—just in time to hear with tolerable nerve and firmness the lumpy, flabby[5], naked feet deliberately descending the stairs again.

I took a candle, not without a tremor. As I crossed the floor I tried to extemporise[6] a prayer, but stopped short to listen, and never finished it. The steps continued. I confess I hesitated for some seconds at the door before I took heart of grace[7] and opened it. When I peeped out the lobby was perfectly empty—there was no monster standing on the staircase; and as the detested sound ceased, I was reassured

---

[1] Exploitive or aggressive military expedition
[2] A mistranslation (literally meaning "listening that cost") of *coute que coute*, French for "cost what it may," or "at any costs" – literally "cost what it costs"
[3] Smacks of a cheap, overly demonstrative brand of Irish whiskey
[4] Fight, shouting match
[5] These corpulent, fleshy feet suggest corruption, overindulgence, sleaziness, sin, and vice
[6] Make up, improvise
[7] *Assured myself of my salvation*

enough to venture forward nearly to the banisters. Horror of horrors! within a stair or two beneath the spot where I stood the unearthly tread smote the floor. My eye caught something in motion; it was about the size of Goliath's[1] foot—it was grey, heavy, and flapped with a dead weight from one step to another. As I am alive, it was the most monstrous grey rat I ever beheld or imagined.

Shakespeare says—"Some men there are cannot abide a gaping pig, and some that are mad if they behold a cat." I went well-nigh out of my wits when I beheld this *rat*; for, laugh at me as you may, it fixed upon me, I thought, a perfectly human expression of malice[2]; and, as it shuffled about and looked up into my face almost from between my feet, I saw, I could swear it—I felt it then, and know it now, the infernal gaze and the accursed countenance of my old friend in the portrait, transfused into the visage of the bloated vermin before me[3].

I bounced into my room again with a feeling of loathing and horror I cannot describe, and locked and bolted my door as if a lion had been at the other side. D—n him or *it*; curse the portrait and its original! I felt in my soul that the rat—yes, the *rat*, the RAT I had just seen, was that evil being in masquerade, and rambling through the house upon some infernal night lark.

§⊃

Next morning I was early trudging through the miry[4] streets; and, among other transactions, posted a peremptory[5] note recalling Tom. On my return, however, I found a note from my absent "chum," announcing his intended return next day. I was doubly rejoiced at

---

[1] The pagan warrior, a giant of nearly ten feet in height, featured in the book of 2 Samuel represents wickedness, corruption, and coarse immorality
[2] Bram Stoker almost lifts this description verbatim in his virtually plagiarized "Judge's House"
[3] Le Fanu has a predilection for familiars, that is, animals that are in actuality the manifestations of evil spirits: in "Squire Toby's Will" it is a bulldog, in "The Familiar" it is an owl
[4] Swampy, deep mud
[5] Demanding, authoritative

this, because I had succeeded in getting rooms; and because the change of scene and return of my comrade were rendered specially pleasant by the last night's half ridiculous half horrible adventure.

I slept extemporaneously in my new quarters in Digges' Street[1] that night, and next morning returned for breakfast to the haunted mansion, where I was certain Tom would call immediately on his arrival.

I was quite right—he came; and almost his first question referred to the primary object of our change of residence.

"Thank God," he said with genuine fervour, on hearing that all was arranged. "On *your* account I am delighted. As to myself, I assure you that no earthly consideration could have induced me ever again to pass a night in this disastrous old house."

"Confound the house!" I ejaculated, with a genuine mixture of fear and detestation, "we have not had a pleasant hour since we came to live here"; and so I went on, and related incidentally my adventure with the plethoric[2] old rat.

"Well, if that were *all*," said my cousin, affecting to make light of the matter, "I don't think I should have minded it very much."

"Ay, but its eye—its countenance, my dear Tom," urged I; "if you had seen *that*, you would have felt it might be *anything* but what it seemed."

"I am inclined to think the best conjurer in such a case would be an able-bodied cat," he said, with a provoking chuckle.

"But let us hear your own adventure," I said tartly.

At this challenge he looked uneasily round him. I had poked up a very unpleasant recollection.

"You shall hear it, Dick; I'll tell it to you," he said. "Begad[3], sir, I should feel quite queer, though, telling it *here*, though we are too strong a body for ghosts to meddle with just now."

Though he spoke this like a joke, I think it was serious calculation. Our Hebe[4] was in a corner of the room, packing our cracked delf tea and dinner-services in a basket. She soon suspended operations, and

---

[1] Some 200 meters away – a 1 minute drive in modern Dublin
[2] Overfull, inflated, inflamed or puffy
[3] *By God!*
[4] Jewess

with mouth and eyes wide open became an absorbed listener. Tom's experiences were told nearly in these words:

"I saw it three times, Dick—three distinct times; and I am perfectly certain it meant me some infernal harm[1]. I was, I say, in danger—

in *extreme* danger; for, if nothing else had happened, my reason would most certainly have failed me, unless I had escaped so soon. Thank God. I *did* escape.

"The first night of this hateful disturbance, I was lying in the attitude of sleep, in that lumbering old bed. I hate to think of it. I was really wide awake, though I had put out my candle, and was lying as quietly as if I had been asleep; and although accidentally restless, my thoughts were running in a cheerful and agreeable channel.

"I think it must have been two o'clock at least when I thought I heard a sound in that—that odious dark recess at the far end of the bedroom. It was as if someone was drawing a piece of cord slowly along the floor, lifting it up, and dropping it softly down again in coils. I sate up once or twice in my bed, but could see nothing, so I concluded it must be mice in the wainscot. I felt no emotion graver than curiosity, and after a few minutes ceased to observe it.

"While lying in this state, strange to say; without at first a suspicion of anything supernatural, on a sudden I saw an old man, rather stout and square, in a sort of roan-red[2] dressing-gown, and with a black cap[3] on his head, moving stiffly and slowly in a diagonal direction, from the recess, across the floor of the bed-room, passing my bed at the foot, and entering the lumber-closet at the left. He had something under his arm; his head hung a little at one side[4]; and merciful God! when I saw his face[5]."

---

[1] Hellish, devil-inspired, a demon's attack

[2] Brownish-red

[3] While passing a death sentence, a judge would don a black cap

[4] As if his neck had been either broken by the fall when he hanged himself, or wrenched by into a rigid angle by the rope

[5] We might assume that Le Fanu spares the reader the specifics, but torments their imagination with the ambiguity – his face must be black and swollen from suffocation

Tom stopped for a while, and then said:

"That awful countenance, which living or dying I never can forget, disclosed what he was[1]. Without turning to the right or left, he passed beside me, and entered the closet by the bed's head.

"While this fearful and indescribable type[2] of death and guilt was passing, I felt that I had no more power to speak or stir than if I had been myself a corpse. For hours after it had disappeared, I was too terrified and weak to move. As soon as daylight came, I took courage, and examined the room, and especially the course which the frightful intruder had seemed to take, but there was not a vestige to indicate anybody's having passed there; no sign of any disturbing agency visible among the lumber that strewed the floor of the closet.

"I now began to recover a little. I was fagged and exhausted, and at last, overpowered by a feverish sleep. I came down late; and finding you out of spirits, on account of your dreams about the portrait, whose *original* I am now certain disclosed himself to me, I did not care to talk about the infernal vision. In fact, I was trying to persuade myself that the whole thing was an illusion, and I did not like to revive in their intensity the hated impressions of the past night—or, to risk the constancy[3] of my scepticism, by recounting the tale of my sufferings.

"It required some nerve, I can tell you, to go to my haunted chamber next night, and lie down quietly in the same bed," continued Tom. "I did so with a degree of trepidation, which, I am not ashamed to say, a very little matter would have sufficed to stimulate to downright panic. This night, however, passed off quietly enough, as also the next; and so too did two or three more. I grew more confident, and began to fancy that I believed in the theories of spectral illusions, with which I had at first vainly tried to impose upon my convictions.

"The apparition had been, indeed, altogether anomalous[4]. It had crossed the room without any recognition of my presence: I had not

---

[1] The disfiguration of his face – whether discolored, oddly wrenched, or otherwise horrifically transformed – leaves no doubt that the man crossing the room has stopped living

[2] Archetype, manifestation, symbol

[3] Faithfulness, dependability

[4] A fluke, an isolated incident

disturbed *it*, and *it* had no mission to *me*. What, then, was the imaginable use of its crossing the room in a visible shape at all? Of course it might have *been* in the closet instead of *going* there, as easily as it introduced itself into the recess without entering the chamber in a shape discernible by the senses. Besides, how the deuce *had* I seen it? It was a dark night; I had no candle; there was no fire; and yet I saw it as distinctly, in colouring and outline, as ever I beheld human form! A cataleptic[1] dream would explain it all; and I was determined that a dream it should be.

"One of the most remarkable phenomena connected with the practice of mendacity[2] is the vast number of deliberate lies we tell ourselves, whom, of all persons, we can least expect to deceive. In all this, I need hardly tell you, Dick, I was simply lying to myself, and did not believe one word of the wretched humbug[3]. Yet I went on, as men will do, like persevering charlatans and impostors, who tire people into credulity by the mere force of reiteration[4]; so I hoped to win myself over at last to a comfortable scepticism about the ghost.

---

[1] That is, a sleeping dream (as opposed to a day dream, or imagined vision)

[2] Lies, falsehoods

[3] Hypocrisy, bullshit

[4] A true gem of literary mechanics lies in this observation: the ghost is that of an English judge who misused and abused his office in Ireland, at the cost of many innocent lives. Le Fanu was deeply aware of the crimes committed by the English against the Irish for several centuries. As an Anglo-Irishman, he was well aware of his divided allegiances, and of the lies that men will tell themselves to avoid unpleasant truths. Ghosts – in literary fiction – are symbolic of the fears, urges, lusts, and anxieties of the unconscious, the (usually shameful or repressed) events of the past, or the true nature of a person, place, or culture which is being publicly denied. Le Fanu lost a parliamentary election the year before he wrote this piece, due in large part to his criticism of the British government's denial and mishandling of the Irish famine. As a conservative Tory, this was certainly a stance which came about after soul-searching and internal struggle. The ghost in "Aungier Street" represents the sins of England against the people of Ireland, and the characters' attempts to deny its existence is tantamount to denying (or avoiding or repressing) the national crimes

"He had not appeared a second time—that certainly was a comfort; and what, after all, did I care for him, and his queer old toggery[1] and strange looks[2]? Not a fig! I was nothing the worse for having seen him, and a good story the better. So I tumbled into bed, put out my candle, and, cheered by a loud drunken quarrel in the back lane, went fast asleep.

"From this deep slumber I awoke with a start. I knew I had had a horrible dream; but what it was I could not remember. My heart was thumping furiously; I felt bewildered and feverish; I sate up in the bed and looked about the room. A broad flood of moonlight came in through the curtainless window; everything was as I had last seen it; and though the domestic squabble in the back lane was, unhappily for me, allayed, I yet could hear a pleasant fellow singing, on his way home, the then popular comic ditty called, 'Murphy Delany.' Taking advantage of this diversion I lay down again, with my face towards the fireplace, and closing my eyes, did my best to think of nothing else but the song, which was every moment growing fainter in the distance:

"*Twas Murphy Delany, so funny and frisky,*
*Stept into a shebeen shop to get his skin*
*full;*
*He reeled out again pretty well lined with*
*whiskey, As fresh as a shamrock, as blind as a*
*bull[3].'*

"The singer, whose condition I dare say resembled that of his hero, was soon too far off to regale my ears any more; and as his music died away, I myself sank into a doze, neither sound nor refreshing. Somehow the song had got into my head, and I went meandering on through the adventures of my respectable fellow-countryman, who, on emerging from the 'shebeen shop[4],' fell into a river, from which he was

---

[1] Clothing
[2] "Strange" may be a bit of an understatement: the man's face looks like that of a hanged corpse
[3] The constant references to whiskey and drinking-to-forget are not accidental – Le Fanu eagerly hopes that we pick up on his cues which indict self-delusion, whether alcoholic or intellectual
[4] A shop that illegally sold liquor without a license

fished up to be 'sat upon' by a coroner's jury, who having learned from a 'horse-doctor' that he was 'dead as a door-nail, so there was an end,' returned their verdict accordingly, just as he returned to his senses, when an angry altercation and a pitched battle between the body and the coroner winds up the lay with due spirit and pleasantry[1].

"Through this ballad I continued with a weary monotony to plod, down to the very last line, and then *da capo*,[2] and so on, in my uncomfortable half-sleep, for how long, I can't conjecture. I found myself at last, however, muttering, '*dead* as a door-nail, so there was an end'; and something like another voice within me, seemed to say, very faintly, but sharply, 'dead! dead! *dead!* and may the Lord have mercy on your soul[3]!' and instantaneously I was wide awake, and staring right before me from the pillow.

"Now—will you believe it, Dick?—I saw the same accursed figure standing full front, and gazing at me with its stony and fiendish countenance, not two yards from the bedside."

Tom stopped here, and wiped the perspiration from his face. I felt very queer. The girl was as pale as Tom; and, assembled as we were in the very scene of these adventures, we were all, I dare say, equally grateful for the clear daylight and the resuming bustle out of doors.

"For about three seconds only I saw it plainly; then it grew indistinct; but, for a long time, there was something like a column of dark vapour where it had been standing between me and the wall; and I felt sure that he was still there[4]. After a good while, this appearance went too. I took my clothes downstairs to the hall, and dressed there, with the

---

[1] The dead, in this comic tune, are not truly dead – not inanimate and spiritually snuffed – but aggressively impose themselves onto the skeptics who deny their existence

[2] Starting over from the top (literally, "at the head" (Italian))

[3] Alarmingly, this echoes the sentence of death by a British judge: "[Full name of the prisoner] you are sentenced to be taken ... to a place of execution where you will be hanged by the neck until dead ... may the Lord have mercy on your soul" – clearly the past is bleeding into the future

[4] Le Fanu – incidentally tapping into the ether theory, which consider ghosts to be made up of the same matter as outer space – suggests that the past never really leaves us, but fades in and out of recollection, always hovering where it can be recovered if noticed

door half open; then went out into the street, and walked about the town till morning, when I came back, in a miserable state of nervousness and exhaustion. I was such a fool, Dick, as to be ashamed to tell you how I came to be so upset. I thought you would laugh at me; especially as I had always talked philosophy, and treated *your* ghosts with contempt. I concluded you would give me no quarter[1]; and so kept my tale of horror to myself.

"Now, Dick, you will hardly believe me, when I assure you, that for many nights after this last experience, I did not go to my room at all. I used to sit up for a while in the drawing-room after you had gone up to your bed; and then steal down softly to the hall-door, let myself out, and sit in the ' Robin Hood ' tavern until the last guest went off; and then I got through the night like a sentry, pacing the streets till morning.

"For more than a week I never slept in bed. I sometimes had a snooze on a form[2] in the 'Robin Hood,' and sometimes a nap in a chair during the day; but regular sleep I had absolutely none.

"I was quite resolved that we should get into another house; but I could not bring myself to tell you the reason, and I somehow put it off from day to day, although my life was, during every hour of this procrastination, rendered as miserable as that of a felon with the constables on his track[3]. I was growing absolutely ill from this wretched mode of life.

"One afternoon I determined to enjoy an hour's sleep upon your bed. I hated mine; so that I had never, except in a stealthy visit every day to unmake it, lest Martha should discover the secret of my nightly absence, entered the ill-omened chamber.

"As ill-luck would have it, you had locked your bedroom, and taken away the key. I went into my own to unsettle the bedclothes, as usual, and give the bed the appearance of having been slept in. Now, a variety of circumstances concurred to bring about the dreadful scene through which I was that night to pass. In the first place, I was literally overpowered with fatigue, and longing for sleep; in the next place, the

---

[1] That is, no mercy – to mock or gloat
[2] Bench
[3] A telling simile: many of the judge's victims were just such sorts of men

effect of this extreme exhaustion upon my nerves resembled that of a narcotic, and rendered me less susceptible than, perhaps I should in any other condition have been, of the exciting fears which had become habitual to me. Then again, a little bit of the window was open, a pleasant freshness pervaded the room, and, to crown all, the cheerful sun of day was making the room quite pleasant[1]. What was to prevent my enjoying an hour's nap *here*? The whole air was resonant with the cheerful hum of life, and the broad matter-of-fact light of day filled every corner of the room.

"I yielded—stifling my qualms—to the almost overpowering temptation; and merely throwing off my coat, and loosening my cravat[2], I lay down, limiting myself to *half*-an-hour's doze in the unwonted[3] enjoyment of a feather bed, a coverlet, and a bolster.

"It was horribly insidious[4]; and the demon, no doubt, marked my infatuated preparations. Dolt[5] that I was, I fancied, with mind and body worn out for want of sleep, and an arrear of a full week's rest to my credit, that such measure as *half*-an-hour's sleep, in such a situation, was possible. My sleep was death-like, long, and dreamless.

"Without a start or fearful sensation of any kind, I waked gently, but completely. It was, as you have good reason to remember, long past midnight—I believe, about two o'clock. When sleep has been deep and long enough to satisfy nature thoroughly, one often wakens in this way, suddenly, tranquilly, and completely.

"There was a figure seated in that lumbering, old sofa-chair, near the

---

[1] Even when times are good and things seem better, if the past has not been resolved or made right, its ramifications can still reach out, like tentacles from a calm and clear ocean. Tom makes the mistake of letting his guard down because the surroundings are seemingly fair, just as many persons assume that events from decades or even centuries previous will have no impact on the present time

[2] Neck-cloth – a predecessor of the necktie, often a strip of fine, white linen knotted intricately

[3] Atypical, uncommon

[4] Menacing, sinister

[5] Simpleton, fool

fireplace[1]. Its back was rather towards me, but I could not be mistaken; it turned slowly round, and, merciful heavens! There was the stony face, with its infernal lineaments[2] of malignity and despair, gloating on me. There was now no doubt as to its consciousness of my presence, and the hellish malice with which it was animated[3], for it arose, and drew close to the bedside. There was a rope about its neck, and the other end, coiled up, it held stiffly in its hand.

"My good angel nerved me[4] for this horrible crisis. I remained for some seconds transfixed by the gaze of this tremendous phantom. He came close to the bed, and appeared on the point of mounting upon it[5]. The next instant I was upon the floor at the far side, and in a moment more was, I don't know how, upon the lobby.

"But the spell was not yet broken; the valley of the shadow of death was not yet traversed. The abhorred phantom was before me there; it was standing near the banisters, stooping a little, and with one end of the rope round its own neck, was poising a noose at the other, as if to

---

[1] The casual comfort – the shameless audacity – of this ghost is its greatest terror: lounging lazily in front of a fireplace, not even bothering to watch its victim ; it owns the house and knows it, and is not even remotely intimidated by his human counterparts – they are furniture to him – mere pets

[2] Facial features

[3] That is to say, the ghost is not just a dead, purposeless mist wafting stupidly from room to room, but a phantom with an earthly mission to cause death – a malignant, murderous intent

[4] *My guardian angel gave me mental strength and courage*

[5] What in God's name would it have *done*? Climbing into bed with Tom would certainly have been the boldest, most invasive thing it could do – not that this spectre has any reservations, sense of decency, shame, or respect for the privacy of his roommates. Beds – by the Victorian era – were private, closed-off areas with connotations of sexual vulnerability (or receptivity). There are certainly homoerotic overtones to this story, and the lustful (for such he is) Judge who walks around in his dressing gown and bare feet, peeking into one man's bedroom and watching the other sleep, compares nicely to the lesbian vampire in Le Fanu's *Carmilla*

133

throw over mine[1]; and while engaged in this baleful pantomime[2], it wore a smile so sensual[3], so unspeakably dreadful, that my senses were nearly overpowered. I saw and remember nothing more, until I found myself in your room.

"I had a wonderful escape, Dick—there is no disputing *that*—an escape for which, while I live, I shall bless the mercy of heaven. No one can conceive or imagine what it is for flesh and blood to stand in the presence of such a thing, but one who has had the terrific experience. Dick, Dick, a shadow has passed over me—a chill has crossed my blood and marrow, and I will never be the same again—never, Dick—never!"

℀

Our handmaid, a mature girl of two-and-fifty, as I have said, stayed her hand[4], as Tom's story proceeded, and by little and little drew near to us, with open mouth, and her brows contracted over her little, beady black eyes, till stealing a glance over her shoulder now and then, she established herself close behind us. During the relation, she had made various earnest comments, in an under-tone; but these and her ejaculations, for the sake of brevity and simplicity, I have omitted in my narration.

"It's often I heard tell of it," she now said, "but I never believed it rightly till now—though, indeed, why should not I? Does not my mother, down there in the lane, know quare[5] stories, God bless us,

---

[1] He apparently hope to attach Tom to himself. It is far grislier that he offers a noose whose other end is still girded about his swollen throat than it would be had he carried a fresh cord coiled around his arm – it is an offer of partnership: become like me, share my vices and evils

[2] A menacing, suggestive action

[3] Passionate, gloating: an expression that is entirely unrestrained and without gentility or kindness – a smile that demonstrates some warped and twisted combination of pride, lust, delight, and desire. Whether genuinely erotic, or simply hungry for blood and souls, or some combination of both, the ghost's attitude is one of eager desire and unsatisfied want

[4] Restrained herself, didn't interrupt

[5] *Queer*

134

beyant[1] telling about it? But you ought not to have slept in the back bedroom. She was loath to let me be going in and out of that room even in the day time, let alone for any Christian[2] to spend the night in it; for sure she says it was his own bedroom."

"*Whose* own bedroom?" we asked, in a breath.

"Why, *his*—the ould Judge's—Judge Horrock's, to be sure, God rest his sowl"; and she looked fearfully round.

"Amen!" I muttered. "But did he die there?"

"Die there! No, not quite *there*," she said. "Shure, was not it over the banisters he hung himself, the ould sinner, God be merciful to us all? And was not it in the alcove they found the handles of the skipping-rope cut off, and the knife where he was settling the cord, God bless us, to hang himself with? It was his housekeeper's daughter owned the rope, my mother often told me, and the child never throve[3] after, and used to be starting up out of her sleep, and screeching in the night time, wid dhrames[4] and frights that cum an her; and they said how it was the speerit of the ould Judge that was tormentin' her; and she used to be roaring and yelling out to hould back the big ould fellow with the crooked neck; and then she'd screech 'Oh, the master! The master! He's stampin' at me, and beckoning to me! Mother, darling, don't let me go!' And so the poor crathure[5] died at last, and the docthers said it was wather on the brain[6], for it was all they could say."

"How long ago was all this?" I asked.

"Oh, then, how would I know?" she answered. "But it must be a wondherful long time ago, for the housekeeper was an ould woman, with a pipe in her mouth, and not a tooth left, and better nor eighty years ould when my mother was first married; and they said she was a

---

[1] *Besides, beyond*

[2] As a Jew in Catholic Ireland, she apparently believes that Christians stand more to suffer at the hands of this ostensibly Christian ghost

[3] Thrived. Was healthy

[4] *With dreams*

[5] *Creature*

[6] The symptoms of hydrocephalus include headaches, vomiting, sleepiness, urinary incontinence, dementia, hallucinations, and hysteria. An understandable diagnosis considering the child's behavior and claims

rale buxom[1], fine-dressed woman when the ould Judge come to his end; an', indeed, my mother's not far from eighty years ould herself this day; and what made it worse for the unnatural ould villain, God rest his soul, to frighten the little girl out of the world the way he did, was what was mostly thought and believed by everyone. My mother says how the poor little crathure was his own child; for he was by all accounts an ould villain every way[2], an' the hangin'est judge that ever was known in Ireland's ground."

"From what you said about the danger of sleeping in that bed-room," said I, " I suppose there were stories about the ghost having appeared there to others."

"Well, there *was* things said—quare things, surely," she answered, as it seemed, with some reluctance. "And why would not there? Sure was it not up in that same room he slept for more than twenty years? and was it not in the *alcove* he got the rope ready that done his own business at last, the way he done many a betther man's[3] in his lifetime?—and was not the body lying in the same bed after death, and put in the coffin there, too, and carried out to his grave from it in Pether's churchyard, after the coroner was done? But there was quare stories—my mother has them all—about how one Nicholas Spaight got into trouble on the head of it."

"And what did they say of this Nicholas Spaight?" I asked. "Oh, for that matther, it's soon told," she answered.

And she certainly did relate a very strange story, which so piqued my curiosity, that I took occasion to visit the ancient lady, her mother, from whom I learned many very curious particulars. Indeed, I am tempted to tell the tale, but my fingers are weary, and I must defer it. But if you wish to hear it another time, I shall do my best.

---

[1] *Very attractive*

[2] He slept with his housekeeper and returned from death to frighten his daughter by her to death. This plot line is much extended in "Mr Justice Harbottle"

[3] The implication is that many of the men he hanged were innocent

When we had heard the strange tale I have *not* told you[1], we put one or two further questions to her about the alleged spectral visitations, to which the house had, ever since the death of the wicked old Judge, been subjected.

"No one ever had luck in it," she told us. "There was always cross accidents, sudden deaths, and short times in it. The first that tuck[2] it was a family—I forget their name—but at any rate there was two young ladies and their papa. He was about sixty, and a stout healthy gentleman as you'd wish to see at that age. Well, he slept in that unlucky back bedroom; and, God between us an' harm! sure enough he was found dead one morning, half out of the bed, with his head as black as a sloe[3], and swelled like a puddin', hanging down near the floor. It was a fit, they said. He was as dead as a mackerel, and so *he* could not say what it was; but the ould people was all sure that it was nothing at all but the ould Judge – God bless us – that frightened him out of his senses and his life together.

"Some time after there was a rich old maiden lady took the house. I don't know which room *she* slept in, but she lived alone; and at any rate, one morning, the servants going down early to their work, found her sitting on the passage-stairs, shivering and talkin' to herself, quite mad; and never a word more could any of *them* or her friends get from her ever afterwards but, 'Don't ask me to go, for I promised to wait for him[4].' They never made out from her who it was she meant by *him*, but of course those that knew all about the ould house were at no loss for the meaning of all that happened to her.

"Then afterwards, when the house was let out in lodgings, there was Micky Byrne that took the same room, with his wife and three little children; and sure I heard Mrs. Byrne myself telling how the children used to be lifted up in the bed at night, she could not see by what

---

[1] Let the reader's imagination wander and speculate – a masterful tactic which serves far better than spelling out the entire backstory (M. R. James, of course, adored this method)

[2] *Rented*

[3] The blackthorn berry – a dark, bluish-black fruit

[4] The ghost appears to have tried to seduce the woman – as he did the housekeeper – because her language suggests a that of a lover's tryst

mains[1]; and
how they were starting and screeching every hour[2], just all as one as
the housekeeper's little girl that died, till at last one night poor Micky
had a dhrop[3] in him, the way he used now and again; and what do you
think in the middle of the night he thought he heard a noise on the
stairs, and being in liquor, nothing less id do him[4] but out he must go
himself to see what was wrong. Well, after that, all she ever heard of
him was himself sayin', 'Oh, God!' and a tumble that shook the very
house; and there, sure enough, he was lying on the lower stairs, under
the lobby, with his neck smashed double undher him, where he was
flung over the banisters."

Then the handmaiden added:

"I'll go down to the lane, and send up Joe Gavvey to pack up the
rest of the taythings[5], and bring all the things across to your new
lodgings."

And so we all sallied out together, each of us breathing more
freely, I have no doubt, as we crossed that ill-omened threshold for
the last time.

Now, I may add thus much, in compliance with the immemorial
usage of the realm of fiction, which sees the hero not only through his
adventures, but fairly out of the world. You must have perceived that
what the flesh, blood, and bone hero of romance proper is to the
regular compounder of fiction, this old house of brick, wood, and
mortar is to the humble recorder of this true tale[6]. I, therefore, relate,
as in duty bound, the catastrophe which ultimately befell it, which was
simply this—that about two years subsequently to my story it was
taken by a quack doctor, who called himself Baron Duhlstoerf, and
filled the parlour windows with bottles of indescribable horrors

---

[1] *Means*
[2] Symptoms consistent with hydrocephalus, casting doubt on the earlier diagnosis
[3] *Drop* (of liquor)
[4] *Would satisfy him*
[5] *Tea things*
[6] It is the house itself which is the actual main character

preserved in brandy[1], and the newspapers with the usual grandiloquent and mendacious[2] advertisements. This gentleman among his virtues did not reckon sobriety, and one night, being overcome with much wine[3], he set fire to his bed curtains, partially burned himself, and totally consumed the house. It was afterwards rebuilt, and for a time an undertaker established himself in the premises[4].

I have now told you my own and Tom's adventures, together with some valuable collateral particulars; and having acquitted myself of my engagement, I wish you a very good night, and pleasant dreams.

---

[1] Biological specimens – e.g. fetuses, tumors, mutations, diseased organs, human heads, etc.

[2] Pretentious and false

[3] The house is ultimately destroyed by a drunk (a vice to which Le Fanu has constantly been referencing as a metaphor for denial, repression, and avoidance of past cultural sins), who also happens to be a liar who misrepresents himself. Le Fanu is clear: the only things more destructive than the sins, lies, vices, and criminality of the past, are those of the present. The present isn't *saved* from the ghost by the quack: the quack (representative of the commercialism, materialism, and consumer fraud that ran rampant during the industrial revolution) is *himself* the next Horrocks of his generation – the great falsifier and maligner

[4] Fittingly, it now has literally become a house for the dead; in the wake of this transparency (it is no longer a house pretending not to board the dead), the hauntings cease. Honesty, genuineness, and acceptance are the anecdotes to this misanthropic spirit

*LIKE Gaskell, Le Fanu wonders what evils might lay dormant for generation after generation, drawing lifeblood and vitality from its descendants. The pattern of English atrocities against the Irish was still storied and centuries-old when Le Fanu wrote "Strange Disturbances." Judge Horrock's sexual deviancy, delight in suffering, and sadistic personality still present a very real and present danger one century after he throttled himself on his love child's jump rope. Unlike most Victorian ghosts – Braddon's for instance – Le Fanu's is not seeking justice or vindication; it is not a wronged soul, it is a wronging soul, gleefully collecting the corpses of its roommates and gathering nourishment from their terror – just as much a vampire as Dracula, or as his real-life inspiration, the Bloody Judge, Lord Jeffrey's. Unjust acts, Le Fanu suggests, can haunt the innocent as well as the guilty, and in a world without definite justice, the supernatural is not always the agent of rectification – it may just as easily perpetuate evil as avenge it. Judge Horrock found his just desserts while his neck twisted under the barrister, but the society that turned a blind eye to his wickedness continued to suffer long after his physical expiration, generation after generation, for their tolerance. But Le Fanu's literary universe was a complex and dynamic one, and evil was just as likely to suffer comeuppance as innocence was to endure persecution: nineteen years later Le Fanu wrote a prequel to this tale, a grisly psychological piece called "Mr. Justice Harbottle" about a hanging judge who is relentlessly haunted and hunted by his victims.*

*OFTEN underrated and under-anthologized, the following story – or more accurately, two stories couched within a frame narrative (we will comment on both, individually) – is perhaps one of Dickens' most complex and thematically dark tales. Often misunderstood and typically criticized for its plot, "To be Read at Dusk" is an intricate study in dualism, repression, fate, and psychological influences on personal identity. Dickens uses the frame narrative – which is disarming in spite of its truly unsettling nature – to commence a conversation on the nature of reality, the source of identity, and the pull of the unconscious – those shadowy things which we avoid or try to deny – on the conscious – the (ostensible) basis of human identity. In the three stories which he twines and threads, Dickens will attempt to cause you to question the power of nurture over nature, of will over fate, and of self over psychology. And then he will turn the tables again.*

---

## TO BE READ AT DUSK
{1852}
*Charles Dickens*

ONE, TWO, THREE, FOUR, FIVE[1]. There were five of them[2].

Five couriers[3], sitting on a bench outside the convent on the summit of

---

[1] Fading in like a shadowy procession flitting through the fog, the central group of this tale already retain the qualities of ghosts – shiftless, airy, and immaterial

[2] "Them" – the subject of this narrative may elucidate the objectivity of these five *"thems"*

[3] Diplomatic messengers. Switzerland, being the geographical hub of Europe, is an understandable place for the representatives of European nations to mingle in between trips. Meeting at the crossroads of Europe, the couriers themselves are go-betweens, strongly suggesting a borderland or a neutral convergence of otherwise opposite entities – in this case, the dead and the living, the natural and the supernatural

the Great St. Bernard[1] in Switzerland, looking at the remote heights, stained by the setting sun as if a mighty quantity of red wine had been broached upon the mountain top, and had not yet had time to sink into the snow[2].

This is not my simile[3]. It was made for the occasion by the stoutest courier, who was a German. None of the others took any more notice of it than they took of me[4], sitting on another bench on the other side of the convent door, smoking my cigar, like them[5], and — also like them — looking at the reddened snow, and at the lonely shed hard by, where the bodies of belated travellers, dug out of it, slowly wither away, knowing no corruption in that cold region[6].

---

[1] The Great St. Bernard Pass (home to the famous Great St. Bernard Pass Hostel), is the third highest road pass in Switzerland, located on the southeastern border, near France and Italy

[2] Kimberly Jackson argues that we are absolutely meant to jump from the simile "red like wine" to "wine like blood" – Dickens' narrator disowns the simile in the next line, allowing the reader to question its appropriateness and to fill in the gap left by "wine" – the mountain, a deadly symbol of mortality and fate, is soaked in the blood of its victims, and Dickens plays with the reader, allowing them to arrive at the conclusion that it is sinister without being heavy handed

[3] Figure of speak used to draw comparisons, employing "like" or "as." Similes play a critical role in Dickens' literary structure – several critics have suggested that this is a ghost story about "likeness" – about similarity, relationship, inversion, and categorical sameness

[4] Initially the narrator is unnoticed – almost ghostlike. That will change

[5] Similes and comparisons are already cropping up – why might Dickens be encouraging juxtaposition between the narrator and the "thems"? This story probes how those things which we insist on (and hope to) disassociating ourselves from – evil, death, corruption... ghosts – are not nearly so neatly compartmentalized. Who are the ghosts and who the men?

[6] Firstly, if Dickens was too deft in using his wine simile, then the "reddened snow" mentioned in this context will undoubtedly conjure something ravenous and sinister. Secondly, Dickens gruesomely explains that beneath that sheet of crimson down are the frozen bodies of unfortunate travelers who have been overtaken by storms. Their bodies, once dug out, are

The wine upon the mountain top soaked in as we looked[1]; the mountain became white; the sky, a very dark blue; the wind rose; and the air turned piercing cold. The five couriers buttoned their rough coats. There being no safer man to imitate in all such proceedings than a courier[2], I buttoned mine.

The mountain in the sunset had stopped the five couriers in a conversation. It is a sublime[3] sight, likely to stop conversation. The mountain being now out of the sunset, they resumed[4]. Not that I had heard any part of their previous discourse; for indeed, I had not then broken away from the American gentleman, in the travellers' parlour of the convent, who, sitting with his face to the fire[5], had undertaken to

---

stacked in a shed like cord wood, where they remain preserved by the extreme cold – the dead encroach on the world of the living in this borderland, failing to decay properly ("knowing no corruption" – one would not immediately be able to identify them as "dead"), and in their grisly proximity to the living, stored in a shed "hard by," within eyesight

[1] Dickens suggests that like the mountain, whose snows hide the dead, and whose scarlet tones imply their nature, the story hides dark secrets about the nature of its characters and literary themes. Like the mountain, which sinks into inoffensive blue, the story, too, will momentarily disarm us, allowing us to ignore what it encloses for the time being

[2] A courier, someone prone to long, exposed travel conditions, would certainly know how to stay warm, and be worth emulating on a chilly Swiss peak

[3] A vision of natural power inspiring awe, fear, dread, admiration, and beauty, such as a violent storm, a vast ocean, an endless desert, or an enormous woodland

[4] Once the uncomfortable nature of the mountain has been disassociated from its visible features – once the blood-red light has faded – the couriers are no longer prevented from continuing their discourse on the relationships of ghosts to men – a topic the reality of which is made abundantly clear by the mountain's gory spectre, rendering such a conversation unnecessary until the vision fades once more, allowing speculation to once more reign

[5] Important: this materialistic capitalist has removed himself as far as possible from the looming phantom of human mortality and moral

realise to me the whole progress of events which had led to the accumulation by the Honourable Ananias Dodger[1] of one of the largest acquisitions of dollars ever made in our country.

'My God!' said the Swiss courier, speaking in French, which I do not hold (as some authors appear to do) to be such an all-sufficient excuse for a naughty word, that I have only to write it in that language to make it innocent[2]; 'if you talk of ghosts — '

'But I DON'T talk of ghosts,' said the German.

'Of what then?' asked the Swiss.

'If I knew of what then,' said the German, 'I should probably know a great deal more[3].'

It was a good answer, I thought, and it made me curious. So, I moved my position to that corner of my bench which was nearest to them, and leaning my back against the convent wall, heard perfectly, without appearing to attend.

'Thunder and lightning[4]!' said the German, warming, 'when a certain man is coming to see you, unexpectedly; and, without his own knowledge, sends some invisible messenger, to put the idea of him into your head all day, what do you call that? When you walk along a crowded street — at Frankfort, Milan, London, Paris — and think that a passing stranger is like your friend Heinrich, and then that another passing stranger is like your friend Heinrich, and so begin to have a strange foreknowledge that presently you'll meet your friend Heinrich — which you do, though you

---

ambiguity, as represented by the mountain. Instead, he thrusts his face into the fire – symbolic of human industry and contrivance

[1] A likely reference to *Oliver Twist's* Artful Dodger – lampooning the morals and virtue of American opportunists – hypocritical shysters who manipulate and scheme in order to accumulate power and wealth

[2] Once more, Dickens conjures the spirit of hypocrisy – "If it's a curse in English, writing it in French does nothing to dilute its genuine import"

[3] They speak not of categorical "ghosts" but of the murky middle country between the living and the dead

[4] *"Donder und Blitzen!"* A traditional German oath (it extends to all German speaking nations, Scandinavians, and the Dutch) used in English literature, most famously employed to name two of the reindeer in "A Visit from St. Nicholas" (so used because of Sinter Klaas' Germano-Dutch etymology)

believed him at Trieste[1] — what do you call THAT?'

'It's not uncommon, either,' murmured the Swiss and the other three.

'Uncommon!' said the German. 'It's as common as cherries in the Black Forest. It's as common as maccaroni at Naples. And Naples reminds me! When the old Marchesa Senzanima shrieks at a card- party on the Chiaja[2] — as I heard and saw her, for it happened in a Bavarian family of mine, and I was overlooking the service that evening — I say, when the old Marchesa starts up at the card-table, white through her rouge, and cries, "My sister in Spain is dead! I felt her cold touch on my back!" — and when that sister IS dead at the moment — what do you call that?'

'Or when the blood of San Gennaro liquefies[3] at the request of the clergy — as all the world knows that it does regularly once a-year, in my native city,' said the Neapolitan courier after a pause, with a comical look, 'what do you call that?'

'THAT!' cried the German. 'Well, I think I know a name for that[4].'

'Miracle?' said the Neapolitan, with the same sly face.

The German merely smoked and laughed; and they all smoked and laughed.

'Bah!' said the German, presently. 'I speak of things that really do happen. When I want to see the conjurer, I pay to see a professed one, and have my money's worth. Very strange things do happen without ghosts[5].

---

[1] A seaport in N.E. Italy – a crossroads (and melting pot) of Slavic, Latin, and German culture

[2] Chiaia : a neighborhood in Naples

[3] Januarius (272 C.E. – 305 C.E.) was an Italian saint. The so-called "Blood Miracle" occurs when a vile of his dried blood reportedly returns to liquid form. This manner of miracle is not uncommon amongst Catholic relics – weeping statues, bleeding paintings, etc. – although hoaxes and natural phenomena explain nearly all of them

[4] Likely a Lutheran, the German – like most Anglican Englishmen – would be almost condescendingly anti-Catholic, viewing relics and related miracles as dangerous superstitions

[5] The ways of ghosts and the ways of men are not, Dickens continues to suggest, mutually exclusive – the line between the natural and supernatural is thin and shaded, for humanity is haunted by its own complex psychological and spiritual nature

145

Ghosts! Giovanni Baptista, tell your story of the English bride. There's no ghost in that, but something full as strange[1]. Will any man tell me what?'

As there was a silence among them, I glanced around. He whom I took to be Baptista was lighting a fresh cigar. He presently went on to speak. He was a Genoese, as I judged.

'The story of the English bride?' said he. 'Basta[2]! one ought not to call so slight a thing a story. Well, it's all one. But it's true. Observe me well, gentlemen, it's true. That which glitters is not always gold; but what I am going to tell, is true.'

He repeated this more than once.

---

*THIS tale is a classic example of the Demon Lover genre – the story of a fated supernatural abduction; it was employed earlier by J. W. von Goethe in "The Erlking" and by Fitz-James O'Brien in "The Demon of the Gibbet." Le Fanu would use the theme in "Schalken the Painter" and "Ultor de Lacy," and this very story would later serve to inspire the classic supernatural works of Rhoda Broughton ("The Man with the Nose") and E. F. Benson ("The Face"). This story is one of split identity – light and darkness, transparency and shadow, Super-Ego and Id – the impossibility of maintaining their separation, and the potentially violent coup that one can have when repressed by the other.*

---

Ten years ago, I took my credentials to an English gentleman at Long's Hotel, in Bond Street, London, who was about to travel — it might be for one year, it might be for two. He approved of them; likewise of me. He was pleased to make inquiry. The testimony that he received was favourable.

---

[1] Rumblings of weird fiction. E. T. A. Hoffmann, Edgar Allan Poe, Goethe, the Brothers Grimm, and several other folklorists, literati, and dramatists had spread tales of the bizarre and uncanny which occur outside of strict literary archetypes such as "ghost" or "vampire," but Dickens extends beyond Victorian conventions by searching out the truly uncanny, nonetheless, and should be applauded for it

[2] Italian: *Stop! Enough!*

He engaged me by the six months, and my entertainment was generous.

He was young, handsome, very happy. He was enamoured of a fair young English lady, with a sufficient fortune, and they were going to be married. It was the wedding-trip[1], in short, that we were going to take. For three months' rest in the hot weather (it was early summer then) he had hired an old place on the Riviera, at an easy distance from my city, Genoa, on the road to Nice. Did I know that place? Yes; I told him I knew it well. It was an old palace with great gardens. It was a little bare, and it was a little dark and gloomy, being close surrounded by trees; but it was spacious, ancient, grand, and on the seashore. He said it had been so described to him exactly, and he was well pleased that I knew it. For its being a little bare of furniture, all such places were. For its being a little gloomy, he had hired it principally for the gardens, and he and my mistress would pass the summer weather in their shade.

'So all goes well, Baptista?' said he.

'Indubitably[2], signore; very well.'

We had a travelling chariot for our journey, newly built for us, and in all respects complete. All we had was complete; we wanted for nothing. The marriage took place. They were happy. I was happy, seeing all so bright, being so well situated, going to my own city, teaching my language in the rumble to the maid, la bella[3] Carolina, whose heart was gay with laughter: who was young and rosy.

The time flew. But I observed — listen to this, I pray[4]! (and here the courier dropped his voice) — I observed my mistress[5] sometimes brooding in a manner very strange; in a frightened manner; in an unhappy manner; with a cloudy, uncertain alarm upon her. I think that I began to notice this when I was walking up hills by the carriage side, and master had gone on in front. At any rate, I remember that it impressed itself upon my mind one evening in the South of France, when she called to me to call master back; and when he came back, and walked for a long way, talking encouragingly and affectionately to her, with his hand upon the

---

[1] A honeymoon
[2] Doubtlessly, without a doubt
[3] The adorable, the lovely
[4] I beg you
[5] Female employer – not a lover

147

open window, and hers in it. Now and then, he laughed in a merry way, as if he were bantering[1] her out of something. By-and-by, she laughed, and then all went well again.

It was curious. I asked la bella Carolina, the pretty little one, *Was mistress unwell?* — No. — *Out of spirits?* — No. — *Fearful of bad roads, or brigands[2]?* — No. And what made it more mysterious was, the pretty little one would not look at me in giving answer, but WOULD look at the view.

But, one day she told me the secret.

'If you must know,' said Carolina, 'I find, from what I have overheard, that mistress is haunted.'

'How haunted?'

'By a dream.'

'What dream?'

'By a dream of a face. For three nights before her marriage, she saw a face in a dream — always the same face, and only One.'

'A terrible face?'

'No. The face of a dark, remarkable-looking man, in black, with black hair and a grey moustache — a handsome man except for a reserved and secret air. Not a face she ever saw, or at all like a face she ever saw. Doing nothing in the dream but looking at her fixedly, out of darkness[3].'

'Does the dream come back?'

'Never. The recollection of it is all her trouble.'

'And why does it trouble her?'

Carolina shook her head.

'That's master's question,' said la bella. 'She don't know. She wonders why, herself. But I heard her tell him, only last night, that if she was to find a picture of that face in our Italian house (which she is afraid she will) she did not know how she could ever bear it.'

---

[1] Using quick, chatty language

[2] Italy was famous for its bandits, highwaymen, and bands of robbers that waylaid rural travel routes, especially those used by foreign tourists and diplomats

[3] The figure is tailored in and surrounded by funereal black – both sinister in its morbid cultural symbolism, and emblematic of Nothingness – cosmic emptiness and spiritual desolation

148

Upon my word I was fearful after this (said the Genoese courier) of our coming to the old palazzo[1], lest some such ill-starred[2] picture should happen to be there. I knew there were many there; and, as we got nearer and nearer to the place, I wished the whole gallery in the crater of Vesuvius[3]. To mend the matter, it was a stormy dismal evening when we, at last, approached that part of the Riviera. It thundered; and the thunder of my city and its environs, rolling among the high hills, is very loud. The lizards ran in and out of the chinks in the broken stone wall of the garden, as if they were frightened; the frogs bubbled and croaked their loudest; the sea-wind moaned, and the wet trees dripped; and the lightning — body of San Lorenzo, how it lightened!

We all know what an old palace in or near Genoa is — how time and the sea air have blotted it — how the drapery painted on the outer walls has peeled off in great flakes of plaster — how the lower windows are darkened with rusty bars of iron — how the courtyard is overgrown with grass — how the outer buildings are dilapidated — how the whole pile seems devoted to ruin. Our palazzo was one of the true kind. It had been shut up close for months. Months? — years! — it had an earthy smell, like a tomb. The scent of the orange trees on the broad back terrace, and of the lemons ripening on the wall, and of some shrubs that grew around a broken fountain, had got into the house somehow, and had never been able to get out again. There was, in every room, an aged smell, grown faint with confinement[4]. It pined in all the cupboards and drawers. In the little rooms of communication between great rooms, it was stifling. If you turned a picture — to come back to the pictures — there it still was, clinging to the wall behind the frame, like a sort of bat[5].

---

[1] Palace, mansion
[2] Cursed, ill-fated
[3] A giant Italian volcano
[4] Confinement – the word evokes repression, sublimation, and the pent up impulses of the unconscious mind. This episode certainly mulls the anxieties of unconscious urges and thoughts
[5] Although *Dracula* is yet to appear in culture, the bat still possessed a leering, lurking cultural currency which saw it as a symbol of devilish perversion – the diabolical, nocturnal foil to the spiritual and melodious bird. Like a bat, repressed terrors hang silently in this house during the

The lattice-blinds were close shut, all over the house. There were two ugly, grey old women in the house, to take care of it; one of them with a spindle, who stood winding and mumbling in the doorway, and who would as soon have let in the devil as the air[1]. Master, mistress, la bella Carolina, and I, went all through the palazzo. I went first, though I have named myself last, opening the windows and the lattice-blinds, and shaking down on myself splashes of rain, and scraps of mortar[2], and now and then a dozing mosquito, or a monstrous, fat, blotchy, Genoese spider[3].

When I had let the evening light into a room, master, mistress, and la bella Carolina, entered. Then, we looked round at all the pictures, and I went forward again into another room. Mistress secretly had great fear of meeting with the likeness of that face — we all had; but there was no such thing. The Madonna and Bambino, San Francisco, San Sebastiano, Venus, Santa Caterina, Angels, Brigands, Friars, Temples at Sunset, Battles, White Horses, Forests, Apostles, Doges, all my old acquaintances many times repeated[4]? — yes. Dark, handsome man in black, reserved and secret, with black hair and grey moustache, looking fixedly at mistress out of darkness? — no[5].

At last we got through all the rooms and all the pictures, and came out

---

daylight of consciousness, only to descend and strike in the blind nocturne of dreams
[1] Symbolic of spiritual purification, truth, speech (confession, testimony), and communication
[2] The mineral cement used to hold building materials together – symbolically, the restraints and regulators of the unconscious mind are crumbling away
[3] Symbolic of dark, venomous, unsightly elements of the unconscious
[4] These are archetypes which represent the romantic, holy, familiar, noble, historic, patriotic, chivalric, manly, maternal, and sacred things that inhabit the middling areas of the Freudian model of consciousness – the Super-Ego: the symbols, ideas, and feelings which inspire good behavior and idealism. The Super-Ego has been widely represented, yes, but the Id – the dark impulses and selfish lusts that we deny or restrict – has failed to appear
[5] As previously mentioned: the Id – the dark impulses and selfish lusts that we deny or restrict – has failed to appear

150

into the gardens. They were pretty well kept, being rented by a gardener, and were large and shady. In one place there was a rustic theatre, open to the sky; the stage a green slope; the coulisses[1], three entrances upon a side, sweet-smelling leafy screens. Mistress moved her bright eyes, even there, as if she looked to see the face come in upon the scene; but all was well.

'Now, Clara[2],' master said, in a low voice, 'you see that it is nothing? You are happy.'

Mistress was much encouraged. She soon accustomed herself to that grim palazzo, and would sing, and play the harp, and copy the old pictures, and stroll with master under the green trees and vines all day. She was beautiful. He was happy. He would laugh and say to me, mounting his horse for his morning ride before the heat:

'All goes well, Baptista!'

'Yes, signore, thank God, very well.'

We kept no company. I took la bella to the Duomo and Annunciata, to the Cafe, to the Opera, to the village Festa, to the Public Garden, to the Day Theatre, to the Marionetti[3]. The pretty little one was charmed with all she saw. She learnt Italian — heavens! miraculously! Was mistress quite forgetful of that dream? I asked Carolina sometimes. Nearly, said la bella — almost. It was wearing out.

One day master received a letter, and called me.

'Baptista!'

'Signore!'

'A gentleman who is presented to me will dine here to-day. He is called the Signor Dellombra[4]. Let me dine like a prince.'

---

[1] Backstage area, or a screen between the stage wings

[2] Importantly, we learn that her name is Clara – from the Latin for *clear, bright, radiant*

[3] Petty amusements: a cathedral; coffee shops; operas; a festival day; a beer garden; stageplays; marionette puppet shows, etc.

[4] A very, *very* sinister omen – his name is Italian for "Of Shadow," "Of Darkness," literally, title included, "Lord Shadow" or "Lord of Shadows." His identity is fused with the concept of hidden things – things invisible but nonetheless extant. Shadows are the opposite of brightness ("Clara"), and Lord Shadow represents Clara's unapparent, repressed inversed, libidinal nature

It was an odd name. I did not know that name. But, there had been many noblemen and gentlemen pursued by Austria on political suspicions, lately, and some names had changed. Perhaps this was one. Altro[1]! Dellombra was as good a name to me as another.

When the Signor Dellombra came to dinner (said the Genoese courier in the low voice, into which he had subsided once before), I showed him into the reception-room, the great sala[2] of the old palazzo. Master received him with cordiality, and presented him to mistress. As she rose, her face changed, she gave a cry, and fell upon the marble floor.

Then, I turned my head to the Signor Dellombra, and saw that he was dressed in black, and had a reserved and secret air, and was a dark, remarkable-looking man, with black hair and a grey moustache.

Master raised mistress in his arms, and carried her to her own room, where I sent la bella Carolina straight. La bella told me afterwards that mistress was nearly terrified to death, and that she wandered in her mind about her dream, all night.

Master was vexed and anxious — almost angry, and yet full of solicitude. The Signor Dellombra was a courtly[3] gentleman, and spoke with great respect and sympathy of mistress's being so ill. The African wind[4] had been blowing for
some days (they had told him at his hotel of the Maltese Cross), and he knew that it was often hurtful. He hoped the beautiful lady would recover soon. He begged permission to retire, and to renew his visit when he should have the happiness of hearing that she was better.

---

[1] Italian: Other

[2] Italian: Room

[3] Refined and aristocratic, with the telltale breeding that identifies him as a high-born noble. Like Dracula, his aristocratic background allows a discussion of the hypocritical perils of privileging wealth, power, class, breeding, gender, and title. Alternatively, it serves to illustrate the elegant persuasion of impulse and passion, which are sometimes played down as crude and thuggish: to the contrary – it can be authoritative, commanding, and alluring

[4] The simoon – a dry, sandy, hurricanical that shuttles through North Africa, across to Southern Europe (especially Italy). Clouded with romance, it is suggestive of passion and lust

153

Master would not allow of this, and they dined alone.

He withdrew early. Next day he called at the gate, on horse-back, to inquire for mistress. He did so two or three times in that week.

What I observed myself, and what la bella Carolina told me, united to explain to me that master had now set his mind on curing mistress of her fanciful terror. He was all kindness, but he was sensible and firm. He reasoned with her, that to encourage such fancies was to invite melancholy, if not madness. That it rested with herself to be herself. That if she once resisted her strange weakness, so successfully as to receive the Signor Dellombra as an English lady would receive any other guest, it was for ever conquered. To make an end, the signore came again, and mistress received him without marked distress (though with constraint and apprehension still), and the evening passed serenely. Master was so delighted with this change, and so anxious to confirm it, that the Signor Dellombra became a constant guest. He was accomplished in pictures, books, and music; and his society, in any grim palazzo, would have been welcome.

I used to notice, many times, that mistress was not quite recovered. She would cast down her eyes and droop her head, before the Signor Dellombra, or would look at him with a terrified and fascinated glance, as if his presence had some evil influence or power upon her. Turning from her to him, I used to see him in the shaded gardens, or the large half-lighted sala, looking, as I might say, 'fixedly upon her out of darkness[1].' But, truly, I had not forgotten la bella Carolina's words describing the face in the dream.

After his second visit I heard master say:

'Now, see, my dear Clara, it's over! Dellombra has come and gone, and your apprehension is broken like glass.'

'Will he — will he ever come again?' asked mistress.

'Again? Why, surely, over and over again! Are you cold?' (she shivered).

'No, dear — but — he terrifies me: are you sure that he need come again?'

'The surer for the question, Clara!' replied master, cheerfully.

But, he was very hopeful of her complete recovery now, and grew more and more so every day. She was beautiful. He was happy.

---

[1] The very image of the lady's vision

154

'All goes well, Baptista?' he would say to me again.

'Yes, signore, thank God; very well.'

We were all (said the Genoese courier, constraining himself to speak a little louder), we were all at Rome for the Carnival. I had been out, all day, with a Sicilian, a friend of mine, and a courier, who was there with an English family. As I returned at night to our hotel, I met the little Carolina, who never stirred from home alone, running distractedly along the Corso[1].

'Carolina! What's the matter?'

'O Baptista! O, for the Lord's sake! where is my mistress?'

'Mistress, Carolina?'

'Gone since morning — told me, when master went out on his day's journey, not to call her, for she was tired with not resting in the night (having been in pain), and would lie in bed until the evening; then get up refreshed. She is gone! — she is gone! Master has come back, broken down the door, and she is gone! My beautiful, my good, my innocent[2] mistress!'

The pretty little one so cried, and raved, and tore herself that I could not have held her, but for her swooning on my arm as if she had been shot. Master came up — in manner, face, or voice, no more the master that I knew, than I was he. He took me (I laid the little one upon her bed in the hotel, and left her with the chamber-women), in a carriage, furiously through the darkness[3], across the desolate Campagna[4]. When it was day, and we stopped at a miserable post-house[5], all the horses had been hired

---

[1] Italian: Course

[2] These positive qualities demonstrate moral homogeneity, good behavior, social respectability, and polite conformity – qualities at odd with the selfish, lustful urges of the Id. It is naturally important that this is her servant's first reaction, to defend her mistress's virtuous reputation, rather than to assume it will be understood. Lord Shadow's influence in the household has clearly alerted at least *her* to her mistress's complex psychological makeup

[3] He begins to acknowledge his wife's turbulent unconscious by acquainting himself with and entering the darkness that he has so long disregarded. It is too late

[4] Italian: countryside, wilderness – implications of vastness

[5] Way station for rest, refreshment, and changing horses

twelve hours ago, and sent away in different directions. Mark me! by the Signor Dellombra, who had passed there in a carriage, with a frightened English lady crouching in one corner[1].

I never heard (said the Genoese courier, drawing a long breath) that she was ever traced beyond that spot. All I know is, that she vanished into infamous oblivion[2], with the dreaded face beside her that she had seen in her dream.

---

*TALES of twins are common throughout literature, and are well-represented in horror, especially by the Doppelgänger, an apparition that – whether physical or psychical – represents the split nature of humanity. Algernon Blackwood ("The Terror of the Twins"), Poe ("William Wilson," "...House of Usher"), and Robert Louis Stevenson ("...Dr Jekyll and Mr Hyde") are just a few of the writers who have employed this motif. The story that follows, while not nearly as elegant as the previous, is perhaps more structurally complicated; it concerns the nature of identity – is it material or is it spiritual? – and the messy, unclear borderlands between Self and Other, between Haunter and Haunted.*

---

'What do you call THAT[3]?' said the German courier, triumphantly.

---

[1] Out of fear or shame? Sometimes I read it one way, others another. Is she an abductee or an accomplice? Certainly Dickens leaves it vague with great intentionality . In either case, Shadow has now become united with Brightness, and the two natures – once forced apart – are now hurdled towards one another in a violent and desperate reunification

[2] Infamous implies a level of lost reputation. Oblivion – like the darkness that houses Lord Shadow – not only hides, but devours. Whatever motives or truths may have been involved in this mystery are now consigned to the same dark void that masks our minds from each other

[3] German and Italian tales of the fantastic are often seen as competing schools, even within English literature, Gothic tales featuring Italian settings were rivaled by those featuring German backdrops. German Gothic is often typified as grotesque – violent, monstrous, brooding, with hate as its

'Ghosts!   There are no ghosts THERE! What do you call this, that I am going to tell you? Ghosts! There are no ghosts HERE!'

I took an engagement once (pursued the German courier) with an English gentleman[1], elderly and a bachelor, to travel through my country, my Fatherland. He was a merchant who traded with my country and knew the language, but who had never been there since he was a boy — as I judge, some sixty years before.

His name was James, and he had a twin-brother[2] John[3], also a bachelor. Between these brothers there was a great affection. They were in business together, at Goodman's Fields, but they did not live together. Mr. James dwelt in Poland Street, turning out of Oxford Street, London; Mr. John resided by Epping Forest[4].

Mr. James and I were to start for Germany in about a week. The exact day depended on business. Mr. John came to Poland Street (where I was staying in the house), to pass that week with Mr. James. But, he said to his brother on the second day, 'I don't feel very well, James. There's not much the matter with me; but I think I am a little gouty[5]. I'll go home and put myself under the care of my old housekeeper, who understands my ways. If I get quite better, I'll come back and see you before you go. If I don't feel well enough to resume my visit where I leave it off, why YOU will come

---

common element – and the Italian Gothic as arabesque – romantic, magical, mysterious, with lust as its common element

[1] Once more, an Englishman is the subject of the tale. Dickens is almost certainly using this international gab fest as an opportunity to critique English culture and hypocrisy

[2] Likeness once more appears in the plot – the two brothers are identical, meaning that while different persons, they nonetheless hold common elements of the same identity

[3] Infamously, James and John, apostles to Jesus, battled over which would have the honor to sit at his right side in the Kingdom of Heaven. Christ chastised their greed and rivalry

[4] Some 27 miles between the two areas

[5] Gout is an inflammation of the feet caused by a welling of uric acid in the lower extremities

and see me before you go[1].' Mr. James, of course, said he would, and they shook hands — both hands, as they always did — and Mr. John ordered out his old-fashioned chariot and rumbled home.

It was on the second night after that — that is to say, the fourth in the week — when I was awoke out of my sound sleep by Mr. James coming into my bedroom in his flannel-gown, with a lighted candle. He sat upon the side of my bed, and looking at me, said:

'Wilhelm, I have reason to think I have got some strange illness upon me.'

I then perceived that there was a very unusual expression in his face.

'Wilhelm,' said he, 'I am not afraid or ashamed to tell you what I might be afraid or ashamed to tell another man. You come from a sensible country[2], where mysterious things are inquired into and are not settled to have been weighed and measured — or to have been unweighable and unmeasurable — or in either case to have been completely disposed of, for all time — ever so many years ago. I have just now seen the phantom

---

[1] A fateful exclamation. While this story lacks the elegance of its predecessor, it deals with a dualism that is perhaps more complicated; John tells James that if he recovers his brother shall see him again, and that if he does not, he shall see his brother. Both men share a facial identity, and to see one is to see the self; they are both distinct individualities and shared partners of a common nature. Dickens once more alludes to the indivisibility of huamnity's complex soup of psychologies, spiritualities, identities, and wills

[2] Germany was infamous for its involvement in the Gothic movement. Stories like those of Goethe, Hoffmann, the Grimms, and Gotthelf were gruesome and weird enough to match Poe, Stoker, and Le Fanu. Being one of the few Protestant regions that did not have a thoroughly successful Enlightenment, avoided humanist influences, and eschewed the republicanization that swept France, Britain, Holland, the United States, and Italy, Germany continued to have a general population that was educated by folklore and superstition rather than Plutarch and Locke, and tales of ghosts, wizards, witchcraft, monsters, vampires, and visions abounded fruitfully in German peasants' cottages and in German intellectuals' libraries alike

of my brother[1].'

I confess (said the German courier) that it gave me a little tingling of the blood to hear it.

'I have just now seen,' Mr. James repeated, looking full at me, that I might see how collected he was, 'the phantom of my brother John. I was sitting up in bed, unable to sleep, when it came into my room, in a white dress, and regarding me earnestly, passed up to the end of the room, glanced at some papers on my writing-desk, turned, and, still looking earnestly at me as it passed the bed, went out at the door. Now, I am not in the least mad, and am not in the least disposed to invest that phantom with any external existence out of myself. I think it is a warning to me that I am ill[2]; and I think I had better be bled[3].'

I got out of bed directly (said the German courier) and began to get on my clothes, begging him not to be alarmed, and telling him that I would go myself to the doctor. I was just ready, when we heard a loud knocking and ringing at the street door. My room being an attic at the back, and Mr. James's being the second-floor room in the front, we went down to his room, and put up the window, to see what was the matter.

'Is that Mr. James?' said a man below, falling back to the opposite side of the way to look up.

'It is,' said Mr. James, 'and you are my brother's man, Robert.'

'Yes, Sir. I am sorry to say, Sir, that Mr. John is ill. He is very bad, Sir. It is even feared that he may be lying at the point of death. He wants to see

---

[1] Or perhaps the phantom of his own self? They are identical, why so sure as to who he saw?

[2] In a sense, he is: John is the one who is ill, but considering their joint identity, when one suffers so does the other. Like Clara and Dellombra who represented the disparate elements of the unconscious – the socially proper and the shunned libido – James and John represent the divided human identity: the physical and the psychical, the tangible and the spiritual. James and John's spiritual identities are unique (or so they think) – one can visit the other supernaturally – but their physical identities are common

[3] The infamous practice of opening a vein and allowing it to momentarily empty was a gambit on the part of pre-Darwinian physicians to balance out the bodily fluids – too much blood was considered the cause of most fevers, diseases, and hysterias

159

you, Sir. I have a chaise here. Pray come to him. Pray lose no time.'

Mr. James and I looked at one another. 'Wilhelm,' said he, 'this is strange. I wish you to come with me!' I helped him to dress, partly there and partly in the chaise; and no grass grew under the horses' iron shoes between Poland Street and the Forest[1].

Now, mind! (said the German courier) I went with Mr. James into his brother's room, and I saw and heard myself what follows.

His brother lay upon his bed, at the upper end of a long bed-chamber. His old housekeeper was there, and others were there: I think three others were there, if not four, and they had been with him since early in the afternoon. He was in white, like the figure — necessarily so, because he had his night-dress on. He looked like the figure — necessarily so, because he looked earnestly at his brother when he saw him come into the room.

But, when his brother reached the bed-side, he slowly raised himself in bed, and looking full upon him, said these words:

'JAMES, YOU HAVE SEEN ME BEFORE, TO-NIGHT— AND YOU KNOW IT![2]'

And so died!

I waited, when the German courier ceased, to hear something said of this strange story. The silence was unbroken. I looked round, and the five couriers were gone: so noiselessly that the ghostly mountain[3] might

---

[1] That is to say, they flew like the wind – to use a simile

[2] James incorrectly mistook the omen to represent a turn in his own health, but death had invaded his brother's physical nature instead. They share a physical identity, but when the body failed to bring about a reunion, the psychical individuation extended itself to his brother. The accusation that John appears to make is that his brother misinterpreted the meaning of his spectral appearance, taking it to foretell disaster to his own body, while the doom was intended for his brothers'. The mistake is due to their shared physicality – an identity thought to split evenly between the material and the spiritual is in fact divided coarsely by a jagged, smeared border that occasions James' failure to respond to his brother's psychic message

[3] Symbolic of mortality and man's ineffectuality in the face of a bizarre, untamable cosmos, the mountain re-dominates the landscape in the

have absorbed them[1] into its eternal snows[2]. By this time, I was by no means in a mood to sit alone in that awful[3] scene, with the chill air coming solemnly upon me — or, if I may tell the truth, to sit alone anywhere. So I went back into the convent- parlour, and, finding the American gentleman still disposed to relate the biography of the Honourable Ananias Dodger, heard it all out.

---

conclusion just as it did in the introduction. You will recall that the couriers were speechless while the sunset poured over its face like spilled wine (sun like wine, wine like blood) because the mountain's encrimsoned face was testimony to the warped chaos of the natural/supernatural worlds, and that once it faded into the blue twilight, their conversation – a debate on the nature of the relationship between the natural and supernatural – was revived, capable of being had while the mountain didn't so obviously attest to the grotesque reality. Now that the conversation has abruptly ceased, the mountain is left looming ominously in the dusk – a closing *"Finis"* that underscores their grim conclusion

[1] Not unlike the bodies of the frozen travelers buried on the mountainside – bodies which, incidentally, might include those of five unfortunate couriers

[2] Just as the narrator began the story as a spectral eavesdropping, unnoticed by his storytellers, he is left alone without a word. The departure is abrupt, jarring, and alienating. Once the object, the narrator becomes the subject – once in control of the narrative, he is now almost helpless to continue it, deciding to return to the greedy American's tales. The couriers may simply have left abruptly, they may have been ghosts themselves, or they may have been visions sent to communicate a message. But one way or another, they are absorbed into the monolithic mountain representing the vast mystery and horror of the unprobed natural world. The universe is indifferent, immense, and prone to deception. Just so is the human mind, Dickens suggests, juxtaposing the vast vista with the labyrinthine psychology of his characters

[3] Both "full of awe" because of the mountain's grand and terrifying sublimity, and "repugnant" because of the corpses that have, throughout time, been absorbed by those eternal snows

*FATE and identity, Dickens suggests, are under the sway of the unconscious, and regardless of our breeding, our higher aspirations, or our conscious desires, reality cannot be altered to fit the needs of the conscience or society. A woman of noble virtue cannot banish the dark impulses of a schizophrenic moral identity; a man whose physical self is shared nebulously with his twin brother cannot rationally expect his psychical self to be neatly split between them; a mountain which is, in reality, bathed in the blood of its victims, cannot be compared to spilled wine without suggesting its true nature; and a party of story tellers bent on arriving at a satisfactory understanding of what is things – ghosts and yet not ghosts – which inhabit the spaces between the natural and the supernatural may not be able to avoid calling attention to their own ambiguous supernaturality. As in "The Signalman" and "The Trial by Murder," Dickens uses the ghost story as a vehicle for illuminating the shadowy territories between unconscious knowledge and conscious denial.*

*THIS queasy tale shares much in common with the gruesome
supernatural universes of Algernon Blackwood, H. P. Lovecraft, and
William Hope Hodgson, and yet its tropes, narrative, and conventions
are decidedly Victorian. Like Le Fanu and Gaskell, O'Donnell (who
published ostensibly true accounts of ghost stories, although any
student of supernatural literature – both literary and veridical – will
consider this a work of fiction, not reporting) uses a truly revolting
haunting to suggest the vast longevity of evil. Long after the actors have
died – long after their very identities have faded into forgetfulness – they
continue to plague one generation after another with their unbearable
pantomime.*

---

# THE TOP ATTIC
## IN PRINGLE'S MANSION, EDINBURGH
### {1911}
### *Elliot O'Donnell*

A CHARMING LADY, MISS SOUTH, informs me that no house
interested her more, as a child, than Pringle's Mansion, Edinburgh.
Pringle's Mansion, by the bye, is not the real name of the house, nor is
the original building still standing—the fact is, my friend has been
obliged to disguise the locality for fear of an action for slander of title,
such as happened in the Egham Case of 1904-7[1].

Miss South never saw—save in a picture—the house that so
fascinated her; but through repeatedly hearing about it from her old
nurse, she felt that she knew it by heart, and used to amuse herself
hour after hour in the nursery, drawing diagrams of the rooms and
passages, which, to make quite realistic, she named and numbered.

There was the Admiral's room, Madame's room, Miss Ophelia's
room, Master Gregory's room, Letty's (the nurse's) room, the cook's

---

[1] This apparently fictitious case is, nonetheless, hardly without precedent:
to spread stories of a haunting about a house which did not revel in the
romance of ghost lore could absolutely merit a civil suit for defamation or
slander

room, the butler's room, the housemaid's room—and—the Haunted Room. The house was very old—probably the sixteenth century—and was concealed from the thoroughfare by a high wall that enclosed it on all sides. It had no garden, only a large yard, covered with faded yellow paving-stones, and containing a well with an old-fashioned roller and bucket[1]. When the well was cleaned out, an event which took place periodically on a certain date, every utensil in the house was called into requisition for ladling out the water, and the Admiral, himself supervising, made every servant in the establishment take an active part in the proceedings. On one of these occasions, the Admiral announced his intention of going down the well in the bucket. That was a rare moment in Letty's life, for when the Admiral had been let down in the bucket, the rope broke!

Indeed, the thought of what the Laird[2] would say when he came up, almost resulted in his not coming up at all. However, some one, rather bolder than the rest, retained sufficient presence of mind to effect a rescue, and the timid ones, thankful enough to survive the explosion, had to be content on "half-rations till further orders."[3]

But in spite of its association with such a martinet[4], and in spite of her ghostly experiences in it, Letty loved the house, and was never tired of singing its praises.

It was a two-storeyed[5] mansion, with roomy cellars but no basement. There were four reception-rooms—all oak-panelled—on the ground floor; numerous kitchen offices, including a cosy housekeeper's room; and a capacious entrance hall, in the centre of which stood a broad oak staircase. The cellars, three in number, and chiefly used as lumber-rooms, were deep down and dank and horrid.

---

[1] The archetypal wishing well as opposed to a 19th century iron pump
[2] Pronounced how it's spelled (rhymes with *aired*) – Scots for "lord," "master"
[3] Being a naval man, the Admiral exacts a naval form of punishment: cutting off their food portions by half
[4] Strict, militaristic disciplinarian, a "drill sergeant"
[5] To fellow Americans: we would say "three storied"; Britons do not count the ground floor

On the first floor[1] eight bedrooms opened on to a gallery[2] overlooking the hall, and the top storey, where the servants slept, consisted solely of attics connected with one another by dark, narrow passages. It was one of these attics that was haunted, although, as a matter of fact, the ghost had been seen in all parts of the house.

When Letty entered the Admiral's service she was but a bairn[3], and had never even heard of ghosts; nor did the other servants apprise her of the hauntings, having received strict injunctions not to do so from the Laird. But Letty's home, humble though it was, had been very bright and cheerful, and the dark precincts of the mansion filled her with dismay. Without exactly knowing why she was afraid, she shrank in terror from descending into the cellars, and felt anything but pleased at the prospect of sleeping alone in an attic. Still nothing occurred to really alarm her till about a month after her arrival. It was early in the evening, soon after twilight, and she had gone down into one of the cellars to look for a boot-jack[4], which the Admiral swore by all that was holy must be found before supper.

Placing the light she had brought with her on a packing-case, she was groping about among the boxes, when she perceived, to her astonishment, that the flame of the candle had suddenly turned blue[5].

---

[1] Again, read: second
[2] Wide, tall, long hallway
[3] Pronounced *BEAR*-ñ – Scots for child, baby, youngling
[4] Small wooden wedge used to pry off riding boots
[5] Blue flame has long been associated with the supernatural, and is referenced to in a variety of folkloric and literary sources, from *Dracula* to "Little Orphant Annie" (An' little Orphant Annie says, when the blaze is blue, / An' the lamp-wick sputters, an' the wind goes woo-oo!). Although the association is difficult to research (many sources employ it; few explain its origin), Leonard Wolf argues for a simple association between will-o'-the-wisps – burning swamp gas and the phosphorescent glow of decaying vegetable and animal matter – which, though rarely seen or documented, is reported to be a low, hazy blue. Will-o'-the-wisps, also called false lights, were known to deceive travelers late at night, giving the impression of a village or farmhouse, but luring them into the heart of the swamp, sometimes to death. This association has carried into the "blue flame

She then felt icy cold, and was much startled on hearing a loud clatter as of some metal instrument on the stone floor in the far-off corner of the cellar. Glancing in the direction of the noise, she saw, looking at her, two eyes—two obliquely set, lurid, light eyes, full of the utmost devilry. Sick with terror and utterly unable to account for what she beheld, she stood stock-still, her limbs refusing to move, her throat parched, her tongue tied. The clanging was repeated, and a shadowy form began slowly to crawl towards her. She dared not afterwards surmise what would have happened to her, had not the Laird himself come down at this moment. At the sound of his stentorian[1] voice the phantasm vanished. But the shock had been too much for Letty; she fainted, and the Admiral, carrying her upstairs as carefully as if she had been his own daughter, gave peremptory[2] orders that she should never again be allowed to go into the cellar alone.

But now that Letty herself had witnessed a manifestation, the other servants no longer felt bound to secrecy, and soon poured into her ears endless accounts of the hauntings.

Every one, they informed her, except Master Gregory and Perkins (the butler) had seen one or other of the ghosts, and the cellar apparition was quite familiar to them all. They also declared that there were other parts of the house quite as badly haunted as the cellar, and it might have been partly owing to these gruesome stories that poor Letty always felt scared, when crossing the passages leading to the attics. As she was hastening down one of them, early one morning, she heard some one running after her. Thinking it was one of the other servants, she turned round, pleased to think that some one else was up early too, and saw to her horror a dreadful-looking object, that seemed to be partly human and partly animal. The body was quite small, and its face bloated, and covered with yellow spots. It had an enormous animal mouth[3], the lips of which, moving furiously without emitting

---

folklore," wherein a bright, yellow candle flame will sour to a cold, sinister blue in the presence of the supernatural

[1] Deep, loud, powerful
[2] Dictatorial, authoritative
[3] Compare to M.R. James' "Casting the Runes"; W. H. Hodgson's "The Haunted *Pampero*"

any sound, showed that the creature was endeavouring to speak but could not[1]. The moment Letty screamed for help the phantasm vanished.

But her worst experience was yet to come. The spare attic which she was told was so badly haunted that no one would sleep in it, was the room next to hers. It was a room Letty could well believe was haunted, for she had never seen another equally gloomy. The ceiling was low and sloping, the window tiny, and the walls exhibited all sorts of odd nooks and crannies. A bed, antique and worm-eaten, stood in one recess, a black oak chest in another, and at right angles with the door, in another recess, stood a wardrobe that used to creak and groan alarmingly every time Letty walked a long the passage. Once she heard a chuckle, a low, diabolical chuckle, which she fancied came from the chest; and once, when the door of the room was open, she caught the glitter of a pair of eyes—the same pale, malevolent eyes that had so frightened her in the cellar. From her earliest childhood Letty had been periodically given to somnambulism[2], and one night, just about a year after she went into service, she got out of bed, and walked, in her sleep, into the Haunted Room. She awoke to find herself standing, cold and shivering, in the middle of the floor, and it was some seconds before she realised where she was. Her horror, when she did discover where she was, is not easily described. The room was bathed in moonlight, and the beams, falling with noticeable brilliancy on each piece of furniture the room contained, at once riveted Letty's attention, and so fascinated her that she found herself utterly unable to move. A terrible and most unusual silence predominated everywhere, and although Letty's senses were wonderfully and painfully on the alert, she could not catch the slightest sound from any of the rooms on the landing.

The night was absolutely still, no breath of wind, no rustle of leaves, no flapping of ivy against the window; yet the door suddenly swung back on its hinges and slammed furiously. Letty felt that this was the work of some supernatural agency, and, fully expecting that the noise

---

[1] The combination of animal stupidity and human intelligence is disturbing in the extreme: it wants to talk and communicate, but is prevented by its beastly vocal instruments
[2] Sleepwalking – a terrible malady to suffer in a haunted house

had awakened the cook, who was a light sleeper (or pretended she was), listened in a fever of excitement to hear her get out of bed and call out. The slightest noise and the spell that held her prisoner would, Letty felt sure, be broken. But the same unbroken silence prevailed. A sudden rustling made Letty glance fearfully at the bed; and she perceived, to her terror, the valance[1] swaying violently, to and fro. Sick with fear, she was now constrained to stare in abject helplessness.

Presently there was a slight, very slight movement on the mattress, the white dust cover rose, and, under it, Letty saw the outlines of what she took to be a human figure, gradually take shape. Hoping, praying, that she was mistaken, and that what appeared to be on the bed was but a trick of her imagination, she continued staring in an agony of anticipation. But the figure remained—extended at full length like a corpse. The minutes slowly passed, a church clock boomed two, and the body moved. Letty's jaw fell, her eyes almost bulged from her head, whilst her fingers closed convulsively on the folds of her night-dress.

The unmistakable sound of breathing now issued from the region of the bed, and the dust-cover commenced slowly to slip aside. Inch by inch it moved, until first of all Letty saw a few wisps of dark hair, then a few more, then a thick cluster; then something white and shining—a protruding forehead; then dark, very dark brows; then two eyelids, yellow, swollen, and fortunately tightly closed; then—a purple conglomeration of Letty knew not what—of anything but what was human. The sight was so monstrous it appalled her; and she was overcome with a species of awe and repulsion, for which the language of mortality has no sufficiently energetic expression. She momentarily forgot that what she looked on was merely superphysical[2], but regarded it as something alive, something that ought to have been a child, comely and healthy as herself—and she hated it. It was an outrage on maternity[3], a blot on nature, a filthy discredit to the house, a blight, a

---

[1] Linen drapery hung over the space between a bed and the floor
[2] Outside of or beyond the nature of physical objects – viz., it *supposedly* cannot touch her
[3] Who or whatever had given birth to or raised it should be horrified and ashamed, Letty thinks

169

sore, a gangrene. It turned over in its sleep, the cover was hurled aside, and a grotesque object, round, pulpy, webbed[1], and of leprous whiteness[2]—an object which Letty could hardly associate with a hand— came groveling out. Letty's stomach heaved; the thing was beastly, indecent, vile, it ought not to live! And the idea of killing flashed through her mind[3].

Boiling over with indignation and absurdly forgetful of her surroundings, she turned round and groped for a stone to smash it. The moonlight on her naked toes brought her to her senses—the thing in the
bed was a devil! Though brought up a member of the Free Church[4], with an abhorrence of anything that could in any way be contorted into Papist practices[5], Letty crossed herself. As she did so, a noise in the passage outside augmented her terror. She strained her ears painfully, and the sound developed into a footstep, soft, light, and surreptitious[6]. It came gently towards the door; it paused outside, and Letty intuitively felt that it was listening. Her suspense was now so intolerable, that it was almost with a feeling of relief that she beheld the door slowly— very slowly—begin to open. A little wider—a little wider—and yet a little wider; but still nothing came. Ah! Letty's heart turned to ice. Another inch, and a shadowy something slipped through and began to wriggle itself stealthily over the floor[7]. Letty tried to divert her gaze, but could not—an irresistible, magnetic attraction kept her eyes glued to

---

[1] Its hands and feet are likely fused together or connected by vestigial webbing

[2] Having the same bleached, splotchy, pulpy complexion of a leper

[3] These thoughts, as we shall soon see, are likely not Letty's. They are thoughts of disgust and shame which drive her towards an unnatural homicidal inclination

[4] That is, the Free Church of Scotland – a Presbyterian sect that reviled the collaboration between church and state and saw Catholicism and all of its rituals, trappings, and superstitions as highly suspicious and heretical

[5] Papist: Roman Catholic

[6] Secretive, attempting to be quiet, creeping

[7] Compare this snakelike behavior to the crawling thing in the cellar; it eschews human locomotion for reptilian slithering

the gradually approaching horror. When within a few feet of her it halted; and again Letty felt it was listening— listening to the breathing on the bed, which was heavy and bestial[1]. Then it twisted round, and Letty watched it crawl into the wardrobe. After this there was a long and anxious wait. Then Letty saw the wardrobe door slyly open, and the eyes of the cellar—inexpressibly baleful[2], and glittering like burnished steel in the strong phosphorescent glow of the moon, peep out— not at her but *through* her—at the object lying on the bed. There were not only eyes, this time, but a form—vague, misty, and irregular, but still with sufficient shape to enable Letty to identify it as that of a woman, tall and thin, and with a total absence of hair, which was emphasised in the most lurid and ghastly fashion. With a snakelike movement, the evil thing slithered out of the wardrobe, and, gliding past Letty, approached the bed. Letty was obliged to follow every proceeding. She saw the thing deftly snatch the bolster[3] from under the sleeping head; noted the gleam of hellish satisfaction in its eyes as it pressed the bolster down; and watched the murdered creature's contortions grow fainter, and fainter, until they finally ceased[4]. The eyes then left the room; and from afar off, away below, in the abysmal cellars of the house, came the sound of digging—faint, very faint, but unquestionably digging. This terminated the grim, phantasmal drama for that night at least, and Letty, chilled to the bone, but thoroughly alert, escaped to her room. She spent her few remaining hours of rest wide-awake, determining never to go to bed again without fastening one of her arms to the iron staples.

With regard the history of the house, Letty never learned anything more remarkable than that, long ago, an idiot child[5] was supposed to

---

[1] Beastlike, inhuman
[2] Threatening, menacing, malicious
[3] Long cylindrical pillow
[4] Here we discover the source of Letty's impulse to euthanatize the deformed child: his mother's infanticidal spirit, which slithers up from the cellars at night to smother her boy
[5] Likely a severely mentally retarded child, possibly – and folklore supports such a suggestion – the inbred result of an incestuous encounter. The child is tremendously deformed at any rate, webbed, disfigured, animal-like, and

have been murdered in the haunted attic—by whom, tradition did not say[1]. The Admiral and his family left Pringle's Mansion the year Letty became Miss South's nurse, and as no one would stay in the house, presumably on account of the hauntings, it was pulled down, and an inexcusably inartistic edifice was erected in its place.

---

misshapen – it is not unlikely that the hideously spotted, animal-mouthed apparition in the hallway was this unfortunate boy's daylight manifestation

[1] "It was an outrage on maternity." Tradition likely does not say because the murderer was either never caught, or the family is ashamed of the truth, or both. Ghost stories in Victorian Britain – especially veridical ones – concerned the reappearance of repressed, secreted, or shameful matters of national, local, or family histories: "the things we try to forget," they suggested, "are the things which will be least likely forgotten." As in "The Old Nurse's Story" and "The Cold Embrace," this appears to be a deep-rooted shame, and while it is trite speculation, we cannot help but suspect the mother, who would resent, even as Letty momentarily did, *this discredit to the house, this outrage on maternity*

172

TERROR and horror intertwine grotesquely in this at first innocuous sketch. But like Nesbit, its brevity is deceiving, because it teems with senseless torments and repulsive evil. The immediate repugnance of O'Donnell's story lies in its casual dramatics: the phantoms are never fully elucidated, the mansion's owners tolerate the visitations without investigating the matter, and the visions are noiselessly doused by the mansion's demolition. The implication is that such horrors could be percolating, unchallenged under any roof. But a deeper layer dwells in the reader's own relationship to the text. We are drawn into the psychological tangles of the Pringle Mansion: we loathe the polypus inbred wriggling in the dark, and we wish it torn away from our presence—to beat its groping hands away from our vulnerable feet, to smash its brains out with the nearest stick of furniture. It is unnatural and repulsive, and our instinct is to destroy it. Only sentences later we infer that our wish has been executed by the serpentine succubus in the closet: our revulsion is manifested in the sinister apparition, and we realize that we share an alliance with a far greater evil than mere physical ugliness. We are ultimately repulsed by our own infanticidal repulsion.

*SYMPATHY was a byword in the Scottish Enlightenment – an intellectual movement that influenced the development of American politics, education, and capitalism. Adam Smith and David Hume were equally fond of the term, which meant "fellow-feeling" – a sense of imaginative empathy wherein a person realized that they could not judge the life or actions of another without first trying to vividly understand the pathos of their situation. Mrs Oliphant was a ghost story writer of the first rate, and like a true Scot inherited a love for sympathy. Her stories are tastefully drenched in psychological complexities, emotional richness, and social commentary. The following novelette, her masterpiece, could be viewed as an allegory of class reactions to sufferings which transcend personal experience. A truly beautiful ghost story – as graceful, elegant, and disquieting as anything in British literature – it rejects the sacred cows of British society (superstition, class, science, and authority) in favor of a truth which Oliphant believes to transcend social rank or intellectual philosophy: the power of sympathy.*

---

# THE OPEN DOOR[1]
## {1881}
## *Mrs. Margaret Oliphant*

I TOOK THE HOUSE OF BRENTWOOD on my return from India in 18--, for the temporary accommodation of my family, until I could find a permanent home for them. It had many advantages which made it peculiarly appropriate. It was within reach of Edinburgh[2]; and my boy Roland, whose education had been considerably neglected, could go in

---

[1] Not to be confused with Mrs J. H. Riddell's "The Open Door" (1882) published the following year. That story is the account of a door which will not remain closed and a poor clerk threatened with unemployment, who volunteers to exorcise the ghost in return for a cash prize

[2] Presumably located within a five to fifteen mile radius of the Scottish capital

174

and out to school; which was thought to be better for him than either leaving home altogether or staying there always with a tutor. The first of these expedients would have seemed preferable to me; the second commended itself to his mother. The doctor, like a judicious man, took the midway between. "Put him on his pony, and let him ride into the High School every morning; it will do him all the good in the world," Dr. Simson said; "and when it is bad weather, there is the train." His mother accepted this solution of the difficulty more easily than I could have hoped; and our pale-faced boy, who had never known anything more invigorating than Simla[1], began to encounter the brisk breezes of the North in the subdued severity of the month of May. Before the time of the vacation in July we had the satisfaction of seeing him begin to acquire something of the brown and ruddy complexion of his schoolfellows. The English system did not commend itself to Scotland in these days. There was no little Eton at Fettes[2]; nor do I think, if there had been, that a genteel exotic of that class would have tempted either my wife or me. The lad was doubly precious to us, being the only one left us of many; and he was fragile in body, we believed, and deeply sensitive in mind. To keep him at home, and yet to send him to school, — to combine the advantages of the two systems, — seemed to be everything that could be desired. The two girls also found at Brentwood everything they wanted. They were near enough to Edinburgh to have masters and lessons as many as they required for completing that never-ending education which the young people seem to require nowadays. Their mother married me when she was younger than Agatha; and I should like to see them improve upon their mother! I myself was then no more than twenty-five, — an age at which I see the young fellows now groping about them, with no notion what they are going to do with their lives. However, I suppose every generation has a conceit of itself which

---

[1] A city in far northern India, formerly the summer capital of British India. The colonel notes that this – one of India's more temperate climates, nestled among misty mountains – is the coldest climate the boy has experienced – a far cry from Scottish Februaries

[2] Fettes College – an independent boarding school founded in 1870 – was known as the Eton of the North. Eton continues to be the most prestigious English boarding school, known for its high standards and success rates

175

elevates it, in its own opinion above that which comes after it.

Brentwood stands on that fine and wealthy slope of country — one of the richest in Scotland — which lies between the Pentland Hills[1] and the Firth[2]. In clear weather you could see the blue gleam — like a bent bow, embracing the wealthy fields and scattered houses — of the great estuary on one side of you; and on the other the blue heights, not gigantic like those we had been used to, but just high enough for all the glories of the atmosphere, the play of clouds, and sweet reflections, which give to a hilly country an interest and a charm which nothing else can emulate. Edinburgh — with its two lesser heights, the Castle and the Calton Hill, its spires and towers piercing through the smoke, and Arthur's Seat lying crouched behind, like a guardian no longer very needful, taking his repose beside the well-beloved charge, which is now, so to speak, able to take care of itself without him — lay at our right hand. From the lawn and drawing-room windows we could see all these varieties of landscape. The color was sometimes a little chilly, but sometimes, also, as animated and full of vicissitude[3] as a drama. I was never tired of it. Its color and freshness revived the eyes which had grown weary of arid plains and blazing skies. It was always cheery, and fresh, and full of repose.

The village of Brentwood lay almost under the house, on the other side of the deep little ravine, down which a stream — which ought to have been a lovely, wild, and frolicsome little river — flowed between its rocks and trees. The river, like so many in that district, had, however, in its earlier life been sacrificed to trade, and was grimy with paper-making[4]. But this did not affect our pleasure in it so much as I have known it to affect other streams. Perhaps our water was more rapid; perhaps less clogged with dirt and refuse. Our side of the dell was

---

[1] A range of hill lands southwest of Edinburgh
[2] The Firth of Forth is an estuary that flows from the North Sea into Edinburgh
[3] Changing, transforming
[4] This river has been polluted by the castoff residue of a paper mill (which uses the water flow to move its energy-generating wheel) – a common industry in Lowland Scotland

charmingly *accidenté*[1], and clothed with fine trees, through which various paths wound down to the river-side and to the village bridge which crossed the stream. The village lay in the hollow, and climbed, with very prosaic[2] houses, the other side. Village architecture does not flourish in Scotland. The blue slates and the gray stone are sworn foes to the picturesque; and though I do not, for my own part, dislike the interior of an old-fashioned pewed and galleried church, with its little family settlements on all sides, the square box outside, with its bit of a spire like a handle to lift it by, is not an improvement to the landscape. Still a cluster of houses on differing elevations, with scraps of garden coming in between, a hedgerow with clothes laid out to dry, the opening of a street with its rural sociability, the women at their doors, the slow wagon lumbering along, gives a centre to the landscape. It was cheerful to look at, and convenient in a hundred ways. Within ourselves we had walks in plenty, the glen being always beautiful in all its phases, whether the woods were green in the spring or ruddy in the autumn. In the park which surrounded the house were the ruins of the former mansion of Brentwood, — a much smaller and less important house than the solid Georgian[3] edifice which we inhabited. The ruins were picturesque, however, and gave importance to the place. Even we, who were but temporary tenants, felt a vague pride in them, as if they somehow reflected a certain consequence upon ourselves[4]. The old building had the remains of a tower, — an indistinguishable mass of mason-work, overgrown with ivy; and the shells of walls attached to this were half filled up with soil. I had never examined it closely, I am ashamed to say. There was a large room, or what had been a large room, with the lower part of the windows still existing, on the principal floor, and underneath

---

[1] French: rough, bumpy, hilly, uneven
[2] Dull, typical
[3] Built circa 1714 – 1830, roughly during the reigns of the four Hanoverian kings named George
[4] A telling comment – the aftermath of the past can have a great influence on the present, even to those who bear very little ancestral relationship to those events. Whether ancient, distant, or near past, the thesis of this tale is that all can have a tremendous influence on the destiny and happiness of future lives. In short – actions have long-felt consequences

other windows, which were perfect, though half filled up with fallen soil, and waving with a wild growth of brambles and chance growths of all kinds. This was the oldest part of all. At a little distance were some very commonplace and disjointed fragments of building, one of them suggesting a certain pathos[1] by its very commonness and the complete wreck which it showed. This was the end of a low gable[2], a bit of gray wall, all incrusted with lichens, in which was a common door-way. Probably it had been a servants' entrance, a back-door, or opening into what are called "the offices" in Scotland. No offices remained to be entered, — pantry and kitchen had all been swept out of being; but there stood the doorway open and vacant, free to all the winds, to the rabbits, and every wild creature. It struck my eye, the first time I went to Brentwood, like a melancholy comment upon a life that was over. A door that led to nothing, — closed once, perhaps, with anxious care, bolted and guarded, now void of any meaning[3]. It impressed me, I remember, from the first; so perhaps it may be said that my mind was prepared to attach to it an importance which nothing justified.

The summer was a very happy period of repose for us all. The warmth of Indian suns was still in our veins. It seemed to us that we could never have enough of the greenness, the dewiness, the freshness of the northern landscape. Even its mists were pleasant to us, taking all the fever out of us, and pouring in vigor and refreshment. In autumn we followed the fashion of the time, and went away for change which we did not in the least require. It was when the family had settled down for the winter, when the days were short and dark, and the rigorous reign of frost upon us, that the incidents occurred which alone could justify me in intruding upon the world my private affairs. These incidents were, however, of so curious a character, that I hope my inevitable references

---

[1] Feeling of deep emotion, especially sympathy or pity (both are etymological relations to the Greek word, *pathos*) – a feeling of pitiable fragility
[2] A wall tapering into a triangular point
[3] A parallel is being drawn between the purposelessness of the derelict door and the purposelessness of life. Ultimately, Oliphant has a more optimistic, albeit tragic, outlook on the long-lasting effects of human life than might be first gleaned from this gloomy comment

to my own family and pressing personal interests will meet with a general pardon[1].

I was absent in London when these events began. In London an old Indian plunges back into the interests with which all his previous life has been associated, and meets old friends at every step. I had been circulating among some half-dozen of these, — enjoying the return to my former life in shadow, though I had been so thankful in substance to throw it aside, — and had missed some of my home letters, what with going down from Friday to Monday to old Benbow's place in the country, and stopping on the way back to dine and sleep at Sellar's and to take a look into Cross's stables, which occupied another day. It is never safe to miss one's letters. In this transitory life, as the Prayer-book[2] says, how can one ever be certain what is going to happen? All was well at home. I knew exactly (I thought) what they would have to say to me: "The weather has been so fine, that Roland has not once gone by train, and he enjoys the ride beyond anything." "Dear papa, be sure that you don't forget anything, but bring us so-and-so, and so-and-so," — a list as long as my arm. Dear girls and dearer mother! I would not for the world have forgotten their commissions, or lost their little letters, for all the Benbows and Crosses in the world.

But I was confident in my home-comfort and peacefulness. When I got back to my club[3], however, three or four letters were lying for me, upon some of which I noticed the "immediate," "urgent," which old-fashioned people and anxious people still believe will influence the post-office and quicken the speed of the mails. I was about to open one of these, when the club porter brought me two telegrams, one of which, he said, had arrived the night before. I opened, as was to be expected, the last first, and this was what I read: "Why don't you come or answer? For God's sake, come. He is much worse." This was a thunderbolt to fall upon a man's head who had one only son, and he the light of his eyes! The other telegram, which I opened with hands trembling so much that I lost time

---

[1] A thoroughly Victorian apology for an approaching lack of candor and propriety – namely a discussion of private family matters
[2] Viz. the Common Book of Prayer, a liturgical, ecclesiastical, and hymn book for the Anglican Church
[3] A gentleman's social club

by my haste, was to much the same purport: "No better; doctor afraid of brain-fever. Calls for you day and night. Let nothing detain you." The first thing I did was to look up the time-tables to see if there was any way of getting off sooner than by the night-train, though I knew well enough there was not; and then I read the letters, which furnished, alas! too clearly, all the details. They told me that the boy had been pale for some time, with a scared look. His mother had noticed it before I left home, but would not say anything to alarm me. This look had increased day by day; and soon it was observed that Roland came home at a wild gallop through the park, his pony panting and in foam, himself "as white as a sheet," but with the perspiration streaming from his forehead. For a long time he had resisted all questioning, but at length had developed such strange changes of mood, showing a reluctance to go to school, a desire to be fetched in the carriage at night, — which was a ridiculous piece of luxury[1], — an unwillingness to go out into the grounds, and nervous start at every sound, that his mother had insisted upon an explanation. When the boy — our boy Roland, who had never known what fear was — began to talk to her of voices he had heard in the park, and shadows that had appeared to him among the ruins, my wife promptly put him to bed and sent for Dr. Simson, which, of course, was the only thing to do.

I hurried off that evening, as may be supposed, with an anxious heart. How I got through the hours before the starting of the train, I cannot tell. We must all be thankful for the quickness of the railway when in anxiety; but to have thrown myself into a post-chaise[2] as soon as horses could be put to, would have been a relief. I got to Edinburgh very early in the blackness of the winter morning, and scarcely dared look the man in the face, at whom I gasped, "What news?" My wife had sent the brougham[3] for me, which I concluded, before the man spoke, was a bad sign. His answer was that stereotyped answer which leaves the imagination so wildly free, — "Just the same." Just the same! What might that mean? The horses seemed to me to creep along the long dark country road. As we dashed through the park, I thought I heard some one moaning among the trees, and clenched my fist at him (whoever he

---

[1] Carriages were wildly expensive to own, upkeep, and operate
[2] A carriage designed for swift travel
[3] Pronounced "broom" – a light, four wheel carriage

180

might be) with fury. Why had the fool of a woman at the gate allowed any one to come in to disturb the quiet of the place? If I had not been in such hot haste to get home, I think I should have stopped the carriage and got out to see what tramp it was that had made an entrance, and chosen my grounds, of all places in the world, — when my boy was ill! — to grumble and groan in. But I had no reason to complain of our slow pace here. The horses flew like lightning along the intervening path, and drew up at the door all panting, as if they had run a race. My wife stood waiting to receive me, with a pale face, and a candle in her hand, which made her look paler still as the wind blew the flame about. "He is sleeping," she said in a whisper, as if her voice might wake him. And I replied, when I could find my voice, also in a whisper, as though the jingling of the horses' furniture[1] and the sound of their hoofs must not have been more dangerous. I stood on the steps with her a moment, almost afraid to go in, now that I was here; and it seemed to me that I saw without observing, if I may say so, that the horses were unwilling to turn round, though their stables lay that way, or that the men were unwilling. These things occurred to me afterwards, though at the moment I was not capable of anything but to ask questions and to hear of the condition of the boy.

I looked at him from the door of his room, for we were afraid to go near, lest we should disturb that blessed sleep. It looked like actual sleep, not the lethargy into which my wife told me he would sometimes fall. She told me everything in the next room, which communicated with his, rising now and then and going to the door of communication; and in this there was much that was very startling and confusing to the mind. It appeared that ever since the winter began — since it was early dark, and night had fallen before his return from school — he had been hearing voices among the ruins: at first only a groaning, he said, at which his pony was as much alarmed as he was, but by degrees a voice.

The tears ran down my wife's cheeks as she described to me how he would start up in the night and cry out, "Oh, mother, let me in! oh, mother, let me in!" with a pathos which rent her heart. And she sitting there all the time, only longing to do everything his heart could desire! But though she would try to soothe him, crying, "You are at home, my

---

[1] The metal clasps, studs, and gears in their equestrian gear

181

darling. I am here. Don't you know me? Your mother is here!" he would only stare at her, and after a while spring up again with the same cry. At other times he would be quite reasonable, she said, asking eagerly when I was coming, but declaring that he must go with me as soon as I did so, "to let them in." "The doctor thinks his nervous system must have received a shock," my wife said. "Oh, Henry, can it be that we have pushed him on too much with his work — a delicate boy like Roland? And what is his work in comparison with his health? Even you would think little of honors or prizes if it hurt the boy's health." Even I! — as if I were an inhuman father sacrificing my child to my ambition[1]. But I would not increase her trouble by taking any notice. After a while they persuaded me to lie down, to rest, and to eat, none of which things had been possible since I received their letters. The mere fact of being on the spot, of course, in itself was a great thing; and when I knew that I could be called in a moment, as soon as he was awake and wanted me, I felt capable, even in the dark, chill morning twilight, to snatch an hour or two's sleep. As it happened, I was so worn out with the strain of anxiety, and he so quieted and consoled by knowing I had come, that I was not disturbed till the afternoon, when the twilight had again settled down. There was just daylight enough to see his face when I went to him; and what a change in a fortnight! He was paler and more worn, I thought, than even in those dreadful days in the plains before we left India. His hair seemed to me to have grown long and lank; his eyes were like blazing lights projecting out of his white face. He got hold of my hand in a cold and tremulous clutch, and waved to everybody to go away. "Go away — even mother," he said; "go away." This went to her heart; for she did not like that even I should have more of the boy's confidence than herself; but my wife has never been a woman to think of herself, and she left us alone[2]. "Are they all gone?" he said eagerly. "They would not let me speak. The doctor treated me as if I were a fool. You know I am not a

---

[1] A prominent element of Oliphant's literary genius is her penchant for probing and depicting domestic psychology with a masterful accuracy – the petty jealousies, anxieties, tender feelings, and endearments of family members are represented in her fiction with a level of depth, grace, and insight that remains unusual even today

[2] Further illustrating the previous note's claims

fool, papa." "Yes, yes, my boy, I know. But you are ill, and quiet is so necessary. You are not only *not* a fool, Roland, but you are reasonable and understand. When you are ill you must deny yourself; you must not do everything that you might do being well."

He waved his thin hand with a sort of indignation. "Then, father, I am not ill," he cried. "Oh, I thought when you came you would not stop me, — you would see the sense of it! What do you think is the matter with me, all of you? Simson is well enough; but he is only a doctor. What do you think is the matter with me? I am no more ill than you are. A doctor, of course, he thinks you are ill the moment he looks at you — that 's what he's there for — and claps you into bed[1]."

"Which is the best place for you at present, my dear boy."

"I made up my mind," cried the little fellow, "that I would stand it till you came home. I said to myself, I won't frighten mother and the girls. But now, father," he cried, half jumping out of bed, "it's not illness: it's a secret."

His eyes shone so wildly, his face was so swept with strong feeling, that my heart sank within me. It could be nothing but fever that did it, and fever had been so fatal[2]. I got him into my arms to put him back into bed. "Roland," I said, humoring the poor child, which I knew was the only way, "if you are going to tell me this secret to do any good, you know you must be quite quiet, and not excite yourself. If you excite yourself, I must not let you speak."

"Yes, father," said the boy. He was quiet directly, like a man[3], as if he quite understood. When I had laid him back on his pillow, he looked up at me with that grateful, sweet look with which children, when they are ill, break one's heart, the water coming into his eyes in his weakness. "I

---

[1] Roland demonstrates a degree of cynical understanding that rapidly attracts the reader's trust, indicating his rationalism, intelligence, and independent spirit – not being childishly won over by Simson's looming role as a cocksure authority figure

[2] The wild claim – "it's not illness: it's a secret" – smacks strongly of delirium, the fatal sort caused by a malarial fever (which had ravaged India)

[3] The understanding and sympathy between father and son is striking, and the tender realism of this mature but loving relationship is the pulse of this uncommon ghost story

was sure as soon as you were here you would know what to do[1]," he said.

"To be sure, my boy. Now keep quiet, and tell it all out like a man." To think I was telling lies to my own child! for I did it only to humor him, thinking, poor little fellow, his brain was wrong.

"Yes, father. Father, there is some one in the park, — some one that has been badly used."

"Hush, my dear; you remember there is to be no excitement. Well, who is this somebody, and who has been ill-using him? We will soon put a stop to that."

"Ah," cried Roland, "but it is not so easy as you think. I don't know who it is. It is just a cry. Oh, if you could hear it! It gets into my head in my sleep. I heard it as clear — as clear; and they think that I am dreaming, or raving perhaps," the boy said, with a sort of disdainful smile[2].

This look of his perplexed me; it was less like fever than I thought. "Are you quite sure you have not dreamed it, Roland?" I said.

"Dreamed? — that!" He was springing up again when he suddenly bethought himself, and lay down flat, with the same sort of smile on his face. "The pony heard it, too," he said. "She jumped as if she had been shot. If I had not grasped at the reins — for I was frightened, father —"

"No shame to you, my boy," said I, though I scarcely knew why[3].

"If I hadn't held to her like a leech, she'd have pitched me over her head, and never drew breath till we were at the door. Did the pony dream it?" he said, with a soft disdain, yet indulgence for my foolishness. Then he added slowly, "It was only a cry the first time, and all the time before you went away. I wouldn't tell you, for it was so wretched[4] to be

---

[1] Heartbreaking indeed: as touching as the child's faith is, both the Colonel and the reader know that it is unfounded: he is as baffled as any of them

[2] Roland is wryly and begrudgingly aware that his claims have been interpreted as lunacy – further developing his persona as an analytical and self-aware prodigy

[3] "I scarcely knew why" – the comment is one that a man might say to a colleague who has admitted feeling fear. A child does not need to be assured of the acceptability of fear, but a proud man might. Roland is becoming a man in his father's eyes, and a reliable narrator in ours

[4] Humiliating, embarrassing

184

frightened. I thought it might be a hare or a rabbit snared[1], and I went in the morning and looked; but there was nothing. It was after you went I heard it really first; and this is what he says." He raised himself on his elbow close to me, and looked me in the face: "'Oh, mother, let me in! oh, mother, let me in!'" As he said the words a mist came over his face, the mouth quivered, the soft features all melted and changed, and when he had ended these pitiful words, dissolved in a shower of heavy tears.

Was it a hallucination? Was it the fever of the brain? Was it the disordered fancy caused by great bodily weakness? How could I tell? I thought it wisest to accept it as if it were all true.

"This is very touching, Roland," I said.

"Oh, if you had just heard it, father! I said to myself, if father heard it he would do something; but mamma, you know, she 's given over to Simson, and that fellow 's a doctor, and never thinks of anything but clapping you into bed."

"We must not blame Simson for being a doctor, Roland[2]."

"No, no," said my boy, with delightful toleration and indulgence; "oh, no; that 's the good of him; that 's what he's for; I know that. But you — you are different; you are just father[3]; and you'll do something — directly, papa, directly; this very night."

"Surely," I said. "No doubt it is some little lost child."

He gave me a sudden, swift look, investigating my face as though to see whether, after all, this was everything my eminence as "father" came to, — no more than that. Then he got hold of my shoulder, clutching it with his thin hand: "Look here," he said, with a quiver in his voice; "suppose it wasn't — living at all!"

"My dear boy, how then could you have heard it?" I said.

He turned away from me with a pettish[4] exclamation, — "As if you

---

[1] The image of a gentle, vulnerable create caught in a devious trap and screaming for help is doubly poignant: it resembles both Roland's unheeded plight and the ghost's

[2] A dash of comic relief

[3] Unlike Simson who is prejudiced by his professional identity, the Colonel is — to Roland — a fully fleshed-out character of sympathy and understanding, capable of adapting intellectually and emotionally to an alien scenario

[4] Pouty, petulant

185

didn't know better than that!"

"Do you want to tell me it is a ghost?" I said.

Roland withdrew his hand; his countenance assumed an aspect of great dignity and gravity; a slight quiver remained about his lips. "Whatever it was — you always said we were not to call names. It was something[1] — in trouble. Oh, father, in terrible trouble!"

"But, my boy," I said (I was at my wits' end), "if it was a child that was lost, or any poor human creature — but, Roland, what do you want me to do?"

"I should know if I was you," said the child eagerly. "That is what I always said to myself, — Father will know. Oh, papa, papa, to have to face it night after night, in such terrible, terrible trouble, and never to be able to do it any good! I don't want to cry; it's like a baby, I know; but what can I do else? Out there all by itself in the ruin, and nobody to help it! I can't bear it! I can't bear it!" cried my generous boy[2]. And in his weakness he burst out, after many attempts to restrain it, into a great childish fit of sobbing and tears.

I do not know that I ever was in a greater perplexity in my life; and afterwards, when I thought of it, there was something comic in it too. It is bad enough to find your child's mind possessed with the conviction that he has seen, or heard, a ghost; but that he should require you to go instantly and help that ghost was the most bewildering experience that had ever come my way. I am a sober man myself, and not superstitious — at least any more than everybody is superstitious. Of course I do not

_____

[1] The humanity of this ghost story is staggeringly uncommon and tender: Roland asserts that whatever the ghost was – prejudice and classification notwithstanding – it is a soul, and that even though it be a ghost, its agony demands humanitarian intervention

[2] Roland is a poster boy for the "sympathy" (a term which at the time more specifically meant "fellow-feeling" – a form of empathy, or of imagining the feelings of another person: imagining walking a mile in another's shoes) that was expounded by the intellectuals of the Scottish Enlightenment (ca. 1688 – 1815), including Hume, Hutcheson, and Adam Smith. They believed that the well-rounded intellectual was also a citizen of humanity, and that logic and intelligence should be tempered with humanity and sympathy for the suffering of others

believe in ghosts; but I don't deny, any more than other people, that there are stories which I cannot pretend to understand[1]. My blood got a sort of chill in my veins at the idea that Roland should be a ghost-seer; for that generally means a hysterical temperament and weak health, and all that men most hate and fear for their children. But that I should take up his ghost and right its wrongs, and save it from its trouble, was such a mission as was enough to confuse any man. I did my best to console my boy without giving any promise of this astonishing kind; but he was too sharp for me: he would have none of my caresses. With sobs breaking in at intervals upon his voice, and the rain-drops hanging on his eyelids, he yet returned to the charge.

"It will be there now! — it will be there all the night! Oh, think, papa, — think if it was me[2]! I can't rest for thinking of it. Don't!" he cried, putting away my hand, — "don't! You go and help it, and mother can take care of me."

"But, Roland, what can I do?"

My boy opened his eyes, which were large with weakness and fever, and gave me a smile such, I think, as sick children only know the secret of. "I was sure you would know as soon as you came. I always said, Father will know. And mother," he cried, with a softening of repose upon his face, his limbs relaxing, his form sinking with a luxurious ease in his bed, — "mother can come and take care of me."

I called her, and saw him turn to her with the complete dependence of a child; and then I went away and left them, as perplexed a man as any in Scotland. I must say, however, I had this consolation, that my mind was greatly eased about Roland. He might be under a hallucination; but his head was clear enough, and I did not think him so ill as everybody else did. The girls were astonished even at the ease with which I took it. "How do you think he is?" they said in a breath, coming round me, laying hold of me. "Not half so ill as I expected," I said; "not very bad at

---

[1] Unlike Simson, the Colonel is fair minded and recognizes the limitations of understanding, while still possessing and practicing a level of skepticism that ensures credibility

[2] "Sympathy" – Roland calls upon his father to practice sympathy by imagining the pain the creature must be suffering in a dearly personal context

all." "Oh, papa, you are a darling!" cried Agatha, kissing me, and crying upon my shoulder; while little Jeanie, who was as pale as Roland, clasped both her arms round mine, and could not speak at all. I knew nothing about it, not half so much as Simson; but they believed in me: they had a feeling that all would go right now. God is very good to you when your children look to you like that. It makes one humble, not proud[1]. I was not worthy of it; and then I recollected that I had to act the part of a father to Roland's ghost, — which made me almost laugh, though I might just as well have cried. It was the strangest mission that ever was intrusted to mortal man.

It was then I remembered suddenly the looks of the men when they turned to take the brougham to the stables in the dark that morning. They had not liked it, and the horses had not liked it. I remembered that even in my anxiety about Roland I had heard them tearing along the avenue back to the stables, and had made a memorandum mentally that I must speak of it. It seemed to me that the best thing I could do was to go to the stables now and make a few inquiries. It is impossible to fathom the minds of rustics[2]; there might be some devilry of practical joking, for anything I knew; or they might have some interest in getting up a bad reputation for the Brentwood avenue[3]. It was getting dark by the time I went out, and nobody who knows the country will need to be told how black is the darkness of a November night under high laurel-bushes and yew-trees. I walked into the heart of the shrubberies two or three times, not seeing a step before me, till I came out upon the broader carriage-road, where the trees opened a little, and there was a faint gray glimmer of sky visible, under which the great limes and elms stood darkling like ghosts; but it grew black again as I approached the corner where the ruins lay. Both eyes and ears were on the alert, as may

---

[1] Oliphant's prowess as a psychology writer shines when describing the nuance of emotion

[2] Rural peasants and menials

[3] While not stated, the implication is smuggling or poaching. J. S. Le Fanu and William Hope Hodgson both wrote stories wherein a haunting was faked – or thought to be faked – in order to clear the way for contraband. It is also a very well-documented method of smugglers during the 18th and 19th centuries – faking supernatural activity to provide privacy

be supposed; but I could see nothing in the absolute gloom, and, so far as I can recollect, I heard nothing. Nevertheless there came a strong impression upon me that somebody was there. It is a sensation which most people have felt. I have seen when it has been strong enough to awake me out of sleep, the sense of some one looking at me. I suppose my imagination had been affected by Roland's story; and the mystery of the darkness is always full of suggestions. I stamped my feet violently on the gravel to rouse myself, and called out sharply, "Who's there?" Nobody answered, nor did I expect any one to answer, but the impression had been made. I was so foolish that I did not like to look back, but went sideways, keeping an eye on the gloom behind. It was with great relief that I spied the light in the stables, making a sort of oasis in the darkness. I walked very quickly into the midst of that lighted and cheerful place, and thought the clank of the groom['s] pail one of the pleasantest sounds I had ever heard. The coachman was the head of this little colony, and it was to his house I went to pursue my investigations. He was a native of the district, and had taken care of the place in the absence of the family for years; it was impossible but that he must know everything that was going on, and all the traditions[2] of the place. The men, I could see, eyed me anxiously when I thus appeared at such an hour among them, and followed me with their eyes to Jarvis's house, where he lived alone with his old wife, their children being all married and out in the world. Mrs. Jarvis met me with anxious questions. How was the poor young gentleman? But the others knew, I could see by their faces, that not even this was the foremost thing in my mind.

ꙅꙩ

"Noises? — ou ay[3], there 'll be noises, — the wind in the trees, and the water soughing down the glen. As for tramps, Cornel, no, there 's little o' that kind o' cattle about here; and Merran at the gate's a careful body." Jarvis moved about with some embarrassment from one leg to another as he spoke. He kept in the shade, and did not look at me more than he

---

[1] A stable worker
[2] Legends, folklore, history
[3] *Oh, aye; oh, yes*

189

could help. Evidently his mind was perturbed, and he had reasons for keeping his own counsel. His wife sat by, giving him a quick look now and then, but saying nothing. The kitchen was very snug and warm and bright, — as different as could be from the chill and mystery of the night outside. "I think you are trifling[1] with me, Jarvis," I said.

"Triflin', Cornel? No me. What would I trifle for? If the deevil himsel was in the auld hoose[2], I have no interest in 't one way or another ——"

"Sandy, hold your peace!" cried his wife imperatively.

"And what am I to hold my peace for, wi' the Cornel standing there asking a' thae[3] questions? I 'm saying, if the deevil himsel ——"

"And I 'm telling ye hold your peace!" cried the woman, in great excitement. "Dark November weather and lang nichts[4], and us that ken a' we ken[5]. How daur ye[6] name — a name that shouldna be spoken?" She threw down her stocking and got up, also in great agitation. "I tellt ye you never could keep it. It 's no a thing that will hide; and the haill toun kens as weel as you or me[7]. Tell the Cornel straight out — or see, I 'll do it. I dinna[8] hold wi' your secrets, and a secret that the haill toun kens!" She snapped her fingers with an air of large disdain. As for Jarvis, ruddy and big as he was, he shrank to nothing before this decided woman. He repeated to her two or three times her own adjuration[9], "Hold your peace!" then, suddenly changing his tone, cried out, "Tell him then, confound ye! I 'll wash my hands o 't[10]. If a' the ghosts in Scotland were in the auld hoose, is that ony concern o' mine?"

After this I elicited without much difficulty the whole story. In the opinion of the Jarvises, and of everybody about, the certainty that the place was haunted was beyond all doubt. As Sandy and his wife warmed

---

[1] Beating around the bush – being difficult
[2] *Old house*
[3] *All of these*
[4] *Long nights*
[5] *Us that know, we know*
[6] *Dare you*
[7] *The whole town knows as well as you and me*
[8] *Do not*
[9] A solemn or desperate appeal
[10] *Of it*

190

to the tale, one tripping up another in their eagerness to tell everything, it gradually developed as distinct a superstition as I ever heard, and not without poetry and pathos[1]. How long it was since the voice had been heard first, nobody could tell with certainty. Jarvis's opinion was that his father, who had been coachman at Brentwood before him, had never heard anything about it, and that the whole thing had arisen within the last ten years, since the complete dismantling of the old house; which was a wonderfully modern date for a tale so well authenticated. According to these witnesses, and to several whom I questioned afterwards, and who were all in perfect agreement, it was only in the months of November and December that "the visitation" occurred. During these months, the darkest of the year, scarcely a night passed without the recurrence of these inexplicable cries. Nothing, it was said, had ever been seen, — at least, nothing that could be identified. Some people, bolder or more imaginative than the others, had seen the darkness moving, Mrs. Jarvis said, with unconscious poetry. It began when night fell, and continued, at intervals, till day broke. Very often it was only an inarticulate cry and moaning, but sometimes the words which had taken possession of my poor boy's fancy had been distinctly audible, — "Oh, mother, let me in!" The Jarvises were not aware that there had ever been any investigation into it. The estate of Brentwood had lapsed into the hands of a distant branch of the family, who had lived but little there; and of the many people who had taken it, as I had done, few had remained through two Decembers. And nobody had taken the trouble to make a very close examination into the facts. "No, no," Jarvis said, shaking his head, "No, no, Cornel. Wha wad[2] set themsels up for a laughin'-stock to a' the country-side, making a wark about a ghost? Naebody believes in ghosts. It bid to be the wind in the trees, the last gentleman said, or some effec' o' the water wrastlin' among the rocks. He said it was a' quite easy explained; but he gave up the hoose. And when you cam, Cornel, we were awfu' anxious you should never hear. What for should I have spoiled the bargain and hairmed[3] the

---

[1] The third time "pathos" is used – it is clearly a crucial philosophical element of this tale
[2] *Who would*
[3] *Harmed*

191

property for no-thing?"

"Do you call my child's life nothing?" I said in the trouble of the moment, unable to restrain myself. "And instead of telling this all to me, you have told it to him, — to a delicate boy, a child unable to sift evidence or judge for himself, a tender-hearted young creature —"

I was walking about the room with an anger all the hotter that I felt it to be most likely quite unjust. My heart was full of bitterness against the stolid retainers of a family who were content to risk other people's children and comfort rather than let a house lie empty. If I had been warned I might have taken precautions, or left the place, or sent Roland away, a hundred things which now I could not do; and here I was with my boy in a brain-fever, and his life, the most precious life on earth, hanging in the balance, dependent on whether or not I could get to the reason of a commonplace ghost-story! I paced about in high wrath, not seeing what I was to do; for to take Roland away, even if he were able to travel, would not settle his agitated mind; and I feared even that a scientific explanation of refracted sound or reverberation, or any other of the easy certainties with which we elder men are silenced, would have very little effect upon the boy.

"Cornel," said Jarvis solemnly, "and she 'll bear me witness, — the young gentleman never heard a word from me — no, nor from either groom or gardener; I 'll gie ye my word for that. In the first place, he's no a lad that invites ye to talk. There are some that are, and some that arena. Some will draw ye on, till ye 've tellt them a' the clatter of the toun, and a' ye ken, and whiles mair[1]. But Maister Roland, his mind 's fu' of his books. He 's aye civil and kind, and a fine lad; but no that sort. And ye see it's for a' our interest, Cornel, that you should stay at Brentwood. I took it upon me mysel to pass the word, — 'No a syllable to Maister Roland, nor to the young leddies[2] — no a syllable.' The women-servants, that have little reason to be out at night, ken little or nothing about it. And some think it grand to have a ghost so long as they 're no in the way of coming across it. If you had been tellt the story to begin with, maybe ye would have thought so yourself."

This was true enough, though it did not throw any light upon my

---

[1] *A while more*

[2] *Ladies,* viz., the daughters

192

perplexity. If we had heard of it to start with, it is possible that all the family would have considered the possession of a ghost a distinct advantage[1]. It is the fashion of the times. We never think what a risk it is to play with young imaginations, but cry out, in the fashionable jargon, "A ghost! — nothing else was wanted to make it perfect." I should not have been above this myself. I should have smiled, of course, at the idea of the ghost at all, but then to feel that it was mine would have pleased my vanity. Oh, yes, I claim no exemption. The girls would have been delighted. I could fancy their eagerness, their interest, and excitement. No; if we had been told, it would have done no good, — we should have made the bargain all the more eagerly, the fools that we are. "And there has been no attempt to investigate it," I said, "to see what it really is?"

"Eh, Cornel," said the coachman's wife, "wha would investigate, as ye call it, a thing that no-body believes in? Ye would be the laughin'-stock of a' the country-side, as my man says."

"But you believe in it," I said, turning upon her hastily. The woman was taken by surprise. She made a step backward out of my way.

"Lord, Cornel, how ye frichten[2] a body! Me! — there's awfu' strange things in this world. An unlearned person doesna ken what to think. But the minister and the gentry they just laugh in your face[3]. Inquire into the thing that is not! Na, na, we just let it be."

"Come with me, Jarvis," I said hastily, "and we'll make an attempt at least. Say nothing to the men or to anybody. I'll come back after dinner, and we'll make a serious attempt to see what it is, if it is anything. If I hear it, — which I doubt, — you may be sure I shall never rest till I make it out. Be ready for me about ten o'clock."

"Me, Cornel!" Jarvis said, in a faint voice. I had not been looking at him in my own preoccupation, but when I did so, I found that the greatest change had come over the fat and ruddy coachman. "Me, Cornel!" he repeated, wiping the perspiration from his brow. His ruddy face hung in flabby folds, his knees knocked together, his voice seemed half

---

[1] Consider Oscar Wilde's "The Canterville Ghost"
[2] *Frighten*
[3] Oliphant often engages in social commentary. In this case presents the first and second estates (aristocrats and clergy) as demeaning and churlish towards the (lower) third estate

193

extinguished in his throat. Then he began to rub his hands and smile upon me in a deprecating, imbecile way. "There 's nothing I wouldna do to pleasure ye, Cornel," taking a step further back. "I 'm sure she kens I've aye said I never had to do with a mair fair, weel-spoken gentleman — " Here Jarvis came to a pause, again looking at me, rubbing his hands.

"Well?" I said.

"But eh, sir!" he went on, with the same imbecile yet insinuating smile, "if ye'll reflect that I am no used to my feet. With a horse atween my legs, or the reins in my hand, I 'm maybe nae worse than other men; but on fit[1], Cornel — It's no the — bogles[2]; — but I 've been cavalry, ye see," with a little hoarse laugh, "a' my life. To face a thing ye didna understan' — on your feet, Cornel."

"Well, sir, if I do it," said I tartly, "why shouldn't you?"

"Eh, Cornel, there 's an awfu' difference. In the first place, ye tramp about the haill[3] countryside, and think naething of it; but a walk tires me mair than a hunard miles' drive; and then ye 're a gentleman, and do your ain pleasure; and you 're no so auld as me; and it 's for your ain bairn[4], ye see, Cornel; and then — — "

"He believes in it, Cornel, and you dinna believe in it," the woman said.

"Will you come with me?" I said, turning to her.

She jumped back, upsetting her chair in her bewilderment. "Me!" with a scream, and then fell into a sort of hysterical laugh. "I wouldna say but what I would go[5]; but what would the folk say to hear of Cornel Mortimer with an auld silly woman at his heels?"

The suggestion made me laugh too, though I had little inclination for it. "I 'm sorry you have so little spirit, Jarvis," I said. "I must find some one else, I suppose."

Jarvis, touched by this, began to remonstrate[6], but I cut him short. My butler was a soldier who had been with me in India, and was not supposed to fear anything, — man or devil, — certainly not the former;

---

[1] *On foot*
[2] *It's not the – bogies* [spooks, ghosts]
[3] *Whole*
[4] *Own child*
[5] *I wouldn't say that I wouldn't be willing to go*
[6] Protest, argue

and I felt that I was losing time. The Jarvises were too thankful to get rid of me. They attended me to the door with the most anxious courtesies. Outside, the two grooms stood close by, a little confused by my sudden exit. I don't know if perhaps they had been listening, — as least standing as near as possible, to catch any scrap of the conversation. I waved my hand to them as I went past, in answer to their salutations, and it was very apparent to me that they also were glad to see me go.

  And it will be thought very strange, but it would be weak not to add, that I myself, though bent on the investigation I have spoken of, pledged to Roland to carry it out, and feeling that my boy's health, perhaps his life, depended on the result of my inquiry, — I felt the most unaccountable reluctance to pass these ruins on my way home. My curiosity was intense; and yet it was all my mind could do to pull my body along. I daresay the scientific people would describe it the other way, and attribute my cowardice to the state of my stomach. I went on; but if I had followed my impulse, I should have turned and bolted. Everything in me seemed to cry out against it: my heart thumped, my pulses all began, like sledge-hammers, beating against my ears and every sensitive part. It was very dark, as I have said; the old house, with its shapeless tower, loomed a heavy mass through the darkness, which was only not entirely so solid as itself. On the other hand, the great dark cedars of which we were so proud seemed to fill up the night. My foot strayed out of the path in my confusion and the gloom together, and I brought myself up with a cry as I felt myself knock against something solid. What was it? The contact with hard stone and lime and prickly bramble-bushes restored me a little to myself. "Oh, it's only the old gable," I said aloud, with a little laugh to reassure myself. The rough feeling of the stones reconciled me. As I groped about thus, I shook off my visionary folly. What so easily explained as that I should have strayed from the path in the darkness? This brought me back to common existence, as if I had been shaken by a wise hand out of all the silliness of superstition. How silly it was, after all! What did it matter which path I took? I laughed again, this time with better heart, when suddenly, in a moment, the blood was chilled in my veins, a shiver stole along my spine, my faculties seemed to forsake me. Close by me, at my side, at my feet, there was a sigh. No, not a groan, not a moaning[1], not anything so tangible, — a perfectly soft, faint, inarticulate sigh. I sprang back, and my heart stopped beating. Mistaken! no, mistake was impossible. I heard it as clearly as I hear myself speak; a long, soft, weary sigh, as if drawn to the utmost, and emptying out a load of sadness that filled the breast. To hear this in the solitude, in the dark, in the night (though it was still early), had an effect which I cannot describe. I feel it now, — something cold creeping over me, up into my hair, and down to my feet, which refused to move. I cried out, with a trembling voice, "Who is there?" as I had done before; but there was no reply. I got home I don't quite know how; but in my mind there was no longer any indifference as to the thing, whatever it was, that haunted these ruins. My scepticism disappeared like a mist. I was as firmly determined that there was something as Roland was. I did not for a moment pretend to myself that it was possible I could be deceived; there were movements and noises which I understood all about, — cracklings of small branches in the frost, and little rolls of gravel on the path, such as have a very eerie sound sometimes, and perplex you with wonder as to who has done it, when there is no real mystery; but I assure you all these little movements of nature don't affect you one bit when there is something. I understood them. I did not understand the sigh. That was not simple nature; there was meaning in it, feeling, the soul of a creature invisible[2]. This is the thing that human nature trembles at, — a creature invisible, yet with sensations, feelings, a power somehow of expressing itself. I had not the same sense of unwillingness to turn my back upon the scene of the mystery which I had experienced in going to the stables; but I almost ran home, impelled by eagerness to get everything done that had to be done, in order to apply myself to finding it out. Bagley was in the hall as usual when I went in. He was always there in the afternoon, always with

---

[1] The sound is not that of anger, sorrow, or any strong emotion – rather, it is the sound of ennui, of deep and morose spiritual exhaustion (read: pathos)
[2] Oliphant juxtaposes measurable Nature with the immeasurable Soul; like Edwards in "Phantom Coach," she is interested in the security that humankind finds in quantification of and dominance over nature, and the existential and psychological terror that occurs when that capacity is defunct

196

the appearance of perfect occupation, yet, so far as I know, never doing anything[1]. The door was open, so that I hurried in without any pause, breathless; but the sight of his calm regard, as he came to help me off with my overcoat, subdued me in a moment. Anything out of the way, anything incomprehensible, faded to nothing in the presence of Bagley. You saw and wondered how he was made: the parting of his hair, the tie of his white neckcloth, the fit of his trousers, all perfect as works of art; but you could see how they were done, which makes all the difference[2]. I flung myself upon him, so to speak, without waiting to note the extreme unlikeness of the man to anything of the kind I meant. "Bagley," I said, "I want you to come out with me to-night to watch for ——"

"Poachers, Colonel?" he said, a gleam of pleasure running all over him.

"No, Bagley; a great deal worse," I cried.

"Yes, Colonel; at what hour, sir?" the man said; but then I had not told him what it was.

It was ten o'clock when we set out. All was perfectly quiet indoors. My wife was with Roland, who had been quite calm, she said, and who (though, no doubt, the fever must run its course) had been better ever since I came. I told Bagley to put on a thick greatcoat over his evening coat, and did the same myself, with strong boots; for the soil was like a sponge, or worse[3]. Talking to him, I almost forgot what we were going to do. It was darker even than it had been before, and Bagley kept very close to me as we went along. I had a small lantern in my hand, which

---

[1] Bagley is a man who is trained in appearance. A military subordinate, he knows how to appear the way he is expected to appear to his superiors, but – as Oliphant so eagerly demonstrates – appearance is quite different from character. He is a study in class and rank, and an indictment of the social training that Victorian society expected of its lower classes; it would have been far better and natural, Oliphant suggests, if Bagley had never adopted the false veneer demanded of him, and if – like the Jarvises – he had been allowed to be genuine to his true character and admit his reservations without fear of social shame

[2] Bagley is a living façade – one that is easily identified and dissected due to its staged nature

[3] Likely peat bogs or – worse – mires: a quicksand-like turf that sucks its victims down

gave us a partial guidance. We had come to the corner where the path turns. On one side was the bowling-green, which the girls had taken possession of for their croquet-ground, — a wonderful enclosure surrounded by high hedges of holly three hundred years old and more; on the other, the ruins. Both were black as night; but before we got so far, there was a little opening in which we could just discern the trees and the lighter line of the road. I thought it best to pause there and take breath. "Bagley," I said, "there is something about these ruins I don't understand. It is there I am going. Keep your eyes open and your wits about you. Be ready to pounce upon any stranger you see, — anything man or woman. Don't hurt, but seize — anything you see." "Colonel," said Bagley, with a little tremor in his breath, "they do say there's things there — as is neither man nor woman." There was no time for words. "Are you game to follow me, my man? that's the question," I said. Bagley fell in without a word[1], and saluted. I knew then I had nothing to fear.

We went, so far as I could guess, exactly as I had come, when I heard that sigh. The darkness, however, was so complete that all marks, as of trees or paths, disappeared. One moment we felt our feet on the gravel, another sinking noiselessly into the slippery grass, that was all. I had shut up my lantern, not wishing to scare any one, whoever it might be. Bagley followed, it seemed to me, exactly in my footsteps as I made my way, as I supposed, towards the mass of the ruined house. We seemed to take a long time groping along seeking this; the squash of the wet soil under our feet was the only thing that marked our progress. After a while I stood still to see, or rather feel, where we were. The darkness was very still, but no stiller than is usual in a winter's night. The sounds I have mentioned — the crackling of twigs, the roll of a pebble, the sound of some rustle in the dead leaves, or creeping creature on the grass — were audible when you listened, all mysterious enough when your mind is disengaged, but to me cheering now as signs of the livingness of nature, even in the death of the frost. As we stood still there came up from the trees in the glen the prolonged hoot of an owl. Bagley started with alarm, being in a state of general nervousness, and not knowing what he

---

[1] Trained to behave, Bagley is – nonetheless – a coward, and his training wears thin in the face of the intangible horrors that his master (whom he looks to for cues) is incapable of understanding

was afraid of. But to me the sound was encouraging and pleasant, being so comprehensible. "An owl," I said, under my breath. "Y—es, Colonel," said Bagley, his teeth chattering. We stood still about five minutes, while it broke into the still brooding of the air, the sound widening out in circles, dying upon the darkness. This sound, which is not a cheerful one, made me almost gay. It was natural, and relieved the tension of the mind[1]. I moved on with new courage, my nervous excitement calming down.

When all at once, quite suddenly, close to us, at our feet, there broke out a cry. I made a spring backwards in the first moment of surprise and horror, and in doing so came sharply against the same rough masonry and brambles that had struck me before. This new sound came upwards from the ground, — a low, moaning, wailing voice, full of suffering and pain. The contrast between it and the hoot of the owl was indescribable, — the one with a wholesome wildness and naturalness that hurt nobody; the other, a sound that made one's blood curdle, full of human misery. With a great deal of fumbling, — for in spite of everything I could do to keep up my courage my hands shook, — I managed to remove the slide of my lantern. The light leaped out like something living, and made the place visible in a moment. We were what would have been inside the ruined building had anything remained but the gable-wall which I have described. It was close to us, the vacant door-way in it going out straight into the blackness outside. The light showed the bit of wall, the ivy glistening upon it in clouds of dark green, the bramble-branches waving, and below, the open door, — a door that led to nothing. It was from this the voice came which died out just as the light flashed upon this strange scene. There was a moment's silence, and then it broke forth again. The sound was so near, so penetrating, so pitiful, that, in the nervous start I gave, the light fell out of my hand. As I groped for it in the dark my hand was clutched by Bagley, who, I think, must have dropped upon his knees; but I was too much perturbed myself to think much of this. He clutched at me in the confusion of his

---

[1] The quantifiable and the natural are friends to the mind which is tormented by the phantoms which exceed human understanding and defy human dominance

200

terror, forgetting all his usual decorum[1]. "For God's sake, what is it, sir?" he gasped. If I yielded, there was evidently an end of both of us. "I can't tell," I said, "any more than you; that's what we 've got to find out. Up, man, up!" I pulled him to his feet. "Will you go round and examine the other side, or will you stay here with the lantern?" Bagley gasped at me with a face of horror. "Can't we stay together, Colonel?" he said; his knees were trembling under him. I pushed him against the corner of the wall, and put the light into his hands. "Stand fast till I come back; shake yourself together, man; let nothing pass you," I said. The voice was within two or three feet of us; of that there could be no doubt.

I went myself to the other side of the wall, keeping close to it. The light shook
in Bagley's hand, but, tremulous though it was, shone out through the vacant door, one oblong block of light marking all the crumbling corners and hanging
masses of foliage. Was that something dark huddled in a heap by the side of it? I pushed forward across the light in the door-way, and fell upon it with my hands; but it was only a juniper-bush growing close against the wall[2]. Meanwhile, the sight of my figure crossing the doorway had brought Bagley's nervous excitement to a height: he flew at me, gripping my shoulder.

---

[1] A pathetically unthinkable breech of etiquette between servant and master. Without the quantifying clarity brought by the light – lost in the blinding darkness – Bagley swarms to his master, whom he trusts to know and understand the world in his place. Used to relying upon the Colonel in this capacity, Bagley's psychological and emotional selves were trained to be disciplined by faith in his leadership, but without that assurance, he collapses physically and mentally, groping for his master like a child for his father

[2] We have reason to doubt the nature of this juniper bush. M. R. James, an admirer of Mrs Oliphant, was known to place suspicious and sickly vegetation in places where the viewer found them oddly repugnant. As they seemed to move, appearing closer (or disappearing altogether at daylight), their sinister nature became more apparent ("Mr Humphreys and his Inheritance" most deftly demonstrates this situation, wherein a character mistakes a voyeuristic ghoul for a misshapen yew tree)

"I've got him, Colonel! I've got him!" he cried, with a voice of sudden exultation. He thought it was a man, and was at once relieved. But at that moment the voice burst forth again between us, at our feet, — more close to us than any separate being could be. He dropped off from me, and fell against the wall, his jaw dropping as if he were dying. I suppose, at the same moment, he saw that it was me whom he had clutched. I, for my part, had scarcely more command of myself. I snatched the light out of his hand, and flashed it all about me wildly. Nothing, — the juniper-bush which I thought I had never seen before, the heavy growth of the glistening ivy, the brambles waving. It was close to my ears now, crying, crying, pleading as if for life. Either I heard the same words Roland had heard, or else, in my excitement, his imagination got possession of mine[1]. The voice went on, growing into distinct articulation, but wavering about, now from one point, now from another, as if the owner of it were moving slowly back and forth. "Mother! mother!" and then an outburst of wailing. As my mind steadied, getting accustomed (as one's mind gets accustomed to anything), it seemed to me as if some uneasy, miserable creature was pacing up and down before a closed door. Sometimes — but that must have been excitement — I thought I heard a sound like knocking, and then another burst, "Oh, mother! mother!" All this close, close to the space where I was standing with my lantern, now before me, now behind me: a creature restless, unhappy, moaning, crying, before the vacant door-way, which no one could either shut or open more.

"Do you hear it, Bagley? do you hear what it is saying?" I cried, stepping in through the door-way. He was lying against the wall, his eyes glazed, half dead with terror. He made a motion of his lips as if to answer me, but no sounds came; then lifted his hand with a curious imperative[2] movement as if ordering me to be silent and listen. And how long I did so I cannot tell. It began to have an interest, an exciting hold upon me, which I could not describe. It seemed to call up visibly a scene any one could understand, — a something shut out, restlessly wandering to and

---

[1] Reality and imagination become blurred, and insanity becomes a tempting escape
[2] Demanding, seriously authoritative – likely he violently waved his hands down or across his mouth

fro; sometimes the voice dropped, as if throwing itself down, sometimes wandered off a few paces, growing sharp and clear. "Oh, mother, let me in! oh, mother, mother, let me in! oh, let me in!" Every word was clear to me. No wonder the boy had gone wild with pity. I tried to steady my mind upon Roland, upon his conviction that I could do something, but my head swam with the excitement, even when I partially overcame the terror. At last the words died away, and there was a sound of sobs and moaning. I cried out, "In the name of God, who are you?" with a kind of feeling in my mind that to use the name of God was profane, seeing that I did not believe in ghosts or anything supernatural; but I did it all the same, and waited, my heart giving a leap of terror lest there should be a reply. Why this should have been I cannot tell, but I had a feeling that if there was an answer it would be more than I could bear. But there was no answer; the moaning went on, and then, as if it had been real, the voice rose a little higher again, the words recommenced, "Oh, mother, let me in! oh, mother, let me in!" with an expression that was heart-breaking to hear.

As if it had been real! What do I mean by that? I suppose I got less alarmed as the thing went on. I began to recover the use of my senses, — I seemed to explain it all to myself by saying that this had once happened, that it was a recollection of a real scene. Why there should have seemed something quite satisfactory and composing in this explanation I cannot tell, but so it was[1]. I began to listen almost as if it had been a play, forgetting Bagley, who, I almost think, had fainted, leaning against the wall. I was startled out of this strange spectatorship that had fallen upon me by the sudden rush of something which made my heart jump once more, a large black figure in the door-way waving its arms. "Come in! come in! come in!" it shouted out hoarsely at the top of a deep bass voice, and then poor Bagley fell down senseless across the threshold. He was less sophisticated[2] than I, — he had not been able to

---

[1] At one time, he conjectures, these words came from the mouth of a living person, in an understandable, observable, natural way. To imagine that this supernatural chaos was at least descended from naturalistic normalcy is correlatively reassuring

[2] Read: socialized to be a member of English high society, which brings education, discipline, and confidence in the ways of the universe (that is to

bear it any longer. I took him for something supernatural, as he took me, and it was some time before I awoke to the necessities of the moment. I remembered only after, that from the time I began to give my attention to the man, I heard the other voice no more. It was some time before I brought him to. It must have been a strange scene: the lantern making a luminous spot in the darkness, the man's white face lying on the black earth, I over him, doing what I could for him. Probably I should have been thought to be murdering him had any one seen us. When at last I succeeded in pouring a little brandy down his throat, he sat up and looked about him wildly. "What's up?" he said; then recognizing me, tried to struggle to his feet with a faint "Beg your pardon, Colonel." I got him home as best I could, making him lean upon my arm. The great fellow was as weak as a child. Fortunately he did not for some time remember what had happened. From the time Bagley fell the voice had stopped, and all was still.

$\wp$

"You've got an epidemic in your house, Colonel," Simson[1] said to me next morning. "What's the meaning of it all? Here's your butler raving about a voice. This will never do, you know; and so far as I can make out,

---

say, the supremacy of God, King, and Country). As a subordinate soldier, Bagley is taught to trust these things, but has not been made a part of them, like English aristocrats, gentry, clerics, and statesmen who imagine themselves a part of a bigger organism: *Dieu et mon droit* – by "God and my (natural) rights" the English upper classes justify their superiority complexes
[1] While the Colonel represents the English aristocracy, the Jarvises the peasantry, and Bagley the serving classes, Simson represents the intellectual class – the learned middle class of lawyers, doctors, academics, and engineers which relies upon intellect and reason in the same way the aristocrats rely upon their "God-given rights," the peasantry upon their superstition, and the subordinates upon their masters. Simson is cold, calculating, and materialistic, rejecting any evidence which discredits his worldview (and hence identity) as false or impossible. Therefore, he is perhaps as useless as the Jarvises or Bagley, although it is his stubborn mind not his shattered nerves which hamstring him

204

you are in it too."

"Yes, I am in it, Doctor. I thought I had better speak to you. Of course you are treating Roland all right, but the boy is not raving, he is as sane as you or me. It's all true."

"As sane as — I — or you. I never thought the boy insane. He's got cerebral excitement, fever. I don't know what you've got. There's something very queer about the look of your eyes[1]."

"Come," said I, "you can't put us all to bed, you know. You had better listen and hear the symptoms in full."

The Doctor shrugged his shoulders, but he listened to me patiently. He did not believe a word of the story, that was clear; but he heard it all from beginning to end. "My dear fellow," he said, "the boy told me just the same. It's an epidemic[2]. When one person falls a victim to this sort of thing, it's as safe as can be, — there's always two or three."

"Then how do you account for it?" I said.

"Oh, account for it! — that's a different matter; there's no accounting for the freaks our brains are subject to. If it's delusion, if it's some trick of the echoes or the winds, — some phonetic[3] disturbance or other —"

"Come with me to-night, and judge for yourself," I said.

Upon this he laughed aloud, then said, "That's not such a bad idea; but it would ruin me forever[4] if it were known that John Simson was ghost-hunting."

"There it is," said I; "you dart down on us who are unlearned with your phonetic disturbances, but you daren't examine what the thing really is for fear of being laughed at. That's science!"

"It's not science, — it's common-sense," said the Doctor. "The thing has delusion on the front of it. It is encouraging an unwholesome tendency

---

[1] Symbolic of understanding, truth, and perception. Indeed, the Colonel's eyes are different: his perspective on the universe has been altered

[2] Mass hysteria – or collective obsessional behavior – is an observed and demonstrated phenomenon where multiple people can be lead (by suggestion) to perceive the same thing, regardless of whether that perception is accurate or even real

[3] Involving the study of human speech

[4] Indeed, Simson's reputation and his very identity are bound up in his skeptical attitude (whether this is true or his own interpretation is not clear)

205

even to examine[1]. What good could come of it? Even if I am convinced, I shouldn't believe[2]."

"I should have said so yesterday; and I don't want you to be convinced or to believe," said I. "If you prove it to be a delusion, I shall be very much obliged to you for one. Come; somebody must go with me."

"You are cool," said the Doctor. "You've disabled this poor fellow of yours, and made him — on that point — a lunatic for life; and now you want to disable me. But, for once, I'll do it. To save appearance, if you'll give me a bed, I'll come over after my last rounds."

It was agreed that I should meet him at the gate, and that we should visit the scene of last night's occurrences before we came to the house, so that nobody might be the wiser. It was scarcely possible to hope that the cause of Bagley's sudden illness should not somehow steal into the knowledge of the servants at least, and it was better that all should be done as quietly as possible. The day seemed to me a very long one. I had to spend a certain part of it with Roland, which was a terrible ordeal for me, for what could I say to the boy? The improvement continued, but he was still in a very precarious state, and the trembling vehemence with which he turned to me when his mother left the room filled me with alarm. "Father?" he said quietly. "Yes, my boy, I am giving my best attention to it; all is being done that I can do. I have not come to any conclusion — yet. I am neglecting nothing you said," I cried. What I could not do was to give his active mind any encouragement to dwell upon the mystery. It was a hard predicament, for some satisfaction had to be given him. He looked at me very wistfully, with the great blue eyes

---

[1] Simson violates the purpose of the scientific method by refusing to investigate the disturbance, claiming that to do so is only to encourage belief, whereas an exposure or rational interpretation would surely do more good than to let the superstition run rampant. His fear is similar to Bagley's: while Bagley feared the infallibility of the aristocracy he has spent his life serving, Simson fears an assault on his materialist philosophy – to even suggest that it is not entirely accurate is to challenge his very identity and his very existence

[2] A severe rejection of a truly scientific mindset which considers evidence and demonstrable testing as the supreme authority. His god is not truly science itself, but materialism

which shone so large and brilliant out of his white and worn face. "You must trust me," I said. "Yes, father. Father understands," he said to himself, as if to soothe some inward doubt. I left him as soon as I could. He was about the most precious thing I had on earth, and his health my first thought; but yet somehow, in the excitement of this other subject, I put that aside, and preferred not to dwell upon Roland, which was the most curious part of it all[1].

That night at eleven I met Simson at the gate. He had come by train, and I let him in gently myself. I had been so much absorbed in the coming experiment that I passed the ruins in going to meet him, almost without thought, if you can understand that. I had my lantern; and he showed me a coil of taper[2] which he had ready for use. "There is nothing like light," he said, in his scoffing tone. It was a very still night, scarcely a sound, but not so dark. We could keep the path without difficulty as we went along. As we approached the spot we could hear a low moaning, broken occasionally by a bitter cry. "Perhaps that is your voice," said the Doctor; "I thought it must be something of the kind. That's a poor brute caught in some of these infernal traps of yours[3]; you'll find it among the bushes somewhere." I said nothing. I felt no particular fear, but a triumphant satisfaction in what was to follow. I led him to the spot where Bagley and I had stood on the previous night. All was silent as a winter night could be, — so silent that we heard far off the sound of the horses in the stables, the shutting of a window at the house. Simson lighted his taper and went peering about, poking into all the corners. We looked like two conspirators lying in wait for some unfortunate traveller;[4] but not a sound broke the quiet. The moaning had stopped

---

[1] Humanitarian stirrings have exceeded paternal stirrings – the care and provision of the lost soul is, Oliphant suggests, the first responsibility of the human spirit

[2] Long, slender wax candle (braided into a "coil") – probably set in a socket

[3] Like Roland, he first suspects a brute (e.g. a hare or rabbit) screaming after being snared in a trap set for small mammals

[4] Previously, the Colonel compared his adventure with Bagley to a sequestered murder. The sinister coloring of the explorers' forays causes the reader to question who is the antagonist and who the victim. Perhaps it is not ghosts who should be feared, but breathing, sinning Man

before we came up; a star or two shone over us in the sky, looking down as if surprised at our strange proceedings. Dr. Simson did nothing but utter subdued laughs under his breath. "I thought as much," he said. "It is just the same with tables[1] and all other kinds of ghostly apparatus; a sceptic's presence stops everything. When I am present nothing ever comes off. How long do you think it will be necessary to stay here? Oh, I don't complain; only when you are satisfied, I am — quite."

I will not deny that I was disappointed beyond measure by this result. It made me look like a credulous[2] fool. It gave the Doctor such a pull over me as nothing else could. I should point all his morals for years to come; and his materialism, his scepticism, would be increased beyond endurance. "It seems, indeed," I said, "that there is to be no — " "Manifestation," he said, laughing; "that is what all the mediums say. No manifestations, in consequence of the presence of an unbeliever." His laugh sounded very uncomfortable[3] to me in the silence; and it was now near midnight. But that laugh seemed the signal; before it died away the moaning we had heard before was resumed. It started from some distance off, and came towards us, nearer and nearer, like some one walking along and moaning to himself. There could be no idea now that it was a hare caught in a trap. The approach was slow, like that of a weak person, with little halts and pauses. We heard it coming along the grass straight towards the vacant door-way. Simson had been a little startled by the first sound. He said hastily, "That child has no business to be out so late." But he felt, as well as I, that this was no child's voice. As it came nearer, he grew silent, and, going to the door-way with his taper, stood looking out towards the sound. The taper being unprotected blew about in the night air, though there was scarcely any wind. I threw the light of my lantern steady and white across the same space. It was in a blaze of light in the midst of the blackness. A little icy thrill had gone over me at

---

[1] Mediums during the 19th century often held séances around tables and used trickery to cause "spectral wrappings" – like the knock of a ghostly hand – to deceive their clients. Questions could be posed to the dead and the knocks (one for *yes,* two for *no*) would satisfy the bereaved
[2] Gullible
[3] His pride is nearly wicked, filling the Colonel with as much apprehension as the ghostly wail

the first sound, but as it came close, I confess that my only feeling was satisfaction. The scoffer could scoff no more. The light touched his own face, and showed a very perplexed countenance. If he was afraid, he concealed it with great success, but he was perplexed. And then all that had happened on the previous night was enacted once more. It fell strangely upon me with a sense of repetition. Every cry, every sob seemed the same as before. I listened almost without any emotion at all in my own person, thinking of its effect upon Simson[1]. He maintained a very bold front, on the whole. All that coming and going of the voice was, if our ears could be trusted, exactly in front of the vacant, blank door-way, blazing full of light, which caught and shone in the glistening leaves of the great hollies at a little distance. Not a rabbit could have crossed the turf without being seen; but there was nothing. After a time, Simson, with a certain caution and bodily reluctance, as it seemed to me, went out with his roll of taper into this space. His figure showed against the holly in full outline. Just at this moment the voice sank, as was its custom, and seemed to fling itself down at the door. Simson recoiled violently, as if some one had come up against him, then turned, and held his taper low, as if examining something. "Do you see anybody?" I cried in a whisper, feeling the chill of nervous panic steal over me at this action. "It 's nothing but a — confounded juniper-bush[2]," he said. This I knew very well to be nonsense, for the juniper-bush was on the other side. He went about after this round and round, poking his taper everywhere, then returned to me on the inner side of the wall. He scoffed no longer; his face was contracted and pale. "How long does this go on?" he whispered to me, like a man who does not wish to interrupt some one who is speaking. I had become too much perturbed myself to remark whether the successions and changes of the voice were the same as last night. It suddenly went out in the air almost as he was speaking, with a soft reiterated sob dying away. If there had been anything to be

---

[1] Sympathy. While this "sympathy" is not terribly sympathetic (being more gloating than pitying), the Colonel uses his imagination to experience Simson's emotions, and thereby neutralizes his fear: sympathy (rather than fear) is the solution to this diabolical riddle

[2] M. R. James surely admired the shifting of the juniper from one side to another – a deft, and masterful touch that suggests far more than it reveals

seen, I should have said that the person was at that moment crouching on the ground close to the door.

We walked home very silent afterwards. It was only when we were in sight of the house that I said, "What do you think of it?" "I can't tell what to think of it," he said quickly. He took — though he was a very temperate[1] man — not the claret[2] I was going to offer him, but some brandy from the tray, and swallowed it almost undiluted[3]. "Mind you, I don't believe a word of it," he said, when he had lighted his candle; "but I can't tell what to think," he turned round to add, when he was half-way upstairs.

All of this, however, did me no good with the solution of my problem. I was to help this weeping, sobbing thing, which was already to me as distinct a personality as anything I knew; or what should I say to Roland? It was on my heart that my boy would die if I could not find some way of helping this creature. You may be surprised that I should speak of it in this way I did not know if it was man or woman; but I no more doubted that it was a soul in pain than I doubted my own being[4]; and it was my business to soothe this pain, — to deliver it, if that was possible. Was ever such a task given to an anxious father trembling for his only boy? I felt in my heart, fantastic as it may appear, that I must fulfil this somehow, or part with my child; and you may conceive that rather than do that I was ready to die. But even my dying would not have advanced me, unless by bringing me into the same world with that seeker at the door.

℘

Next morning Simson was out before breakfast, and came in with evident signs of the damp grass on his boots, and a look of worry and weariness, which did not say much for the night he had passed[5]. He

---

[1] That is to say, he did not drink liquor often if ever

[2] Red Burgundy wine – highly popular in Britain between the reigns of Henry VIII and Victoria

[3] Brandy is a spirit made of distilled wine, containing around 40-60% alcohol

[4] Sympathy of a most concentrated form

[5] He has, it would seem, been walking fitfully outside rather than sleeping

210

improved a little after breakfast, and visited his two patients, — for Bagley was still an invalid[1]. I went out with him on his way to the train, to hear what he had to say about the boy. "He is going on very well," he said; "there are no complications as yet. But mind you, that's not a boy to be trifled with, Mortimer. Not a word to him about last night." I had to tell him then of my last interview with Roland, and of the impossible demand he had made upon me, by which, though he tried to laugh, he was much discomposed, as I could see. "We must just perjure ourselves all round," he said, "and swear you exorcised it;" but the man was too kind-hearted to be satisfied with that. "It's frightfully serious for you, Mortimer. I can't laugh as I should like to. I wish I saw a way out of it, for your sake. By the way," he added shortly, "didn't you notice that juniper-bush on the left-hand side?" "There was one on the right hand of the door. I noticed you made that mistake last night." "Mistake!" he cried, with a curious low laugh, pulling up the collar of his coat as though he felt the cold, — "there's no juniper there this morning, left or right. Just go and see." As he stepped into the train a few minutes after, he looked back upon me and beckoned me for a parting word. "I'm coming back to-night," he said.

I don't think I had any feeling about this as I turned away from that common bustle of the railway which made my private preoccupations feel so strangely out of date. There had been a distinct satisfaction in my mind before, that his scepticism had been so entirely defeated. But the more serious part of the matter pressed upon me now. I went straight from the railway to the manse[2], which stood on a little plateau on the side of the river opposite to the woods or Brentwood. The minister was one of a class which is not so common in Scotland as it used to be[3]. He

---

[1] Bagley has had a nervous breakdown, and (like the maid – a fellow servant – in "Nothing But the Truth," is in danger of losing his mind)
[2] The house of a Presbyterian minister – a Protestant denomination wildly popular in Scotland
[3] The Colonel (a status-trusting aristocrat), the Jarvises (superstition-trusting peasants), Bagley (an authority-trusting subordinate), and Simson (a material-trusting bourgeoisie) have been joined by Moncrieff, a cleric whose trust is in sympathy and compassion. Together, these figures represent the

was a man of good family, well educated in the Scotch way, strong in philosophy, not so strong in Greek[1], strongest of all in experience, — a man who had "come across," in the course of his life, most people of note that had ever been in Scotland, and who was said to be very sound in doctrine, without infringing the toleration with which old men, who are good men, are generally endowed. He was old-fashioned; perhaps he did not think so much about the troublous problems of theology as many of the young men, nor ask himself any hard questions about the Confession of Faith[2]; but he understood human nature, which is perhaps better. He received me with a cordial welcome. "Come away, Colonel Mortimer," he said; "I 'm all the more glad to see you, that I feel it's a good sign for the boy. He's doing well? — God be praised, — and the Lord bless him and keep him. He has many a poor body's prayers[3], and that can do nobody harm."

"He will need them all, Dr. Moncrieff," I said, "and your counsel too." And I told him the story, — more than I had told Simson. The old clergyman listened to me with many suppressed exclamations, and at the end the water stood in his eyes.

"That's just beautiful," he said. "I do not mind to have heard anything like it; it's as fine as Burns[4] when he wished deliverance to one — that is prayed for in no kirk[5]. Ay, ay! so he would have you console the poor lost spirit? God bless the boy! There's something more than common in that, Colonel Mortimer. And also the faith of him in his father! — I would like to put that into a sermon." Then the old gentleman gave me

---

classes, identities, and faiths of British society in the Victorian Age, and their various responses and anxieties are telling

[1] Necessary for exegetical study of the New Testament, which was written in *Koine* Greek

[2] The creed (doctrine and beliefs) of the church

[3] That is to say, many in the community (such as the Jarvises) are praying for Roland

[4] Robert Burns (1759 – 1796) was a Romantic poet whose poetry – often written in the Scots dialect – is to Scotland what Goethe is to Germany, Shakespeare to England, and Frost to the United States. "Auld Lang Syne" is his most well-known piece

[5] Church

212

an alarmed look, and said, "No, no; I was not meaning a sermon; but I must write it down for the 'Children's Record.'" I saw the thought that passed through his mind. Either he thought, or he feared I would think, of a funeral sermon. You may believe this did not make me more cheerful.

I can scarcely say that Dr. Moncrieff gave me any advice. How could any one advise on such a subject? But he said, "I think I'll come too. I 'm an old man; I 'm less liable to be frightened than those that are further off the world unseen. It behooves me to think of my own journey there[1]. I've no cut-and-dry beliefs on the subject[2]. I'll come too; and maybe at the moment the Lord will put into our heads what to do."

This gave me a little comfort, — more than Simson had given me. To be clear about the cause of it was not my grand desire. It was another thing that was in my mind, — my boy. As for the poor soul at the open door, I had no more doubt, as I have said, of its existence than I had of my own. It was no ghost to me. I knew the creature, and it was in trouble. That was my feeling about it, as it was Roland's. To hear it first was a great shock to my nerves, but not now; a man will get accustomed to anything. But to do something for it was the great problem; how was I to be serviceable to a being that was invisible, that was mortal no longer? "Maybe at the moment the Lord will put it into our heads." This is very old-fashioned phraseology, and a week before, most likely, I should have smiled (though always with kindness) at Dr. Moncrieff's credulity; but there was a great comfort, whether rational or otherwise I cannot say, in the mere sound of the words.

The road to the station and the village lay through the glen, not by the ruins; but though the sunshine and the fresh air, and the beauty of the trees, and the sound of the water were all very soothing to the spirits, my mind was so full of my own subject that I could not refrain from turning to the right hand as I got to the top of the glen, and going straight to the

---

[1] Being older, he is – arguably – closer to death, and should therefore be both less afraid and more interested in communing with one who has already gone to his nearing destination

[2] Unlike Simson, who is a materialist zealot, Moncrieff is not a spiritualist zealot (despite his profession, which embraces the Beyond), but a fair-minded man

213

place which I may call the scene of all my thoughts. It was lying full in the sunshine, like all the rest of the world. The ruined gable looked due east[1], and in the present aspect of the sun the light streamed down through the door-way as our lantern had done, throwing a flood of light upon the damp grass beyond. There was a strange suggestion in the open door, — so futile, a kind of emblem of vanity: all free around, so that you could go where you pleased, and yet that semblance of an enclosure, — that way of entrance, unnecessary, leading to nothing[2]. And why any creature should pray and weep to get in — to nothing, or be kept out — by nothing! You could not dwell upon it, or it made your brain go round. I remembered, however, what Simson said about the juniper, with a little smile on my own mind as to the inaccuracy of recollection which even a scientific man will be guilty of. I could see now the light of my lantern gleaming upon the wet glistening surface of the spiky leaves at the right hand, — and he ready to go to the stake for it that it was the left! I went round to make sure. And then I saw what he had said. Right or left there was no juniper at all! I was confounded by this, though it was entirely a matter of detail: nothing at all, — a bush of brambles waving, the grass growing up to the very walls. But after all, though it gave me a shock for a moment, what did that matter? There were marks as if a number of footsteps had been up and down in front of the door, but these might have been our steps; and all was bright and peaceful and still. I poked about the other ruin — the larger ruins of the old house — for some time, as I had done before. There were marks upon the grass here and there — I could not call them footsteps — all about; but that told for nothing one way or another. I had examined the ruined rooms closely the first day. They were half filled up with soil and debris, withered brackens and bramble, — no refuge for any one there. It vexed me that Jarvis should see me coming from that spot when he came up to me for his orders. I don't know whether my nocturnal expeditions had got wind among the servants. But there was a

---

[1] A direction symbolic of resurrection and rebirth – return from death and salvation

[2] Another depressing meditation on the futility of mankind's endeavors – of the mockery of our ambitions and statuses (such as those which arbitrarily divide the Jarvises and the Mortimers)

significant look in his face. Something in it I felt was like my own sensation when Simson in the midst of his scepticism was struck dumb. Jarvis felt satisfied that his veracity had been put beyond question[1]. I never spoke to a servant of mine in such a peremptory[2] tone before. I sent him away "with a flea in his lug[3]," as the man described it afterwards. Interference of any kind was intolerable to me at such a moment.

But what was strangest of all was, that I could not face Roland. I did not go up to his room, as I would have naturally done, at once. This the girls could not understand. They saw there was some mystery in it. "Mother has gone to lie down." Agatha said: "he has had such a good night." "But he wants you so, papa!" cried little Jeanie, always with her two arms embracing mine in a pretty way she had. I was obliged to go at last, but what could I say? I could only kiss him, and tell him to keep still, — that I was doing all I could. There is something mystical about the patience of a child. "It will come all right, won't it, father?" he said. "God grant it may! I hope so, Roland." "Oh, yes, it will come all right." Perhaps he understood that in the midst of my anxiety I could not stay with him as I should have done otherwise. But the girls were more surprised than it is possible to describe. They looked at me with wondering eyes. "If I were ill, papa, and you only stayed with me a moment, I should break my heart," said Agatha. But the boy had a sympathetic feeling[4]. He knew that of my own will I would not have done it. I shut myself up in the library, where I could not rest, but kept pacing up and down like a caged beast. What could I do? and if I could do nothing, what would become of my boy? These were the questions that, without ceasing, pursued each other through my mind. Simson came out to dinner, and when the house was all still, and most of the servants in bed, we went out and met Dr. Moncrieff, as we had appointed, at the head of the glen. Simson, for his part, was disposed to scoff at the Doctor. "If there are to be any spells you know, I'll cut the whole concern," he said. I did not make him any

---

[1] Jarvis is – in a spiritual sense – justified, and placed on level with the Colonel who was earlier skeptical and demeaning
[2] Dictatorial, authoritarian
[3] *Ear*
[4] Roland understands his father's situation – through sympathy

215

reply. I had not invited him; he could go or come as he pleased. He was very talkative, far more so than suited my humor, as we went on. "One thing is certain, you know; there must be some human agency," he said. "It is all bosh¹ about apparitions. I never have investigated the laws of sound to any great extent, and there's a great deal in ventriloquism that we don't know much about." "If it's the same to you," I said, "I wish you'd keep all that to yourself, Simson. It doesn't suit my state of mind." "Oh, I hope I know how to respect idiosyncrasy²," he said. The very tone of his voice irritated me beyond measure. These scientific fellows, I wonder people put up with them as they do, when you have no mind for their cold-blooded confidence³. Dr. Moncrieff met us about eleven o'clock, the same time as on the previous night. He was a large man, with a venerable countenance and white hair, — old, but in full vigor, and thinking less of a cold night walk than many a younger man. He had his lantern, as I had. We were fully provided with means of lighting the place, and we were all of us resolute men. We had a rapid consultation as we went up, and the result was that we divided to different posts. Dr. Moncrieff remained inside the wall — if you can call that inside where there was no wall but one. Simson placed himself on the side next the ruins, so as to intercept any communication with the old house, which was what his mind was fixed upon. I was posted on the other side. To say that nothing could come near without being seen was self-evident. It had been so also on the previous night. Now with our three lights in the midst of the darkness, the whole place seemed illuminated. Dr. Moncrieff's lantern, which was a large one, without any means of shutting up⁴, — an old-fashioned lantern with a pierced and ornamental top, — shone steadily, the rays shooting out of it upward into the gloom. He placed it on the grass, where the middle of the room, if this had been a room, would have been. The usual effect of the light streaming out of

---

¹ Rubbish
² Eccentricity, oddness
³ Simson is entirely lacking in sympathy. His mission is to resist the pull of the world on his heart, and to remain steadfast regardless of exterior conditions – his is a stony, unmoving, fixed universe, unlike the dynamic, fluid cosmos that Moncrieff and Mortimer detect
⁴ Indicative of his character: genuine, unrestricted, generous, and open

the door-way was prevented by the illumination which Simson and I on either side supplied. With these differences, everything seemed as on the previous night. And what occurred was exactly the same, with the same air of repetition, point for point, as I had formerly remarked. I declare that it seemed to me as if I were pushed against, put aside, by the owner of the voice as he paced up and down in his trouble, — though these are perfectly futile words, seeing that the stream of light from my lantern, and that from Simson's taper, lay broad and clear, without a shadow, without the smallest break, across the entire breadth of the grass. I had ceased even to be alarmed, for my part. My heart was rent with pity and trouble, — pity for the poor suffering human creature that moaned and pleaded so, and trouble for myself and my boy. God! if I could not find any help, — and what help could I find? — Roland would die.

We were all perfectly still till the first outburst was exhausted, as I knew, by experience, it would be. Dr. Moncrieff, to whom it was new, was quite motionless on the other side of the wall, as we were in our places. My heart had remained almost at its usual beating during the voice. I was used to it; it did not rouse all my pulses as it did at first. But just as it threw itself sobbing at the door (I cannot use other words), there suddenly came something which sent the blood coursing through my veins, and my heart into my mouth. It was a voice inside the wall, — the minister's well-known voice. I would have been prepared for it in any kind of adjuration[1], but I was not prepared for what I heard. It came out with a sort of stammering, as if too much moved for utterance. "Willie, Willie! Oh, God preserve us! is it you?"

These simple words had an effect upon me that the voice of the invisible creature had ceased to have. I thought the old man, whom I had brought into this danger, had gone mad with terror. I made a dash round to the other side of the wall, half crazed myself with the thought. He was standing where I had left him, his shadow thrown vague and large upon the grass by the lantern which stood at his feet. I lifted my own light to see his face as I rushed forward. He was very pale, his eyes wet and glistening, his mouth quivering with parted lips. He neither saw nor heard me. We that had gone through this experience before, had

---

[1] Solemn or desperate plea, as in a prayer

crouched towards each other to get a little strength to bear it. But he was not even aware that I was there. His whole being seemed absorbed in anxiety and tenderness. He held out his hands, which trembled, but it seemed to me with eagerness, not fear[1]. He went on speaking all the time. "Willie, if it is you, — and it's you, if it is not a delusion of Satan, — Willie, lad! why come ye here fright'ing them that know you not? Why came ye not to me?"

He seemed to wait for an answer. When his voice ceased, his countenance, every line moving, continued to speak. Simson gave me another terrible shock, stealing into the open door-way with his light, as much awe-stricken, as wildly curious, as I. But the minister resumed, without seeing Simson, speaking to some one else. His voice took a tone of expostulation[2]:—

"Is this right to come here? Your mother's gone with your name on her lips. Do you think she would ever close her door on her own lad? Do ye think the Lord will close the door, ye faint-hearted creature? No! — I forbid ye! I forbid ye!" cried the old man. The sobbing voice had begun to resume its cries. He made a step forward, calling out the last words in a voice of command. "I forbid ye! Cry out no more to man. Go home, ye wandering spirit! go home! Do you hear me? — me that christened ye, that have struggled with ye, that have wrestled for ye with the Lord!" Here the loud tones of his voice sank into tenderness. "And her too, poor woman! poor woman! her you are calling upon. She's no[3] here. You'll find her with the Lord. Go there and seek her, not here. Do you hear me, lad? go after her there. He'll let you in, though it's late[4]. Man, take heart! if you will lie and sob and greet, let it be at heaven's gate, and no your poor mother's ruined door."

---

[1] The power of sympathy is shown to arouse tenderness and banish fear – to overthrow self-interest and self-preservation with fellow-feeling and empathy
[2] Earnest and kindly protest or chiding
[3] *Not*
[4] "Therefore the LORD will wait, that He may be gracious to you; And therefore He will be exalted, that He may have mercy on you. For the LORD *is* a God of justice; Blessed *are* all those who wait for Him" ISAIAH 30:18 (NKJV)

He stopped to get his breath; and the voice had stopped, not as it had done before, when its time was exhausted and all its repetitions said, but with a sobbing catch in the breath as if overruled. Then the minister spoke again, "Are you hearing me, Will? Oh, laddie, you've liked the beggarly elements all your days. Be done with them now. Go home to the Father — the Father[1]! Are you hearing me?" Here the old man sank down upon his knees, his face raised upwards, his hands held up with a tremble in them, all white in the light in the midst of the darkness[2]. I resisted as long as I could, though I cannot tell why[3]; then I, too, dropped upon my knees. Simson all the time stood in the door-way, with an expression in his face such as words could not tell, his under lip dropped, his eyes wild, staring. It seemed to be to him, that image of blank ignorance and wonder, that we were praying. All the time the voice, with a low arrested sobbing, lay just where he was standing, as I thought.

"Lord," the minister said, — "Lord, take him into Thy everlasting habitations. The mother he cries to is with Thee. Who can open to him but Thee? Lord, when is it too late for Thee, or what is too hard for Thee? Lord, let that woman there draw him inower[4]! Let her draw him inower!"

I sprang forward to catch something in my arms that flung itself wildly within the door. The illusion was so strong, that I never paused till I felt my forehead graze against the wall and my hands clutch the ground, — for there was nobody there to save from falling, as in my foolishness I thought. Simson held out his hand to me to help me up. He was trembling and cold, his lower lip hanging, his speech almost inarticulate. "It's gone," he said, stammering, — "it's gone!" We leaned upon each other for a moment, trembling so much, both of us, that the whole scene trembled as if it were going to dissolve and disappear; and yet as long as I live I will never forget it, — the shining of the strange lights, the blackness all round, the kneeling figure with all the whiteness

---

[1] Viz. God
[2] Moncrieff is situated to represent the single pathway to truth and redemption in a sea of darkness and hopelessness
[3] Pride in his social station (*my* analysis)
[4] *In to her*

219

of the light concentrated on its white venerable head and uplifted hands. A strange solemn stillness seemed to close all round us. By intervals a single syllable, "Lord! Lord!" came from the old minister's lips. He saw none of us, nor thought of us. I never knew how long we stood, like sentinels guarding him at his prayers, holding our lights in a confused dazed way, not knowing what we did. But at last he rose from his knees, and standing up at his full height, raised his arms, as the Scotch manner is at the end of a religious service, and solemnly gave the apostolical benediction[1], — to what? to the silent earth, the dark woods, the wide breathing atmosphere[2]; for we were but spectators gasping an Amen!

It seemed to me that it must be the middle of the night, as we all walked back. It was in reality very late. Dr. Moncrieff put his arm into mine. He walked slowly, with an air of exhaustion. It was as if we were coming from a death-bed. Something hushed and solemnized the very air. There was that sense of relief in it which there always is at the end of a death-struggle. And nature, persistent, never daunted, came back in all of us, as we returned into the ways of life. We said nothing to each other, indeed, for a time; but when we got clear of the trees and reached the opening near the house, where we could see the sky, Dr. Moncrieff himself was the first to speak. "I must be going," he said; "it's very late, I 'm afraid. I will go down the glen, as I came."

"But not alone. I am going with you, Doctor."

"Well, I will not oppose it. I am an old man, and agitation wearies more than work. Yes; I'll be thankful of your arm. To-night, Colonel, you've done me more good turns than one."

I pressed his hand on my arm, not feeling able to speak. But Simson, who turned with us, and who had gone along all this time with his taper flaring, in entire unconsciousness, came to himself, apparently at the

---

[1] "The grace of the Lord Jesus Christ, and the love of God, and the communion of the Holy Ghost, be with you all" (2 Corinthians 13:14)
[2] Nature is depicted as mute and dead, with the atmosphere – representing the world of spirits and spirituality – brimming with an awful sentience, breathing like a great, watching Thing

sound of our voices[1], and put out that wild little torch with a quick movement, as if of shame[2]. "Let me carry your lantern," he said; "it is heavy." He recovered with a spring; and in a moment, from the awe-stricken spectator he had been, became himself, sceptical and cynical. "I should like to ask you a question," he said. "Do you believe in Purgatory[3], Doctor? It 's not in the tenets of the Church[4], so far as I know."

"Sir," said Dr. Moncrieff, "an old man like me is sometimes not very sure what he believes. There is just one thing I am certain of — and that is the loving-kindness of God[5]."

"But I thought that was in this life. I am no theologian —"

"Sir," said the old man again, with a tremor in him which I could feel going over all his frame, "if I saw a friend of mine within the gates of hell, I would not despair but his Father would take him by the hand still, if he cried like yon[6]."

"I allow it is very strange, very strange. I cannot see through it. That there must be human agency, I feel sure. Doctor, what made you decide upon the person and the name?"

The minister put out his hand with the impatience which a man might show if he were asked how he recognized his brother. "Tuts[7]!" he said, in familiar speech; then more solemnly, "How should I not recognize a person that I know better — far better — than I know you?"

"Then you saw the man?"

Dr. Moncrieff made no reply. He moved his hand again with a little impatient movement, and walked on, leaning heavily on my arm. And

---

[1] Natural, quantifiable things – he has returned to his element of materialism
[2] Symbolically, he douses his faith out of shame
[3] A ghostly, unhappy realm in Christian (particularly Catholic) mythology, said to be between Heaven and Hell where the unbaptized, virtuous pagans, and sinful Christians are said to wander for a period of penance before being admitted to Heaven (sometimes for eternity)
[4] The (Presbyterian) Church of Scotland
[5] The divinity of sympathy
[6] *Yonder one – that one out there*
[7] "For shame!" An expression of impatience, disdain, or annoyance

221

we went on for a long time without another word, threading the dark paths, which were steep and slippery with the damp of the winter. The air was very still, — not more than enough to make a faint sighing in the branches, which mingled with the sound of the water to which we were descending. When we spoke again, it was about indifferent matters, — about the height of the river, and the recent rains. We parted with the minister at his own door, where his old housekeeper appeared in great perturbation[1], waiting for him. "Eh, me, minister! the young gentleman will be worse?" she cried.

"Far from that — better. God bless him!" Dr. Moncrieff said.

I think if Simson had begun again to me with his questions, I should have pitched him over the rocks as we returned up the glen; but he was silent, by a good inspiration[2]. And the sky was clearer than it had been for many nights, shining high over the trees, with here and there a star faintly gleaming through the wilderness of dark and bare branches. The air, as I have said, was very soft in them, with a subdued and peaceful cadence. It was real, like every natural sound, and came to us like a hush of peace and relief I thought there was a sound in it as of the breath of a sleeper, and it seemed clear to me that Roland must be sleeping, satisfied and calm. We went up to his room when we went in. There we found the complete hush of rest. My wife looked up out of a doze, and gave me a smile: "I think he is a great deal better; but you are very late," she said in a whisper, shading the light with her hand that the Doctor might see his patient. The boy had got back something like his own color. He woke as we stood all round his bed. His eyes had the happy, half-awakened look of childhood, glad to shut again, yet pleased with the interruption and glimmer of the light. I stooped over him and kissed his forehead, which was moist and cool[3]. "All is well, Roland," I said. He looked up at me with a glance of pleasure, and took my hand and laid his cheek upon it, and so went to sleep.

ॐ

---

[1] Alarm, worry

[2] That is, by a good stroke of fate, or by the power of a good influence (e.g. angel, spirit)

[3] The fever is vanishing

222

For some nights after, I watched among the ruins, spending all the dark hours up to midnight patrolling about the bit of wall which was associated with so many emotions; but I heard nothing, and saw nothing beyond the quiet course of nature; nor, so far as I am aware, has anything been heard again. Dr. Moncrieff gave me the history of the youth, whom he never hesitated to name. I did not ask, as Simson did, how he recognized him. He had been a prodigal[1], — weak, foolish, easily imposed upon, and "led away," as people say[2]. All that we had heard had passed actually in life, the Doctor said. The young man had come home thus a day or two after his mother died, — who was no more than the housekeeper in the old house, — and distracted with the news, had thrown himself down at the door and called upon her to let him in. The old man could scarcely speak of it for tears. To me it seemed as if — Heaven help us, how little do we know about anything! — a scene like that might impress itself somehow upon the hidden heart of nature. I do not pretend to know how, but the repetition had struck me at the time as, in its terrible strangeness and incomprehensibility, almost mechanical, — as if the unseen actor could not exceed or vary, but was bound to re-enact the whole. One thing that struck me, however, greatly, was the likeness between the old minister and my boy in the manner of regarding these strange phenomena. Dr. Moncrieff was not terrified, as I had been myself, and all the rest of us. It was no "ghost," as I fear we all vulgarly[3] considered it, to him, — but a poor creature whom he knew under these conditions, just as he had known him in the flesh, having no doubt of his identity. And to Roland it was the same. This spirit in pain, — if it was a spirit, — this voice out of the unseen, — was a poor fellow-creature in misery, to be succored[4] and helped out of his trouble, to my boy[5]. He spoke to me quite frankly about it when he got

---

[1] A rebellious, contrarian person
[2] That is, ruled by his impulses
[3] With inappropriate, unrefined, or uneducated ignorance
[4] Aided, assisted
[5] Sympathy is incompatible with fear, because fear is the action of ignorance – we fear that which we do not know or understand – and sympathy is the

better. "I knew father would find out some way," he said. And this was when he was strong and well, and an idea that he would turn hysterical or become a seer of visions had happily passed away.

ɕɔ

I must add one curious fact, which does not seem to me to have any relation to the above, but which Simson made great use of, as the human agency which he was determined to find somehow. We had examined the ruins very closely at the time of these occurrences; but afterwards, when all was over, as we went casually about them one Sunday afternoon in the idleness of that unemployed day, Simson with his stick penetrated an old window which had been entirely blocked up with fallen soil. He jumped down into it in great excitement, and called me to follow. There we found a little hole, — for it was more a hole than a room, — entirely hidden under the ivy and ruins, in which there was a quantity of straw laid in a corner, as if some one had made a bed there, and some remains of crusts about the floor. Some one had lodged there, and not very long before, he made out; and that this unknown being was the author of all the mysterious sounds we heard he is convinced. "I told you it was human agency," he said triumphantly. He forgets, I suppose, how he and I stood with our lights, seeing nothing, while the space between us was audibly traversed by something that could speak, and sob, and suffer. There is no argument with men of this kind. He is ready to get up a laugh against me on this slender ground. "I was puzzled myself, — I could not make it out, — but I always felt convinced human agency was at the bottom of it. And here it is, — and a clever fellow he must have been," the Doctor says. Bagley left my service as soon as he got well. He assured me it was no want of respect[1], but he could not stand "them kind of things;" and the man was so shaken and ghastly that I was glad

---

action of empathic imagination – to creatively experience and understand a stranger, or another soul

[1] Hardly, as this unnecessary comment proves: Bagley is bound to respect authority, and has been deeply shaken by his experiences due to the Colonel's shared helplessness

to give him a present[1] and let him go. For my own part, I made a point of staying out the time — two years — for which I had taken Brentwood; but I did not renew my tenancy. By that time we had settled, and found for ourselves a pleasant home of our own.

I must add, that when the Doctor defies me[2], I can always bring back gravity to his countenance[3], and a pause in his railing[4], when I remind him of the juniper-bush. To me that was a matter of little importance. I could believe I was mistaken. I did not care about it one way or other; but on his mind the effect was different. The miserable voice, the spirit in pain, he could think of as the result of ventriloquism, or reverberation, or — anything you please: an elaborate prolonged hoax, executed somehow by the tramp that had found a lodging in the old tower; but the juniper-bush staggered him[5]. Things have effects so different on the minds of different men[6].

---

[1] A tradition between masters and faithful servants who retire – either an item of some worth such as a silver watch or shaving mug, or a generous financial reward
[2] The new home is – it would appear – still within the vicinity
[3] Seriousness to his face
[4] Protestations and complaints – teasing
[5] The bush – an ostensibly tangible item, capable of quantification – crosses both the spiritual realms and the materialism that Simson adores. He could scoff at a spiritual manifestation because it lacks materiality, but the observable behavior of this bush (presumably the crouching figure of Willie) intrudes into the material world, and casts a shadow on Simson's confidence in his interpretation of the events
[6] A statement which evinces sympathy – the ability to imagine another's feelings and thoughts

*TO the very end, Oliphant weaves a story rich in psychological feeling, graceful elegance, and emotional power. Like Gaskell and Broughton, she saw fit to overturn prejudices of class and society in favor of the universal bond of the human spirit – something simultaneously beautiful and terrifying – which transcends the blandly simplistic conventions of socio-economic status, gender, or nationality. The Open Door is a rich landscape of human vanity, compassion, and fear, which roots through a wide range of ultimately futile worldviews before unearthing sympathy and compassion, which finally bring peace to a tortured human spirit. Likewise, Oliphant suggests that the forces and authorities which we often cling to, expecting to be saved from our anxieties and from which we derive our existential identities (we are members of our class, men of science, servants of our countries, sons of our fathers, confident in our traditions) are helpless against the dark nights of the human soul – that rather than deriving externally hope and exterior definition, we should seek within, that by sympathy, by identifying the basic humanity that unites us (rather than dividing, compartmentalizing) of a common spirit, we can derive security and self-definition. Kingdoms and classes are finite and fallible, she warns, but the shared bond of suffering – of fear and vulnerability – may ironically prove to be the means by which humanity can allude its deepest anxieties, and brighten its darkest nights.*

*IF you were passing through a coastal town in Southern England in the 1890s, perhaps leaving your apartment (hopefully not a semi-detached) in London's West End to visit a cousin in Plymouth, you might have heard this story when the coach stopped to change horses. Hardy creates a world that is pleasant and relatable, and we feel like we know the residents and the customs as well as the creaky turnstiles and breezy hedgerows after only a few pages. All of this makes its somber subject all the more tragic.*

## THE SUPERSTITIOUS MAN'S STORY
### {1891}
### *Thomas Hardy*

"THERE WAS SOMETHING VERY STRANGE about William's death—very strange indeed!" sighed a melancholy man in the back of the van[1]. It was the seedman's[2] father, who had hitherto kept silence.

"And what might that have been?" asked Mr Lackland.

"William, as you may know, was a curious, silent man; you could feel when he came near 'ee; and if he was in the house or anywhere behind you without your seeing him, there seemed to be something clammy in the air, as if a cellar door opened close by your elbow[3]. Well, one Sunday, at a time that William was in very good health to all appearance, the bell that was ringing for church went very heavy all of a sudden; the sexton[4], who told me o't, said he had not known the bell go

---

[1] A shaded, sometimes entirely enclosed horse-drawn cart with seating for multiple passengers

[2] Or seedsman. One who sells seeds and grains, usually to farmers for spring planting

[3] William appears to have a remarkable nature. That he already seems to belong to the world of the dead makes the narrative more believable and the ending more fitting, though less ironic

[4] Custodian of a church, its properties, and its graveyard, charged with their maintenance

227

so heavy in his hand for years—it was just as if the gudgeons[1] wanted oiling. That was on the Sunday, as I say.

"During the week after, it chanced that William's wife was staying up late one night to finish her ironing, she doing the washing for Mr and Mrs Hardcome. Her husband had finished his supper, and gone to bed as usual some hour or two before. While she ironed she heard him coming downstairs; he stopped to put on his boots at the stair-foot, where he always left them, and then came on into the living-room where she was ironing, passing through it towards the door, this being the only way from the staircase to the outside of the house. No word was said on either side, William not being a man given to much speaking, and his wife being occupied with her work. He went out and closed the door behind him. As her husband had now and then gone out in this way at night before when unwell, or unable to sleep for want of a pipe, she took no particular notice, and continued at her ironing. This she finished shortly after, and, as he had not come in, she waited awhile for him, putting away the irons and things, and preparing the table for his breakfast in the morning. Still he did not return, but supposing him not far off, and wanting to go to bed herself, tired as she was, she left the door unbarred and went to the stairs, after writing on the back of the door with chalk: *Mind and do the door* (because he was a forgetful man).

"To her great surprise, and I might say alarm, on reaching the foot of the stairs his boots were standing there as they always stood when he had gone to rest. Going up to their chamber, she found him in bed sleeping as sound as a rock. How he could have got back again without her seeing or hearing him was beyond her comprehension. It could only have been by passing behind her very quietly while she was bumping with the iron. But this notion did not satisfy her: it was surely impossible that she should not have seen him come in through a room so small. She could not unravel the mystery, and felt very queer and uncomfortable about it. However, she would not disturb him to question him then, and went to bed herself.

"He rose and left for his work very early the next morning, before she was awake, and she waited his return to breakfast with much anxiety

---

[1] Sockets upon which the bell is swung

228

for an explanation, for thinking over the matter by daylight made it seem only the more startling. When he came in to the meal he said, before she could put her question, 'What's the meaning of them words chalked on the door?'

"She told him, and asked him about his going out the night before. William declared that he had never left the bedroom after entering it, having in fact undressed, lain down, and fallen asleep directly, never once waking till the clock struck five, and he rose up to go to his labour.

"Betty Privett was as certain in her own mind that he did go out as she was of her own existence, and was little less certain that he did not return. She felt too disturbed to argue with him, and let the subject drop as though she must have been mistaken. When she was walking down Longpuddle Street[1] later in the day she met Jim Weedle's daughter Nancy, and said: 'Well Nancy, you do look sleepy to-day!'

"'Yes, Mrs Privett,' said Nancy. 'Now, don't tell anybody, but I don't mind letting you know what the reason o't is. Last night, being Old Midsummer Eve[2], some of us church porch[3], and didn't get home till near one.'

"'Did ye?' says Mrs Privett. 'Old Midsummer yesterday was it?

---

[1] Longpuddle is a fictional village invented by Thomas Hardy for his Longpuddle Series of stories. It is located in the Piddle River Valley in Dorset on England's southern coast

[2] Midsummer Eve takes place on June 23 and is recognized across Europe (and former colonies such as Brazil) – especially in Scandinavia, Central Europe, and Britain – as a day when the veil between the invisible and visible worlds recedes, allowing for a plethora of supernatural activity. Also known as St. John's Eve, it is the inspiration for Modest Mussorgsky's 1872 composition made famous by Disney's *Fantasia*. Originally named *St. John's Night on the Bare Mountain*, it is commonly shortened to *Night on Bald Mountain*. Comparable ghostly holidays in Europe include the witches' mass Wulpurgisnacht (April 30 - May 1), Christmas Eve, Michaelmas (September 29), and Hallow-Mass, or Hallowe'en (October 31)

[3] The lobby of many churches was used to store the sidearms of parishioners (weapons were not permitted inside), and was called the porch. To "church porch" is to loiter and tarry about the porch

230

Faith, I didn't think whe'r 'twas[1] Midsummer or Michaelmas[2]; I'd too much work to do.'

"'Yes. And we were frightened enough, I can tell 'ee by what we saw.' "'What did ye see?'

"(You may not remember, sir[3], having gone off to foreign parts so young, that on Midsummer Night it is believed hereabout that the faint shapes of all the folk in the parish who are going to be at death's door within the year can be seen entering the church. Those who get over their illness come out again after awhile; those that are doomed to die do not return.)

"'What did you see?' asked William's wife.

"'Well,' says Nancy, backwardly—'we needn't tell what we saw or who we saw.'

"'You saw my husband,' said Betty Privettin a quiet way.

"'Well, since you put it so,' says Nancy, hanging fire[4], 'we—thought we did see him; but it was darkish and we was frightened, and of course it might not have been he.'

"'Nancy, you needn't mind letting it out, though 'tis kept back in kindness. And he didn't come out of the church again: I know it as well as you.'

"Nancy did not answer yes or no to that, and no more was said. But three days after, William Privett was mowing[5] with John Chiles in Mr Hardcome's meadow, and in the heat of the day they sat down to their

---

[1] "By my Faith, I couldn't have told you whether it was…"
[2] Michaelmas, or St. Michael's Mass, occurs on September 29 (coincidentally sharing a week with the autumn equinox and thus overlapping, like St. John's Eve, Christmas, and All Hallows Eve with pagan rites and rituals). It commemorates the archangel Michael's casting Satan from heaven and naturally is endowed with a supernatural history and lore of its own
[3] The seedman's father addresses the listener, presumably a man who has either sought fortune or soldiered in North America or one of the British colonies in Africa, Asia, or Australia
[4] Pausing at a critical moment; building suspense
[5] Cutting tall grass with a scythe, to dry and feed as hay to livestock during winter months

bit o' lunch under a tree, and empty their flagon[1]. Afterwards both of 'em fell asleep as they sat. John Chiles was the first to wake, and, as he looked towards his fellow-mower, he saw one of those great white miller's-souls as we call 'em—that is to say, a miller moth[2]—come from William's open mouth while he slept and fly straight away[3]. John thought it odd enough, as William had worked in a mill for several years when he was a boy. He then looked at the sun, and found by the place o't that they had slept a long while, and, as William did not wake, John called to him and said it was high time to begin work again. He took no notice, and then John went up and shook him and found he was dead[4].

"Now on that very day old Philip Hookhorn was down at Longpuddle Spring, dipping up a pitcher of water; and, as he turned away, who should he see coming down to the spring on the other side but William, looking very pale and old. This surprised Philip Hookhorn very much, for years before that time William's little son—his only child—had been drowned in that spring while at play there, and this had so preyed upon William's mind that he'd never been seen near the spring afterwards, and had been known to go half a mile out of his way to avoid the place[5]. On enquiry, it was found that William in body could not have stood by the spring, being in the mead[6] two miles off; and it also came out that at the time at which he was seen at the spring

---

[1] A flask, probably filled with water cut with wine or a spirit – rum, brandy, or whiskey

[2] This moth receives its name from its snowy-white appearance – like a miller bleached with flour dust – and is the subject of a number of rural superstitions regarding omens of death

[3] Symbolically, the soul has left the body. Literally, a live, breathing man will not likely allow a large moth to climb into and out of his mouth, even if asleep; the image is unsettling

[4] Arguably of hyperthermia – heatstroke caused by the hot summer sun, exacerbated by liquor

[5] Apparently in death William is either trying to reunite with his son, or confronting, acknowledging, and accepting the deep emotional pain he avoided in life

[6] Meadow, grasslands

was the very time when he died."

"A rather melancholy story," observed the emigrant[1], after a minute's silence.

"Yes, yes. Well, we must take ups and downs together," said the seedman's father.

---

*THOMAS Hardy does not terrify or revolt us; his story is heavy and sullen with pathos. Rather than portraying the conquest of human agency over ghostly machinations, Hardy delves into the solemn smothering of a man by supernatural provenance, without either resistance or objection. Shuffling through a quiet life, William is snuffed unceremoniously, and his spiritual reflection is seen shambling by the well that swallowed his son. Human life, Hardy offers, is a slow, ambling, but often abbreviated, trailing off into time without theatrics like a streak of soot above an extinguished fire.*

---

[1] The listener, once more

HORROR *is perhaps best dictated to the senses – to the animal rather than the intellectual faculties. Amelia B. Edwards shoots for both in this cerebrally visceral tale by cushioning a quaint, fireside chat with a scholar of the natural and supernatural between two lonely, agonizing experiences of fear. The first is an experience that anyone might have when a car breaks down in an unfamiliar county on a winter night. The second is a vision that most can only say to have viewed – and smelled – in their nightmares. It is the intellect behind its construction that projects this story directly into the soft underbelly of irrational human terror. Like Wells, Edwards (whom E. F. Bleiler ranks amongst Le Fanu and Broughton as one of the Victorian's best supernaturalists) introduces us to a bleak landscape in a bleak universe – one hostile to humanity and devoid of help or guidance.*

## THE PHANTOM COACH
### OR, THE NORTH MAIL
### {1864}
### *Amelia B. Edwards*

THE CIRCUMSTANCES I AM ABOUT TO RELATE to you have truth to recommend them. They happened to myself, and my recollection of them is as vivid as if they had taken place only yesterday. Twenty years, however, have gone by since that night[1]. During those twenty years I have told the story to but one other person. I tell it now with a reluctance which I find it difficult to overcome. All I entreat, meanwhile, is that you will abstain from forcing your own conclusions upon me. I want nothing explained away. I desire no arguments. My mind on this subject is quite made up, and, having the testimony of my own senses to rely upon, I prefer to abide by it.

Well! It was just twenty years ago, and within a day or two of the end

---

[1] Setting of the narrative can be supposed in the vicinity of 1835 - 1845

234

of the grouse season[1]. I had been out all day with my gun, and had had no sport to speak of. The wind was due east; the month, December; the place, a bleak wide moor[2] in the far north of England. And I had lost my way. It was not a pleasant place in which to lose one's way, with the first feathery flakes of a coming snowstorm just fluttering down upon the heather, and the leaden evening closing in all around. I shaded my eyes with my hand, and staled anxiously into the gathering darkness, where the purple moorland melted into a range of low hills, some ten or twelve miles distant. Not the faintest smoke-wreath, not the tiniest cultivated patch, or fence, or sheep-track, met my eyes in any direction[3]. There was nothing for it but to walk on, and take my chance of finding what shelter I could, by the way. So I shouldered my gun[4] again, and pushed wearily forward; for I had been on foot since an hour after daybreak, and had eaten nothing since breakfast.

Meanwhile, the snow began to come down with ominous steadiness, and the wind fell. After this, the cold became more intense, and the night came rapidly up[5]. As for me, my prospects darkened with the darkening sky, and my heart grew heavy as I thought how my young wife was already watching for me through the window of our little inn parlour, and thought of all the suffering in store for her throughout this weary night. We had been married four months, and, having spent

---

[1] The hunting season for grouse – a bird similar to the pheasant and quail – lasted from 12 August to 10 December according to the 1831 Game Act. Our plot occurs in the first week of December
[2] Desolate tracks of heath, grassland, hill country, notable for their un-arable soil, rocky landscape, course shrubbery, and lack of trees. Typically used for grazing by herdsmen
[3] The landscape suggests the manner of universe that this story represents: one in which the will and ingenuity of mankind is absent, dominated by the harsh assertiveness of nature and – by extension – the supernatural. No trace of human interference is discernable in this wasteland, and the sense of isolation, helplessness, and inferiority grows only stronger as the narrator becomes stranded in the moonscape of alien moorland
[4] Most likely a single-barrel shotgun discharged by a percussion cap lock
[5] Rather than welcome him, nature lethally conspires against him

235

our autumn in the Highlands[1], were now lodging in a remote little village situated just on the verge of the great English moorlands. We were very much in love, and, of course, very happy. This morning, when we parted, she had implored me to return before dusk, and I had promised her that I would. What would I not have given to have kept my word!

Even now, weary as I was, I felt that with a supper, an hour's rest, and a guide, I might still get back to her before midnight, if only guide and shelter could be found.

And all this time, the snow fell and the night thickened. I stopped and shouted every now and then, but my shouts seemed only to make the silence deeper. Then a vague sense of uneasiness came upon me, and I began to remember stories of travellers who had walked on and on in the falling snow until, wearied out, they were fain to lie down and sleep their lives away. Would it be possible, I asked myself, to keep on thus through all the long dark night? Would there not come a time when my limbs must fail, and my resolution give way? When I, too, must sleep the sleep of death. Death! I shuddered. How hard to die just now, when life lay all so bright before me! How hard for my darling, whose whole loving heart but that thought was not to be borne! To banish it, I shouted again, louder and longer, and then listened eagerly. Was my shout answered, or did I only fancy that I heard a far-off cry? I halloed again, and again the echo followed. Then a wavering speck of light came suddenly out of the dark, shifting, disappearing, growing momentarily nearer and brighter[2]. Running towards it at full speed, I found myself, to my great joy, face to face with an old man and a lantern.

"Thank God!" was the exclamation that burst involuntarily from my lips. Blinking and frowning, he lifted his lantern and peered into my

---

[1] A traditional destination for marriage and honeymooners in Britain

[2] Such is the power and brilliance of human agency in this bleak cosmos: a pinpoint of light barely fighting off the rapacious and expanding darkness. It compares nicely to the cosmicism of Algernon Blackwood, whose universe was sometimes mystical and sublime, but often hostile and stifling towards errant human beings who dared to drift away from the clustered pockets of civilization into the vast, unpeopled domains of nature

face. "What for?" growled he, sulkily.

"Well—for you. I began to fear I should be lost in the snow."

"Eh, then, folks do get cast away hereabouts fra' time to time, an' what's to hinder you from bein' cast away likewise, if the Lord's so minded[1]?"

"If the Lord is so minded that you and I shall be lost together, friend, we must submit," I replied; "but I don't mean to be lost without you. How far am I now from Dwolding?"

"A gude twenty mile, more or less." "And the nearest village?"

"The nearest village is Wyke[2], an' that's twelve mile t'other side." "Where do you live, then?"

"Out yonder," said he, with a vague[3] jerk of the lantern. "You're going home, I presume?"

"Maybe I am."

"Then I'm going with you."

The old man shook his head, and rubbed his nose reflectively with the handle of the lantern.

"It ain't o' no use," growled he. "He 'ont let you in—not he."

"We'll see about that," I replied, briskly. "Who is He?"

"The master."

"Who is the master?"

"That's nowt[4] to you," was the unceremonious reply.

"Well, well; you lead the way, and I'll engage that the master shall give me shelter and a supper to-night."

---

[1] God is not portrayed as the self-sacrificing Trinity of the New Testament, but as the faceless, disinterested deity of pagan mythology – indifferent to human concerns and just as likely to lure a man to an ironic and tragic end as to recover him from disaster

[2] A village in the vicinity of Bradford, West Yorkshire, in the central area of Northern England

[3] His instructions – and thus his reassurance – are vague, just as the nature of the universe, God, and humanity are vague in this nocturnal void

[4] "No one"

237

"Eh, you can try him[1]!" muttered my reluctant guide; and, still shaking his head, he hobbled, gnome-like, away through the falling snow. A large mass loomed up presently out of the darkness, and a huge dog rushed out, barking furiously.

"Is this the house?" I asked.

"Ay, it's the house. Down, Bey!"

And he fumbled in his pocket for the key. I drew up close behind him, prepared to lose no chance of entrance, and saw in the little circle of light shed by the lantern that the door was heavily studded with iron nails, like the door of a prison[2]. In another minute he had turned the key and I had pushed past him into the house.

Once inside, I looked round with curiosity, and found myself in a great raftered hall, which served, apparently, a variety of uses. One end was piled to the roof with corn, like a barn. The other was stored with flour-sacks, agricultural implements, casks, and all kinds of miscellaneous lumber; while from the beams overhead hung rows of hams, flitches[3], and bunches of dried herbs for winter use. In the centre of the floor stood some huge object gauntly dressed in a dingy wrapping-cloth, and reaching half way to the rafters. Lifting a corner of this cloth, I saw, to my surprise, a telescope of very considerable size, mounted on a rude movable platform, with four small wheels. The tube was made of painted wood, bound round with bands of metal rudely fashioned; the speculum[4], so far as I could estimate its size in the dim light, measured at least fifteen inches in diameter. While I was yet examining the instrument, and asking myself whether it was not the work of some self-taught optician, a bell rang sharply.

"That's for you," said my guide, with a malicious grin. "Yonder's his

---

[1] That the Master – who is described in almost godlike terms – is the only source of intelligence and comfort in the area is reflective of the theological themes of this tale: God's favor, protection, and even His reasonability are not to be taken for granted or expected; the divine is not compassionate and merciful, but whimsical, pugnacious, and unsociable

[2] A telling description of ambiguity – salvation and life might been damnation and confinement

[3] Unsliced bacon

[4] Mirror of the telescope

room." He pointed to a low black door at the opposite side of the hall.
I crossed
over, rapped somewhat loudly, and went in, without waiting for an
invitation. A huge, white-haired old man rose from a table covered
with books and papers, and confronted me sternly.

"Who are you?" said he. "How came you here? What do you
want?" "James Murray, barrister-at-law[1]. On foot across the moor.
Meat, drink,
and sleep."

He bent his bushy brows into a portentous frown.

"Mine is not a house of entertainment," he said, haughtily. "Jacob,
how dared you admit this stranger?"

"I didn't admit him," grumbled the old man. "He followed me over
the muir, and shouldered his way in before me. I'm no match for six
foot two."

"And pray, sir, by what right have you forced an entrance into my
house?" "The same by which I should have clung to your boat, if I
were drowning.
The right of self-
preservation." "Self-
preservation?"

"There's an inch of snow on the ground already," I replied, briefly;
"and it would be deep enough to cover my body before daybreak."

He strode to the window, pulled aside a heavy black curtain, and
looked out.

"It is true," he said. "You can stay, if you choose, till morning[2]. Jacob,
serve the supper."

With this he waved me to a seat, resumed his own, and became at
once absorbed in the studies from which I had disturbed him.

I placed my gun in a corner, drew a chair to the hearth, and examined

---

[1] Unlike a solicitor, a barrister is a specialist in courtroom proceedings, an
expert legal mind who is often engaged by solicitors – personal lawyers – on
their clients' behalves

[2] Another ominous note: *if you choose…* Why would he possibly prefer to
die than commune with this crabby intellectual? The glimpse of the universe
that the Master will provide might be the reason for this insane notion

my quarters at leisure. Smaller and less incongruous in its arrangements than the hall, this room contained, nevertheless, much to awaken my curiosity. The floor was carpetless. The whitewashed walls were in parts scrawled over with strange diagrams, and in others covered with shelves crowded with philosophical instruments, the uses of many of which were unknown to me. On one side of the fireplace, stood a bookcase filled with dingy folios; on the other, a small organ, fantastically decorated with painted carvings of mediæval saints and devils. Through the half-opened door of a cupboard at the further end of the room, I saw a long array of geological specimens, surgical preparations, crucibles, retorts[1], and jars of chemicals; while on the mantelshelf beside me, amid a number of small objects, stood a model of the solar system, a small galvanic battery, and a microscope[2]. Every chair had its burden. Every corner was heaped high with books. The very floor was littered over with maps, casts, papers, tracings, and learned lumber of all conceivable kinds.

I stared about me with an amazement increased by every fresh object upon which my eyes chanced to rest. So strange a room I had never seen; yet seemed it stranger still, to find such a room in a lone farmhouse amid those wild and solitary moors! Over and over again, I looked from my host to his surroundings, and from his surroundings back to my host, asking myself who and what he could be? His head was singularly fine; but it was more the head of a poet than of a philosopher[3]. Broad in the temples, prominent over the eyes, and clothed with a rough profusion of perfectly white hair, it had all the ideality and much of the ruggedness that characterises the head of

---

[1] Glassware used in chemistry for the distillation process
[2] The Master is shown to be a practitioner of natural philosophy, astronomy, biology, engineering, physics, geology, medicine, and surgery – a better expert on the nature of the universe – its inner workings and philosophical character – could not be imagined
[3] He is well-rounded indeed: deeply schooled in the sciences, but by nature creative and insightful – an artist as well as a scientist, representing the gamut of human knowledge

240

Louis von Beethoven[1]. There were the same deep lines about the mouth, and the same stern furrows in the brow. There was the same concentration of expression. While I was yet observing him, the door opened, and Jacob brought in the supper. His master then closed his book, rose, and with more courtesy of manner than he had yet shown, invited me to the table.

A dish of ham and eggs, a loaf of brown bread, and a bottle of admirable sherry[2], were placed before me.

"I have but the homeliest farmhouse fare to offer you, sir," said my entertainer. "Your appetite, I trust, will make up for the deficiencies of our larder[3]."

I had already fallen upon the viands[4], and now protested, with the enthusiasm of a starving sportsman, that I had never eaten anything so delicious.

He bowed stiffly, and sat down to his own supper, which consisted, primitively, of a jug of milk and a basin of porridge. We ate in silence, and, when we had done, Jacob removed the tray. I then drew my chair back to the fireside. My host, somewhat to my surprise, did the same, and turning abruptly towards me, said:

"Sir, I have lived here in strict retirement for three-and-twenty years. During that time, I have not seen as many strange faces, and I have not read a single newspaper. You are the first stranger who has crossed my threshold for more than four years. Will you favour me with a few words of information respecting that outer world from which I have parted company so long[5]?"

---

[1] *Ludwig van* Beethoven (Ludwig is the German equivalent of Louis) (1770 – 1827) was the most notable composer of the early Romantic period, notable for introducing a level of violent expression and complex psychological and emotional articulation to Western music. This comparison helps to round out the Master as an emotionally as well as intellectually formidable figure

[2] Fortified white wine from Spain

[3] A cool container or cellar for keeping food – a primitive ice box

[4] Victuals – food items

[5] The Master is the overlord of a world between the living and the dead, and his domain is a perfect arena to experience the middle ground that blends the natural and supernatural

"Pray interrogate me," I replied. "I am heartily at your service."
He bent his head in acknowledgment; leaned forward, with his elbows resting on his knees and his chin supported in the palms of his hands; stared fixedly into the fire; and proceeded to question me.

His inquiries related chiefly to scientific matters, with the later progress of which, as applied to the practical purposes of life, he was almost wholly unacquainted. No student of science myself, I replied as well as my slight information permitted; but the task was far from easy, and I was much relieved when, passing from interrogation to discussion, he began pouring forth his own conclusions upon the facts which I had been attempting to place before him. He talked, and I listened spellbound. He talked till I believe he almost forgot my presence, and only thought aloud. I had never heard anything like it then; I have never heard anything like it since. Familiar with all systems of all philosophies, subtle in analysis, bold in generalisation, he poured forth his thoughts in an uninterrupted stream, and, still leaning forward in the same moody attitude with his eyes fixed upon the fire, wandered from topic to topic, from speculation to speculation, like an inspired dreamer. From practical science to mental philosophy; from electricity in the wire to electricity in the nerve[1]; from Watts to Mesmer, from Mesmer to Reichenbach, from Reichenbach to Swedenborg, Spinoza, Condillac, Descartes, Berkeley, Aristotle, Plato, and the Magi and mystics of the East[2], were transitions which, however

---

[1] An authority on both practical and medical science
[2] Isaac Watts was an English theologian and logician; Franz Mesmer was a German physician and astronomer who developed the theory of animal magnetism (AKA mesmerism); C. L. von Reichenbach was a German chemist, geologist, metallurgist, naturalist, industrialist, and philosopher; Emanuel Swedenbourg was a Swedish scientist, philosopher, theologian, revelator, and notable Christian mystic who advanced many mystical theories of the supernatural (claiming that he could freely visit heaven and hell, angels and demons, among other things); Baruch Spinoza was a Dutch philosopher, metaphysician, pantheist, and student of the nature of existence; Etienne Bonnot de Condillac was a French philosopher, psychologist, and epistemologist (student of the scope of knowledge); Rene Descartes was a French philosopher, metaphysician, and mathematician – the "Father of

bewildering in their variety and scope, seemed easy and harmonious upon
his lips as sequences in music. By-and-by—I forget now by what link of conjecture or illustration—he passed on to that field which lies beyond the boundary line of even conjectural philosophy, and reaches no man knows whither[1]. He spoke of the soul and its aspirations; of the spirit and its powers; of second sight; of prophecy; of those phenomena which, under the names of ghosts, spectres, and supernatural appearances, have been denied by the sceptics and attested by the credulous, of all ages[2].

"The world," he said, "grows hourly more and more sceptical of all that lies beyond its own narrow radius; and our men of science foster the fatal tendency. They condemn as fable all that resists experiment. They reject as false all that cannot be brought to the test of the laboratory or the dissecting-room. Against what superstition have they waged so long and obstinate a war, as against the belief in apparitions? And yet what superstition has maintained its hold upon the minds of men so long and so firmly? Show me any fact in physics, in history, in archæology, which is supported by testimony so wide and so various. Attested by all races of men, in all ages, and in all climates, by the soberest sages of antiquity, by the rudest savage of to-day, by the Christian, the Pagan, the Pantheist, the Materialist[3], this phenomenon

---

Western Philosophy"; George Berkeley was an Anglo-Irish philosopher – a student of Descartes – who argued that perception is false: that material items are figments of imagination, that perception-is-existence; Aristotle and Plato are the founders of the Western school of philosophy whose teachings sought to define essence, reality, and character; the Magi were Zoroastrian priests, magicians, philosophers, astronomers, astrologists, and mystics in ancient Persia known for their esoteric and mystical philosophies on fate and divination
[1] A fitting subject for a man who symbolically occupies the boundary between life and death – supernatural and natural, visible and invisible
[2] Shown to be an expert on the physical world, the Master's musings on the *metaphysical* world are therefore more credible
[3] Pagans (polytheists such as Hindus and Romans), Christians, Pantheists (those who believe that all things have a divine element, such as Native American religions), and Materialists (those who believe only in what can be

243

is treated as a nursery tale by the philosophers of our century. Circumstantial evidence weighs with them as a feather in the balance. The comparison of causes with effects, however valuable in physical science, is put aside as worthless and unreliable. The evidence of competent witnesses, however conclusive in a court of justice, counts for nothing. He who pauses before he pronounces, is condemned as a trifler. He who believes, is a dreamer or a fool."

He spoke with bitterness, and, having said thus, relapsed for some minutes into silence. Presently he raised his head from his hands, and added, with an altered voice and manner, "I, sir, paused, investigated, believed, and was not ashamed to state my convictions to the world. I, too, was branded as a visionary, held up to ridicule by my contemporaries, and hooted from that field of science in which I had laboured with honour during all the best years of my life. These things happened just three-and-twenty years ago. Since then, I have lived as you see me living now, and the world has forgotten me, as I have forgotten the world. You have my history."

"It is a very sad one," I murmured, scarcely knowing what to answer. "It is a very common one," he replied. "I have only suffered for the truth, as many a better and wiser man has suffered before me."

He rose, as if desirous of ending the conversation, and went over to the window.

"It has ceased snowing," he observed, as he dropped the curtain, and came back to the fireside.

"Ceased!" I exclaimed, starting eagerly to my feet. "Oh, if it were only possible--but no! it is hopeless. Even if I could find my way across the moor, I could not walk twenty miles to-night."

"Walk twenty miles to-night!" repeated my host. "What are you thinking of?"

"Of my wife," I replied, impatiently. "Of my young wife, who does not know that I have lost my way, and who is at this moment breaking her heart with suspense and terror."

"Where is she?"

"At Dwolding, twenty miles away."

---

materially measured and observed, such as atheists and nonreligious persons) are certainly disparate spiritual perspectives

"At Dwolding," he echoed, thoughtfully. "Yes, the distance, it is true, is twenty miles; but—are you so very anxious to save the next six or eight hours?"

"So very, very anxious, that I would give ten guineas[1] at this moment for a guide and a horse."

"Your wish can be gratified at a less costly rate," said he, smiling. "The night mail[2] from the north[3], which changes horses at Dwolding, passes within five miles of this spot, and will be due at a certain cross-road in about an hour and a quarter. If Jacob were to go with you across the moor, and put you into the old coach-road, you could find your way, I suppose, to where it joins the new one?"

"Easily—gladly."

He smiled again, rang the bell, gave the old servant his directions, and, taking a bottle of whisky and a wineglass from the cupboard in which he kept his chemicals, said:

"The snow lies deep, and it will be difficult walking to-night on the moor. A glass of usquebaugh[4] before you start?"

I would have declined the spirit, but he pressed it on me, and I drank it. It went down my throat like liquid flame, and almost took my breath away.

"It is strong," he said; "but it will help to keep out the cold. And now you have no moments to spare. Good night!"

I thanked him for his hospitality, and would have shaken hands, but that he had turned away before I could finish my sentence. In another

---

[1] Nearly $1,000 USD (2014)

[2] A carriage drawn by four horses which carried mail deliveries between regions on regular routes. Along with interior seating for four passengers, the coach was manned by a guard armed with a blunderbuss and pistols (a Royal Mail employee who sat at the rear), a driver and an shotgun-armed assistant (riding at the front). The coaches were famed for their fast pace (they only travelled at night – to avoid traffic – and only stopped to deliver the mail). They were, however, notoriously uncomfortable, being primarily made to convey the post

[3] The north mail – a mail coach making the journey from London to York along the Great North Road (the modern day A1 Road in Britain), which shuttled mail from London to York, from York to London

[4] Gaelic: whisky, pronounced us-*kwi*-BAH

245

minute I had traversed the hall, Jacob had locked the outer door behind me, and we were out on the wide white moor[1].

Although the wind had fallen, it was still bitterly cold. Not a star glimmered in the black vault overhead[2]. Not a sound, save the rapid crunching of the snow beneath our feet, disturbed the heavy stillness of the night. Jacob, not too well pleased with his mission, shambled on before in sullen silence, his lantern in his hand, and his shadow at his feet. I followed, with my gun over my shoulder, as little inclined for conversation as himself. My thoughts were full of my late host. His voice yet rang in my ears. His eloquence yet held my imagination captive. I remember to this day, with surprise, how my over-excited brain retained whole sentences and parts of sentences, troops of brilliant images, and fragments of splendid reasoning, in the very words in which he had uttered them. Musing thus over what I had heard, and striving to recall a lost link here and there, I strode on at the heels of my guide, absorbed and unobservant.   Presently—at the end, as it seemed to me, of only a few minutes—he came to a sudden halt, and said:

"Yon's your road. Keep the stone fence to your right hand, and you can't fail of the way."

"This, then, is the old coach-road[3]?" "Ay, 'tis the old coach-road."

"And how far do I go, before I reach the crossroads?" "Nigh upon three mile."

I pulled out my purse, and he became more communicative.

"The road's a fair road enough," said he, "for foot passengers; but

---

[1] Previously the "purple" moor – with heather and (albeit course) life – the moor is now white with snow – cold, unfeeling, featureless, evocative of a heartless, hostile universe brimming with ubiquitous energy

[2] Stars represent spiritual transcendence, hope, and aspiration. None is to be found

[3] The road originally ran between Mansfield and Richmond, but was altered to York. The leg that he will ultimately encounter is between the stops at Halifax and Skipton, west of Leeds

'twas over steep and narrow for the northern traffic. You'll mind where the parapet's[1] broken away, close again the sign-post. It's never been mended since the accident."

"What accident?"

"Eh, the night mail pitched right over into the valley below—a gude fifty feet an' more—just at the worst bit o' road in the whole county."

"Horrible! Were many lives lost?"

"All. Four were found dead, and t'other two died next morning[2]."

"How long is it since this happened?"

"Just nine year[3]."

"Near the sign-post, you say? I will bear it in mind. Good night."

"Gude night, sir, and thankee." Jacob pocketed his half-crown[4], made a faint pretence of touching his hat[5], and trudged back by the way he had come.

I watched the light of his lantern till it quite disappeared, and then turned to pursue my way alone. This was no longer matter of the slightest difficulty, for, despite the dead darkness overhead, the line of stone fence showed distinctly enough against the pale gleam of the snow. How silent it seemed now, with only my footsteps to listen to; how silent and how solitary! A strange disagreeable sense of loneliness stole over me. I walked faster. I hummed a fragment of a tune. I cast up enormous sums in my head, and accumulated them at compound interest[6]. I did my best, in short, to forget the startling speculations to which I had but just been listening, and, to some extent, I succeeded.

---

[1] Guardrail

[2] Three passengers, a Royal Mail guard, a shotgunner, and a driver

[3] We may place this event at roughly 1825 - 1835

[4] Roughly $30 USD (2014)

[5] Human respect is entirely foreign to Jacob, who fits in keenly with this misanthropic moors

[6] By doing arithmetic, James is executing an exercise that human beings use to quantify – and thereby understand and control – the laws of the universe. Algebra, arithmetic, and geometry have long been seen and used (e.g. by the Freemasons) as symbols of wisdom, divinity, and transcendence over animal stupidity. This futile effort to assert his cosmic importance leaves James unsettled and stunned

Meanwhile the night air seemed to become colder and colder, and though I walked fast I found it impossible to keep myself warm. My feet were like ice. I lost sensation in my hands, and grasped my gun mechanically. I even breathed with difficulty, as though, instead of traversing a quiet north country highway, I were scaling the uppermost heights of some gigantic Alp. This last symptom became presently so distressing, that I was forced to stop for a few minutes, and lean against the stone fence. As I did so, I chanced to look back up the road, and there, to my infinite relief, I saw a distant point of light, like the gleam of an approaching lantern. I at first concluded that Jacob had retraced his steps and followed me; but even as the conjecture presented itself, a second light flashed into sight—a light evidently parallel with the first, and approaching at the same rate of motion[1]. It needed no second thought to show me that these must be the carriage-lamps of some private vehicle, though it seemed strange that any private vehicle should take a road professedly disused and dangerous

There could be no doubt, however, of the fact, for the lamps grew larger and brighter every moment, and I even fancied I could already see the dark outline of the carriage between them. It was coming up very fast, and quite noiselessly, the snow being nearly a foot deep under the wheels.

And now the body of the vehicle became distinctly visible behind the lamps. It looked strangely lofty. A sudden suspicion flashed upon me. Was it possible that I had passed the cross-roads in the dark without observing the sign-post, and could this be the very coach which I had come to meet?

No need to ask myself that question a second time, for here it came round the bend of the road, guard and driver, one outside passenger, and four steaming greys[2], all wrapped in a soft haze of light, through which the lamps blazed out, like a pair of fiery meteors[3].

I jumped forward, waved my hat, and shouted. The mail came down

---

[1] Coaches employed large, powerful lamps on both sides
[2] Horses
[3] Traditionally, meteors are seen as omens of otherworldly significance  -- a fitting simile

at full speed, and passed me. For a moment I feared that I had not been seen or heard, but it was only for a moment. The coachman pulled up; the guard, muffled to the eyes in capes and comforters, and apparently sound asleep in the rumble[1], neither answered my hail nor made the slightest effort to dismount; the outside passenger did not even turn his head. I opened the door for myself, and looked in. There were but three travellers inside, so I stepped in, shut the door, slipped into the vacant corner, and congratulated myself on my good fortune.

The atmosphere of the coach seemed, if possible, colder than that of the outer air, and was pervaded by a singularly damp and disagreeable smell. I looked round at my fellow-passengers. They were all three, men, and all silent. They did not seem to be asleep, but each leaned back in his corner of the vehicle, as if absorbed in his own reflections. I attempted to open a conversation.

"How intensely cold it is to-night," I said, addressing my opposite neighbour.

He lifted his head, looked at me, but made no reply.

"The winter," I added, "seems to have begun in earnest."

Although the corner in which he sat was so dim that I could distinguish none of his features very clearly, I saw that his eyes were still turned full upon me. And yet he answered never a word.

At any other time I should have felt, and perhaps expressed, some annoyance, but at the moment I felt too ill to do either. The icy coldness of the night air had struck a chill to my very marrow, and the strange smell inside the coach was affecting me with an intolerable nausea. I shivered from head to foot, and, turning to my left-hand neighbour, asked if he had any objection to an open window?

He neither spoke nor stirred.

I repeated the question somewhat more loudly, but with the same result. Then I lost patience, and let the sash down[2]. As I did so, the leather strap broke in my hand, and I observed that the glass was covered with a thick coat of mildew, the accumulation, apparently, of years. My attention being thus drawn to the condition of the coach, I

---

[1] A seat at the rear of the coach
[2] Pulled down the interior window sash

examined it more narrowly, and saw by the uncertain light of the outer lamps that it was in the last stage of dilapidation. Every part of it was not only out of repair, but in a condition of decay. The sashes splintered at a touch. The leather fittings were crusted over with mould, and literally rotting from the woodwork. The floor was almost breaking away beneath my feet. The whole machine, in short, was foul with damp, and had evidently been dragged from some outhouse[1] in which it had been mouldering away for years, to do another day or two of duty on the road.

I turned to the third passenger, whom I had not yet addressed, and hazarded one more remark.

"This coach," I said, "is in a deplorable condition. The regular mail, I suppose, is under repair?"

He moved his head slowly, and looked me in the face, without speaking a word. I shall never forget that look while I live. I turned cold at heart under it. I turn cold at heart even now when I recall it. His eyes glowed with a fiery unnatural lustre. His face was livid[2] as the face of a corpse. His bloodless lips were drawn back as if in the agony of death, and showed the gleaming teeth between.

The words that I was about to utter died upon my lips, and a strange horror—a dreadful horror—came upon me. My sight had by this time become used to the gloom of the coach, and I could see with tolerable distinctness. I turned to my opposite neighbour. He, too, was looking at me, with the same startling pallor in his face, and the same stony glitter in his eyes. I passed my hand across my brow. I turned to the passenger on the seat beside my own, and saw—oh Heaven! how shall I describe what I saw? I saw that he was no living man—that none of them were living men, like myself! A pale phosphorescent light—the light of putrefaction—played upon their awful faces; upon their hair, dank with the dews of the grave; upon their clothes, earth-stained and dropping to pieces; upon their hands, which were as the hands of corpses long buried. Only their eyes, their terrible eyes, were living[3];

---

[1] Storage shed
[2] Leaden – bluish-gray, dull purple
[3] Eyes indicate truth and conviction -- their eyes prove and attest to the reality of the situation

and those eyes were all turned menacingly upon me!

A shriek of terror, a wild unintelligible cry for help and mercy; burst from my lips as I flung myself against the door, and strove in vain to open it.

In that single instant, brief and vivid as a landscape beheld in the flash of summer lightning, I saw the moon shining down through a rift of stormy cloud—the ghastly sign-post rearing its warning finger by the wayside— the broken parapet—the plunging horses—the black gulf below. Then, the coach reeled like a ship at sea. Then, came a mighty crash—a sense of crushing pain—and then, darkness.

֍

It seemed as if years had gone by when I awoke one morning from a deep sleep, and found my wife watching by my bedside I will pass over the scene that ensued, and give you, in half a dozen words, the tale she told me with tears of thanksgiving. I had fallen over a precipice, close against the junction of the old coach-road and the new, and had only been saved from certain death by lighting upon a deep snowdrift that had accumulated at the foot of the rock beneath. In this snowdrift I was discovered at daybreak[1], by a couple of shepherds, who carried me to the nearest shelter, and brought a surgeon to my aid. The surgeon found me in a state of raving delirium, with a broken arm and a compound fracture of the skull. The letters in my pocket-book showed my name and address; my wife was summoned to nurse me; and, thanks to youth and a fine constitution, I came out of danger at last. The place of my fall, I need scarcely say, was precisely that at which a frightful accident had happened to the north mail nine years before.

I never told my wife the fearful events which I have just related to you. I told the surgeon who attended me; but he treated the whole adventure as a mere dream born of the fever in my brain. We discussed the question over and over again, until we found that we

---

[1] Likely – according to the account of time passed at the Master's – just an hour or so after the accident, otherwise he surely would have succumbed to hypothermia

could discuss it with temper[1] no longer, and then we dropped it. Others may form what conclusions they please—I know that twenty years ago I was the fourth inside passenger in that Phantom Coach.

---

*EDWARDS' chilling tale is – especially in its climactic scene – a montage of masterful atmospherics. A blend of shadowy scenes weave one into the other, culminating in the pungent horror awaiting in the phantom coach. Tension builds and depresses like a road bobbing along a series of moorland hills. While it may be argued that the middle section fails to set up the conclusion, the antique metaphysician suspends the reality of the frosted air and the pensive wife waiting at home. Upon entering his candle-lit domain the protagonist is ushered into a world previously invisible to him – one which is only too real once he exits. The wasted desolation of the moor country minimizes human agency and enhances the threat of the outer unknown. The cosmic terror of the outerspaces and unbroken landscapes – of impersonal snow and all-consuming night – is temporarily deflated by the appearance of a lantern and the safety of the philosopher's hearth. The temporary respite may seem jarring and unnecessary, but it is an essential transition: before the conversation in the cabin, the north country is a bleak, uninhabited cosmos – a threat of its own, godless and teeming with spiritual hostility. After conversing with the exiled academic, however, the blackness he returns to is now the domain of the once-invisible world: the universe is no longer the same to him, no longer warm and promising, but cold and consuming: he is indeed the "fourth inside passenger in that Phantom Coach" a fellow passenger on a grisly journey, finally conscious of his awful status in the universe.*

---

[1] Without fighting or becoming passionate

VIRTUALLY unrivalled in his generation as a writer of ghost stories (even afterward, only H. Russell Wakefield, Robert Aickman, and Ramsey Campbell approach him in literary prowess), M. R. James excelled at nuance, suggestion, and the psychology of fear. James wrote stories that featured a tense, slow-burning dread, which steadily increased until the thing of horror thrust its head into the protagonist's reeling face. "Lost Hearts" was among James' first stories, and (other than the wartime allegory "A Warning to the Curious") represents his most cynical and somber work. Like "The Old Nurse's Story," it follows an orphan whose wealthy guardian ironically poses a very real danger to his life. However, in the world that young Stephen inhabits, there is no protective nurse-maid to guard him – it is a world where adults are either clueless enablers or sinister threats; it is a world without moral authority, a world stripped of protections and devoid of benevolence, where the vulnerable must fend for themselves, and the innocent are in peril.

<hr>

# LOST HEARTS
## {1895}
## *M. R. James*

IT WAS, AS FAR AS I CAN ASCERTAIN, in September of the year 1811 that a post-chaise[1] drew up before the door of Aswarby Hall, in the heart of Lincolnshire[2]. The little boy who was the only passenger in the chaise, and who jumped out as soon as it had stopped, looked about him with the keenest curiosity during the short interval that elapsed between the ringing of the bell and the opening of the hall door. He saw a tall, square, red-brick house, built in the reign of Anne[3]; a stone-pillared porch had

---

[1] A speedy, four-wheeled carriage, driven by four horses and accommodating four passengers
[2] A large, historic region on the east-central coast of England
[3] 1702 – 1714. This style of architecture, beloved by several design-minded writers of horror fiction (including H. P. Lovecraft and M. R. James) was known for its simple elegance and for being the archetypal style of the English manor house

254

been added in the purer classical style of 1790; the windows of the house were many, tall and narrow, with small panes and thick white woodwork. A pediment[1], pierced with a round window, crowned the front. There were wings to right and left, connected by curious glazed galleries, supported by colonnades[2], with the central block. These wings plainly contained the stables and offices of the house. Each was surmounted by an ornamental cupola[3] with a gilded vane[4].

An evening light shone on the building, making the window-panes glow like so many fires. Away from the Hall in front stretched a flat park studded with oaks and fringed with firs, which stood out against the sky. The clock in the church-tower, buried in trees on the edge of the park, only its golden weather-cock catching the light, was striking six, and the sound came gently beating down the wind. It was altogether a pleasant impression, though tinged with the sort of melancholy appropriate to an evening in early autumn, that was conveyed to the mind of the boy who was standing in the porch waiting for the door to open to him.

The post-chaise had brought him from Warwickshire[5], where, some six months before, he had been left an orphan[6]. Now, owing to the generous offer of his elderly cousin, Mr Abney, he had come to live at Aswarby. The offer was unexpected, because all who knew anything of Mr Abney looked upon him as a somewhat austere recluse, into whose steady-going household the advent of a small boy would import a new and, it seemed, incongruous element. The truth is that very little was known of Mr Abney's pursuits or temper. The Professor of Greek at Cambridge[7] had been heard to say that no one knew more of the religious beliefs of the

---

[1] Triangular area on the face of a building, below the roof, above the entrance, often upheld by columns
[2] Sequence of columns
[3] A small, ornamental tower on the spine of a roof – used for ventilation or as a bell tower
[4] Ornamented weather device used to indicate the direction of the wind
[5] Small county is central England
[6] Charles Dickens was James' most revered author. Stephen is an archetypal Dickensian character – a plucky orphan who encounters decadent adults and faces perils bravely, innocently, and with moral confidence
[7] James' alma mater and longtime employer

later pagans[1] than did the owner of Aswarby. Certainly his library contained all the then available books bearing on the Mysteries, the Orphic poems, the worship of Mithras, and the Neo–Platonists[2]. In the marble-paved hall stood a fine group[3] of Mithras slaying a bull, which had been imported from the Levant at great expense by the owner. He had contributed a description of it to the Gentleman's Magazine, and he had written a remarkable series of articles in the Critical Museum on the superstitions of the Romans of the Lower Empire[4]. He was looked upon, in fine, as a man wrapped up in his books, and it was a matter of great surprise among his neighbours that he should ever have heard of his orphan cousin, Stephen Elliott, much more that he should have volunteered to make him an inmate of Aswarby Hall.

Whatever may have been expected by his neighbours, it is certain that Mr Abney — the tall, the thin, the austere — seemed inclined to give his young cousin a kindly reception. The moment the front-door was opened he darted out of his study, rubbing his hands with delight.

'How are you, my boy? — how are you? How old are you?' said he — 'that is, you are not too much tired, I hope, by your journey to eat your supper?'

'No, thank you, sir,' said Master Elliott; 'I am pretty well.'

'That's a good lad,' said Mr Abney. 'And how old are you, my boy?'
It seemed a little odd that he should have asked the question twice in the first two minutes of their acquaintance.

'I'm twelve years old next birthday, sir,' said Stephen.

'And when is your birthday, my dear boy? Eleventh of September, eh?

---

[1] The Greeks, Romans, Egyptians, etc. circa, 400 B.C.E. – 400 C.E.; Late Antiquity
[2] The Mystery Religions were a series of secretive, ritualistic cults that thrived in Greco-Roman culture shrouded in suspicion and dread; the Orphic poems are texts related to the Mystery cult of Orpheus, who was said to descend into hell in search of his deceased lover, Eurydice; another Mystery cult, this one devoted to the Zoroastrian god Mithra – the all-seeing protector of truth; Neo-Platonism was a period of mystical philosophy that arose during the 3rd Century C.E.
[3] Statue consisting of more than one figure
[4] The eastern part of the Roman Empire dominated by Byzantium

That's well — that's very well. Nearly a year hence, isn't it? I like — ha, ha! — I like to get these things down in my book. Sure it's twelve? Certain?'

'Yes, quite sure, sir.'

'Well, well! Take him to Mrs Bunch's room, Parkes, and let him have his tea — supper[1] — whatever it is.'

'Yes, sir,' answered the staid Mr Parkes; and conducted Stephen to the lower regions[2].

Mrs Bunch was the most comfortable and human person whom Stephen had as yet met at Aswarby. She made him completely at home; they were great friends in a quarter of an hour: and great friends they remained. Mrs Bunch had been born in the neighbourhood some fifty-five years before the date of Stephen's arrival, and her residence at the Hall was of twenty years' standing. Consequently, if anyone knew the ins and outs of the house and the district, Mrs Bunch knew them; and she was by no means disinclined to communicate her information.

Certainly there were plenty of things about the Hall and the Hall gardens which Stephen, who was of an adventurous and inquiring turn, was anxious to have explained to him. 'Who built the temple[3] at the end of the laurel walk? Who was the old man whose picture hung on the staircase, sitting at a table, with a skull under his hand?' These and many similar points were cleared up by the resources of Mrs Bunch's powerful intellect. There were others, however, of which the explanations furnished were less satisfactory.

One November evening Stephen was sitting by the fire in the housekeeper's room reflecting on his surroundings.

'Is Mr Abney a good man, and will he go to heaven?' he suddenly asked, with the peculiar confidence which children possess in the ability of their

---

[1] Abney is profoundly aloof and absorbed in his esoteric research, unaware of what meal would be appropriate to the time of day – either tea (three-to-fourish) or supper (six-to-sevenish)

[2] Ominous – meaning the kitchen and the operational quarters, but also a euphemism for hell

[3] Many Jamesian villains install temple-like, pagan edifices or objects on their grounds. Like the antagonists in "Count Magnus" and "Mr Humphrey's Inheritance," Abney introduces an element of long-dead pagan beliefs into the bucolic, English landscape

257

elders to settle these questions, the decision of which is believed to be reserved for other tribunals.

'Good? — bless the child!' said Mrs Bunch. 'Master's as kind a soul as ever I see! Didn't I never tell you of the little boy as he took in out of the street, as you may say, this seven years back? and the little girl, two years after I first come here?'

'No. Do tell me all about them, Mrs Bunch — now, this minute[1]!'

'Well,' said Mrs Bunch, 'the little girl I don't seem to recollect so much about. I know master brought her back with him from his walk one day, and give orders to Mrs Ellis, as was housekeeper then, as she should be took every care with. And the pore child hadn't no one belonging to her — she told me so her own self — and here she lived with us a matter of three weeks it might be; and then, whether she were somethink of a gipsy[2] in her blood or what not, but one morning she out of her bed afore any of us had opened a eye, and neither track nor yet trace of her have I set eyes on since. Master was wonderful put about, and had all the ponds dragged; but it's my belief she was had away by[3] them gipsies, for there was singing round the house for as much as an hour the night she went, and Parkes, he declare as he heard them a-calling in the woods all that afternoon[4]. Dear, dear! a hodd child she was, so silent in her ways and all, but I was wonderful taken up with her, so domesticated she was — surprising[5].'

'And what about the little boy?' said Stephen.

'Ah, that pore boy!' sighed Mrs Bunch. 'He were a foreigner — Jevanny[6]

---

[1] We are left in the dark as to whether Stephen is aware of the danger lurking around him – he seems simultaneously naïve and insightful. This bursting eagerness might fortify the later interpretation: he appears desperate to assure himself of Abney's good character

[2] Potentially either a member of the Romani people or one of the Irish Travellers, or Pavee, a sect of ethnically Irish wanderers who, like the Romani, are tradition-conscious nomads

[3] Kidnapped – although murder might also be implied

[4] Keep this account in mind when we draw towards the plot's conclusion

[5] Gypsies were unfairly stereotyped as wild, animalistic, and thuggish

[6] Anglicization of a Lincolnshire dialect's interpretation of the Italian name *Giovanni*

he called hisself — and he come a-tweaking his 'urdy-gurdy[1] round and about the drive one winter day, and master 'ad him in that minute, and ast all about where he came from, and how old he was, and how he made his way, and where was his relatives, and all as kind as heart could wish. But it went the same way with him. They're a hunruly lot, them foreign nations[2], I do suppose, and he was off one fine morning just the same as the girl. Why he went and what he done was our question for as much as a year after; for he never took his 'urdy-gurdy, and there it lays on the shelf.'

The remainder of the evening was spent by Stephen in miscellaneous cross-examination of Mrs Bunch and in efforts to extract a tune from the hurdy-gurdy.

That night he had a curious dream. At the end of the passage at the top of the house, in which his bedroom was situated, there was an old disused bathroom. It was kept locked, but the upper half of the door was glazed, and, since the muslin curtains which used to hang there had long been gone, you could look in and see the lead-lined bath affixed to the wall on the right hand, with its head towards the window.

On the night of which I am speaking, Stephen Elliott found himself, as he thought, looking through the glazed door. The moon was shining through the window, and he was gazing at a figure which lay in the bath.

His description of what he saw reminds me of what I once beheld myself in the famous vaults of St Michan's Church in Dublin[3], which possesses the horrid property of preserving corpses from decay for centuries. A

---

[1] A hurdy-gurdy is a mechanized stringed instrument played by cranking a rosin-covered wheel – something of a mechanical violin bow – that rubs against the strings. Melodies are played by pressing down on keys. It is something of a string accordion, and the sound is not unlike that of a bagpipe. Popular throughout Europe, but particularly in France, Southern and Eastern-Europe

[2] Her ethnocentric xenophobia is deeply ironic: the true fiend is her respectable English master

[3] The humidity, atmosphere, and steady source of natural gases that permeate the macabre crypts below this medieval church have mummified the corpses interred there; they are left looking quite dead, but still sound enough to resemble a shriveled, leathery human figure

figure inexpressibly thin and pathetic[1], of a dusty leaden colour, enveloped in a shroud-like garment, the thin lips crooked into a faint and dreadful smile, the hands pressed tightly over the region of the heart.

As he looked upon it, a distant, almost inaudible moan seemed to issue from its lips, and the arms began to stir. The terror of the sight forced Stephen backwards and he awoke to the fact that he was indeed standing on the cold boarded floor of the passage in the full light of the moon[2]. With a courage which I do not think can be common among boys of his age, he went to the door of the bathroom to ascertain if the figure of his dreams were really there. It was not, and he went back to bed.

Mrs Bunch was much impressed next morning by his story, and went so far as to replace the muslin curtain over the glazed door of the bathroom. Mr Abney, moreover, to whom he confided his experiences at breakfast, was greatly interested and made notes of the matter in what he called 'his book'.

The spring equinox[3] was approaching, as Mr Abney frequently reminded his cousin, adding that this had been always considered by the ancients to be a critical time for the young[4]: that Stephen would do well to take care of himself, and to shut his bedroom window at night; and that

---

[1] Although truly horrifying, the figure is largely characterized as eliciting pity, sympathy, and pathos; her portrayal is one of acute vulnerability, exposure, and neglect

[2] Having sleepwalked during the course of his dream. The juxtaposition is chilling, and literarily brilliant, as it calls into question the nature of reality – what is the dream and what is the truth? The sainted guardian of orphans, or the grisly corpse in the bath?

[3] March 20 (or 21) is the time when the daytime and nighttime share equal duration during the spring. As with most remarkable cycles of nature, it is a popular anniversary in mysticism, and is accompanied by superstitions, speculations, and folklore in nearly every global culture

[4] The half-light and half-dark of those 24 hours are used to symbolize the turning point from youth to maturity for those at the crossroads between childhood and adulthood (namely, twelve year olds, thirteen being seen by many cultures as a milestone of maturation )

Censorinus[1] had some valuable remarks on the subject. Two incidents that occurred about this time made an impression upon Stephen's mind.

The first was after an unusually uneasy and oppressed night that he had passed — though he could not recall any particular dream that he had had.

The following evening Mrs Bunch was occupying herself in mending his nightgown.

'Gracious me, Master Stephen!' she broke forth rather irritably, 'how do you manage to tear your nightdress all to flinders this way? Look here, sir, what trouble you do give to poor servants that have to darn and mend after you!'

There was indeed a most destructive and apparently wanton series of slits or scorings in the garment, which would undoubtedly require a skilful needle to make good. They were confined to the left side of the chest — long, parallel slits about six inches in length, some of them not quite piercing the texture of the linen[2]. Stephen could only express his entire ignorance of their origin: he was sure they were not there the night before.

'But,' he said, 'Mrs Bunch, they are just the same as the scratches on the outside of my bedroom door: and I'm sure I never had anything to do with making them.'

Mrs Bunch gazed at him open-mouthed, then snatched up a candle, departed hastily from the room, and was heard making her way upstairs. In a few minutes she came down.

'Well,' she said, 'Master Stephen, it's a funny thing to me how them marks and scratches can 'a' come there — too high up for any cat or dog to 'ave made 'em, much less a rat: for all the world like a Chinaman's

---

[1] A Roman grammarian (fl. 250 C.E.) known for his miscellaneous writings on the influence of the stars and genii, religious rites, astronomy, antiquarian subjects and Greek philosophy

[2] The first two fingers on the human hand have the most force, followed by the third and the thumb, and lastly by the fourth. Grooves left by human fingers will not be uniform in pressure

finger-nails[1], as my uncle in the tea-trade used to tell us of when we was girls together. I wouldn't say nothing to master[2], not if I was you, Master Stephen, my dear; and just turn the key of the door when you go to your bed.'

'I always do, Mrs Bunch, as soon as I've said my prayers[3].'

'Ah, that's a good child: always say your prayers, and then no one can't hurt you[4].'

Herewith Mrs Bunch addressed herself to mending the injured nightgown, with intervals of meditation, until bed-time. This was on a Friday night in March, 1812.

On the following evening the usual duet of Stephen and Mrs Bunch was augmented by the sudden arrival of Mr Parkes, the butler, who as a rule kept himself rather to himself in his own pantry. He did not see that Stephen was there: he was, moreover, flustered and less slow of speech than was his wont.

---

[1] Some Chinese nobles were known to grow out their nails to prodigious lengths (a demonstration of their lives of luxury; manual laborers' nails would break if left uncut)

[2] Whether or not Bunch is consciously complicit in her master's doings (and this is doubtful – she seems quite duped), she is nonetheless apparently aware that mentioning certain goings-on might awaken an uncomfortable mood in him, and she steers Stephen from alerting him to the *obviously* sinister development knowing that the master would not take kindly to the intelligence

[3] A pious, Anglican lad – as much as Tiny Tim or David Copperfield – who stands in direct juxtaposition to his sociopathic, pagan uncle

[4] A warning that is both sinister and sad. Sinister because it was surely not on Stephen's mind (nor would it need to be if someone wasn't *actively* trying to hurt him) and sad because – as many commentators have noted – this is one of James' most pessimistic, cynical stories, one which watches a virtuous child adrift in a world where adults are oblivious, negligent, and abusive, where the promises and expectations of a happy childhood are not to be taken for granted – indeed, no, they are false promises, and while Stephen may have an opportunity to save himself, it is mere chance, and not in anyway related to his piety; prayer alone will not save him when his own uncle is (metaphorically) fattening him up to be devoured

'Master may get up his own wine, if he likes, of an evening,' was his first remark. 'Either I do it in the daytime or not at all, Mrs Bunch. I don't know what it may be: very like it's the rats, or the wind got into the cellars; but I'm not so young as I was, and I can't go through with it as I have done[1].'

'Well, Mr Parkes, you know it is a surprising place for the rats, is the Hall.'

'I'm not denying that, Mrs Bunch; and, to be sure, many a time I've heard the tale from the men in the shipyards about the rat that could speak. I never laid no confidence in that before; but tonight, if I'd demeaned myself to lay my ear to the door of the further bin, I could pretty much have heard what they was saying.'

'Oh, there, Mr Parkes, I've no patience with your fancies! Rats talking in the wine-cellar indeed!'

'Well, Mrs Bunch, I've no wish to argue with you: all I say is, if you choose to go to the far bin, and lay your ear to the door, you may prove my words this minute.'

'What nonsense you do talk, Mr Parkes — not fit for children to listen to! Why, you'll be frightening Master Stephen there out of his wits.'

'What! Master Stephen?' said Parkes, awaking to the consciousness of the boy's presence. 'Master Stephen knows well enough when I'm a-playing a joke with you, Mrs Bunch[2].'

In fact, Master Stephen knew much too well to suppose that Mr Parkes had in the first instance intended a joke. He was interested, not altogether pleasantly, in the situation; but all his questions were unsuccessful in inducing the butler to give any more detailed account of his experiences in the wine-cellar.

80

---

[1] There is a long tradition amongst this staff of inconveniently inexplicable phenomena

[2] The air of intrigue and conspiracy is becoming unbearably obvious; although he may seem naïve, Stephen is almost certainly aware that his safety is precarious in this house. Candor and honesty would be a much greater favor to the child than "protecting" him with cover stories and excuses

We have now arrived at March 24, 1812. It was a day of curious experiences for Stephen: a windy, noisy day, which filled the house and the gardens with a restless impression. As Stephen stood by the fence of the grounds, and looked out into the park, he felt as if an endless procession of unseen people were sweeping past him on the wind, borne on resistlessly and aimlessly, vainly striving to stop themselves, to catch at something that might arrest their flight and bring them once again into contact with the living world of which they had formed a part[1]. After luncheon that day Mr Abney said: 'Stephen, my boy, do you think you could manage to come to me tonight as late as eleven o'clock in my study? I shall be busy until that time, and I wish to show you something connected with your future life[2] which it is most important that you should know. You are not to mention this matter to Mrs Bunch nor to anyone else in
the house[3]; and you had better go to your room at the usual time.'

Here was a new excitement added to life: Stephen eagerly grasped at the opportunity of sitting up till eleven o'clock. He looked in at the library door on his way upstairs that evening, and saw a brazier[4], which he had often noticed in the corner of the room, moved out before the fire; an old silver-gilt cup[5] stood on the table, filled with red wine, and some written sheets of paper lay near it.
Mr Abney was sprinkling some incense on the brazier from a round silver

---

[1] A parade of spirits that resembles the flying column of elementals in Blackwood's later-published "The Willows." James later suggests that the beings sensed here are indeed elementals – spirits, not of human beings, but of nature and natural processes, favored by mystics and alchemists as supernatural agents capable of being subjected to servitude
[2] Indeed?
[3] Intrigue. Conspiracy. Secrecy. The house is redolent with denial and mistrust
[4] An iron framework that holds live coals and is often used to heat irons or to burn materials – both possibilities have a decidedly sinister tone about them
[5] Silver cups were are are often used in rituals of great importance – usually the passing of a cup filled with a ceremonial fluid (wine, blood, tinctures) around a fraternal gathering

box as Stephen passed, but did not seem to notice his step.

The wind had fallen, and there was a still night and a full moon. At about ten o'clock Stephen was standing at the open window of his bedroom, looking out over the country. Still as the night was, the mysterious population of the distant moon-lit woods was not yet lulled to rest. From time to time strange cries as of lost and despairing wanderers sounded from across the mere. They might be the notes of owls or water-birds, yet they did not quite resemble either sound. Were not they coming nearer? Now they sounded from the nearer side of the water, and in a few moments they seemed to be floating about among the shrubberies. Then they ceased; but just as Stephen was thinking of shutting the window and resuming his reading of *Robinson Crusoe*[1], he caught sight of two figures standing on the gravelled terrace that ran along the garden side of the Hall — the figures of a boy and girl, as it seemed; they stood side by side, looking up at the windows. Something in the form of the girl recalled irresistibly his dream of the figure in the bath. The boy inspired him with more acute fear.

Whilst the girl stood still, half smiling, with her hands clasped over her heart, the boy, a thin shape, with black hair and ragged clothing, raised his arms in the air with an appearance of menace and of unappeasable hunger and longing[2]. The moon shone upon his almost transparent hands, and Stephen saw that the nails were fearfully long and that the light shone through them. As he stood with his arms thus raised, he disclosed a terrifying spectacle. On the left side of his chest there opened

---

[1] Daniel Defoe's 1719 novel of self-reliance, piety, adventure, and survival was a favorite of many literati, including Robert Louis Stevenson, Charles Dickens, and M. R. James. It is a paean to self-reliance, and is not haplessly referenced to by James: like Crusoe, Stephen finds himself shipwrecked and marooned in a hostile, pagan landscape where he is forced to use insight, observation, and critical thinking to evade disaster

[2] He has taken after his adoptive guardian, who lusts after knowledge, power, and life. Like many ghosts, Giovanni has become a manifestation of the emotions and vices that contributed to his demise. Consider a Dickensian analog: when Scrooge is shown Want and Ignorance – two bestial wastrels said to be his children, nurtured into vile ugliness by his Ignorance of Want

a black and gaping rent; and there fell upon Stephen's brain, rather than upon his ear, the impression of one of those hungry and desolate cries that he had heard resounding over the woods of Aswarby all that evening. In another moment this dreadful pair had moved swiftly and noiselessly over the dry gravel[1], and he saw them no more.

Inexpressibly frightened as he was, he determined to take his candle and go down to Mr Abney's study, for the hour appointed for their meeting was near at hand[2]. The study or library opened out of the front-hall on one side, and Stephen, urged on by his terrors, did not take long in getting there. To effect an entrance was not so easy. It was not locked, he felt sure, for the key was on the outside of the door as usual. His repeated knocks produced no answer. Mr Abney was engaged: he was speaking. What! why did he try to cry out? and why was the cry choked in his throat? Had he, too, seen the mysterious children? But now everything was quiet, and the door yielded to Stephen's terrified and frantic pushing.

ℰↄ

On the table in Mr Abney's study certain papers were found which explained the situation to Stephen Elliott when he was of an age to understand them. The most important sentences were as follows:

'It was a belief very strongly and generally held by the ancients — of whose wisdom in these matters I have had such experience as induces me to place confidence in their assertions — that by enacting certain processes, which to us moderns have something of a barbaric complexion[3], a very remarkable enlightenment of the spiritual faculties in man may be attained: that, for example, by absorbing the personalities of a certain number of his fellow-creatures, an individual may gain a complete ascendancy over those orders of spiritual beings which control

---

[1] A difficult feat for a mortal
[2] Once more we must ask: is Stephen a naïve dolt or a brave cynic? Wobbling stupidly to his death, or courageously attempting not to arouse suspicion while keeping a level head?
[3] Human sacrifice indeed has something of a barbaric complexion

the elemental forces of our universe[1].

'It is recorded of Simon Magus[2] that he was able to fly in the air, to become invisible, or to assume any form he pleased, by the agency of the soul of a boy whom, to use the libellous phrase employed by the author of the Clementine Recognitions[3], he had "murdered". I find it set down, moreover, with considerable detail in the writings of Hermes Trismegistus[4], that similar happy results may be produced by the absorption of the hearts of not less than three human beings below the age of twenty-one years. To the testing of the truth of this receipt I have devoted the greater part of the last twenty years, selecting as the corpora vilia[5] of my experiment such persons as could conveniently be removed without occasioning a sensible gap in society[6]. The first step I effected by the removal of one Phoebe Stanley, a girl of gipsy extraction, on March 24, 1792. The second, by the removal of a wandering Italian lad, named Giovanni Paoli, on the night of March 23, 1805. The final "victim"— to employ a word repugnant in the highest degree to my feelings — must be my cousin, Stephen Elliott. His day must be this March 24, 1812.

'The best means of effecting the required absorption is to remove the

---

[1] Indeed, an ancient theory associated with the Mysteries and with other sinister cults, fellowships, disciplines, and magic

[2] Simon the Sorcerer was a magician and occultist who converted to Christianity (Acts 8)

[3] A religious anthology supposedly compiled by a scholar named Clement, purporting to be a series of discourses made by the Apostle Peter, who challenged Simon Magus's sorcery

[4] "Thrice-Greatest" Hermes is the purported author of the core religious texts of Hermeticism, an esoteric tradition of philosophy and religion which emerged at the same time as Christianity and Gnosticism. It was rediscovered during the Renaissance, and its emphasis on liberality, openmindedness, and independence greatly influenced the tide of humanism during the Renaissance, Reformation, and Enlightenment

[5] Latin: "worthless bodies." Plural of *corpus vile*. Meaning, a person, animal, or thing treated as expendable, to therefore use as an experimental subject regardless of whatever loss or damage it may suffer in the process

[6] A sociopathic, almost genocidal attitude

heart from the living subject[1], to reduce it to ashes[2], and to mingle them with about a pint of some red wine[3], preferably port[4]. The remains of the first two subjects, at least, it will be well to conceal: a disused bathroom or wine-cellar will be found convenient for such a purpose. Some annoyance may be experienced from the psychic portion of the subjects, which popular language dignifies with the name of ghosts. But the man of philosophic temperament — to whom alone the experiment is appropriate — will be little prone to attach importance to the feeble efforts of these beings to wreak their vengeance on him. I contemplate with the liveliest satisfaction the enlarged and emancipated existence which the experiment, if successful, will confer on me; not only placing me beyond the reach of human justice (so-called), but eliminating to a great extent the prospect of death itself[5].'

℘

Mr Abney was found in his chair, his head thrown back, his face stamped with an expression of rage, fright, and mortal pain[6]. In his left

---

[1] It must be reinforced: he removes the still-beating heart of the still-living child. This is not simple murder followed with postmortem mutilation – the man is breaking the ribs and tearing the flesh off of the chest of a screaming child before plucking out their palpitating heart
[2] Ergo, brazier
[3] Ergo, silver cup
[4] A decidedly, quintessentially English selection (fortified red wine) – almost certainly chosen by James to juxtapose his bourgeois drinking preference with an infanticidal cult-ritual
[5] While his experiments may seem somewhat based in hobby and discipline, make no mistake: the ultimate goal is immortality and invincibility – to become a god
[6] Rage: indignation at the rebellion of his "corpora villia" – his worthless bodies; Fear: his hubris and chiding of ghosts appear to have been all too hasty; Mortal pain: James is intentional with his word choice – the pain is mortal, the man is mortal, his death is mortal

side was a terrible lacerated wound, exposing the heart[1]. There was no blood on his hands, and a long knife that lay on the table was perfectly clean. A savage wild-cat might have inflicted the injuries. The window of the study was open, and it was the opinion of the coroner that Mr Abney had met his death by the agency of some wild creature. But Stephen Elliott's study of the papers I have quoted led him to a very different conclusion.

---

[1] It was not taken. Several explanations exist: Moral Commentary and Symbolism -- the heart could have been found worthless – a testimony to his moral disease; Act of Implication and Revenge – the the children may have wanted merely to disfigure, shame, or implicate their murderer, rather than practically seeking a heart; Disappointing Discovery – the heart may not have achieved the desired effect – they had hoped for restoration but found only continuing death and abandonment, leaving it behind in despair

WHETHER a naïve and susceptible victim or a brave and watchful tactician, Stephen is caught in a hostile environment where the most vulnerable members of society – children, foreigners, orphans, females – are preyed upon by those with the most power, with seeming impunity. No external agency steps in to defend them; the police do not arrive at the eleventh hour; the government fails to provide guidance; religion does nothing to prevent the abuser. Ultimately, the victims themselves must rise up against their oppressor, since their society allows such atrocities to go unnoticed. The weak can expect no defender, and the abused must choose between submission and self-defense, because no one can be counted on to act on their behalf. James' stories almost always expose uncommon horrors festering beneath a facade of everyday normalcy: charred corpses prowl in lovely hedge mazes, sweaty faces protrude from rose gardens in midday, and a dollhouse teems with murderous ghosts. In the midst of a quintessentially English background – a country manor, the seat of a rural scholar – pagan dangers lurk and thrive. His universe – the one which made him famous as a first rate writer of ghost stories – is not one of clear boundaries between good and evil, but one in which the two merge and blend, trespass and encroach. While Stephen was fortunate to escape a hideous death, we cannot avoid the fact that two others were not so fortunate: just as they were stripped of their hearts, their world is one bereft of sensitivity, compassion, and morality.

*LIKE "Nothing But the Truth," the following tale is an example of Broughton's brilliant ability to infuse the dreadful into the domestic. Another story built on a foundation of witty letters between two women, it is, nonetheless, quite different. The setting is rural, the threat – although suggested by the supernatural – is all too physical: a vicious and sloppy murder at the edge of a reaping hook. In this sense, it also pairs wonderfully with Nesbit's "The Semi-Detached," because both are tales of precognitive dreams which stand to prevent a grisly butchering. And like Nesbit, who fogs her story with the tension of scandal and sexuality, Broughton darkens her sunny pastures with resentment and passive aggression between two friends who begin the story desperately missing one another's company. Hidden realities weave their way through the story like an adder through tall grass – behind a loving friend may dwell an envious rival, behind a pastoral cottage might lurk a house of horror, and behind an unremarkable face might brew the plots of a murderer.*

---

# BEHOLD, IT WAS A DREAM[1]!
## {1872}
## *Rhoda Broughton*

### CHAPTER I.

YESTERDAY MORNING I RECEIVED the following letter:

Weston House, Caulfield[2], ------shire.

"MY DEAR DINAH,--You must come: I scorn all your excuses, and see through their flimsiness. I have no doubt that you are much better amused in Dublin, frolicking round ball rooms with a succession of

---

[1] The title arrives from 1 Kings 3:15, following a vision where God grants King Solomon's request for wisdom, the scribe writes: "And Solomon awoke; and behold, *it was* a dream..." The theme is fitting given Dinah's vision – she, like Solomon, is granted wisdom from a supernatural source through the conduit of a dream

[2] Fictitious

272

horse-soldiers[1], and watching her Majesty's household troops play Polo in the Phoenix Park[2], but no matter--you must come. We have no particular inducements to hold out. We lead an exclusively bucolic[3], cow-milking, pig-fattening, roast-mutton-eating and to-bed-at-ten-o'clock-going life; but no matter--you must come. I want you to see how happy two dull elderly people may be, with no special brightness in their lot to make them so. My old man[4]--he is surprisingly ugly at the first glance, but grows upon one afterwards--sends you his respects, and bids me say that he will meet you at any station on any day at any hour of the day or night. If you succeed in evading our persistence this time, you will be a cleverer woman than I take you for.

"Ever yours affectionately,

"*August* 15*th.*

"JANE WATSON.

"P.S.--We will invite our little scarlet-headed curate[5] to dinner to meet you, so as to soften your fall from the society of the Plungers[6]."

This is my answer:

"MY DEAR JANE,--Kill the fat calf in all haste, and put the bake meats into the oven, for I will come. Do not, however, imagine that I am moved thereunto by the prospect of the bright-headed curate. Believe me, my dear, I am as yet at a distance of ten long good years from an addiction to the minor clergy. If I survive the crossing of that seething, heaving, tumbling abomination, St. George's Channel[7], you may expect me on

---

[1] Cavalrymen

[2] A fashionable park including fields and woodlands, of some 1,750 acres in Dublin

[3] Romantically rural, pastoral

[4] Yes, her husband

[5] Parish vicar

[6] Heavy gamblers

[7] The channel between Eastern Ireland and Wales

273

Tuesday next. I have been groping for hours in 'Bradshaw's'[1] darkness that may be felt, and I have arrived at length at this twilight result, that I may arrive at your station at 6.55 P.M. But the ways of 'Bradshaw' are not our ways, and I may either rush violently past or never attain it. If I do, and if on my arrival I see some rustic vehicle, guided by a startlingly ugly gentleman, awaiting me, I shall know from your wifely description that it is your 'old man.' Till Tuesday, then,

"Affectionately yours,

"*August 17th.*

"DINAH BELLAIRS.

I am as good as my word; on Tuesday I set off. For four mortal hours and a half I am disastrously, hideously, diabolically sick. For four hours and a half I curse the day on which I was born, the day on which Jane Watson was born, the day on which her old man was born, and lastly-- but oh! not, not leastly--the day and the dock on which and in which the *Leinster's*[2] plunging, courtseying, throbbing body was born. On arriving at Holyhead[3], feeling convinced from my sensations that, as the French say, I touch my last hour, I indistinctly request to be allowed to stay on board and die, then and there; but as the stewardess and my maid take a different view of my situation, and insist upon forcing my cloak and bonnet on my dying body and limp head, I at length succeed in staggering on deck and off the accursed boat. I am then well shaken up for two or three hours in the Irish mail[4], and after crawling along a slow by-line[5] for two or three hours more, am at length, at 6:55, landed, battered, tired, dust-blacked and qualmish, at the little roadside station of Caulfield. My maid and I are the only passengers who descend. The train snorts its slow way onwards, and I am left gazing at the calm crimson death of the August sun, and smelling the sweet peas in the station-master's garden border. I look round in search of Jane's

---

[1] *Bradshaw's Guide*. A series of railway timetables and guidebooks published 1839 - 1961
[2] A packet ship crossing the channel (Leinster is port on the Irish side)
[3] A major Welsh seaport corresponding to Leinster
[4] The mail train – a small, cheap, rickety passage
[5] Minor train route

promised tax-cart[1], and steel my nerves for the contemplation of her old man's unlovely features. But the only vehicle which I see is a tiny two-wheeled pony carriage, drawn by a small and tub-shaped bay pony and driven by a lady in a hat, whose face is turned expectantly towards me. I go up and recognise my friend, whom I have not seen for two years--not since before she fell in with her old man and espoused him.

"I thought it safest, after all, to come myself," she says with a bright laugh. "My old man looked so handsome this morning, that I thought you would never recognise him from my description. Get in, dear, and let us trot home as quickly as we can."

I comply, and for the next half hour sit (while the cool evening wind is blowing the dust off my hot and jaded face) stealing amazed glances at my companion's cheery features. Cheery! That is the very last word that, excepting in an ironical sense, any one would have applied to my friend Jane two years ago. Two years ago Jane was thirty-five, the elderly eldest daughter of a large family[2], hustled into obscurity, jostled, shelved, by half a dozen younger, fresher sisters; an elderly girl addicted to lachrymose verse[3] about the gone and the dead and the for-ever-lost. Apparently the gone has come back, the dead resuscitated, the for-ever-lost been found again. The peaky sour virgin is transformed into a gracious matron with a kindly, comely face, pleasure making and pleasure feeling. Oh, Happiness, what powder, or paste, or milk of roses, can make old cheeks young again in the cunning way that you do? If you would but bide steadily with us we might live for ever, always young and always handsome[4].

My musings on Jane's metamorphosis, combined with a tired headache, make me somewhat silent, and indeed there is mostly a slackness of conversation between the two dearest allies on first meeting after absence--a sort of hesitating shiver before plunging into the sea of

---

[1] Or spring cart. A rough, open, two wheeled farmer's cart
[2] Daughters were expected to marry off in order of birth, and typically married between 22 and 28. To be the 35 year-old eldest daughter of a large family was truly an awkward situation (compare to Charlotte Lucas in *Pride and Prejudice*)
[3] Teary, depressing poetry
[4] Broughton begins to lay out her signature tripwire of cosmic irony

talk that both know to lie in readiness for them.

"Have you got your harvest in yet?" I ask, more for the sake of not utterly holding my tongue than from any profound interest in the subject, as we jog briskly along between the yellow cornfields, where the dry bound sheaves are standing in golden rows in the red sunset light.

"Not yet," answers Jane; "we have only just begun to cut some of it. However, thank God, the weather looks as settled as possible; there is not a streak of watery lilac in the west."

My headache is almost gone and I am beginning to think kindly of dinner--a subject from which all day until now my mind has hastily turned with a sensation of hideous inward revolt--by the time that the fat pony pulls up before the old-world dark porch of a modest little house, which has bashfully hidden its original face under a veil of crowded clematis flowers and stalwart ivy. Set as in a picture-frame by the large drooped ivy-leaves, I see a tall and moderately hard-featured gentleman of middle age, perhaps, of the two, rather inclining towards elderly, smiling at us a little shyly.

"This is my old man," cries Jane, stepping gaily out, and giving him a friendly introductory pat on the shoulder. "Old man, this is Dinah."

Having thus been made known to each other we shake hands, but neither of us can arrive at anything pretty to say. Then I follow Jane into her little house, the little house for which she has so happily exchanged her tenth part of the large and noisy paternal mansion. It is an old house, and everything about it has the moderate shabbiness of old age and long and careful wear. Little thick-walled rooms, dark and cool, with flowers and flower scents lying in wait for you everywhere--a silent, fragrant, childless house. To me, who have had oily locomotives snorting and racing through my head all day, its dumb sweetness seems like heaven[1].

"And now that we have, secured you, we do not mean to let you go in a

---

[1] Truly, truly bucolic; the rural cottage is drawn straight from sentimental, pastoral art of the pre-Raphaelites and the Romantics. It is a cozy, dreamy respite for Jane, who – while childless and likely to remain so – has been saved from being a burden and an embarrassment to her family. Her home is comfortable, modest, quaint, and domestic, almost Edenic. But the garden has a serpent lurking in it

hurry," says Jane hospitably that night at bedtime, lighting the candles on my dressing-table.

"You are determined to make my mouth water, I see," say I, interrupting a yawn to laugh. "Lone, lorn[1] me, who have neither old man, nor dear little house, nor any prospect of ultimately attaining either."

"But if you honestly are not bored you will stay with us a good bit?" she says, laying her hand with kind entreaty on my sleeve.

"St. George's Channel is not lightly to be faced again."

"Perhaps I shall stay until you are obliged to go away yourselves to get rid of me," return I, smiling. "Such things have happened. Yes, without joking, I will stay a month. Then, by the end of a month, if you have not found me out thoroughly, I think I may pass among men for a more amiable woman than I have ever yet had the reputation of."

A quarter of an hour later I am laying down my head among soft and snow-white pillows, and saying to myself that this delicious sensation of utter drowsy repose, of soft darkness and odorous quiet, is cheaply purchased even by the ridiculous anguish which my own sufferings and--hardly less than my own sufferings--the demoniac sights and sounds afforded by my fellow passengers, caused me on board the accursed *Leinster*,

"Built in the eclipse, and rigged with curses dark[2]."

## CHAPTER II.

"WELL, I cannot say that you look much rested," says Jane next morning, coming in to greet me, smiling and fresh--(yes, sceptic of

---

[1] Lonesome, forgotten, abandoned (*forlorn*)

[2] From John Milton's (1608 -1674) "Lycidas," a funeral poem about the death of a dear friend who drowned in the Irish Sea off the coast of Wales, angrily blaming those that looked away and ignored his plight — unquestionably fitting for this story, both geographically and thematically. The reference is to the fateful ship that sent Milton's friend to his death; while Dinah uses the line in reference to the rickety Leinster, it is to the seemingly sweet cottage that Broughton hopes to draw our attention to: built in a dark hour and nailed together with curses

eighteen, even a woman of thirty-seven may look fresh in a print gown on an August morning, when she has a well of lasting quiet happiness inside her[1],)--coming in with a bunch of creamy *gloire de Dijons*[2] in her hand for the breakfast table. "You look infinitely more fagged[3] than you did when I left you last night!"

"Do I?" say I rather faintly.

"I am afraid you did not sleep much?" suggests Jane, a little crestfallen at the insult to her feather beds implied by my wakefulness. "Some people never can sleep the first night in a strange bed, and I stupidly forgot to ask whether you liked the feather bed or mattress at the top."

"Yes, I did sleep," I answer gloomily. "I wish to heaven I had not."

"Wish--to--heaven--you--had--not?" repeats Jane slowly, with a slight astonished pause between each word. "My dear child, for what other purpose did you go to bed?"

"I--I--had bad dreams," say I, shuddering a little and then taking her hand, roses and all, in mine. "Dear Jane, do not think me quite run mad, but--but--have you got a 'Bradshaw' in the house?"

"A 'Bradshaw?' What on earth do you want with 'Bradshaw?'" says my hostess, her face lengthening considerably and a slight tincture of natural coldness coming into her tone.

"I know it seems rude--insultingly rude," say I, still holding her hand and speaking almost lachrymosely[4]; "but do you know, my dear, I really am afraid that--that--I shall have to leave you--to-day?"

"To leave us?" repeats she, withdrawing her hand and growing angrily red. "What! when not twenty-four hours ago you settled to stay a month with us? What have we done between then and now to disgust you with us?"

"Nothing--nothing," cry I eagerly; "how can you suggest such a thing? I never had a kinder welcome nor ever saw a place that charmed me more; but--but"

---

[1] Broughton (32 at the time), who never married, bitterly chides the hypothetical 18 year old girls reading her story, who might prioritize youth, viewing maturity and beauty as mutually exclusive
[2] Beautiful peach-colored roses
[3] Fatigued, exhausted as if from running
[4] Tearfully

"But what?" asks June, her colour subsiding and looking a little mollified[1].

"It is best to tell the truth, I suppose," say I sighing, "even though I know that you will laugh at me--will call me vapourish--sottishly[2] superstitious; but I had an awful and hideous dream last night."

"Is that all?" she says, looking relieved, and beginning to arrange her roses in an old china bowl. "And do you think that all dreams are confined to this house? I never heard before of their affecting any one special place more than another. Perhaps no sooner are you back in Dublin, in your own room and your own bed, than you will have a still worse and uglier one."

I shake my head. "But it was about this house--about you."

"About me?" she says, with an accent of a little aroused interest.

"About you and your husband," I answer earnestly. "Shall I tell it you? Whether you say 'Yes' or 'No' I must. Perhaps it came as a warning; such things have happened. Yes, say what you will, I cannot believe that any vision so consistent--so tangibly real and utterly free from the jumbled incongruities and unlikelinesses of ordinary dreams--could have meant nothing. Shall I begin?"

"By all means," answers Mrs. Watson[3], sitting down in an arm-chair and smiling easily. "I am quite prepared to listen--and disbelieve."

"You know," say I, narratively, coming and standing close before her, "how utterly tired out I was when you left me last night. I could hardly answer your questions for yawning. I do not think that I was ten minutes in getting into bed, and it seemed like heaven when I laid my head down on the pillow. I felt as if I should sleep till the Day of Judgment. Well, you know, when one is asleep one has of course no measure of time, and I have no idea what hour it was really; but at some time, in the blackest and darkest of the night, I seemed to wake. It appeared as if a noise had woke me--a noise which at first neither frightened nor surprised me in the least, but which seemed quite natural, and which I accounted for in the muddled drowsy way in which one does account for things when

---

[1] Pacified, soothed

[2] As of a drunk

[3] Suddenly a formal tone – the friends are now in a much less casual situation, and Dinah regards her with starchy respect

279

half asleep. But as I gradually grew to fuller consciousness I found out, with a cold shudder, that the noise I heard was not one that belonged to the night; nothing that one could lay on wind in the chimney, or mice behind the wainscot, or ill-fitting boards. It was a sound of muffled struggling, and once I heard a sort of choked strangled cry. I sat up in bed, perfectly numbed with fright, and for a moment could hear nothing for the singing of the blood in my head and the loud battering of my heart against my side. Then I thought that if it were anything bad--if I were going to be murdered--I had at least rather be in the light than the dark, and see in what sort of shape my fate was coming, so I slid out of bed and threw my dressing-gown over my shoulders. I had stupidly forgotten, in my weariness over night, to put the matches by the bedside, and could not for the life of me recollect where they were. Also, my knowledge of the geography of the room was so small that in the utter blackness, without even the palest, greyest ray from the window to help me, I was by no means sure in which direction the door lay. I can feel now the pain of the blow I gave this right side against the sharp corner of the table in passing; I was quite surprised this morning not to find the mark of a bruise there. At last, in my groping I came upon the handle and turned the key in the lock. It gave a little squeak, and again I stopped for a moment, overcome by ungovernable fear. Then I silently opened the door and looked out. You know that your door is exactly opposite mine. By the line of red light underneath it, I could see that at all events some one was awake and astir within, for the light was brighter than that given by a night-light[1]. By the broader band of red light[2] on the right side of it I could also perceive that the door was ajar. I stood stock still and listened. The two sounds of struggling and chokedly crying had both ceased. All the noise that remained was that as of some person quietly moving about on unbooted feet. 'Perhaps Jane's dog Smut is ill and she is sitting up with it; she was saying last night, I remember, that

---

[1] A small candle or tea light

[2] By using terms like "the blood singing in my ears" and by referring the light – which many would more generally describe as yellow or orange – as red, Broughton underscores Dinah's initial instinct: there is bloody murder going on

she was afraid it was beginning with the distemper[1]. Perhaps either she or her old man have been taken with some trifling temporary sickness. Perhaps the noise of crying out that I certainly heard was one of them fighting with a nightmare.' Trying, by such like suggestions, to hearten myself up, I stole across the passage and peeped in"----

I pause in my narrative[2].
"Well?" says Jane, a little impatiently.
She has dropped her flowers. They lie in odorous dewy confusion in her lap. She is listening rather eagerly. I cover my face with my hands. "Oh! My dear," I cry, "I do not think I can go on. It was too dreadful! Now that I am telling it I seem to be doing and hearing it over again"----
"I do not call it very kind to keep me on the rack," she says, with a rather forced laugh. "Probably I am imagining something much worse than the reality. For heaven's sake speak up! What did you see?"
I take hold of her hand and continue "You know that in your room the bed exactly faces the door. Well, when I looked in, looked in with eyes blinking at first, and dazzled by the long darkness they had been in, it seemed to me as if that bed were only one horrible sheet of crimson; but as my sight grew clearer I saw what it was that caused that frightful impression of universal red"--again I pause with a gasp and feeling of oppressed breathing.
"Go on! go on!" cries my companion, leaning forward, and speaking with some petulance[3]. "Are you never going to get to the point?"
"Jane," say I solemnly, "do not laugh at me, nor poohpooh me, for it is God's truth--as clearly and vividly as I see you now, strong, flourishing, and alive, so clearly, so vividly, with no more of dream haziness nor of contradiction in details than there is in the view I now have of this room and of you--I saw you both--you and your husband, lying dead--murdered--drowned in your own blood!"
"What, both of us?" she says, trying to laugh, but her healthy cheek has rather paled.

---

[1] Viral disease common to house pets
[2] Present tense makes an already tense sentence interrupting an already tense story even tenser
[3] Grouchiness, irritability

"Both of you," I answer, with growing excitement. "You, Jane, had evidently been the one first attacked--taken off in your sleep--for you were lying just as you would have lain in slumber, only that across your throat from there to there" (touching first one ear and then the other), "there was a huge and yawning gash."

"Pleasant," replies she, with a slight shiver.

"I never saw any one dead," continue I earnestly, "never until last night. I had not the faintest idea how dead people looked, even people who died quietly, nor has any picture ever given me at all a clear conception of death's dread look. How then could I have imagined the hideous contraction and distortion of feature, the staring starting open eyes--glazed yet agonised--the tightly clenched teeth that go to make up the picture, that is now, this very minute standing out in ugly vividness before my mind's eye?" I stop, but she does not avail herself of the pause to make any remark, neither does she look any longer at all laughingly inclined. "And yet," continue I, with a voice shaken by emotion, "it was you, very you, not partly you and partly some one else, as is mostly the case in dreams, but as much you, as the you I am touching now" laying my finger on her arm as I speak).

"And my old man, Robin," says poor Jane, rather tearfully, after a moment's silence, "what about him? Did you see him? Was he dead too?"

"It was evidently he whom I had heard struggling and crying," I answer with a strong shudder, which I cannot keep down, "for it was clear that he had fought for his life. He was lying half on the bed and half on the floor, and one clenched hand was grasping a great piece of the sheet; he was lying head downwards, as if, after his last struggle, he had fallen forwards. All his grey hair was reddened and stained, and I could see that the rift in his throat was as deep as that in yours."

"I wish you would stop," cries Jane, pale as ashes, and speaking with an accent of unwilling, terror; "you are making me quite sick!"

"I must finish," I answer earnestly, "since it has come in time I am sure it has come for some purpose. Listen to me till the end; it is very near." She does not speak, and I take her silence for assent. "I was staring at you both in a stony way," I go on, "feeling--if I felt at all--that I was turning idiotic[1] with horror--standing in exactly the same spot, with my neck craned to look round the door, and my eyes unable to stir from that hideous scarlet bed, when a slight noise, as of some one cautiously stepping on the carpet, turned my stony terror into a living quivering agony. I looked and saw a man with his back towards me walking across the room from the bed to the dressing-table. He was dressed in the dirty fustian[2] of an ordinary workman, and in his hand he held a red wet sickle[3]. When he reached the dressing-table he laid it down on the floor beside him, and began to collect all the rings, open the cases of the bracelets, and hurry the trinkets of all sorts into his pockets. While he was thus busy I caught a full view of the reflection of the face in the glass"-- I stop for breath, my heart is panting almost as hardly as it seemed to pant during the awful moments I am describing."

"What was he like--what was he like?" cries Jane, greatly excited. "Did you see him distinctly enough to recollect his features again? Would you know him again if you saw him?"

"Should I know my own face if I saw it in the glass?" I ask scornfully. "I see every line of it now more clearly than I do yours, though that is before my eyes, and the other only before my memory"----

"Well, what was he like?--be quick, for heaven's sake[4]."

"The first moment that I caught sight of him," continue I, speaking quickly, "I felt certain that he was Irish; to no other nationality could such a type of face have belonged. His wild rough hair fell down over his forehead, reaching his shagged and overhanging brows. He had the wide grinning slit of a mouth--the long nose, the cunningly twinkling eyes-- that one so often sees, in combination with a shambling gait and ragged tail-coat, at the railway stations or in the harvest fields at this time of year." A pause. "I do not know how it came to me," I go on presently;

---

[1] Insane

[2] Hardy, twilled cloth, often dark in color

[3] The curved blade of this hand tool would require a brutal hacking and ripping action rather than the typical slicing of a knife – the murders would be unbearably heinous

[4] While annoying, Dinah's perforated narrative, jolted with pauses and delays, acutely mounts the tension in a way that can only be described as masterful

"but I felt as convinced as if I had been told--as if I had known it for a positive fact--that he was one of your own labourers'--one of your own harvest men. Have you any Irishmen working for you?"

"Of course we have[2]," answers Jane, rather sharply, "but that proves nothing. Do not they, as you observed just now, come over in droves at this time of year for the harvest?"

"I am sorry," say I, sighing. "I wish you had not. Well, let me finish; I have just done--I had been holding the door-handle mechanically in my hand; I suppose I pulled it unconsciously towards me, for the door hinge creaked a little, but quite audibly. To my unspeakable horror the man turned round and saw me. Good God! he would cut my throat too with that red, red reaping hook! I tried to get into the passage and lock the door, but the key was on the inside. I tried to scream, I tried to run; but voice and legs disobeyed me. The bed and room and man began to dance before me; a black earthquake seemed to swallow me up, and I suppose I fell down in a swoon. When I awoke really the blessed morning had come, and a robin was singing outside my window on an apple bough. There--you have it all, and now let me look for a 'Bradshaw,' for I am so frightened and unhinged that go I must."

## CHAPTER III.

"I MUST own that it has taken away appetite," I say, with rather a sickly smile, as we sit round the breakfast table. "I assure you that I mean no insult to your fresh eggs and bread-and-butter, but I simply cannot eat."

"It certainly was an exceptionally dreadful dream," says Jane, whose colour has returned, and who is a good deal fortified and reassured by

---

[1] The Watsons may appear to live in a peasants cottage, but they are in fact well-off (albeit middle classed) farmers who hire workers to take in the harvest, mend repairs, tend to the crops, and care for the livestock and machinery. Such men – unskilled agricultural laborers – would typically be barely above the very lowest of Victorian classes

[2] Living so close to the most important British port on the Irish Sea, it is only natural that they should have a handful of Irish laborers in their employment – likely runaway sailors, men eager to avoid the Irish police, dock rats, unemployed stevedores, or foreclosed upon land tenets

the influences of breakfast and of her husband's scepticism; for a condensed and shortened version of my dream has been told to him, and he has easily laughed it to scorn. "Exceptionally dreadful, chiefly from its extreme consistency and precision of detail. But still, you know, dear, one has had hideous dreams oneself times out of mind and they never came, to anything. I remember once I dreamt that all my teeth came out in my mouth at once--double ones and all; but that was ten years ago, and they still keep their situations, nor did I about that time lose any friend, which they say such a dream is a sign of."

"You say that some unaccountable instinct told you that the hero of your dream was one of my own men," says Robin, turning towards me with a covert smile of benevolent contempt for my superstitiousness; "did not I understand you to say so?"

"Yes," reply I, not in the least shaken by his hardly-veiled disbelief. "I do not know how it came to me, but I was as much persuaded of that, and am so still, as I am of my own identity."

"I will tell you of a plan then to prove the truth of your vision," returns he, smiling. "I will take you through the fields this morning and you shall see all my men at work, both the ordinary staff and the harvest casuals, Irish and all. If amongst them you find the counterpart of Jane's and my murderer (a smile) I will promise then--no, not even then can I promise to believe you, for there is such a family likeness between all Irishmen, at all events between all the Irishmen that one sees out of Ireland."

"Take me," I say eagerly, jumping up; "now, this minute! You cannot be more anxious nor half so anxious to prove me a false prophet as I am to be proved one."

"I am quite at your service," he answers, "as soon as you please. Jenny, get your hat and come too."

"And if we do not find him," says Jane, smiling playfully--" I think I am growing pretty easy on that head--you will promise to eat a great deal of luncheon and never mention 'Bradshaw' again?"

"I promise," reply I gravely. "And if, on the other hand, we do find him, you will promise to put no more obstacles in the way of my going, but will let me depart in peace without taking any offence thereat?"

"It is a bargain," she says gaily. "Witness, Robin."

So we set off in the bright dewiness of the morning; on our walk over

286

Robin's farm. It is a grand harvest day, and the whitened sheaves are everywhere, drying, drying in the genial sun[1]. We have been walking for an hour and both Jane and I are rather tired. The sun beats with all his late-summer strength on our heads and takes the force and spring out of our hot limbs.

"The hour of triumph is approaching," says Robin, with a quiet smile, as we draw near an open gate through which a loaded wain, shedding, ripe wheat ears from its abundance as it crawls along, is passing. "And time for it too; it is a quarter past twelve and you have been on your legs for fully an hour. Miss Bellairs, you must make haste and find the murderer, for there is only one more field to do it in."

"Is not there?" I cry eagerly. "Oh, I am glad! Thank God, I begin to breathe again."

"We pass through the open gate and begin to tread across the stubble for almost the last load has gone."

"We must get nearer the hedge," says Robin, "or you will not see their faces; they are all at dinner."

We do as he suggests. In the shadow of the hedge we walk close in front of the row of heated labourers, who, sitting or lying on the hedge bank, are eating unattractive looking dinners. I scan one face after another--honest bovine[2] English faces. I have seen a hundred thousand faces like each one of the faces now before me--very like but the exact counterpart of none. We are getting to the end of the row, I beginning to feel rather ashamed, though infinitely relieved, and to smile at my own expense. I look again, and my heart suddenly stands still and turns to stone within me. He is there!--not a handsbreadth from me! Great God! how well I have remembered his face, even to the unsightly smallpox seams[3], the shagged locks, the grinning slit mouth, the little sly base eyes. He is employed in no murderous occupation now; he is harmlessly cutting hunks of coarse bread and fat cold bacon with a clasp knife; but yet I have no more doubt that it is he--he whom I saw with

---

[1] The fresh grass was shorn when it reached an agreeable height, and left to dry in the sun, producing hay to feed livestock in the winter. It was, of course, mown with scythes *and sickles*
[2] Cowlike
[3] Smallpox leaves scars that resemble craggy creases in the flesh

287

the crimsoned sickle in his stained hand--than I have that it is I who am stonily, shiveringly, staring at him.

"Well, Miss Bellairs, who was right?" asks Robin's cheery voice at my elbow. "Perish Bradshaw and all his labyrinths! Are you satisfied now? Good heavens!" (catching a sudden sight of my face) "How white you are! Do you mean to say that you have found him at last? Impossible!"

"Yes, I have found him," I answer in a low and unsteady tone. "I knew I should. Look, there he is!--close to us, the third from the end."

I turn away my head, unable to bear the hideous recollections and associations that the sight of the man calls up, and I suppose that they both look.

"Are you sure that you are not letting your imagination carry you away?" asks he presently, in a tone of gentle kindly remonstrance. "As I said before, these fellows are all so much alike, they have all the same look of debased squalid cunning. Oblige me by looking once again, so as to be quite sure."     I obey. Reluctantly I look at him once again. Apparently becoming aware that he is the object of our notice, he lifts his small dull eyes and looks back at me. It is the same face--they are the same eyes that turned from the plundered dressing-table to catch sight of me last night.

"There is no mistake," I answer, shuddering from head to foot. "Take me away, please--as quick as you can--out of the field--home!"

They comply, and over the hot fields and through the hot noon air we step silently homewards. As we reach the cool and ivied porch of the house I speak for the first time.

"You believe me now?"

He hesitates. "I was staggered for a moment, I will own," he answers, with candid gravity; "but I have been thinking it over and on reflection I have come to the conclusion that the highly excited state of your imagination is answerable for the heightening of the resemblance which exists between all the Irish of that class into an identity with the particular Irishman you dreamed of, and whose face (by your own showing) you only saw dimly reflected in the glass."

"Not dimly," repeat I, emphatically, "unless I now see that Sun dimly" (pointing to him as he gloriously, blindingly, blazes from the sky). You will not be warned by me, then?" I continue passionately, after an interval. "You will run the risk of my dream coming true--you will stay

288

on here in spite of it? Oh, if I could persuade you to go from home--anywhere--anywhere--for a time, until the danger was past!"

"And leave the harvest to itself?" answers he, with a smile of quiet sarcasm; "be a loser of two hundred or three hundred pounds, probably, and a laughing-stock to my acquaintance into the bargain, and all for--what? A dream a fancy--a nightmare!"

"But do you know anything of the man?--of his antecedents[1]?--of his character?" I persist eagerly.

He shrugs he shoulders.

"Nothing whatever; nothing to his disadvantage, certainly. He came over with a lot of others a fortnight ago, and I engaged him for the harvesting. For anything I have heard to the contrary, he is a simple inoffensive fellow enough."

I am silenced, but not convinced. I turn to Jane. "You remember your promise: you will now put no more hindrances in the way of my going?"

"You do not mean to say that you are going, really?" says Jane, who is looking rather awed by what she calls the surprising coincidence but is still a good deal heartened up by her husband's want of faith.

"I do," reply I, emphatically. "I should go stark staring mad if I were to sleep another night in that room. I shall go to Chester[2] to-night, and cross to-morrow from Holyhead."

I do as I say. I make my maid, to her extreme surprise, repack my just unpacked wardrobe and take an afternoon train to Chester. As I drive away with bag and baggage down the leafy lane, I look back and see my two friends standing at their gate. Jane is leaning her head on her old man's shoulder, and looking rather wistfully after me: an expression of mingled regret for my departure and vexation at my folly clouding their kind and happy faces. At least my last living recollection of them is a pleasant one[3].

CHAPTER IV.

---

[1] Family, background

[2] An English port city in Cheshire, near the border of Wales

[3] These last two sentences are simply masterful, firstly in evoking a highly realistic mental image worthy of E. Nesbit, and secondly is spelling out DOOM in casual a way as to give the reader genuine shivers of dread

THE joy with which my family welcome my return is largely mingled with surprise, but still more largely with curiosity, as to the cause of my so sudden reappearance. But I keep my own counsel. I have a reluctance to give the real reason, and possess no inventive faculty in the way of lying, so I give none. I say, "I am back: is not that enough for you? Set your minds at rest, for that is as much as you will ever know about the matter."

For one thing, I am occasionally rather ashamed of my conduct. It is not that the impression produced by my dream is effaced[1], but that absence and distance from the scene and the persons of it have produced their natural weakening effect. Once or twice during the voyage, when writhing in laughable torments in the ladies' cabin of the steam~boat, I said to myself, "Most likely you are a fool!" I therefore continually ward off the cross-questionings of my family with what defensive armour of silence and evasion I may.

"I feel convinced it was the husband," says one of my sisters, after a long catechism[2], which, as usual, has resulted in nothing. "You are too loyal to your friend to own it, but I always felt sure that any man who could take compassion on that poor peevish[3] old[4] Jane must be some wonderful freak of nature. Come, confess. Is not he a cross between an orang-outang and a Methodist parson[5]?"

"He is nothing of the kind," reply I, in some heat, recalling the libelled[6] Robin's clean fresh-coloured human face. "You will be very lucky if you ever secure any one half so kind, pleasant, and gentleman-like."

Three days after my return, I receive a letter from Jane:

Weston House, Caulfield.

---

[1] Obliterated, removed

[2] In this case, a long list or summary of beliefs

[3] Crabby

[4] It is terribly sad that Jane has indeed found a loving match, but that her years as a confirmed spinster have earned her the disdain and displeasure of her younger, marriageable peers

[5] Known for being mirthless bores

[6] Slandered

"MY DEAR DINAH,--I hope you are safe home again, and that you have made up your mind that two crossings of St. George's Channel within forty-eight hours are almost as bad as having your throat cut, according to the programme[1] you laid out for us. I have good news for you. Our murderer elect is gone. After hearing of the connection that there was to lie between us[2], Robin naturally was rather interested in him, and found out his name, which is the melodious one of Watty Doolan After asking his name he asked other things about him, and finding that he never did a stroke of work and was inclined to be tipsy and quarrelsome he paid and packed him off at once. He is now on the way back to his native shores, and if he murder anybody it will be you my dear[3]. Good-bye, Dinah. Hardly yet have I forgiven you[4] for the way in which you frightened me with your graphic description of poor Robin and me, with our heads loose and waggling.

"Ever yours affectionately,
"JANE WATSON."

I fold up this note with a feeling of exceeding relief, and a thorough faith that I have been a superstitious hysterical fool. More resolved than ever am I to keep the reason for my return profoundly secret from my family. The next morning but one we are all in the breakfast-room after breakfast, hanging about, and looking at the papers. My sister has just thrown down the *Times*, with a pettish[5] exclamation that there is nothing in it and that it really is not worthwhile paying threepence[6] a day to see nothing but advertisements and police reports. I pick it up as she throws it down, and look listlessly[7] over its tall columns from top to

---

[1] This is to say, according to the drama in which you have told us we will have roles
[2] The sarcasm is fluid and caustic; she still treasures the friendship, but her venomous passive-aggression is bitter to the taste
[3] My editor's hand is restrained from merely writing "wow…" Reeking of bitter annoyance
[4] Indeed not
[5] Grouchy, moody
[6] $2.74 in USD (2014)
[7] Lethargically, lazily

291

bottom. Suddenly my listlessness vanishes. What is this that I am reading?--this in staring capitals?

"SHOCKING TRAGEDY AT CAULFIELD.--DOUBLE MURDER."

I am in the middle of the paragraph before I realise what it is.

"From an early hour of the morning this village has been the scene of deep and painful excitement in consequence of the discovery of the atrocious murder of Mr. and Mrs. Watson, of Weston House, two of its most respected inhabitants. It appears that the deceased had retired to rest on Tuesday night at their usual hour, and in their usual health and spirits. The housemaid, on going to call them at the accustomed hour on Wednesday morning, received no answer, in spite of repeated knocking. She therefore at length opened the door and entered. The rest of the servants, attracted by her cries, rushed to the spot, and found the unfortunate gentleman and lady lying on the bed with their throats cut from ear to ear. Life must have been extinct for some hours, as they were both perfectly cold. The room presented a hideous spectacle, being literally swimming in blood. A reaping hook, evidently the instrument with which the crime was perpetrated, was picked up near the door. An Irish labourer of the name of Watty Doolan, discharged by the lamented gentleman a few days ago on account of misconduct, has already been arrested on strong suspicion, as at an early hour on Wednesday morning he was seen by a farm labourer, who was going to his work, washing his waistcoat at a retired spot in the stream which flows through the meadows below the scene of the murder. On being apprehended and searched, several small articles of jewelry, identified as having belonged to Mr. Watson, were discovered in his possession."

I drop the paper and sink into a chair, feeling deadly sick. So you see that my dream came true, after all. The facts narrated in the above story occurred in Ireland. The only liberty I have taken with them is in transplanting them to England[1].

---

[1] Like "Nothing But the Truth's" "This is a true story," we have to wonder why Broughton would deflate a terrific climax with this talk of transplanting

BROUGHTON'S horror stories almost always involve the doom lurking behind the peaceful, and are, in that sense, typically meditations on the unconscious – replete with fears, hates, pettiness, and lust – churning beneath the exteriors of social normalcy: loved ones envy one another, gentlemen restrain rapacious urges, ladies wish misery on their friends, the classiest townhouse in Mayfair may be the den of a demon, and the most idyllic cottage in the fairest valley may prove the perfect setting for a relentless slaughter. Dreams, Broughton suggests – the unconscious, instinct, intuition – may be more real and trustworthy than cold, hard facts, and the gut feelings that seem silly when weighed against logic and reason, may be a better source of guidance. "Behold, it was a Dream!" follows the pitfalls of pride, the importance of trust, and the unreliability of appearances. Her two chief characters fall out of friendship as one departs the other in pursuit of intuition. The newlywed who wishes to show off her escape from spinsterhood to a Dinah – likely, it seems, to remain an old maid – is incensed by her friend's inability to be impressed, and the true mission of their reunion is exposed for what it was: bragging rights. Self deprecating references to her "ugly old man" and simple little cottage are not what they seem, and Jane is less concerned with Dinah's peace of mind and more annoyed at the failure of her chance to show off. Likewise the dream is shown to be reality, and the nightmare truth. Things are not as they always seem, Broughton sadly warns, whether cottages, laborers, or friendships.

---

the action to England. Perhaps it is a misguided attempt to establish veracity, but it is certainly unnecessary

ALGERNON BLACKWOOD, *famed for his weird fiction and cosmic spiritualism, was also a very talented writer of ghost stories. He commonly utilized physical and psychological vulnerability to evoke high terror, but its usage in the following episode is laden with questions of masculinity and socializations of gender. The principle character, a secretary named Johnson, finds himself stalked and dominated by the psychic impressions left by a man who brutally killed and butchered a woman. Blackwood's particular use of feminizing descriptors ("girlish," "like a girl") and mannerisms places Johnson in jeopardy of finding himself isolated in the periphery of a society which had polarized standards for masculinity, prosecuted homosexual behavior with the law, and largely ignored its existence and the social problems and abuses which rose from its marginalization – the Cleveland Street Scandal and the trial of Oscar Wilde were only two events in Blackwood's recent memory which highlighted Victorian society's volatility to (and denial of) what we now might refer to queer culture: the entire gamut of gender identification, from uncloseted homosexuality to straight men with mannerisms and constitutions which fall outside of society's definitions, expectations, and ideals of male identity. Falling outside of the stereotype of Victorian masculinity, regardless of his sexual orientation, Johnson is vulnerable: unprotected by the fraternity of British manhood, and subject to its abuses.*

---

# THE KIT-BAG
{1908}
*Algernon Blackwood*

WHEN THE WORDS 'NOT GUILTY' SOUNDED through the crowded courtroom that dark December afternoon, Arthur Wilbraham, the great criminal KC[1], and

---

[1] King's Counsel – a senior jurist appointed by letters patent to be "one of His Majesty's Counsel learned in the law." During the reign of a queen the designation is changed to "Q.C."

leader for the triumphant defence, was represented by his junior; but Johnson, his private secretary, carried the verdict across to his chambers like lightning.

'It's what we expected, I think,' said the barrister[1], without emotion; 'and, personally, I am glad the case is over.' There was no particular sign of pleasure that his defence of John Turk[2], the murderer, on a plea of insanity, had been successful, for no doubt he felt, as everybody who had watched the case felt, that no man had ever better deserved the gallows.

'I'm glad too,' said Johnson. He had sat in the court for ten days watching the face of the man who had carried out with callous detail one of the most brutal and cold-blooded murders of recent years.

The counsel glanced up at his secretary. They were more than employer and
employed; for family and other reasons, they were friends. 'Ah, I remember; yes,' he said with a kind smile, 'and you want to get away for Christmas? You're going to skate and ski in the Alps[3], aren't you? If I was your age I'd come with you.'

---

[1] Lawyer – literally, a member of the bar

[2] As a reporter, Blackwood was called upon to cover sensational cases, often of a grisly nature. He not infrequently used crime, criminals, and psychopathy in his fiction. Perhaps most famous is his tour-de-force of crime writing, "Max Hensig – Bacteriologist and Murderer," a thriller about a German expert in microbes who, after being found not guilty in the death of his wife, begins to stalk a reporter who covered his case

[3] As with his other wintry stories "The Occupant of the Room" and "The Glamour of the Snow," the allure of snowy mountains acts as a motif in "The Kit-Bag"

Johnson laughed shortly. He was a young man of twenty-six, with a delicate face like a girl's[1]. 'I can catch the morning boat[2] now,' he said; 'but that's not the reason I'm glad the trial is over. I'm glad it's over because I've seen the last of that man's dreadful face. It positively haunted me. Bat white skin, with the black hair brushed low over the forehead, is a thing I shall never forget, and the description of the way the dismembered body was crammed and packed with lime[3] into that—'

'Don't dwell on it, my dear fellow,' interrupted the other, looking at him curiously out of his keen eyes, 'don't think about it. Such pictures have a trick of coming back when one least wants them.' He paused a moment. 'Now go,' he added presently, 'and enjoy your holiday. I shall want all your energy for my Parliamentary[4] work when you get back. And don't break your neck skiing[5].'

Johnson shook hands and took his leave. At the door he turned suddenly.

'I knew there was something I wanted to ask you,' he said. 'Would you

---

[1] "Kit-Bag" introduces an intriguing element of gender into its plot. Johnson, almost immediately portrayed as being somewhat effeminate and fragile will find himself haunted by the ghost of a man who butchered a woman and stuffed her into a bag. Like many writers of horror from this period (M.R. James, Henry James, H.P. Lovecraft, E.F. Benson, R.H. Benson), questions have arisen as to what Blackwood's sexual identity may have been. A lifelong bachelor who preferred the rousing company of men (much like James and Lovecraft), Blackwood has been interpreted by some as having homosexual or bisexual inclinations. Nonetheless, the particularly blatant feminizing of Johnson raises questions in gender theory and queer theory regardless of Blackwood's sexual identification

[2] That is, the packet crossing the English Channel between Dover and Calais

[3] Quicklime – calcium oxide – is a caustic mineral compound often used to speed decomposition

[4] Likely either a campaign to run for a Parliamentary seat, or a legal case with Parliamentary ramifications

[5] An ominous warning, setting the tone of lurking danger

mind lending me one of your kit-bags[1]? It's too late to get one tonight, and I leave in the morning before the shops are open.'

'Of course; I'll send Henry over with it to your rooms. You shall have it the moment I get home.'

'I promise to take great care of it,' said Johnson gratefully, delighted to think that within thirty hours he would be nearing the brilliant sunshine of the high Alps in winter. Be thought of that criminal court was like an evil dream in his mind.

He dined at his club and went on to Bloomsbury[2], where he occupied the top floor in one of those old, gaunt houses in which the rooms are large and lofty. The floor below his own was vacant and unfurnished, and below that were other lodgers whom he did not know[3]. It was cheerless, and he looked forward heartily to a change. The night was even more cheerless: it was miserable, and few people were about. A cold, sleety rain was driving down the streets before the keenest[4] east wind he had ever felt. It howled dismally among the big, gloomy houses of the great squares, and when he reached his rooms he heard it whistling and shouting over the world of black roofs beyond his windows.

In the hall he met his landlady, shading a candle from the draughts with
her thin hand. 'This come by a man from Mr Wilbr'im's, sir.'

---

[1] A large canvas bag shaped like a tube, closed at one end; the open end is often pierced with a series of brass rings through which a bar or drawstring can be threaded to secure it closed. Often associated with rugged travel, the military, and sports – notably all stereotypical male activities, especially before World War II. That Johnson does not own one may be seen as symbolic of his perceived immasculinity, both in a social sense (a man wanting to rough it in the mountains "should" already own one) and in a Freudian sense (he lacks a "bag" and must ask to borrow one)

[2] A neighborhood in Central London – very posh, and noted for its many elegant parks

[3] Loneliness, isolation, and lack of immediate relationships once more haunts a Blackwood character

[4] Sharpest

She pointed to what was evidently the kit-bag, and Johnson thanked her

and took it upstairs with him. 'I shall be going abroad in the morning for ten days, Mrs Monks,' he said. 'I'll leave an address for letters.'

'And I hope you'll 'ave a merry Christmas, sir,' she said, in a raucous, wheezy voice that suggested spirits[1], 'and better weather than this.'

'I hope so too,' replied her lodger, shuddering a little as the wind went roaring down the street outside.

When he got upstairs he heard the sleet volleying against the window panes. He put his kettle on to make a cup of hot coffee, and then set about putting a few things in order for his absence. 'And now I must pack—such as my packing is,' he laughed to himself, and set to work at once.

He liked the packing, for it brought the snowy mountains so vividly before him, and made him forget the unpleasant scenes of the past ten days. Besides, it was not elaborate in nature. His friend had lent him the very thing—a stout canvas kit-bag, sack-shaped, with holes round the neck for the brass bar and padlock. It was a bit shapeless, true, and not much to look at, but its capacity was unlimited, and there was no need to pack carefully. He shoved in his waterproof coat, his fur cap and gloves, his skates and climbing boots, his sweaters, snow-boots, and ear-caps; and then on the top of these he piled his woolen shirts and underwear, his thick socks, puttees[2], and knickerbockers[3]. The dress suit came next, in case the hotel people dressed for dinner, and then, thinking of the best way to pack his white shirts, he paused a moment to reflect. 'That's the worst of these kit-bags,' he mused vaguely, standing in the centre of the sitting-room, where he had come to fetch some string.

It was after ten o'clock. A furious gust of wind rattled the windows as though to hurry him up, and he thought with pity of the poor Londoners whose Christmas would be spent in such a climate, whilst

---

[1] That is, drunkenness

[2] Strips of wool wrapped like bandages around the foreleg – commonly used by soldiers of WWI

[3] Baggy, knee-length trousers commonly used for leisure or sports (stereotypically so by golfers)

he was skimming over snowy slopes in bright sunshine, and dancing in the evening with rosy-checked girls—Ah! that reminded him; he must put in his dancing-pumps[1] and evening socks. He crossed over from his sitting-room to the cupboard on the landing where he kept his linen.

And as he did so he heard someone coming softly up the stairs.

He stood still a moment on the landing to listen. It was Mrs Monks's step, he thought; she must he coming up with the last post. But then the steps ceased suddenly, and he heard no more. They were at least two flights down, and he came to the conclusion they were too heavy to be those of his bibulous landlady. No doubt they belonged to a late lodger who had mistaken his floor. He went into his bedroom and packed his pumps and dress-shirts as best he could.

The kit-bag by this time was two-thirds full, and stood upright on its own base like a sack of flour. For the first time he noticed that it was old and dirty, the canvas faded and worn, and that it had obviously been subjected to rather rough treatment. It was not a very nice bag to have sent him—certainly not a new one, or one that his chief valued. He gave the matter a passing thought, and went on with his packing. Once or twice, however, he caught himself wondering who it could have been wandering down below, for Mrs Monks had not come up with letters, and the floor was empty and unfurnished. From time to time, moreover, he was almost certain he heard a soft tread of someone padding about over the bare boards—cautiously, stealthily, as silently as possible—and, further, that the sounds had been lately coming distinctly nearer.

For the first time in his life he began to feel a little creepy[2]. Then, as though to emphasize this feeling, an odd thing happened: as he left the bedroom, having, just packed his recalcitrant[3] white shirts, he noticed that the top of the kit-bag lopped over towards him with an

---

[1] While pumps were not synonymous with women's footwear in the early 20th century, they did maintain a foppish, pretentious, girlish association which would have identified Johnson as being – if nothing else – somewhat fussy about his appearance, and possibly needed to boost his height with extended heels

[2] "Creeped out," spooked

[3] In this context, difficult to pack

extraordinary resemblance to a human face. The camas fell into a fold like a nose and forehead, and the brass rings for the padlock just filled the position of the eyes. A shadow—or was it a travel stain? for he could not tell exactly—looked like hair. It gave him rather a turn[1], for it was so absurdly, so outrageously, like the face of John Turk the murderer.

He laughed, and went into the front room, where the light was stronger.

'That horrid case has got on my mind,' he thought; 'I shall be glad of a change of scene and air.' In the sitting-room, however, he was not pleased to hear again that stealthy tread upon the stairs, and to realize that it was much closer than before, as well as unmistakably real. And this time he got up and went out to see who it could be creeping about on the upper staircase at so late an hour.

But the sound ceased; there was no one visible on the stairs. He went to the floor below, not without trepidation, and turned on the electric light to make sure that no one was hiding in the empty rooms of the unoccupied suite. There was not a stick of furniture large enough to hide a dog. Then he called over the banisters to Mrs Monks, but there was no answer, and his voice echoed down into the dark vault of the house, and was lost in the roar of the gale that howled outside. Everyone was in bed and asleep—everyone except himself and the owner of this soft and stealthy tread.

'My absurd imagination, I suppose,' he thought. 'It must have been the wind after all, although—it seemed so *very* real and close, I thought.' He went back to his packing. It was by this time getting on towards midnight. He drank his coffee up and lit another pipe—the last before turning in. It is difficult to say exactly at what point fear begins, when the causes of that fear are not plainly before the eyes[2]. Impressions gather on the surface of the mind, film by film, as ice gathers upon the surface of still water, but often so lightly that they claim no definite recognition from the consciousness. Then a point is

---

[1] Causing a double-take or a pause to reflect

[2] Fear is being piped into Johnson's mind not by distinct visual cues, but by subtle psychological encroachments. Blackwood has developed a sadistically playful, predatory spirit which circles its prey until the ultimate moment

reached where the accumulated impressions become a definite emotion, and the mind realizes that something has happened. With something of a start, Johnson suddenly recognized that he felt nervous—oddly nervous; also, that for some time past the causes of this feeling had been gathering slowly in his mind, but that he had only just reached the point where he was forced to acknowledge them.

It was a singular and curious malaise[1] that had come over him, and he hardly knew what to make of it. He felt as though he were doing something that was strongly objected to by another person, another person, moreover, who had some right to object. It was a most disturbing and disagreeable feeling, not unlike the persistent promptings of conscience: almost, in fact, as if he were doing something he knew to be wrong. Yet, though he searched vigorously and honestly in his mind, he could nowhere lay his finger upon the secret of this growing uneasiness, and it perplexed him. More, it distressed and frightened him.

'Pure nerves, I suppose,' he said aloud with a forced laugh. 'Mountain air will cure all that! Ah,' he added, still speaking to himself, 'and that reminds me—my snow-glasses[2].'

He was standing by the door of the bedroom during this brief soliloquy[3], and as he passed quickly towards the sitting-room to fetch them from the cupboard he saw out of the corner of his eye the indistinct outline of a figure standing on the stairs, a few feet from the top. It was someone in a stooping position, with one hand on the banisters, and the face peering up towards the landing. And at the same moment he heard a shuffling footstep. The person who had been creeping about below all this time had at last come up to his own floor. Who in the world could it be? And what in the name of Heaven did he want[4]?

Johnson caught his breath sharply and stood stock still. Then, after a few seconds' hesitation, he found his courage, and turned to investigate. The stairs, he saw to his utter amazement, were

---

[1] Discontent, discomfort, unease
[2] Snow goggles
[3] A speech given to no one in particular – talking out loud to oneself
[4] Compare to the motif of "lurker-in-the-stair-well" used in "The Listener"

empty; there was no one. He felt a series of cold shivers run over him, and something about the muscles of his legs gave a little and grew weak. For the space of several minutes he peered steadily into the shadows that congregated about the top of the staircase where he had seen the figure, and then he walked fast—almost ran, in fact—into the light of the front room; but hardly had he passed inside the doorway when he heard someone come up the stairs behind him with a quick bound and go swiftly into

his bedroom. It was a heavy, but at the same time a stealthy footstep— the tread of somebody who did not wish to be seen. And it was at this precise moment that the nervousness he had hitherto experienced leaped the boundary line, and entered the state of fear, almost of acute, unreasoning fear. Before it turned into terror there was a further boundary to cross, and beyond that again lay the region of pure horror. Johnson's position was an unenviable one.

'By Jove[1]! That was someone on the stairs, then,' he muttered, his flesh crawling all over; 'and whoever it was has now gone into my bedroom.' His

delicate, pale face[2] turned absolutely white, and for some minutes he hardly knew what to think or do. Then he realized intuitively that delay only set a premium upon fear; and he crossed the landing boldly and went straight into the other room, where, a few seconds before, the steps had disappeared.

'Who's there? Is that you, Mrs Monks?' he called aloud, as he went, and heard the first half of his words echo down the empty stairs, while the second half fell dead against the curtains in a room that apparently held no other human figure than his own.

'Who's there?' he called again, in a voice unnecessarily loud and that only just held firm. 'What do you want here?'

The curtains swayed very slightly, and, as he saw it, his heart felt as if it almost missed a beat; yet he dashed forward and drew them aside with a rush. A window, streaming with rain, was all that met his gaze. He continued his search, but in vain; the cupboards held nothing but rows of clothes, hanging motionless; and under the bed there was no

---

[1] "In God's name!" – a euphemism
[2] Another feminizing touch

sign of anyone hiding. He stepped backwards into the middle of the room, and, as he did so, something all but tripped him up. Turning with a sudden spring of alarm he saw—the kit-bag.

'Odd!' he thought. 'That's not where I left it!' A few moments before it had surely been on his right, between the bed and the bath; he did not remember having moved it. It was very curious. What in the world was the matter with everything? Had all of his senses gone queer? A terrific gust of wind tore at the windows, dashing the sleet against the glass with the force of small gunshot, and then fled away howling dismally over the waste of Bloomsbury roofs. A sudden vision of the Channel next day rose in his mind and recalled him sharply to realities.

'There's no one here at any rate; that's quite clear!' he exclaimed aloud.

Yet at the time he uttered them he knew perfectly well that his words were not true and that he did not believe them himself. He felt exactly as though someone was hiding close about him, watching all his movements, trying to hinder his packing in some way. 'And two of my senses,' he added, keeping up the pretence, 'have played me the most absurd tricks: the steps I heard and the figure I saw were both entirely imaginary.'

He went back to the front room, poked the fire into a blaze, and sat down before it to think. What impressed him more than anything else was the fact that the kit-bag was no longer where he had left at. It had been dragged nearer to the door.

What happened afterwards that night happened, of course, to a man already excited by fear, and was perceived by a mind that had not the full and proper control, therefore, of the senses. Outwardly, Johnson remained calm and master of himself to the end, pretending to the very last that everything he witnessed had a natural explanation, or was merely delusions of his tired nerves. But inwardly, in his very heart, he knew all along that someone had been hiding downstairs in the empty suite when he came in, that this person had watched his opportunity and then stealthily made his way up to the bedroom, and that all he saw and heard afterwards, from the moving of the kit-bag to—well, to the other things this story has to tell—were caused directly by the presence of this invisible person.

304

And it was here, just when he most desired to keep his mind and thoughts
controlled, that the vivid pictures received day after day upon the mental plates exposed in the courtroom of the Old Bailey, came strongly to light and developed themselves in the dark room of his inner vision. Unpleasant, haunting memories have a way of coming to life again just when the mind least desires them—in the silent watches of the night, on sleepless pillows, during the lonely hours spent by sick and dying beds. And so now, in the same way, Johnson saw nothing but the dreadful face of John Turk, the murderer, lowering at him from every corner of his mental field of vision; the white skin, the evil eyes, and the fringe of black hair low over the forehead. All the pictures of those ten days in court crowded back into his mind unbidden, and very vivid.

'This is all rubbish and nerves,' he exclaimed at length, springing with sudden energy from his chair. 'I shall finish my packing and go to bed. I'm overwrought[1], overtired. No doubt, at this rate I shall hear steps and things all night!'

But his face was deadly white all the same. He snatched up his field-glasses[2] and walked across to the bedroom, humming a music-hall song[3] as he went—a trifle too loud to be natural; and the instant he crossed the threshold and stood within the room something turned cold about his heart, and he felt that every hair on his head stood up.

The kit-bag lay close in front of him, several feet nearer to the door than he had left it, and just over its crumpled top he saw a head and face slowly sinking down out of sight as though someone were crouching behind it to hide, and at the same moment a sound like a long-drawn sigh was distinctly audible in the still air about him between the gusts of the storm outside.

---

[1] Tense, stressed, overworked
[2] Binoculars
[3] The Edwardian version of a cheap pop song – something common and peppy

Johnson had more courage and will-power than the girlish indecision[1] of his face indicated; but at first such a wave of terror came over him that for some seconds he could do nothing but stand and stare. A violent trembling ran down his back and legs, and he was conscious of a foolish, almost a hysterical[2], impulse to scream aloud. That sigh seemed in his very ear, and the air still quivered with it. It was unmistakably a human sigh.

'Who's there?' he said at length, finding his voice; but thought he meant to speak with loud decision, the tones came out instead in a faint whisper, for he had partly lost the control of his tongue and lips.

He stepped forward, so that he could see all round and over the kit-bag.

Of course there was nothing there, nothing but the faded carpet and the bulging canvas sides. He put out his hands and threw open the mouth of the sack where it had fallen over, being only three parts full, and then he saw for the first time that round the inside, some six inches from the top, there ran a broad smear of dull crimson. It was an old and faded blood stain. He uttered a scream, and drew hack his hands as if they had been burnt. At the same moment the kit-bag gave a faint, but unmistakable, lurch forward towards the door.

Johnson collapsed backwards, searching with his hands for the support of something solid, and the door, being further behind him than he realized, received his weight just in time to prevent his falling, and shut to with

---

[1] Once more referred to as girlish, Johnson rebounds and attempts to produce reserves of firm resolution. Blackwood here implies that Johnson may make an easy target – that regardless of his interior strengths, his exterior appearance and carriage exude a sense of helplessness, weakness, and dreamy naïveté

[2] "Hysterical" was a clinical term used by Victorian and early twentieth century physicians and psychologists. Literally meaning "affliction of the uterus," it was assumed that extreme bouts of irrational emotion in women were caused by disturbances in the womb. Although the usage had long since lost its literally usage (Freud had studied cases of "hysteria" in both sexes), the femininity of the word would not be lost on contemporaries

306

a resounding bang. At the same moment the swinging of his left arm accidentally touched the electric switch, and the light in the room went out.

It was an awkward and disagreeable predicament, and if Johnson had not been possessed of real pluck[1] he might have done all manner of foolish things[2]. As it was, however, he pulled himself together, and groped furiously for the little brass knob to turn the light on again. But the rapid closing of the door had set the coats hanging on it a-swinging, and his fingers became entangled in a confusion of sleeves and pockets, so that it was some moments before he found the switch. And in those few moments of bewilderment and terror two things happened that sent him beyond recall over the boundary into the region of genuine horror—he distinctly heard the kit-bag shuffling heavily across the floor in jerks, and close in front of his face sounded once again the sigh of a human being.

In his anguished efforts to find the brass button on the wall he nearly scraped the nails from his fingers, but even then, in those frenzied moments of alarm—so swift and alert are the impressions of a mind keyed-up by a vivid emotion—he had time to realize that he dreaded the return of the light, and that it might be better for him to stay hidden in the merciful screen of darkness. It was but the impulse of a moment, however, and before he had time to act upon it he had yielded automatically to the original desire, and the room was flooded again with light.

But the second instinct had been right. It would have been better for him to have stayed in the shelter of the kind darkness. For there, close before him, bending over the half-packed kit-bag, clear as life in the merciless glare of the electric light, stood the figure of John Turk, the murderer. Not three feet from him the man stood, the fringe of black hair marked plainly against the pallor of the forehead, the whole horrible presentment of the scoundrel, as vivid as he had seen him day

---

[1] Courage, resolve

[2] The subtle implication here is that he might have given into hysterics and gone mad, or found a way to destroy himself – perhaps by leaping out of the window

after day in the Old Bailey, when he stood there in the dock, cynical and callous, under the very shadow of the gallows.

In a flash Johnson realized what it all meant: the dirty and much-used bag; the smear of crimson within the top; the dreadful stretched condition of the bulging sides. He remembered how the victim's body had been stuffed into a canvas bag for burial, the ghastly, dismembered fragments forced with lime into this very bag; and the bag itself produced as evidence—it all came back to him as clear as day...

Very softly and stealthily his hand groped behind him for the handle of the door, but before he could actually turn it the very thing that he most of all dreaded came about, and John Turk lifted his devil's face and looked at him. At the same moment that heavy sigh passed through the air of the room, formulated somehow into words: 'It's my bag. And I want it.'

Johnson just remembered clawing the door open, and then falling in a heap upon the floor of the landing, as he tried frantically to make his way into the front room.

He remained unconscious for a long time, and it was still dark when he opened his eyes and realized that he was lying, stiff and bruised, on the cold boards. Then the memory of what he had seen rushed back into his mind, and he promptly fainted again. When he woke the second time the wintry dawn was just beginning to peep in at the windows, painting the stairs a cheerless, dismal grey, and he managed to crawl into the front room, and cover himself with an overcoat in the armchair, where at length he fell asleep.

A great clamour woke him. He recognized Mrs Monks's voice, loud and voluble.

'What! You ain't been to bed, sir! Are you ill, or has anything 'appened?

And there's an urgent gentleman to see you, though it ain't seven o'clock yet, and—'

'Who is it?' he stammered. 'I'm all right, thanks. Fell asleep in my chair, I suppose.'

'Someone from Mr Wilb'rim's, and he says he ought to see you quick before you go abroad, and I told him—'

'Show him up, please, at once,' said Johnson, whose head was whirling, and his mind was still full of dreadful visions.

308

Mr Wilbraham's man came in with many apologies, and explained briefly and quickly that an absurd mistake had been made, and that the wrong kit-bag had been sent over the night before.

'Henry somehow got hold of the one that came over from the courtoom, and
Mr Wilbraham only discovered it when he saw his own lying in his room, and asked why it had not gone to you,' the man said.

'Oh!' said Johnson stupidly.

'And he must have brought you the one from the murder case instead, sir,
I'm afraid,' the man continued, without the ghost of an expression on his face. "The one John Turk packed the dead body in. Mr Wilbraham's awful upset about it, sir, and told me to come over first thing this morning with the right one, as you were leaving by the boat.'

He pointed to a clean-looking kit-bag on the floor, which he had just brought. 'And I was to bring the other one back, sir,' he added casually.

For some minutes Johnson could not find his voice. At last he pointed in the direction of his bedroom. 'Perhaps you would kindly unpack it for me.
Just empty the things out on the floor.'

The man disappeared into the other room, and was gone for five minutes.
Johnson heard the shifting to and fro of the bag, and the rattle of the skates and boots being unpacked.

' Thank you, sir,' the man said, returning with the bag folded over his arm. 'And can I do anything more to help you, sir?'

'What is it?' asked Johnson, seeing that he still had something he wished to say.

The man shuffled and looked mysterious. 'Beg pardon, sir, but knowing your interest in the Turk case, I thought you'd maybe like to know what's
happened—'

'Yes.'

'John Turk killed hisself last night with poison immediately on getting his release, and he left a note for Mr Wilbraham saying as he'd be much obliged if they'd have him put away, same as the woman he murdered, in the old kit-hag.'

'What time—did he do it?' asked Johnson.
'Ten o'clock last night, sir, the warder says.'

---

*JOHNSON'S alienation may have mirrored Blackwood's own struggle to feel secure within the solid boundaries of Victorian masculinity: a member of the boy's club of New York journalism, and party to several perilous hunting expeditions into eastern Canada's woolly frontier, he was granted admission into a variety of male societies renowned for their machismo, posturing, and codes of manly standoffishness. In such situations, hints of femininity, sensitivity, or lack of nerve could spell professional and social peril. In the Canadian wilds they could spell desertion or death. Mike Ashley – in his foundational biography, An Extraordinary Life – suggests that Blackwood's lifelong bachelorhood and apparent later-life celibacy was due to an abysmal homosexual affair, a fact which he would have been eager to hide from his cronies in North America. Johnson – physiologically and constitutionally coded as anti-masculine – is neither afforded the hearty and inclusive fraternity of his peers, nor is he spared the predatory attentions of Turk, a man who butchered a woman and escaped the death penalty (assisted by Wilbraham's professional fraternity). Failing to fit in is lonely, painful, frustrating, and confusing. Failing to belong to the privileged class is also dangerous. Johnson is unable to shake Turk's subjecting gaze from his memory – it is dominating, challenging, and belittling. Away from the protection of his socially honored friends, nothing can restrain the threat that Turk represents from spilling over from unconscious insecurity to supernatural manifestation: namely, the threat of being recognized as different, stripped of the securities that homogeneity offers.*

NO collection of Victorian ghost stories would be complete without a glance into the British relationship with colonialism. Rudyard Kipling's "At the End of the Passage" and B.M. Croker's "'To Let'" are brilliant examples of how invading a foreign culture can conjure ghosts of guilt and regret in a heart once filled with imperialistic hubris, thirsty for wealth or adventure. Sir Arthur Conan Doyle was keenly aware of the disasters incurred by empire. Try to think of a single Sherlock Holmes adventure that didn't somehow involve a current (The Sign of Four, "The Speckled Band," "The Crooked Man") or former (A Study in Scarlet, Hound of the Baskervilles, "The Five Orange Pips") British colony – the dangers Holmes faces are almost always caused by the shadowy relationship between Britain and a colony. Dabbling in the affairs of another culture transforms the intruder – for better or worse – and the colonizer stands to become haunted by the ghosts of shame and rage that work their way back home. This story – despite its anglicized spellings and misconceptions (see footnotes) – is a rich study in colonial sins haunting the guilt -burdened malefactor in the perceived safety of the English countryside. The only cure to imperial crimes, Doyle suggests, is complete reimbursement, or – if the transgression is otherwise irredeemable – a "reasonable compromise."

---

## THE BROWN HAND
{1899}
### Sir Arthur Conan Doyle

EVERYONE KNOWS THAT SIR DOMINICK HOLDEN, the famous

---

[1] No further than the title and race has become an issue worth probing. Much like his similarly titled and hugely unpopular Sherlock Holmes tale, "The Yellow Face" (1893), Doyle immediately leaps to otherness in a bid to attract readership. There are very, very few Holmes stories that do not use either the colonies or former colonies to add an effect of drama to their plots. And yet, it is unfair to brand Doyle a blatant racist: this haunting does little to enhance the glory of British imperialism and much to decry it

Indian surgeon, made me his heir, and that his death changed me in an hour from a hard-working and impecunious young man to a well-to-do landed proprietor.

Many know also that there were at least five people between the inheritance and me, and that Sir Dominick's selection appeared to be altogether arbitrary and whimsical. I can assure them, however, that they are quite mistaken, and that, although I only knew Sir Dominick in the closing years of his life, there were, none the less, very real reasons why he should show his goodwill towards me. As a matter of fact, though I say it myself, no man ever did more for another than I did for my Indian uncle. I cannot expect the story to be believed, but it is so singular[1] that I should feel that it was a breach of duty if I did not put it upon record—so here it is, and your belief or incredulity is your own affair.

Sir Dominick Holden, C.B., K.C.S.I.[2], and I don't know what besides, was the most distinguished Indian surgeon of his day. In the Army originally, he afterwards settled down into civil practice in Bombay[3], and visited, as a
consultant, every part of India. His name is best remembered in connection with the Oriental Hospital, which he founded and supported. The time came, however, when his iron constitution began to show signs of the long strain to which he had subjected it, and his brother practitioners (who were not, perhaps, entirely disinterested upon the point) were unanimous in recommending him to return to England. He held on so long as he could, but at last he developed nervous symptoms of a very pronounced character, and so came back, a broken man, to his native county of Wiltshire[4]. He bought a considerable estate with an ancient manor-house upon the edge of Salisbury Plain[5], and devoted his old age to the study of Comparative

---

[1] A favorite Holmesian term of Doyle's – unique, unparalleled, bizarre
[2] Knighthoods. C.B. represents a Companion of the Order of Bath. K.C.S.I. represents a Knight Commander of the Order of the Star of India
[3] Mumbai. Located on the east coast of central India on the Arabian Sea
[4] Grassy, rolling county in southern England – due west of London – home to the town of Salisbury and the nearby prehistoric monoliths of Stonehenge
[5] No more purely English – and simultaneously foreboding – setting could be imagined

Pathology[1], which had been his learned hobby all his life, and in which he was a foremost authority.

We of the family were, as may be imagined, much excited by the news of the return of this rich and childless uncle to England. On his part, although by no means exuberant in his hospitality, he showed some sense of his duty to his relations, and each of us in turn had an invitation to visit him. From the accounts of my cousins it appeared to be a melancholy business, and it was with mixed feelings that I at last received my own summons to appear at Rodenhurst. My wife was so carefully excluded in the invitation that my first impulse was to refuse it, but the interests of the children had to be considered, and so, with her consent, I set out one October afternoon upon my visit to Wiltshire, with little thought of what that visit was to entail.

My uncle's estate was situated where the arable[2] land of the plains begins to swell upwards into the rounded chalk hills which are characteristic of the county. As I drove from Dinton Station in the waning light of that autumn day, I was impressed by the weird[3] nature of the scenery. The few scattered cottages of the peasants were so dwarfed by the huge evidences of prehistoric life that the present appeared to be a dream and the past to be the obtrusive and masterful reality. The road wound through the valleys, formed by a succession of grassy hills, and the summit of each was cut and carved into the most elaborate fortifications, some circular, and some square, but all on a scale which has defied the winds and the rains of many centuries. Some call them Roman and some British, but their true origin and the reasons for this particular tract of country being so interlaced with entrenchments have never been finally made clear[4]. Here and there on the long, smooth, olive-coloured slopes there rose small, rounded barrows or tumuli[5]. Beneath them lie the cremated ashes of the race which cut so deeply into the hills, but their graves tell us nothing save

---

[1] The comparative study of diseases across types and classes
[2] Suitable for farming
[3] Evoking the mystical, bizarre, and supernatural
[4] Both early Britons and Roman legions constructed earthwork fortifications along the coasts of Britain. The Roman fort of Cunetio was discovered in Wiltshire in 1940 after an aerial photograph of farmland revealed its traces
[5] Prehistoric mounds of earth covering burial plots

that a jar full of dust represents the man who once laboured under the sun[1].

It was through this weird country that I approached my uncle's residence of Rodenhurst, and the house was, as I found, in due keeping with its surroundings. Two broken and weather-stained pillars, each surmounted by a mutilated heraldic emblem[2], flanked the entrance to a neglected drive. A cold wind whistled through the elms which lined it, and the air was full of the drifting leaves. At the far end, under the gloomy arch of trees, a single yellow lamp burned steadily. In the dim half-light of the coming night I saw a long, low building stretching out two irregular wings, with deep eaves, a sloping gambrel roof[3], and walls which were criss-crossed with timber balks in the fashion of the Tudors. The cheery light of a fire flickered in the broad, latticed window to the left of the low-porched door, and this, as it proved, marked the study of my uncle, for it was thither that I was led by his butler in order to make my host's acquaintance.

He was cowering over his fire, for the moist chill of an English autumn had set him shivering. His lamp was unlit, and I only saw the red glow of the embers beating upon a huge, craggy face, with a Red Indian[4] nose and cheek, and deep furrows and seams from eye to chin, the sinister marks of hidden volcanic fires. He sprang up at my entrance with something of an old-world courtesy and welcomed me warmly to Rodenhurst. At the same time I was conscious, as the lamp was carried in, that it was a very critical pair of light-blue eyes which looked out at me from under shaggy eyebrows, like scouts beneath a bush, and that this outlandish uncle of mine was carefully reading off my character with all the ease of a practised observer and an experienced man of the world.

For my part I looked at him, and looked again, for I had never seen a man whose appearance was more fitted to hold one's attention. His

---

[1] A melancholy meditation indeed – the theme of works (such as Sir Dominick's charity) as being worthless is already drumming loudly
[2] A family crest or other design
[3] A roof typical of a Dutch colonial house or an American barn, with two sloping sides
[4] American Indian, that is to say

figure was the framework of a giant, but he had fallen away until his coat dangled straight down in a shocking fashion from a pair of broad and bony shoulders. All his limbs were huge yet emaciated, and I could not take my gaze from his knobby wrists, and long, gnarled hands. But his eyes—those peering, light-blue eyes—they were the most arrestive of any of his peculiarities. It was not their colour alone, nor was it the ambush of hair in which they lurked; but it was the expression which I read in them. For the appearance and bearing of the man were masterful, and one expected a certain corresponding arrogance in his eyes, but instead of that I read the look which tells of a spirit cowed and crushed, the furtive[1], expectant look of the dog whose master has taken the whip from the rack. I formed my own medical diagnosis upon one glance at those critical and yet appealing eyes. I believed that he was stricken with some mortal ailment, that he knew himself to be exposed to sudden death, and that he lived in terror of it. Such was my judgment—a false one, as the event showed; but I mention it that it may help you to realize the look which I read in his eyes.

My uncle's welcome was, as I have said, a courteous one, and in an hour or so I found myself seated between him and his wife at a comfortable dinner, with curious, pungent delicacies upon the table, and a stealthy, quick-eyed Oriental waiter behind his chair. The old couple had come round to that tragic imitation of the dawn of life when husband and wife, having lost or scattered all those who were their intimates, find themselves face to face and alone once more, their work done, and the end nearing fast. Those who have reached that stage in sweetness and love, who can change their winter into a gentle, Indian summer[2], have come as victors through the ordeal of life. Lady Holden was a small, alert woman with a kindly eye, and her expression as she glanced at him was a certificate of character to her husband. And yet, though I read a mutual love in their glances, I read also mutual horror, and recognized in her face some reflection of that stealthy fear which I had detected in his. Their talk was sometimes merry and sometimes sad, but there was a forced note in their

---

[1] Secretive
[2] A term that refers to an autumn where a pleasant heat wave appears after the first frost

merriment and a naturalness in their sadness which told me that a heavy heart beat upon either side of me.

We were sitting over our first glass of wine, and the servants had left the room, when the conversation took a turn which produced a remarkable effect upon my host and hostess. I cannot recall what it was which started the topic of the supernatural, but it ended in my showing them that the abnormal in psychical experiences was a subject to which I had, like many neurologists, devoted a great deal of attention. I concluded by narrating my experiences when, as a member of the Psychical Research Society[1], I had formed one of a committee of three who spent the night in a haunted house. Our adventures were neither exciting nor convincing, but, such as it was, the story appeared to interest my auditors in a remarkable degree. They listened with an eager silence, and I caught a look of intelligence between them which I could not understand. Lady Holden immediately afterwards rose and left the room.

Sir Dominick pushed the cigar-box over to me, and we smoked for some little time in silence. That huge, bony hand of his was twitching as he raised it with his cheroot[2] to his lips, and I felt that the man's nerves were vibrating like fiddle-strings. My instincts told me that he was on the verge of some intimate confidence, and I feared to speak lest I should interrupt it. At last he turned towards me with a spasmodic gesture like a man who throws his last scruple to the winds.

"From the little that I have seen of you it appears to me, Dr. Hardacre," said he, "that you are the very man I have wanted to meet."

"I am delighted to hear it, sir."

---

[1] Formed in 1882, this society of paranormal investigators included Doyle, Sigmund Freud, W.B. Yeats, Carl Jung, and many other luminaries. Its self-proclaimed mission was to understand "events and abilities commonly described as psychic or paranormal by promoting and supporting important research in this area" and to "examine allegedly paranormal phenomena in a scientific and unbiased way"

[2] A large cigar with both ends cut flush rather than tapering. They are traditionally associated with India and, in particular, Burma, where they remain popular

"Your head seems to be cool and steady. You will acquit me of any desire to flatter you, for the circumstances are too serious to permit of insincerities. You have some special knowledge upon these subjects, and you evidently view them from that philosophical standpoint which robs them of all vulgar[1] terror. I presume that the sight of an apparition would not seriously discompose you?"

"I think not, sir."

"Would even interest you, perhaps?" "Most intensely."

"As a psychical observer, you would probably investigate it in as impersonal a fashion as an astronomer investigates a wandering comet?"

"Precisely."

He gave a heavy sigh.

"Believe me, Dr. Hardacre, there was a time when I could have spoken as you do now. My nerve was a byword in India. Even the Mutiny[2] never shook it for an instant. And yet you see what I am reduced to—the most timorous[3] man, perhaps, in all this county of Wiltshire. Do not speak too bravely upon this subject, or you may find yourself subjected to as long-drawn a test as I am—a test which can only end in the madhouse or the grave."

I waited patiently until he should see fit to go farther in his confidence. His preamble had, I need not say, filled me with interest and expectation. "For some years, Dr. Hardacre," he continued, "my life and that of my wife have been made miserable by a cause which is so grotesque that it borders upon the ludicrous. And yet familiarity has never made it more easy to bear—on the contrary, as time passes my nerves become more worn and shattered by the constant

---

[1] Lower-classed, uneducated

[2] The Indian Rebellion of 1857 occurred when Indian soldiers in service to the British East India Company mutinied. It began over a rumor that the paper cartridges soldiers had to bite off to load their rifles were greased in pig and cow fat – offensive to both Muslims and Hindus respectively. The conflict was far from civil, being vicious, bloody, and inhuman. Massacres of surrendered garrisons, torture, and mass executions clouded the year with unforgettable violence

[3] Nervous, timid

attrition. If you have no physical fears, Dr. Hardacre, I should very much value your opinion upon this phenomenon which troubles us so."

"For what it is worth my opinion is entirely at your service. May I ask the nature of the phenomenon?"

"I think that your experiences will have a higher evidential value if you are not told in advance what you may expect to encounter. You are yourself aware of the quibbles of unconscious cerebration and subjective impressions with which a scientific sceptic may throw a doubt upon your statement. It would be as well to guard against them in advance[1]."

"What shall I do, then?"

"I will tell you. Would you mind following me this way?" He led me out of the dining-room and down a long passage until we came to a terminal door. Inside there was a large, bare room fitted as a laboratory, with numerous scientific instruments and bottles. A shelf ran along one side, upon which there stood a long line of glass jars containing pathological and anatomical specimens[2].

"You see that I still dabble in some of my old studies," said Sir Dominick. "These jars are the remains of what was once a most excellent collection, but unfortunately I lost the greater part of them when my house was burned down in Bombay in '92. It was a most unfortunate affair for me—in more ways than one. I had examples of many rare conditions, and my splenic collection was probably unique. These are the survivors."

I glanced over them, and saw that they really were of a very great value and rarity from a pathological point of view: bloated organs, gaping cysts, distorted bones, odious parasites—a singular exhibition of the products of India[3].

---

[1] Rhetoric undoubtedly lifted from the SPR's playbook – applying scientific process to supernaturalism naturally assists in developing veracity, respect, and credibility

[2] Tumors, diseased organs, deformed fetuses, and anatomical anomalies are likely candidates

[3] The "products of India" are repulsive, hateful, parasitic deformities – Doyle seems to suggest that Britain's dalliances in colonialism (and in India's case,

"There is, as you see, a small settee[1] here," said my host. "It was far from our intention to offer a guest so meagre an accommodation, but since affairs have taken this turn, it would be a great kindness upon your part if you would consent to spend the night in this apartment. I beg that you will not hesitate to let me know if the idea should be at all repugnant to you."

"On the contrary," I said, "it is most acceptable."

"My own room is the second on the left, so that if you should feel that you are in need of company a call would always bring me to your side."

"I trust that I shall not be compelled to disturb you."

"It is unlikely that I shall be asleep. I do not sleep much. Do not hesitate to summon me."

And so with this agreement we joined Lady Holden in the drawing-room and talked of lighter things. It was no affectation upon my part to say that the prospect of my night's adventure was an agreeable one. I have no pretence to greater physical courage than my neighbours, but familiarity with a subject robs it of those vague and undefined terrors which are the most appalling to the imaginative mind. The human brain is capable of only one strong emotion at a time, and if it be filled with curiosity or scientific enthusiasm, there is no room for fear. It is true that I had my uncle's assurance that he had himself originally taken this point of view, but I reflected that the break-down of his nervous system might be due to his forty years in

---

brutal colonialism) have come back to haunt the national conscience, and that, like Indian parasites revoltingly pickled in a British study, these moral shames have not remained neatly behind in their country of origin

[1] Comfortable seat for two persons

India as much as to any psychical experiences which had befallen him. I at least was sound in nerve and brain, and it was with something of the pleasurable thrill of anticipation with which the sportsman takes his position beside the haunt of his game that I shut the laboratory door behind me, and partially undressing, lay down upon the rug-covered settee.

It was not an ideal atmosphere for a bedroom. The air was heavy with many chemical odours, that of methylated spirit[1] predominating. Nor were the decorations of my chamber very sedative[2]. The odious line of glass jars with their relics of disease and suffering[3] stretched in front of my very eyes. There was no blind to the window, and a three-quarter moon streamed its white light into the room, tracing a silver square with filigree[4] lattices upon the opposite wall. When I had extinguished my candle this one bright patch in the midst of the general gloom had certainly an eerie and discomposing aspect. A rigid and absolute silence reigned throughout the old house, so that the low swish of the branches in the garden came softly and smoothly to my ears. It may have been the hypnotic lullaby of this gentle susurrus[5], or it may have been the result of my tiring day, but after many dozings and many efforts to regain my clearness of perception, I fell at last into a deep and dreamless sleep.

I was awakened by some sound in the room, and I instantly raised myself upon my elbow on the couch. Some hours had passed, for the square patch upon the wall had slid downwards and sideways until it lay obliquely at the end of my bed. The rest of the room was in deep shadow. At first I could see nothing, presently, as my eyes became accustomed to the faint light, I was aware, with a thrill which all my

---

[1] Denatured alcohol; ethanol laced with caustic additives to discourage drinking, with many uses in the industrial, medical, commercial, and janitorial fields – in this case, pickling tissue
[2] Relaxing, conducive to sleep
[3] "relics of disease and suffering..." once more we are reminded that the impact of colonialism in India has not been one-sided – the British public is conscious of their shame and guilt
[4] Delicate metalwork
[5] Whimpering, murmuring noise

scientific absorption could not entirely prevent, that something was moving slowly along the line of the wall. A gentle, shuffling sound, as of soft slippers, came to my ears, and I dimly discerned a human figure walking stealthily from the direction of the door. As it emerged into the patch of moonlight I saw very clearly what it was and how it was employed. It was a man, short and squat, dressed in some sort of dark-grey gown, which hung straight from his shoulders to his feet. The moon shone upon the side of his face, and I saw that it was chocolate-brown in colour, with a ball of black hair like a woman's at the back of his head. He walked slowly, and his eyes were cast upwards towards the line of bottles which contained those gruesome remnants of humanity. He seemed to examine each jar with attention, and then to pass on to the next. When he had come to the end of the line, immediately opposite my bed, he stopped, faced me, threw up his hands with a gesture of despair, and vanished from my sight.

I have said that he threw up his hands, but I should have said his arms, for as he assumed that attitude of despair I observed a singular peculiarity about his appearance. He had only one hand! As the sleeves drooped down from the upflung arms I saw the left plainly, but the right ended in a knobby and unsightly[1] stump. In every other way his appearance was so natural, and I had both seen and heard him so clearly, that I could easily have believed that he was an Indian servant of Sir Dominick's who had come into my room in search of something. It was only his sudden disappearance which suggested anything more sinister to me. As it was I sprang from my couch, lit a candle, and examined the whole room carefully. There were no signs of my visitor, and I was forced to conclude that there had really been something outside the normal laws of Nature in his appearance. I lay awake for the remainder of the night, but nothing else occurred to disturb me.

I am an early riser, but my uncle was an even earlier one, for I found him pacing up and down the lawn at the side of the house. He ran towards me in his eagerness when he saw me come out from the door.

---

[1] *Unsightly*. Once more, Doyle evinces feelings of discomfort, shame, repulsion, and "unsightliness" that could be compared to the national conscience of the United Kingdom in the later stages of British imperialism

"Well, well!" he cried. "Did you see him?" "An Indian with one hand?"

"Precisely."

"Yes, I saw him"—and I told him all that occurred. When I had finished, he led the way into his study.

"We have a little time before breakfast," said he. "It will suffice to give you an explanation of this extraordinary affair—so far as I can explain that which is essentially inexplicable. In the first place, when I tell you that for four years I have never passed one single night, either in Bombay, aboard ship, or here in England without my sleep being broken by this fellow, you will understand why it is that I am a wreck of my former self. His programme[1] is always the same. He appears by my bedside, shakes me roughly by the shoulder, passes from my room into the laboratory, walks slowly along the line of my bottles, and then vanishes. For more than a thousand times he has gone through the same routine."

"What does he want?"

"He wants his hand."

"His hand?"

"Yes, it came about in this way. I was summoned to Peshawur[2] for a consultation some ten years ago, and while there I was asked to look at the hand of a native who was passing through with an Afghan caravan. The fellow came from some mountain tribe living away at the back of beyond somewhere on the other side of Kaffiristan[3]. He talked a bastard Pushtoo[4], and it was all I could do to understand him. He was suffering from a soft sarcomatous[5] swelling of one of the metacarpal[6] joints, and I made him realize that it was only by losing his hand that he could hope to save his life. After much persuasion he consented to the operation, and he asked me, when it was over, what fee I

---

[1] Schedule, agenda, routine
[2] *Peshawar* is a city situated in northeast Pakistan, near the Afghani border

[3] *Kāfiristān* is a historical region in southeastern Afghanistan
[4] *Pashto* is a central Asian language also loosely called Afghani
[5] A malignant tumor rising from connective tissues
[6] Situated between the wrist and fingers

demanded. The poor fellow was almost a beggar, so that the idea of a fee was absurd, but I answered in jest that my fee should be his hand, and that I proposed to add it to my pathological collection.

"To my surprise he demurred very much to the suggestion, and he explained that according to his religion it was an all-important matter that the body should be reunited after death, and so make a perfect dwelling for the spirit. The belief is, of course, an old one, and the mummies of the Egyptians arose from an analogous superstition. I answered him that his hand was already off, and asked him how he intended to preserve it. He replied that he would pickle it in salt and carry it about with him. I suggested that it might be safer in my keeping than in his, and that I had better means than salt for preserving it. On realizing that I really intended to carefully keep it, his opposition vanished instantly. 'But remember, sahib[1],' said he, 'I shall want it back when I am dead.' I laughed at the remark, and so the matter ended. I returned to my practice, and he no doubt in the course of time was able to continue his journey to Afghanistan.

"Well, as I told you last night, I had a bad fire in my house at Bombay. Half of it was burned down, and, amongst other things, my pathological collection was largely destroyed. What you see are the poor remains of it. The hand of the hillman went with the rest, but I gave the matter no particular thought at the time. That was six years ago.

"Four years ago—two years after the fire—I was awakened one night by a furious tugging at my sleeve. I sat up under the impression that my favourite mastiff was trying to arouse me. Instead of this, I saw my Indian patient of long ago, dressed in the long, grey gown which was the badge of his people. He was holding up his stump and looking reproachfully at me. He then went over to my bottles, which at that time I kept in my room, and he examined them carefully, after which he gave a gesture of anger and vanished. I realized that he had just died, and that he had come to claim my promise that I should keep his limb in safety for him.

"Well, there you have it all, Dr. Hardacre. Every night at the same

---

[1] South Indian address to a respectable man (cf. *mynheer, mein Herr, monsieur, senior*)

hour for four years this performance has been repeated. It is a simple thing in itself, but it has worn me out like water dropping on a stone. It has brought a vile insomnia with it, for I cannot sleep now for the expectation of his coming. It has poisoned my old age and that of my wife, who has been the sharer in this great trouble. But there is the breakfast gong, and she will be waiting impatiently to know how it fared with you last night. We are both much indebted to you for your gallantry, for it takes something from the weight of our misfortune when we share it, even for a single night, with a friend, and it reassures us to our sanity, which we are sometimes driven to question."

This was the curious narrative which Sir Dominick confided to me— a story which to many would have appeared to be a grotesque impossibility, but which, after my experience of the night before, and my previous knowledge of such things, I was prepared to accept as an absolute fact. I thought deeply over the matter, and brought the whole range of my reading and experience to bear over it. After breakfast, I surprised my host and hostess by announcing that I was returning to London by the next train. "My dear doctor," cried Sir Dominick in great distress, "you make me feel that I have been guilty of a gross breach of hospitality in intruding this unfortunate matter upon you. I should have borne my own burden."

"It is, indeed, that matter which is taking me to London," I answered; "but you are mistaken, I assure you, if you think that my experience of last night was an unpleasant one to me. On the contrary, I am about to ask your permission to return in the evening and spend one more night in your laboratory. I am very eager to see this visitor once again."

My uncle was exceedingly anxious to know what I was about to do, but my fears of raising false hopes prevented me from telling him. I was back in my own consulting-room a little after luncheon, and was confirming my memory of a passage in a recent book upon occultism which had arrested my attention when I read it.

"In the case of earth-bound spirits," said my authority, "some one dominant idea obsessing them at the hour of death is sufficient to hold them in this material world. They are the amphibia of this life and of the next, capable of passing from one to the other as the turtle passes from land to water. The causes which may bind a soul so strongly to a life which its body has abandoned are any violent emotion. Avarice, revenge, anxiety, love, and pity have all been known to have this effect. As a rule it springs from some unfulfilled wish, and when the wish has been fulfilled the material bond relaxes. There are many cases upon record which show the singular persistence of these visitors, and also their disappearance when their wishes have been fulfilled, or in some cases when a reasonable compromise has been effected."[1]

"*A reasonable compromise effected*"—those were the words which I had brooded over all the morning, and which I now verified in the original. No actual atonement could be made here—but a reasonable compromise! I made my way as fast as a train could take me to the Shadwell Seamen's Hospital, where my old friend Jack Hewett was house-surgeon. Without explaining the situation I made him understand what it was that I wanted.

"A brown man's hand!" said he, in amazement. "What in the world do you want that for?"

"Never mind. I'll tell you some day. I know that your wards are full of Indians."

"I should think so. But a hand—" He thought a little, and then struck a bell.

"Travers," said he to a student-dresser, "what became of the hands of the Lascar[2] which we took off yesterday? I mean the fellow from the East India Dock who got caught in the steam winch."

"They are in the *post-mortem* room, sir."

"Just pack one of them in antiseptics and give it to Dr. Hardacre."

And so I found myself back at Rodenhurst before dinner with this curious outcome of my day in town. I still said nothing to Sir Dominick, but I slept that night in the laboratory, and I placed the Lascar's hand in one of the glass jars at the end of my couch.

So interested was I in the result of my experiment that sleep was out of the question. I sat with a shaded lamp beside me and waited patiently for my visitor. This time I saw him clearly from the first. He

---

[1] This is a very excellent summarization of the principle theory – both in literature and among 19th century spiritualists – of who ghosts are and why they remain. A more concise but exhaustive explanation could not be hoped for

[2] A southeast Indian menial worker – in this case, a sailor

appeared beside the door, nebulous[1] for an instant, and then hardening into as distinct an outline as any living man. The slippers beneath his grey gown were red and heelless, which accounted for the low, shuffling sound which he made as he walked. As on the previous night he passed slowly along the line of bottles until he paused before that which contained the hand. He reached up to it, his whole figure quivering with expectation, took it down, examined it eagerly, and then, with a face which was convulsed with fury and disappointment, he hurled it down on the floor. There was a crash which resounded throughout the house, and when I looked up the mutilated Indian had disappeared. A moment later my door flew open and Sir Dominick rushed in.

"You are not hurt?" he cried.

"No—but deeply disappointed."

He looked in astonishment at the splinters of glass, and the brown hand lying upon the floor.

"Good God!" he cried. "What is this?"

I told him my idea and its wretched sequel. He listened intently, but shook his head.

"It was well thought of," said he, "but I fear that there is no such easy end to my sufferings. But one thing I now insist upon. It is that you shall never again upon any pretext occupy this room. My fears that something might have happened to you—when I heard that crash—have been the most acute of all the agonies which I have undergone. I will not expose myself to a repetition of it."

He allowed me, however, to spend the remainder of the night where I was, and I lay there worrying over the problem and lamenting my own failure. With the first light of morning there was the Lascar's hand still lying upon the floor to remind me of my fiasco. I lay looking at it—and as I lay suddenly an idea flew like a bullet through my head and brought me quivering with excitement out of my couch. I raised the grim relic from where it had fallen. Yes, it was indeed so. The hand was the *left* hand of the Lascar.

By the first train I was on my way to town, and hurried at once to the

---

[1] Unclear, hazy

327

Seamen's Hospital. I remembered that both hands of the Lascar had been amputated, but I was terrified lest the precious organ which I was in search of might have been already consumed in the crematory[1]. My suspense was soon ended. It had still been preserved in the *post-mortem* room. And so I returned to Rodenhurst in the evening with my mission accomplished and the material for a fresh experiment.

But Sir Dominick Holden would not hear of my occupying the laboratory again. To all my entreaties he turned a deaf ear. It offended his sense of hospitality, and he could no longer permit it. I left the hand, therefore, as I had done its fellow the night before, and I occupied a comfortable bedroom in another portion of the house, some distance from the scene of my adventures.

But in spite of that my sleep was not destined to be uninterrupted. In the dead of night my host burst into my room, a lamp in his hand. His huge, gaunt figure was enveloped in a loose dressing-gown, and his whole appearance might certainly have seemed more formidable to a weak-nerved man than that of the Indian of the night before. But it was not his entrance so much as his expression which amazed me. He had turned suddenly younger by twenty years at the least. His eyes were shining, his features radiant, and he waved one hand in triumph over his head. I sat up astounded, staring sleepily at this extraordinary visitor. But his words soon drove the sleep from my eyes.

"We have done it! We have succeeded!" he shouted. "My dear Hardacre, how can I ever in this world repay you?"

"You don't mean to say that it is all right?"

"Indeed I do. I was sure that you would not mind being awakened to hear such blessed news."

"Mind! I should think not indeed. But is it really certain?"

"I have no doubt whatever upon the point. I owe you such a debt, my dear nephew, as I have never owed a man before, and never expected to. What can I possibly do for you that is commensurate[2]? Providence must have sent you to my rescue. You have saved both my reason and my life, for another six months of this must have seen me

---

[1] Furnace where unclaimed bodies were cremated
[2] A proportional favor in return

either in a cell[1] or a coffin. And my wife—it was wearing her out before my eyes. Never could I have believed that any human being could have lifted this burden off me." He seized my hand and wrung it in his bony grip.

"It was only an experiment—a forlorn hope—but I am delighted from my heart that it has succeeded. But how do you know that it is all right? Have you seen something?"

He seated himself at the foot of my bed.

"I have seen enough," said he. "It satisfies me that I shall be troubled no more. What has passed is easily told. You know that at a certain hour this creature always comes to me. To-night he arrived at the usual time, and aroused me with even more violence than is his custom. I can only surmise that his disappointment of last night increased the bitterness of his anger against me. He looked angrily at me, and then went on his usual round. But in a few minutes I saw him, for the fist time since this persecution began, return to my chamber. He was smiling. I saw the gleam of his white teeth through the dim light. He stood facing me at the end of my bed, and three times he made the low Eastern salaam[2] which is their solemn leave-taking. And the third time that he bowed he raised his arms over his head, and I saw his *two* hands outstretched in the air. So he vanished, and, as I believe, for ever."

So that is the curious experience which won me the affection and the gratitude of my celebrated uncle, the famous Indian surgeon. His anticipations were realised, and never again was he disturbed by the visits of the restless hillman in search of his lost member. Sir Dominick and Lady Holden spent a very happy old age, unclouded, so far as I know, by any trouble, and they finally died during the great influenza epidemic[3] within a few weeks of each other. In his lifetime he always turned to me for advice in everything which concerned that English life of which he knew so little; and I aided him also in the purchase and

---

[1] At a madhouse

[2] A deep bow with the right hand on the forehead commonly practiced in Muslim cultures, *salām* meaning "peace" in Arabic

[3] The Russian Flu of 1889-1890 swept across Europe, the Americas, and Asia taking the lives of some one million people. It remains the earliest flu pandemic in recorded history

development of his estates. It was no great surprise to me, therefore, that I found myself eventually promoted over the heads of five exasperated cousins, and changed in a single day from a hard-working country doctor into the head of an important Wiltshire family. I, at least, have reason to bless the memory of the man with the brown hand, and the day when I was fortunate enough to relieve Rodenhurst of his unwelcome presence.

---

*INFUSING his ghost tale with a taste of the logic and deduction of Sherlock Holmes, Conan Doyle provides a solution to race relations in the British Empire – making symbolic reparations in place of irredeemable losses to Anglo-Saxon colonial ventures. Life and limb may not be replicable, but suitable compensations and national gestures of apology can be made. Other Doyle ghost stories ("The Leather Funnel," "Captain of the Polestar," and "How it Happened" being three) have far grimmer plots, but this one attempts to exorcise a social ill rather than take the pessimistic stance that many colonial ghost stories (see: Kipling) strike. Images of decayed invaders feature prominently in the landscape with its Roman ruins, foreshadowing the Empire's ghostly fate if left unaltered, draping the plot in a dreary pall of constricting doom. While the specter is certainly not duped into believing the replacement hand to be the original, it responds to a respectful effort to right the wrong (no pun intended). After this the suffocating vapors dissipate from the English countryside. A similar effort, Doyle ventures, would exorcise the demons of the spiritually anemic Victorian society.*

ON *June 9, 1865 at 3:13 in the afternoon, an elderly Charles Dickens was travelling by train with his mistress and her mother in southeastern England when the Folkestone-to-London train derailed near Staplehurst due to a signalman's negligence. The Staplehurst Rail Crash took the lives of ten and left forty injured – some of whom died in Dickens' arms. The author was traumatized. He lost his voice for two weeks afterward, and avoided trains with phobic anxiety. Dying five years later on June 9, 1870, Dickens, as his son stated, "never fully recovered" from the shock. Written a year after the disaster, this cathartic ghost tale features a responsible signalman haunted in an emotionally exhaustive sense by Dickens' own wasting phantom: the helplessness to save life in spite of one's best efforts. The titular railroadman's angst mirrors Dickens' eerily. He is a man who accepts his unnecessarily menial role in society, not daring to change his station or aspire to better himself. "The Signal-Man" is a grim and chilling study both in man's desperate inability to alter the fates of others, and in his stubborn unwillingness to affect the one life which he may reasonably hope to better, or even save: his own.*

---

## THE SIGNAL-MAN[1]
{1866}
### Charles Dickens

"HALLOA! BELOW THERE[2]!"

When he[3] heard a voice thus calling to him, he was standing at the

---

[1] An employee of the railroad transport network who operates the signals from a signal box overlooking the rails in order to control the movement of trains

[2] "Bellow *there*" – Immediately, separation and isolation are thematically introduced

[3] Although the story is told in first person, it begins in third – the signalman is instantly made the tale's focus – a solitary man who is the object rather than the subject of human society

door of his box[1], with a flag in his hand, furled round its short pole. One would have thought, considering the nature of the ground, that he could not have doubted from what quarter the voice came; but instead of looking up to where I stood on the top of the steep cutting[2] nearly over his head, he turned himself about, and looked down the Line. There was something remarkable in his manner of doing so, though I could not have said for my life what. But I know it was remarkable enough to attract my notice, even though his figure was foreshortened and shadowed, down in the deep trench, and mine was high above him, so steeped in the glow of an angry sunset[3], that I had shaded my eyes with my hand before I saw him at all.

"Halloa! Below!"

From looking down the Line, he turned himself about again, and, raising his eyes, saw my figure high above him.

"Is there any path by which I can come down and speak to you?"

He looked up at me without replying, and I looked down at him without pressing him too soon with a repetition of my idle question. Just then there came a vague vibration in the earth and air[4], quickly changing into a violent pulsation, and an oncoming rush that caused

---

[1] Usually a small brick building with large windows on three sides, elevated high over the tracks to allow the signalman a means of warmth, shelter, and perspective, allowing him to see the rails in both directions. From here he operates mechanical (telegram signals raised by pulleys) and manual (flags and colored lanterns) signals in order to direct engineers or warn of danger. Bells engaged by passing locomotives communicated when a train was approaching, and telegraphs communicated between signal boxes down the line and from conductors' cabooses

[2] A hill or rock formation that has been transfixed (or "cut through") to allow for a narrow road, canal, or railway track to pass through an otherwise impassible landscape

[3] Sunsets are usually typified as beautiful – sublime at the worst – and seen as having a spiritual, even religious quality. That the sunset is "angry" informs us of the manner of universe that this tale is set in: hostile, indifferent, malicious

[4] The very elements – earth and air, physical and psychical, material and spiritual – are disturbed in this chaotic environment where industry has violated nature

me to start back, as though it had force to draw me down. When such vapour as rose to my height from this rapid train had passed me, and was skimming away over the landscape, I looked down again, and saw him refurling the flag he had shown while the train went by.

I repeated my inquiry. After a pause, during which he seemed to regard me with fixed attention, he motioned with his rolled-up flag towards a point on my level, some two or three hundred yards distant. I called down to him, "All right!" and made for that point. There, by dint of looking closely about me, I found a rough zigzag descending path notched out, which I followed.

The cutting was extremely deep, and unusually precipitate[1]. It was made through a clammy stone, that became oozier and wetter as I went down. For these reasons, I found the way long enough to give me time to recall a singular air of reluctance or compulsion[2] with which he had pointed out the path.

When I came down low enough upon the zigzag descent to see him again, I saw that he was standing between the rails on the way by which the train had lately passed, in an attitude as if he were waiting for me to appear. He had his left hand at his chin, and that left elbow rested on his right hand, crossed over his breast. His attitude was one of such expectation and watchfulness that I stopped a moment, wondering at it.

I resumed my downward way, and stepping out upon the level of the railroad, and drawing nearer to him, saw that he was a dark, sallow man, with a dark beard and rather heavy eyebrows[3]. His post was in as solitary and dismal a place as ever I saw. On either side, a dripping-wet wall of jagged stone, excluding all view but a strip of sky[4]; the perspective one way only a crooked prolongation of this great

---

[1] Sudden, steep – it is difficult to reach this sad, isolated man in his spiritual banishment

[2] The signalman is comfortable in his alienation – resistant to accepting company

[3] An earthy, almost underworldly appearance – his exterior matches his surroundings, indicating the nature of his spirit: remote and hidden

[4] Read: heaven, spiritual health, transcendence of the soul over sin, dread, and misery

dungeon; the shorter perspective in the other direction terminating in a gloomy red light[1], and the gloomier entrance to a black tunnel[2], in whose massive architecture there was a barbarous, depressing, and forbidding air. So little sunlight ever found its way to this spot, that it had an earthy, deadly smell; and so much cold wind rushed through it, that it struck chill to me, as if I had left the natural world.

Before he stirred, I was near enough to him to have touched him. Not even then removing his eyes from mine, he stepped back one step, and lifted his hand.

This was a lonesome post to occupy (I said), and it had riveted my attention when I looked down from up yonder. A visitor was a rarity, I should suppose; not an unwelcome rarity, I hoped? In me, he merely saw a man who had been shut up within narrow limits all his life, and who, being at last set free, had a newly-awakened interest in these great works. To such purpose I spoke to him; but I am far from sure of the terms I used; for, besides that I am not happy in opening any conversation, there was something in the man that daunted me.

He directed a most curious look towards the red light near the tunnel's mouth, and looked all about it, as if something were missing from it, and then looked at me.

That light was part of his charge? Was it not?

He answered in a low voice,—"Don't you know it is[3]?"

The monstrous thought came into my mind, as I perused the fixed eyes and the saturnine[4] face, that this was a spirit, not a man. I have speculated since, whether there may have been infection in his mind[5].

---

[1] A hellish tint suggesting blood and damnation -- the only light (read: illumination, truth, spiritual clarity) in this gravelike place comes from a soullessly practical, industrial tool

[2] Symbolic of the unconscious, the cosmic void

[3] The exchange is bizarre and redolent with subtextual meaning. The narrator questions the signalman's responsibility for the manufactured illumination, and the operator responds defensively, asserting his ownership of and comfort with the subterranean world

[4] Gloomy, morose

[5] This questioning of the signalman's sanity casts him as a somewhat unreliable narrator

In my turn, I stepped back. But in making the action, I detected in his eyes some latent fear of me. This put the monstrous thought to flight.

"You look at me," I said, forcing a smile, "as if you had a dread of me." "I was doubtful," he returned, "whether I had seen you before." "Where?"

He pointed to the red light he had looked at.

"There?" I said.

Intently watchful of me, he replied (but without sound), "Yes."

"My good fellow, what should I do there? However, be that as it may, I never was there, you may swear."

"I think I may," he rejoined. "Yes; I am sure I may."

His manner cleared, like my own. He replied to my remarks with readiness, and in well-chosen words. Had he much to do there? Yes; that was to say, he had enough responsibility to bear; but exactness and watchfulness were what was required of him[1], and of actual work—manual labour—he had next to none. To change that signal, to trim those lights, and to turn this iron handle now and then, was all he had to do under that head. Regarding those many long and lonely hours of which I seemed to make so much, he could only say that the routine of his life had shaped itself into that form, and he had grown used to it. He had taught himself a language down here,—if only to know it by sight, and to have formed his own crude ideas of its pronunciation, could be called learning it[2]. He had also worked at fractions and decimals, and tried a little algebra; but he was, and had been as a boy, a poor hand at figures. Was it necessary for him when on duty always to remain in that channel of damp air, and could he never rise into the sunshine from between those high stone walls?

---

[1] The signalman is a paragon of Victorian duty – a watchful, alert, industrious exemplar of British expectations for the lower-middle class and public servants. He attends to his duties unquestioningly, performing them with a passion that confines his soul to his work

[2] He has learned a language (likely French or German, possibly Italian), but only by sight; he has no expectations of speaking it to another human soul, only of reading the sterile print

Why, that depended upon times and circumstances[1]. Under some conditions there would be less upon the Line than under others, and the same held good as to certain hours of the day and night. In bright weather, he did choose occasions for getting a little above these lower shadows; but, being at all times liable to be called by his electric bell, and at such times listening for it with redoubled anxiety, the relief was less than I would suppose.

He took me into his box, where there was a fire, a desk for an official book in which he had to make certain entries, a telegraphic instrument with its dial, face, and needles, and the little bell of which he had spoken. On my trusting that he would excuse the remark that he had been well educated, and (I hoped I might say without offence) perhaps educated above that station[2], he observed that instances of slight incongruity[3] in such wise would rarely be found wanting among large bodies of men; that he had heard it was so in workhouses, in the police force, even in that last desperate resource, the army; and that he knew it was so, more or less, in any great railway staff[4]. He had been, when young (if I could believe it, sitting in that hut,—he scarcely could), a student of natural philosophy[5], and had attended lectures; but he had run wild, misused his opportunities, gone down, and never risen again[6].

---

[1] His physical, psychological, and spiritual well-being is restrained by the duties of his job, and he happily forfeits their care in the pursuit of his responsibilities

[2] Critically, the signalman has demonstrated that he is capable of elevating himself beyond his job. Having educated himself beyond the expectations of a minor railway functionary, he could – if he so chose – remove himself from the grave-like cutting

[3] Inappropriateness

[4] The signalman's excuse is that he is not an anomaly, and that his education would do him no good because plenty of equally knowledable men continue to toil as lower middle class functionaries in the nation's service organizations

[5] The philosophical study of nature and the physical universe – in a word, science, but with an inclination towards theoretical philosophy

[6] A typical Dickensian character, the signalman has been diverted from a more personally and spiritually fulfilling life by the forces of society and the

He had no complaint to offer about that. He had made his bed, and he lay upon it. It was far too late to make another[1]. All that I have here condensed he said in a quiet manner, with his grave, dark regards divided between me and the fire. He threw in the word, "Sir," from time to time, and especially when he referred to his youth,—as though to request me to understand that he claimed to be nothing but what I found him[2]. He was several times interrupted by the little bell, and had to read off messages, and send replies. Once he had to stand without the door, and display a flag as a train passed, and make some verbal communication to the driver. In the discharge of his duties, I observed him to be remarkably exact and vigilant, breaking off his discourse at a syllable, and remaining silent until what he had to do was done[3].

In a word, I should have set this man down as one of the safest of men to be employed in that capacity, but for the circumstance that while he was speaking to me he twice broke off with a fallen colour, turned his face towards the little bell when it did NOT ring, opened the door of the hut (which was kept shut to exclude the unhealthy damp), and looked out towards the red light near the mouth of the tunnel. On both of those occasions, he came back to the fire with the inexplicable air upon him which I had remarked, without being able to define, when we were so far asunder.

Said I, when I rose to leave him, "You almost make me think that I have met with a contented man."

(I am afraid I must acknowledge that I said it to lead him on[4].)

---

industrial revolution, and has become mired in a depressing and dehumanizing occupation that pits vital nature against cold industry

[1] Psychologists would say that the signalman has an exterior locus of power: he believes that he is at the mercy of a hostile world and that his actions to benefit himself will be useless. In short, he is a pessimist who resists any suggestion that he act to improve his life

[2] Although he is demonstrably more than a minion of the railway, he resists any possibilities

[3] Efficient, dutiful – an obedient underling to the class-conscious demands of society

[4] The signalman avoids honest conversation, so the narrator attempt to lure him into a dialog

"I believe I used to be so," he rejoined, in the low voice in which he had first spoken; "but I am troubled, sir, I am troubled."

He would have recalled the words if he could. He had said them, however, and I took them up quickly.

"With what? What is your trouble?"

"It is very difficult to impart, sir. It is very, very difficult to speak of. If ever you make me another visit, I will try to tell you."

"But I expressly intend to make you another visit. Say, when shall it be?" "I go off early in the morning, and I shall be on again at ten to-morrow night, sir."

"I will come at eleven."

He thanked me, and went out at the door with me. "I'll show my white light, sir," he said, in his peculiar low voice, "till you have found the way up. When you have found it, don't call out! And when you are at the top, don't call out!"

His manner seemed to make the place strike colder to me, but I said no more than, "Very well."

"And when you come down to-morrow night, don't call out! Let me ask you a parting question. What made you cry, 'Halloa! Below there!' to-night?"

"Heaven knows," said I. "I cried something to that effect—"

"Not to that effect, sir. Those were the very words. I know them well." "Admit those were the very words. I said them, no doubt, because I saw you below."

"For no other reason?"

"What other reason could I possibly have?"

"You had no feeling that they were conveyed to you in any supernatural way?"

"No."

He wished me good-night, and held up his light. I walked by the side of the down Line of rails (with a very disagreeable sensation of a train coming behind me[1]) until I found the path. It was easier to mount than to descend, and I got back to my inn without any adventure.

Punctual to my appointment, I placed my foot on the first notch of the zigzag next night, as the distant clocks were striking eleven. He was waiting for me at the bottom, with his white light on. "I have not called out," I said, when we came close together; "may I speak now?"

"By all means, sir."

"Good-night, then, and here's my hand." "Good-night, sir, and here's mine." With that we walked side by side to his box, entered it, closed the door, and sat down by the fire.

"I have made up my mind, sir," he began, bending forward as soon as we were seated, and speaking in a tone but a little above a whisper, "that you shall not have to ask me twice what troubles me. I took you for some one else yesterday evening. That troubles me."

"That mistake?"

"No. That some one else." "Who is it?"

"I don't know." "Like me?"

"I don't know. I never saw the face. The left arm is across the face, and the right arm is waved,—violently waved. This way."

I followed his action with my eyes, and it was the action of an arm gesticulating, with the utmost passion and vehemence, "For God's sake, clear the way!"

"One moonlight night," said the man, "I was sitting here, when I heard a voice cry, 'Halloa! Below there!' I started up, looked from that door, and saw this. Some one else standing by the red light near the tunnel, waving as I just now showed you.

---

[1] A tremendously eerie and ominous experience the suggests the presence of a great, hurtling force of destruction lurking in the signalman's underworld, and prefiguring events to come

339

The voice seemed hoarse with shouting, and it cried,

'Look out! Look out!' And then again, 'Halloa! Below there! Look out!' I caught up my lamp, turned it on red[1], and ran towards the figure, calling, 'What's wrong? What has happened? Where?' It stood just outside the blackness of the tunnel. I advanced so close upon it that I wondered at its keeping the sleeve across its eyes. I ran right up at it, and had my hand stretched out to pull the sleeve away, when it was gone."

"Into the tunnel?" said I.

"No. I ran on into the tunnel, five hundred yards. I stopped, and held my lamp above my head, and saw the figures of the measured distance, and saw the wet stains stealing down the walls and trickling through the arch. I ran out again faster than I had run in (for I had a mortal abhorrence of the place upon me[2]), and I looked all round the red light with my own red light, and I went up the iron ladder to the gallery atop of it, and I came down again, and ran back here. I telegraphed both ways[3], 'An alarm has been given. Is anything wrong?' The answer came back, both ways, 'All well.'"

Resisting the slow touch of a frozen finger tracing out my spine, I showed him how that this figure must be a deception of his sense of sight; and how that figures, originating in disease of the delicate nerves that minister to the functions of the eye[4], were known to have often troubled patients, some of whom had become conscious of the nature of their affliction, and had even proved it by experiments upon themselves. "As to an imaginary cry," said I, "do but listen for a moment to the wind in this unnatural valley while we speak so low,

---

[1] A sign of warning or distress to oncoming trains – *"Beware!"*

[2] Very telling – the signalman, despite his protests of contentment, is made tremendously uncomfortable by this symbolic reminder of the unconscious – replete with regrets, fears, anxieties, and anger

[3] Separated by a matter of several miles, signal boxes lined the railroad. The signalman telegraphs his colleagues on either side, but neither reports trouble

[4] Politely, and sugarcoated with jargon, the narrator advances his theory that the signalman might be going insane

and to the wild harp[1] it makes of the telegraph wires."

That was all very well, he returned, after we had sat listening for a while, and he ought to know something of the wind and the wires,—he who so often passed long winter nights there, alone and watching. But he would beg to remark that he had not finished.

I asked his pardon, and he slowly added these words, touching my arm,—

"Within six hours after the Appearance, the memorable accident on this Line happened, and within ten hours the dead and wounded were brought along through the tunnel over the spot where the figure had stood.[2]"

A disagreeable shudder crept over me, but I did my best against it. It was not to be denied, I rejoined, that this was a remarkable

---

[1] An Aeolian harp – famously the subject of Coleridge's "Ode" – is a form of wind chime that creates pleasant notes as the wind crosses its strings ; it is associated with the idea of nature producing designs of spirit (much like nature appears to be producing the signalman's apparition out of thin air)

[2] On 25 August 1861, three locomotives left Brighton in southern England within only minutes of one another. As a result of complicated miscommunications between the signalmen at the opposite ends of a tunnel through which all three were due to travel, the bloodiest train wreck in British history up to that date occurred. Not wanting the second train to plow into the first as both flew into the Clayton Tunnel, the first signalman urged the second train that a train was already in the tunnel by rushing out of his box and flagging the engineer down. But both trains shuttled into the tunnel despite his warnings. The signalman on the other side of the tunnel, seeing the first train pass through safely, signaled all clear, which the first signalman took to mean both engines had made it out. Tragically, the second train had seen the flag in time to stop before hitting the first, and was in the act of backing out of the tunnel. Thinking that both trains were cleared, the first signalman signaled "all-clear" to the third locomotive which plowed through the reversing second train, killing 23 and wounding 176. Many of the deaths were particularly gruesome, being caused by scalding from the steam or incineration from the coals from the obliterated engine that bored into the passenger cabins. This is almost certainly the event that inspired Dickens' first tragedy

coincidence, calculated deeply to impress his mind. But it was unquestionable that remarkable coincidences did continually occur, and they must be taken into account in dealing with such a subject. Though to be sure I must admit, I added (for I thought I saw that he was going to bring the objection to bear upon me), men of common sense did not allow much for coincidences in making the ordinary calculations of life.

He again begged to remark that he had not finished.

I again begged his pardon for being betrayed into interruptions.

"This," he said, again laying his hand upon my arm, and glancing over his shoulder with hollow eyes, "was just a year ago. Six or seven months passed, and I had recovered from the surprise and shock, when one morning, as the day was breaking, I, standing at the door, looked towards the red light, and saw the spectre again." He stopped, with a fixed look at me.

"Did it cry out?"

"No. It was
silent."

"Did it wave its arm?"

"No. It leaned against the shaft of the light, with both hands before the face. Like this."

Once more I followed his action with my eyes. It was an action of mourning. I have seen such an attitude in stone figures on tombs.

"Did you go up to it?"

"I came in and sat down, partly to collect my thoughts, partly because it had turned me faint. When I went to the door again, daylight was above me, and the ghost was gone."

"But nothing followed? Nothing came of this?"

He touched me on the arm with his forefinger twice or thrice giving a ghastly nod each time:—

"That very day, as a train came out of the tunnel, I noticed, at a carriage window on my side, what looked like a confusion of hands and heads, and something waved. I saw it just in time to signal the driver, Stop! He shut off, and put his brake on, but the train drifted past here a hundred and fifty yards or more. I ran after it, and, as I went along, heard terrible screams and cries. A beautiful young lady had died

343

instantaneously in one of the compartments, and was brought in here, and laid down on this floor between us."

Involuntarily I pushed my chair back, as I looked from the boards at which he pointed to himself.

"True, sir. True. Precisely as it happened, so I tell it you."

I could think of nothing to say, to any purpose, and my mouth was very dry. The wind and the wires took up the story with a long lamenting wail.

He resumed. "Now, sir, mark this, and judge how my mind is troubled. The spectre came back a week ago. Ever since, it has been there, now and again, by fits and starts."

"At the light?"

"At the Danger-light[1]."

"What does it seem to do?"

He repeated, if possible with increased passion and vehemence, that former gesticulation of, "For God's sake, clear the way!"

Then he went on. "I have no peace or rest for it. It calls to me, for many minutes together, in an agonised manner, 'Below there! Look out! Look out!'

It stands waving to me. It rings my little bell—"

I caught at that. "Did it ring your bell yesterday evening when I was here, and you went to the door?"

"Twice."

"Why, see," said I, "how your imagination misleads you. My eyes were on the bell, and my ears were open to the bell, and if I am a living man, it did NOT ring at those times. No, nor at any other time, except when it was rung in the natural course of physical things by the station communicating with you."

---

[1] In one sense, that the ghost haunts the danger-light is only natural – it is a harbinger of danger. In other, it is more nuanced, laying the onus of responsibility at the feet of the railway, the industrialism that has forged this subterranean hell by violating nature and dehumanizing menial men like the signalman. The danger-light is the manufactured sun of the railway – symbolically, its truth, its gospel – and the ghost haunts this "gospel" of industrialism, blaming it for the tragedies – both physical and spiritual – that occur in the bowels of the cutting

He shook his head. "I have never made a mistake as to that yet, sir. I have never confused the spectre's ring with the man's. The ghost's ring is a strange vibration in the bell that it derives from nothing else, and I have not asserted that the bell stirs to the eye. I don't wonder that you failed to hear it. But *I* heard it."

"And did the spectre seem to be there, when you looked out?"

"It WAS there."

"Both times?"

He repeated firmly: "Both times."

"Will you come to the door with me, and look for it now?"

He bit his under lip as though he were somewhat unwilling, but arose. I opened the door, and stood on the step, while he stood in the doorway. There was the Danger-light. There was the dismal mouth of the tunnel. There were the high, wet stone walls of the cutting. There were the stars above them[1].

"Do you see it?" I asked him, taking particular note of his face. His eyes were prominent and strained, but not very much more so, perhaps, than my own had been when I had directed them earnestly towards the same spot.

"No," he answered. "It is not there."

"Agreed," said I.

We went in again, shut the door, and resumed our seats. I was thinking how best to improve this advantage, if it might be called one, when he took up the conversation in such a matter-of-course way, so assuming that there could be no serious question of fact between us, that I felt myself placed in the weakest of positions.

"By this time you will fully understand, sir," he said, "that what troubles me so dreadfully is the question, What does the spectre mean?"

I was not sure, I told him, that I did fully understand.

"What is its warning against?" he said, ruminating, with his eyes on the fire, and only by times turning them on me. "What is the danger? Where is the danger? There is danger overhanging somewhere on the

---

[1] Stars, like daylight sky, symbolize spiritual health, transcendence, and heaven – something beyond reach in the miserable cutting

Line. Some dreadful calamity will happen. It is not to be doubted this third time, after what has gone before. But surely this is a cruel haunting of *me*. What can *I* do[1]?"

He pulled out his handkerchief, and wiped the drops from his heated forehead.

"If I telegraph Danger, on either side of me, or on both, I can give no reason for it," he went on, wiping the palms of his hands. "I should get into trouble, and do no good. They would think I was mad. This is the way it would work,—Message: 'Danger! Take care!' Answer: 'What Danger? Where?' Message: 'Don't know. But, for God's sake, take care!' They would displace me. What else could they do?"

His pain of mind was most pitiable to see. It was the mental torture of a conscientious man, oppressed beyond endurance by an unintelligible responsibility involving life.

"When it first stood under the Danger-light," he went on, putting his dark hair back from his head, and drawing his hands outward across and across his temples in an extremity of feverish distress, "why not tell me where that accident was to happen,—if it must happen? Why not tell me how it could be averted,—if it could have been averted? When on its second coming it hid its face, why not tell me, instead, 'She is going to die. Let them keep her at home'? If it came, on those two occasions, only to show me that its warnings were true, and so to prepare me for the third, why not warn me plainly now? And I, Lord help me! A mere poor signal-man on this solitary station[2]! Why not go to somebody with credit to be believed,

---

[1] Overwhelmed by his sense of responsibility, the signalman is failing to understand that he cannot possibly be held responsible for all such things in a scenario such as this, but he takes his job duties seriously to the point of masochism, and languishes under the guilt that he projects onto himself from the standpoint of the railway company. It must surely be his fault, he reasons, because his sole task on earth is to ensure safety on the line. While his concern is certainly in part humanitarian, it is undoubtedly fueled by a sense of obligation and obedience to the company, from whom he derives his self-worth, identity, and soul

[2] The signalman's torments stem from his comfort in isolation: he does not ask to partake in the affairs of men, only to do his duty. But this self-

and power to act?"

When I saw him in this state, I saw that for the poor man's sake, as well as for the public safety[1], what I had to do for the time was to compose his mind. Therefore, setting aside all question of reality or unreality between us, I represented to him that whoever thoroughly discharged his duty must do well, and that at least it was his comfort that he understood his duty, though he did not understand these confounding Appearances. In this effort I succeeded far better than in the attempt to reason him out of his conviction. He became calm; the occupations incidental to his post as the night advanced began to make larger demands on his attention: and I left him at two in the morning. I had offered to stay through the night, but he would not hear of it.

That I more than once looked back at the red light as I ascended the pathway, that I did not like the red light[2], and that I should have slept but poorly if my bed had been under it, I see no reason to conceal. Nor did I like the two sequences of the accident and the dead girl. I see no reason to conceal that either[3].

But what ran most in my thoughts was the consideration how ought

---

banishment cannot protect him from the inevitability of being touched by human traumas and events. Emotion and social congress is, perhaps more than prevention, the message of the ghost. Remove yourself from here; resurrect yourself and rejoin the flock of mankind. As the poor man himself observes, there was absolutely no chance that he could have influenced the second tragedy – the ghost's appearance seems to serve more as an indictment of the society and culture, and as a call to re-humanize himself before he too is destroyed. The warning is unheeded

[1] If he is insane or maddened by anxiety, the next accident might be due to his negligence

[2] Note, the red light is absolutely not portrayed as a simple, innocuous prop. It is the symbol of the soul of an industrial nation that dehumanizes its citizens and violates the realm of nature (i.e., the cutting), and the narrator is sensitive to its sinister nature

[3] The narrator explains that he is not ashamed that he is unsettled by what might be a genuine haunting, and what – in either case – is certainly a series of tragedies

I to act, having become the recipient of this disclosure[1]? I had proved the man to be intelligent, vigilant, painstaking, and exact; but how long might he remain so, in his state of mind[2]? Though in a subordinate position, still he held a most important trust, and would I (for instance) like to stake my own life on the chances of his continuing to execute it with precision?

Unable to overcome a feeling that there would be something treacherous in my communicating what he had told me to his superiors in the Company, without first being plain with himself and proposing a middle course to him, I ultimately resolved to offer to accompany him (otherwise keeping his secret for the present) to the wisest medical practitioner we could hear of in those parts, and to take his opinion. A change in his time of duty would come round next night, he had apprised me, and he would be off an hour or two after sunrise, and on again soon after sunset. I had appointed to return accordingly.

Next evening was a lovely evening, and I walked out early to enjoy it. The sun was not yet quite down when I traversed the field-path near the top of the deep cutting. I would extend my walk for an hour, I said to myself, half an hour on and half an hour back, and it would then be time to go to my signal-man's box.

Before pursuing my stroll, I stepped to the brink, and mechanically looked down, from the point from which I had first seen him. I cannot describe the thrill that seized upon me, when, close at the mouth of the tunnel, I saw the appearance of a man, with his left sleeve across his eyes, passionately waving his right arm.

The nameless horror that oppressed me passed in a moment, for in a moment I saw that this appearance of a man was a man indeed, and that there was a little group of other men, standing at a short distance, to whom he seemed to be rehearsing the gesture he made. The

---

[1] He begins to inherit the signalman's crippling responsibility

[2] The menial workmen that keep the nation running are not robots or machinery, Dickens asserts: no, they are psychologically complicated, and may become infected by the dehumanizing contagion of their isolated existences

Danger-light was not yet lighted[1]. Against its shaft, a little low hut, entirely new to me, had been made of some wooden supports and tarpaulin. It looked no bigger than a bed.

With an irresistible sense that something was wrong,—with a flashing self-reproachful fear that fatal mischief had come of my leaving the man there, and causing no one to be sent to overlook or correct what he did,—I descended the notched path with all the speed I could make.

"What is the matter?" I asked the men "Signal-man[2] killed this morning, sir." "Not the man belonging to that box?" "Yes, sir." "Not the man I know?"

"You will recognise him, sir, if you knew him," said the man who spoke for the others, solemnly uncovering his own head, and raising an end of the tarpaulin, "for his face is quite composed."

"O, how did this happen, how did this happen?" I asked, turning from one to another as the hut closed in again.

"He was cut down by an engine, sir. No man in England knew his work better[3]. But somehow he was not clear of the outer rail. It was just at broad day. He had struck the light, and had the lamp in his hand. As the engine came out of the tunnel, his back was towards her, and she cut him down. That man drove her, and was showing how it happened. Show the gentleman, Tom."

---

[1] Almost as if its mission to destroy and squelch had been completed, the light is darkened

[2] Not "*The* signal-man," not "John (or Bob or Jack or Will) the Signal-man..." "Signal-man." His identity is seen as indivisible with his work. He is not viewed as a soul or a mind or a heart, but as a job. As "signal-man"

[3] It is no mistake that Dickens qualifies the signalman by his nation: he is described as one of the best of his kind in the entire nation – an exemplar of duty and responsibility – and yet he is mowed down like dry fodder by the machinery of his dehumanizing occupation. If this is the fate of the best in the country – to be tortured with self-doubt, anxiety, and misery – what then are the psychological and spiritual conditions of the rest of Victorian Britain's menials like?

The man, who wore a rough dark dress, stepped back to his former place at the mouth of the tunnel.

"Coming round the curve in the tunnel, sir," he said, "I saw him at the end, like as if I saw him down a perspective-glass[1]. There was no time to check speed, and I knew him to be very careful. As he didn't seem to take heed of the whistle[2], I shut it off when we were running down upon him, and called to him as loud as I could call."

"What did you say?"

"I said, 'Below there! Look out! Look out! For God's sake, clear the way!' "

I started.

"Ah! it was a dreadful time, sir. I never left off calling to him. I put

---

[1] A mounted magnifying glass used to examine pictures, giving them a 3-D appearance. The tunnel objectifies the signalman – just as the first lines of the story do – framing him in its ravenous gaze. When looking into it, he saw only blackness, stains, and murk – the crude blots of a turbulent unconscious – but from the other end he (the supposed viewer) becomes the viewed. It brings to mind Nietzsche's famous comment "when you gaze long into an abyss, the abyss gazes also into you"

[2] Perhaps the most outstanding mystery of "The Signal-Man" is the scenario of the signalman's death. Why was he so effortlessly mowed down? What was he doing standing in the tunnel's mouth? It stands to reason that while the train barreled down the tunnel he was staring into its recesses. This is curious, since the signalman had "a mortal abhorrence" of the place, which symbolically represents the forbidding turbulence and desolation of his troubled unconscious. Staring fixedly into this dark mirror, possibly – though not necessarily – lured there by the apparition, the signalman is caught off guard while in an existential stupor. The signalman's sole solace in his diabolical surroundings is the assurance that his job matters, that his dedication and obedience have been done faithfully in pursuit of a noble calling. But the red light at the tunnel's face – like the green one across from Jay Gatsby's mansion – is a flase light, luring him onto the rocks of a crisis in purpose and identity, and we may wonder if the full import of this reality has dawned on him while gazing into the brooding tunnel. Fixatedly stunned by the reality of his alienation and cosmic insignificance, he is absorbed in existential terror when the train cuts him down

this arm before my eyes not to see, and I waved this arm to the last; but it was no use."

Without prolonging the narrative to dwell on any one of its curious circumstances more than on any other, I may, in closing it, point out the coincidence that the warning of the Engine-Driver included, not only the words which the unfortunate Signal-man had repeated to me as haunting him, but also the words which I myself—not he—had attached, and that only in my own mind, to the gesticulation he had imitated[1].

----

*DICKENS lures us into a Dantean purgatory where the abilities and realities of willpower, personal agency, and human transcendence are repeatedly called into question and affirmed – doubted and established. The signalman is simultaneously helpless and empowered, incapable of altering fate and amply armed to release himself from approaching destruction. This humble functionary – a man who willing works below the station of his intellectual ability, resisting upward mobility on the grounds of obligation – presents a chilling indictment of the British cult of status and duty (he is cut from the same cloth as Oliphant's devoted servant, Bagley). As he learned from his own life-rattling brush with death, Dickens avows that the only thing which we can be held responsible for in life is our own fate. The signalman tortures himself over his failure at duty, but fails to remove himself (in spite of his mobilizing capabilities) from his station, stubbornly standing at the helm of a floundering ship due to his stunting and self-deprecating fetish for*

----

[1] His demise was the tragedy the ghost foretold, and critics have pointed out that while the previous disasters were beyond his control, this final one was indeed within his power to divert

duty. In his final moments, the nervous little man is run down while staring into the tunnel's black mouth – a void which suggests the other end of his purgatory, a hell which ultimately swallows him when he refuses to ascend to the available salvation yawning above him. Like Bagley, the railroad-man is either unwilling or incapable of questioning the status of his menial station or the infallibility of his masters, and (as Dickens wants us to understand) a society which urges its best and brightest to settle for what they are allowed, will ultimately sink into a hell which devours individuality and crushes potential. Dickens does not hesitate to doubt the cruel riptides of life – as he learned at Staplehurst, it can suddenly surge and consume, and we cannot expect to save everyone or be responsible for the whims of fate – but he charges his readership: if you can save no one else, at least save yourself – ascend, transcend, rise above what life deals you, or be prepared to be destroyed; when we are given a chance to better our lives – when warnings and opportunities come – we must understand that the abyss is close behind.

*WHILE Nebit's couple in "The Semi-Detached" was clouded in disapproval and scandal, these spouses are cozy, charming, and romantic: they are two genuinely loving, relatable spouses, still snuggled together in a honeymooner mentality. Pet names like "wifie" and "dearest" and the petty anxieties of domestic concerns such as blacking boots and cleaning dishes make this country setting vastly different from the urbane West-Enders. But chaotic supernatural hazards menace their love-nest as surely as the vision of the ripped throat haunted the apartment in London. Failure to take heed of sincere advice – even to the slightest degree – Nesbit suggests, can rob us of all we hold dear, leaving us wiser but sadder... if we manage to survive. Like Edwards, James, Broughton, and Wells, Nesbit constructs a universe in chaos, one deaf to entreaty and blind to love, a heartless, merciless, misanthropic cosmos that crushes hope and smothers love.*

## MAN-SIZE IN MARBLE
{1893}
### *Edith Nesbit*

ALTHOUGH EVERY WORD OF THIS STORY is as true as despair, I do not expect people to believe it. Nowadays a "rational explanation" is required before belief is possible. Let me then, at once, offer the "rational explanation" which finds most favour among those who have heard the tale of my life's tragedy. It is held that we were "under a delusion," Laura and I, on that 31st of October[1]; and that this supposition places the whole matter on a satisfactory and believable basis. The reader can judge, when he, too, has heard my story, how far this is an "explanation," and in what sense it is "rational." There were three who took part in this: Laura and I and another man. The other man still lives, and can speak to the truth of the least credible part of my story.

I never in my life knew what it was to have as much money as I required to supply the most ordinary needs—good colours[2], books, and

---

[1] Hallowe'en Night, of course
[2] Art supplies

cab-fares— and when we were married we knew quite well that we should only be able to live at all by "strict punctuality and attention to business[1]." I used to paint in those days, and Laura used to write, and we felt sure we could keep the pot at least simmering[2]. Living in town was out of the question, so we went to look for a cottage in the country, which should be at once sanitary and picturesque. So rarely do these two qualities meet in one cottage that our search was for some time quite fruitless. We tried advertisements, but most of the desirable rural residences which we did look at proved to be lacking in both essentials, and when a cottage chanced to have drains it always had stucco as well and was shaped like a tea-caddy[3]. And if we found a vine or rose-covered porch, corruption invariably lurked within[4]. Our minds got so befogged by the eloquence of house-agents and the rival disadvantages of the fever-traps and outrages to beauty which we had seen and scorned, that I very much doubt whether either of us, on our wedding morning, knew the difference between a house and a haystack. But when we got away from friends and house-agents, on our honeymoon, our wits grew clear again, and we knew a pretty cottage when at last we saw one. It was at Brenzett[5]—a little village set on a hill over against the southern marshes. We had gone there, from the seaside village where we were staying, to see the church, and two fields from the church we found this cottage. It stood quite by itself, about two miles from the village. It was a long, low building, with rooms sticking out in unexpected places. There was a bit of stone-work—ivy-covered and moss-grown, just two old rooms, all that was left of a big house that had once stood there—and round this stone-work the house had grown

---

[1] Our narrator aligns with the Victorian ethos of no nonsense and level-headedness -- a reliable narrator for a supernatural story
[2] That is, make a livelihood off of these little jobs – keep themselves fed
[3] A box or jar used to store tea – typically shaped like a shoe box
[4] A favorite theme of Nesbit's (and Broughton's): loveliness can conceal wickedness, and nothing is invulnerable to the ubiquitous assaults of human evil and cosmic tragedy
[5] In Kent, in southeast England – a pastoral country village, home to some 400 inhabitants

up. Stripped of its roses and jasmine it would have been hideous[1]. As it stood it was charming, and after a brief examination we took it. It was absurdly cheap. The rest of our honeymoon we spent in grubbing about in second-hand shops in the county town, picking up bits of old oak and Chippendale[2] chairs for our furnishing. We wound up with a run up to town and a visit to Liberty's, and soon the low oak-beamed lattice-windowed rooms began to be home. There was a jolly old-fashioned garden, with grass paths, and no end of hollyhocks and sunflowers, and big lilies. From the window you could see the marsh-pastures, and beyond them the blue, thin line of the sea. We were as happy as the summer was glorious, and settled down into work sooner than we ourselves expected. I was never tired of sketching the view and the wonderful cloud effects from the open lattice, and Laura would sit at the table and write verses about them, in which I mostly played the part of foreground.

We got a tall old peasant woman to do for us. Her face and figure were good, though her cooking was of the homeliest; but she understood all about gardening, and told us all the old names of the coppices[3] and cornfields, and the stories of the smugglers and highwaymen, and, better still, of the "things that walked," and of the "sights" which met one in lonely glens of a starlight night. She was a great comfort to us, because Laura hated housekeeping as much as I loved folklore, and we soon came to leave all the domestic business to Mrs. Dorman, and to use her legends in little magazine stories which brought in the jingling guinea[4].

We had three months of married happiness, and did not have a single quarrel. One October evening I had been down to smoke a pipe with the doctor—our only neighbour—a pleasant young Irishman. Laura had stayed at home to finish a comic sketch of a village episode

---

[1] External trappings dress up what is in reality a "hideous" thing. Nesbit suggests that the way something is *made* to seem can often distract us from what it in reality is

[2] Fine furniture made after the craftsmanship of the 18th century joiner, Thomas Chippendale

[3] Small glens of woodland maintained and preserved as sources of wood

[4] A gold coin worth one pound, one shilling, or £1.05

for the Monthly Marplot. I left her laughing over her own jokes, and came in to find her a crumpled heap of pale muslin weeping on the window seat.

"Good heavens, my darling, what's the matter?" I cried, taking her in my arms. She leaned her little dark head against my shoulder and went on crying. I had never seen her cry before—we had always been so happy, you see—and I felt sure some frightful misfortune had happened.

"What is the matter? Do speak." "It's Mrs. Dorman," she sobbed.

"What has she done?" I inquired, immensely relieved.

"She says she must go before the end of the month, and she says her niece is ill; she's gone down to see her now, but I don't believe that's the reason, because her niece is always ill. I believe someone has been setting her against us. Her manner was so queer—"

"Never mind, Pussy," I said; "whatever you do, don't cry, or I shall have to cry too, to keep you in countenance, and then you'll never respect your man again!"

She dried her eyes obediently on my handkerchief, and even smiled faintly.

"But you see," she went on, "it is really serious, because these village people are so sheepy[1], and if one won't do a thing you may be quite sure none of the others will. And I shall have to cook the dinners, and wash up the hateful greasy plates; and you'll have to carry cans of water about, and clean the boots and knives—and we shall never have any time for work, or earn any money, or anything. We shall have to work all day, and only be able to rest when we are waiting for the kettle to boil!"

I represented to her that even if we had to perform these duties, the day would still present some margin for other toils and recreations. But she refused to see the matter in any but the greyest light. She was very unreasonable, my Laura, but I could not have loved her any more if she

---

[1] Senseless, easily spooked, illogical

had been as reasonable as Whately[1].

"I'll speak to Mrs. Dorman when she comes back, and see if I can't come to terms with her," I said. "Perhaps she wants a rise in her screw[2]. It will be all right. Let's walk up to the church."

The church was a large and lonely one, and we loved to go there, especially upon bright nights. The path skirted a wood, cut through it once, and ran along the crest of the hill through two meadows, and round the churchyard wall, over which the old yews loomed in black masses of shadow. This path, which was partly paved, was called "the bier-balk[3]," for it had long been the way by which the corpses had been carried to burial. The churchyard was richly treed, and was shaded by great elms which stood just outside and stretched their majestic arms in benediction[4] over the happy dead. A large, low porch let one into the building by a Norman[5] doorway and a heavy oak door studded with iron. Inside, the arches rose into darkness, and between them the reticulated[6] windows, which stood out white in the moonlight. In the

---

[1] Richard Whatley (1787 - 1863) was an English economist, logician, and theologian

[2] An increase of pay or a decrease of hours or work — literally, that she wants a torture device loosened (the same metaphor is referenced in the title of "The Turn of the Screw," wherein the implication is that the device is tightened, and with it the dramatic tension)

[3] A bier being a conveyance or platform for a coffin

[4] A blessing or wish for peace, literally "words of goodness"

[5] A crash course in British history: the original Britons (today the Welsh) were pushed to the west by invading Germanic tribes — the Saxons and Angles — who reigned in England for centuries. But in 1066 the French Normans invaded England in the Norman Conquest, under William the Conqueror. The Normans were depicted in English folklore and literature (e.g. *Ivanhoe* and the legends of Robin Hood) as ruthless thugs and abusers who disrespected Anglo-Saxon culture and sensibilities. Ultimately, the feudal Anglo-Saxon barons rose up against what they viewed as Norman abuses of power, and forced King John (of Robin Hood infamy) to sign the Magna Carta, assuring them of their rights, limiting the powers of the throne, and fortifying the national identity of "Englishmen"

[6] Richly decorated, made up of a network of geometric shapes

chancel[1], the windows were of rich glass, which showed in faint light their noble colouring, and made the black oak of the choir pews hardly more solid than the shadows. But on each side of the altar lay a grey marble figure of a knight in full plate armour lying upon a low slab, with hands held up in everlasting prayer, and these figures, oddly enough, were always to be seen if there was any glimmer of light in the church[2]. Their names were lost[3], but the peasants told of them that they had been fierce and wicked men, marauders by land and sea, who had been the scourge of their time, and had been guilty of deeds so foul that the house they had lived in—the big house, by the way, that had stood on the site of our cottage—had been stricken by lightning and the vengeance of Heaven. But for all that, the gold of their heirs had bought them a place in the church[4]. Looking at the bad hard faces reproduced in the marble, this story was easily believed.

The church looked at its best and weirdest on that night, for the shadows of the yew trees fell through the windows upon the floor of the nave[5] and touched the pillars with tattered shade. We sat down together without speaking, and watched the solemn beauty of the old church, with some of that awe which inspired its early builders. We walked to the chancel and looked at the sleeping warriors. Then we rested some time on the stone seat in the porch, looking out over the stretch of quiet moonlit meadows, feeling in every fibre of our being

---

[1] Space surrounding the altar in the sanctuary

[2] Amidst all the finery and lush décor, only two things are impossible to avoid: the statues of the wicked knights. Nesbit implies that despite our attempts to fancify or glaze over the crimes of the past, they will feature prominently in our collective unconscious

[3] Names may fade, details be lost, and facts be muddled, but character and legacy are more difficult to expunge. Inhumanities have a far longer psychological shelf life than virtues

[4] Materialism, wealth, and power were enough to purchase a place for these two men in the holy sanctuary, falsifying their character and forging their legacy. And yet, the legends continue: even power cannot obstruct wickedness, and money cannot procure a reputation

[5] The main part of a church sanctuary – the central area extending from the entry to the altar

the peace of the night and of our happy love; and came away at last with a sense that even scrubbing and blackleading[1] were but small troubles at their worst[2].

Mrs. Dorman had come back from the village, and I at once invited her to a tête-à-tête[3].

"Now, Mrs. Dorman," I said, when I had got her into my painting room, "what's all this about your not staying with us?"

"I should be glad to get away, sir, before the end of the month," she answered, with her usual placid dignity.

"Have you any fault to find, Mrs. Dorman?"

"None at all, sir; you and your lady have always been most kind, I'm sure—"

"Well, what is it? Are your wages not high enough?" "No, sir, I gets quite enough."

"Then why not stay?"

"I'd rather not"—with some hesitation—"my niece is ill." "But your niece has been ill ever since we came."

No answer. There was a long and awkward silence. I broke it. "Can't you stay for another month?" I asked.

"No, sir. I'm bound to go by Thursday." And this was Monday!

"Well, I must say, I think you might have let us know before. There's no time now to get any one else, and your mistress is not fit to do heavy housework. Can't you stay till next week?"

"I might be able to come back next week."

I was now convinced that all she wanted was a brief holiday, which we should have been willing enough to let her have, as soon as we could get a substitute.

"But why must you go this week?" I persisted. "Come, out with it."

---

[1] To polish with black graphite (pencil lead) – typically used to clean cast iron tools like skillets

[2] At this story's most tender, this is its moral: forget the petty annoyances of life; appreciate the love and affection that you have at your disposal while you can, because there are far more menacing things in the universe than chores, and far more precious commodities than paychecks

[3] Interview or discussion – literally a mouth-to-mouth, or a face-to-face

Mrs. Dorman drew the little shawl, which she always wore, tightly across her bosom, as though she were cold. Then she said, with a sort of effort— "They say, sir, as this was a big house in Catholic times[1], and there was a many deeds done here."

The nature of the "deeds[2]" might be vaguely inferred from the inflection of Mrs. Dorman's voice—which was enough to make one's blood run cold. I was glad that Laura was not in the room[3]. She was always nervous, as highly-strung natures are[4], and I felt that these tales about our house, told by this old peasant woman, with her impressive manner and contagious credulity, might have made our home less dear to my wife.

"Tell me all about it, Mrs. Dorman," I said; "you needn't mind about telling me. I'm not like the young people who make fun of such things." Which was partly true.

---

[1] Before the English reformation, circa 1530 – 1560

[2] By the end of the story it will have become apparent that many of these unspeakable "deeds" were sexual in nature, and above all violent. Rape, as in "The Semi-Detached" and several of Nesbit's other supernatural tales ("John Charrington's Wedding," etc.) is a lurking threat that – while unnamed and merely alluded to – darkens the ostensibly wholesome and happy lives of her (either sexually or – as in "Semi-Detached" – violently) repressed characters

[3] By sheltering Laura, her husband inadvertently is complicit in her own rapacious destruction. A reader might view her cripplingly neurotic nervousness as suggestive of some form of psychological repression. She might be better served by treating her with adultlike frankness. But by shielding her from the realities of the world – one in which rape and murder are realistic concerns – he only enables her squeamish disposition and jelly-like, fragile psychology

[4] Such a description can almost always be interpreted as a literary codification of psychological repression. Not necessarily sexual, it may suggest repression of the will, of the heart, of desire, of ambition, or any number of things. What is clear, however, is that Laura is an incomplete character, who for some reason is denying an element of her own nature. The conclusion implies that her anxieties surround an aversion to physical (and sexual) vulnerability

"Well, sir"—she sank her voice—"you may have seen in the church, beside the altar, two shapes[1]."

"You mean the effigies of the knights in armour," I said cheerfully.

"I mean them two bodies, drawed out man-size in marble[2]," she returned, and I had to admit that her description was a thousand times more graphic than mine, to say nothing of a certain weird force and uncanniness about the phrase "drawed out man-size in marble."

"They do say, as on All Saints' Eve[3] them two bodies sits up on their slabs, and gets off of them, and then walks down the aisle, in their marble"— (another good phrase, Mrs. Dorman)—"and as the church clock strikes eleven they walks out of the church door, and over the graves, and along the bier-balk, and if it's a wet night there's the marks of their feet in the morning."

"And where do they go?" I asked, rather fascinated.

"They comes back here to their home, sir, and if any one meets them—" "Well, what then?" I asked.

But no—not another word could I get from her, save that her niece was ill and she must go. After what I had heard I scorned to discuss the niece, and tried to get from Mrs. Dorman more details of the legend. I could get nothing but warnings.

---

[1] She does not say "statues." She says "shapes." The archetypes that fill our collective unconscious are not restricted by time or place, and while the two statues are indeed physically bound by their physical nature, she suggests that they are not static statues, but fluid suggestions – symbols of something that transcends art or history, something living and mobile

[2] Implying that whatever they represent – in one sense sexual violence, in another bald human wickedness – is not restricted to the forms they occupy, but is rather transferable between human beings. Any living man can adopt their virtues, because they are not statues of dead men, but representations of a very dark and hateful component of the human condition – a man-sized evil that is neither uncommon or mythic, but a real and present danger

[3] November 1 is All Saints' Day (or All Hallows' Day, or Hallowmas) – the day set aside in Christian tradition to pray for and to all of those who are saints – known or unknown. Hallowe'en – literally All Hallows' Evening – is the evening before

"Whatever you do, sir, lock the door early on All Saints' Eve, and make the cross-sign over the doorstep and on the windows."

"But has any one ever seen these things?" I persisted.

"That's not for me to say. I know what I know, sir."

"Well, who was here last year?"

"No one, sir; the lady as owned the house only stayed here in summer, and she always went to London a full month afore the night. And I'm sorry to inconvenience you and your lady, but my niece is ill and I must go on Thursday."

I could have shaken her for her absurd reiteration of that obvious fiction, after she had told me her real reasons.

She was determined to go, nor could our united entreaties move her in the least.

I did not tell Laura the legend of the shapes that "walked in their marble," partly because a legend concerning our house might perhaps trouble my wife, and partly, I think, from some more occult reason[1]. This was not quite the same to me as any other story, and I did not want to talk about it till the day was over. I had very soon ceased to think of the legend, however. I was painting a portrait of Laura[2], against the lattice window, and I could not think of much else. I had got a splendid background of yellow and grey sunset, and was working away with enthusiasm at her lace. On Thursday Mrs. Dorman went. She relented, at parting, so far as to say—

"Don't you put yourself about too much, ma'am, and if there's any little thing I can do next week, I'm sure I shan't mind."

---

[1] He suggests that something supernatural may have influenced him to hold his tongue -- ostensibly because Laura's being kept in the dark on this matter is directly to blame for her ultimate fate. On another level, we might view this as an excuse on the part of a man who is all too aware of the ramifications of coddling his wife

[2] Like the relationship between the spouses in Edgar Allan Poe's "The Oval Portrait," the artist-husband may be accused of over-idealizing his wife, whom he tries to capture in art. Both men fail to appreciate the dynamic, fragile humanity of their wives. Distracted by the spiritual ideals they are drawn to, they are unavailable when to provide for their spouses' emotional and physical needs when they are necessary

From which I inferred that she wished to come back to us after Hallowe'en. Up to the last she adhered to the fiction of the niece with touching fidelity.

Thursday passed off pretty well. Laura showed marked ability in the matter of steak and potatoes, and I confess that my knives, and the plates, which I insisted upon washing, were better done than I had dared to expect. Friday came. It is about what happened on that Friday that this is written. I wonder if I should have believed it, if any one had told it to me. I will write the story of it as quickly and plainly as I can. Everything that happened on that day is burnt into my brain. I shall not forget anything, nor leave anything out.

I got up early, I remember, and lighted the kitchen fire, and had just achieved a smoky success, when my little wife came running down, as sunny and sweet as the clear October morning itself. We prepared breakfast together, and found it very good fun. The housework was soon done, and when brushes and brooms and pails were quiet again, the house was still indeed. It is wonderful what a difference one makes in a house. We really missed Mrs. Dorman, quite apart from considerations concerning pots and pans. We spent the day in dusting our books and putting them straight, and dined gaily on cold steak and coffee. Laura was, if possible, brighter and gayer and sweeter than usual, and I began to think that a little domestic toil was really good for her. We had never been so merry since we were married, and the walk we had that afternoon was, I think, the happiest time of all my life. When we had watched the deep scarlet clouds slowly pale into leaden grey against a pale-green sky, and saw the white mists curl up along the hedgerows in the distant marsh, we came back to the house, silently, hand in hand.

"You are sad, my darling," I said, half-jestingly, as we sat down together in our little parlour. I expected a disclaimer, for my own silence had been the silence of complete happiness. To my surprise she said—

"Yes. I think I am sad, or rather I am uneasy. I don't think I'm very well. I have shivered three or four times since we came in, and it is not cold, is it?"

"No," I said, and hoped it was not a chill caught from the treacherous mists that roll up from the marshes in the dying light. No—she said, she did not think so. Then, after a silence, she spoke suddenly—

"Do you ever have presentiments of evil?"

"No," I said, smiling, "and I shouldn't believe in them if I had."

"I do," she went on; "the night my father died I knew it, though he was right away in the north of Scotland." I did not answer in words.

She sat looking at the fire for some time in silence, gently stroking my hand. At last she sprang up, came behind me, and, drawing my head back, kissed me.

"There, it's over now," she said. "What a baby I am! Come, light the candles, and we'll have some of these new Rubinstein[1] duets."

And we spent a happy hour or two at the piano.

At about half-past ten I began to long for the good-night pipe, but Laura looked so white that I felt it would be brutal of me to fill our sitting-room with the fumes of strong cavendish[2].

"I'll take my pipe outside," I
said. "Let me come, too."

"No, sweetheart, not to-night; you're much too tired[3]. I shan't be long. Get to bed, or I shall have an invalid to nurse to-morrow as well as the boots to clean."

I kissed her and was turning to go, when she flung her arms round my neck, and held me as if she would never let me go again. I stroked her hair. "Come, Pussy, you're over-tired. The housework has been too much for you."

She loosened her clasp a little and drew a deep breath.

"No. We've been very happy to-day, Jack, haven't we? Don't stay out too long."

"I won't, my dearie."

I strolled out of the front door, leaving it unlatched[4]. What a night it

---

[1] Anton Grigorevich Rubinstein (1829 – 1894), a Russian pianist and composer

[2] Strong pipe tobacco, specially cut and cured to produce a stronger flavor

[3] A patronizing presumption that will prove disastrous

[4] His cardinal failing is that he is too certain of his control over the forces of the universe. He fails to appreciate the fragility of life and the cruel whims of fate and the cosmos

was! The jagged masses of heavy dark cloud were rolling at intervals from horizon to horizon, and thin white wreaths covered the stars. Through all the rush of the cloud river, the moon swam, breasting the waves and disappearing again in the darkness. When now and again her light reached the woodlands they seemed to be slowly and noiselessly waving in time to the swing of the clouds above them. There was a strange grey light over all the earth; the fields had that shadowy bloom over them which only comes from the marriage of dew and moonshine, or frost and starlight.

I walked up and down, drinking in the beauty of the quiet earth and the changing sky. The night was absolutely silent. Nothing seemed to be abroad. There was no scurrying of rabbits, or twitter of the half-asleep birds. And though the clouds went sailing across the sky, the wind that drove them never came low enough to rustle the dead leaves in the woodland paths. Across the meadows I could see the church tower standing out black and grey against the sky. I walked there thinking over our three months of happiness—and of my wife, her dear eyes, her loving ways. Oh, my little girl! my own little girl; what a vision came then of a long, glad life for you and me together!

I heard a bell-beat from the church. Eleven already! I turned to go in, but the night held me. I could not go back into our little warm rooms yet. I would go up to the church. I felt vaguely that it would be good to carry my love and thankfulness to the sanctuary whither so many loads of sorrow and gladness had been borne by the men and women of the dead years.

I looked in at the low window as I went by. Laura was half lying on her chair in front of the fire. I could not see her face, only her little head showed dark against the pale blue wall. She was quite still. Asleep, no doubt. My heart reached out to her, as I went on. There must be a God, I thought, and a God who was good[1]. How otherwise could anything so sweet and dear as she have ever been imagined?

I walked slowly along the edge of the wood. A sound broke the stillness of the night, it was a rustling in the wood. I stopped and listened. The sound stopped too. I went on, and now distinctly heard another step than mine answer mine like an echo. It was a poacher or a

---

[1] The conclusion conflicts with this assessment

wood-stealer, most likely, for these were not unknown in our Arcadian[1] neighbourhood. But whoever it was, he was a fool not to step more lightly[2]. I turned into the wood, and now the footstep seemed to come from the path I had just left. It must be an echo, I thought. The wood looked perfect in the moonlight. The large dying ferns and the brushwood showed where through thinning foliage the pale light came down. The tree trunks stood up like Gothic columns all around me[3]. They reminded me of the church, and I turned into the bier-balk, and passed through the corpse-gate between the graves to the low porch. I paused for a moment on the stone seat where Laura and I had watched the fading landscape. Then I noticed that the door of the church was open, and I blamed myself for having left it unlatched the other night[4]. We were the only people who ever cared to come to the church except on Sundays, and I was vexed to think that through our carelessness the damp autumn airs had had a chance of getting in and injuring the old fabric[5]. I went in. It will seem strange, perhaps, that I should have gone half-way up the aisle before I remembered—with a sudden chill, followed by as sudden a rush of self-contempt—that this was the very day and hour when, according to tradition, the "shapes drawed out man-size in marble" began to walk. Having thus remembered the legend, and remembered it with a shiver, of which I was ashamed, I could not do otherwise than walk up towards the altar, just to look at the figures—as I said to myself; really what I wanted was to assure myself, first, that I did not believe the legend, and, secondly, that it was not true. I was rather glad that I had come. I thought now I could tell Mrs. Dorman how vain her fancies were, and how peacefully the marble

---

[1] Having a charming woodland quality

[2] Bold indeed – someone who truly is not afraid to be heard or noticed, someone without fear or reservations, tramping brashly over underbrush with thuggish nonchalance

[3] Calling into question: which is the holy place, the church or the wood, and which is the protective space, the church or the wood? Is this church truly a sanctuary?

[4] Not the door he should be concerned about leaving unlatched

[5] Again, the most valuable treasure he has left vulnerable is at home, not in the church

figures slept on through the ghastly hour. With my hands in my pockets I passed up the aisle. In the grey dim light the eastern end of the church looked larger than usual, and the arches above the two tombs looked larger too. The moon came out and showed me the reason. I stopped short, my heart gave a leap that nearly choked me, and then sank sickeningly.

The "bodies drawed out man-size" were gone, and their marble slabs lay wide and bare in the vague moonlight that slanted through the east window.

Were they really gone? or was I mad? Clenching my nerves, I stooped and passed my hand over the smooth slabs, and felt their flat unbroken surface. Had some one taken the things away? Was it some vile practical joke? I would make sure, anyway. In an instant I had made a torch of a newspaper, which happened to be in my pocket, and lighting it held it high above my head. Its yellow glare illuminated the dark arches and those slabs. The figures were gone. And I was alone in the church; or was I alone[1]?

And then a horror seized me, a horror indefinable and indescribable--an overwhelming certainty of supreme and accomplished calamity[2]. I flung down the torch and tore along the aisle and out through the porch, biting my lips as I ran to keep myself from shrieking aloud. Oh, was I mad--or what was this that possessed me? I leaped the churchyard wall and took the straight cut across the fields, led by the light from our windows. Just as I got over the first stile, a dark figure seemed to spring out of the ground. Mad still with that certainty of misfortune, I made for the thing that stood in my path, shouting, "Get out of the way, can't you!"

But my push met with a more vigorous resistance than I had expected. My arms were caught just above the elbow and held as in a vice, and the raw-boned Irish doctor actually shook me.

---

[1] Suddenly reality – and security – is called into question. While he is certainly alone – there is nothing to suggest otherwise – he can longer take his security (or that of his universe, or wife) for granted

[2] The hostile universe has suddenly revealed itself in all its horrific reality: victorious and unstoppable. Nesbit calls it an "accomplished calamity." The destruction is certain – already done, already finalized and irreversible

"Would ye?" he cried, in his own unmistakable accents—
"would ye, then?"

"Let me go, you fool," I gasped. "The marble figures have gone
from the church; I tell you they've gone."

He broke into a ringing laugh. "I'll have to give ye a draught to-
morrow, I see. Ye've bin smoking too much and listening to old wives'
tales."

"I tell you, I've seen the bare slabs."

"Well, come back with me. I'm going up to old Palmer's—his
daughter's ill; we'll look in at the church and let me see the bare
slabs."

"You go, if you like," I said, a little less frantic for his laughter; "I'm
going home to my wife."

"Rubbish, man," said he; "d'ye think I'll permit of that? Are ye to go
saying all yer life that ye've seen solid marble endowed with vitality,
and me to go all me life saying ye were a coward? No, sir—ye shan't do
ut."

The night air—a human voice—and I think also the physical contact
with this six feet of solid common sense, brought me back a little to
my ordinary self, and the word "coward" was a mental shower-bath.

"Come on, then," I said sullenly; "perhaps you're right."

He still held my arm tightly. We got over the stile and back to the
church. All was still as death. The place smelt very damp and earthy[1].
We walked up the aisle. I am not ashamed to confess that I shut my
eyes: I knew the figures would not be there. I heard Kelly strike a
match.

"Here they are, ye see, right enough; ye've been dreaming or
drinking, asking yer pardon for the imputation."

I opened my eyes. By Kelly's expiring vesta[2] I saw two shapes
lying "in their marble" on their slabs. I drew a deep breath, and
caught his hand.

"I'm awfully indebted to you," I said. "It must have been some trick
of light, or I have been working rather hard, perhaps that's it. Do you
know, I was quite convinced they were gone."

---

[1] Suggesting the domain of the grave – death is ruler in this universe
[2] Swan vestas – a brand of strike-anywhere matches, made of wooden splits
dipped in wax

369

"I'm aware of that," he answered rather grimly; "ye'll have to be careful of that brain of yours, my friend, I assure ye."

He was leaning over and looking at the right-hand figure, whose stony face was the most villainous and deadly in expression.

"By Jove," he said, "something has been afoot here—this hand is broken." "That won't account for my impression," I objected.

And so it was. I was certain that it had been perfect the last time Laura and I had been there.

"Perhaps some one has tried to remove them," said the young doctor. "Too much painting and tobacco will account for that, well enough."

"Come along," I said, "or my wife will be getting anxious. You'll come in and have a drop of whisky and drink confusion to ghosts and better sense to me."

"I ought to go up to Palmer's, but it's so late now I'd best leave it till the morning," he replied. "I was kept late at the Union[1], and I've had to see a lot of people since. All right, I'll come back with ye."

I think he fancied I needed him more than did Palmer's girl, so, discussing how such an illusion could have been possible, and deducing from this experience large generalities concerning ghostly apparitions, we walked up to our cottage. We saw, as we walked up the garden-path, that bright light streamed out of the front door, and presently saw that the parlour door was open too. Had she gone out?

"Come in," I said, and Dr. Kelly followed me into the parlour. It was all ablaze with candles, not only the wax ones, but at least a dozen guttering[2], glaring tallow dips[3], stuck in vases and ornaments in unlikely places[4]. Light, I knew, was Laura's remedy for nervousness.

---

[1] A gentleman's club

[2] Flickering unhealthily or weakly – suggestive of an expiring life or a dying spirit

[3] An improvised candle – a strip of cloth or twine placed in a saucer of tallow grease, and lit, creating a very clean, white light

[4] Apparently a desperate, frantic attempt to stave off the darkness – or scare off an intruder. The method of lighting appears haphazard, random, and unnatural

Poor child! Why had I left her? Brute that I was[1].

We glanced round the room, and at first we did not see her. The window was open, and the draught set all the candles flaring one way. Her chair was empty and her handkerchief and book lay on the floor. I turned to the window. There, in the recess of the window, I saw her. Oh, my child, my love, had she gone to that window to watch for me? And what had come into the room behind her? To what had she turned with that look of frantic fear and horror? Oh, my little one, had she thought that it was I whose step she heard, and turned to meet— what?

She had fallen back across a table in the window, and her body lay half on it and half on the window-seat, and her head hung down over the table, the brown hair loosened and fallen to the carpet[2]. Her lips were drawn back, and her eyes wide, wide open. They saw nothing now. What had they seen last?

The doctor moved towards her, but I pushed him aside and sprang to her; caught her in my arms and cried—

"It's all right, Laura! I've got you safe, wifie."

She fell into my arms in a heap. I clasped her and kissed her, and called her by all her pet names, but I think I knew all the time that she was dead.

Her hands were tightly clenched. In one of them she held something fast. When I was quite sure that she was dead, and that nothing mattered at all any more, I let him open her hand to see what she held.

It was a grey marble finger.

---

[1] To some degree, he accepts a level of complicity in his wife's ravishing

[2] A sexually vulnerable position. The loose hair is especially suggestive, often used in 19th century literature to imply violation

REGARDLESS *of its advances – of science and civility, manners and law – society remains vulnerable to the same ruthless passions which prowled boldly through it during its infancy. Nesbit used "The Semi-Detached" to expose the chaos that can brew in the urban heart of affluence, and sends her gun-shy protagonist packing for the simple domesticity of the English countryside. In this thematic foil – which, like "Semi-Detached," pairs agreeably with Broughton's "Behold, it was a Dream!" – she tears the idyllic mask from a rural retreat, exposing a misanthropic energy, ripe with thoughtless lust and bursting with psychopathic glee. The couple is sweet and careful, selecting their honeymoon cabin with precision and mindfulness. Their lives are frugal and sensible, yet romantic and tender. They are the very embodiment of tidy, middle-classed Englishness, which so caringly merges dutiful pragmatism with a cultivated aesthetic. Their universe is manicured and purposeful, and yet the sky above their considerate kingdom is torn to shreds, and evil things peer through and crush them. The universe is harsh, sudden, and sadistic, and haunted by the wickedness of mankind; though six centuries may pass, the living nature of the rapacious knights still roams. They do not represent a mythic or godlike evil, but one real, tangible, and contemporary – man-sized sins that beat in men's hearts and stew in their brains. There also dwells in this story, a moral sentiment prominent in the works of Poe, especially "The Oval Portrait." Both stories feature an artist who adores his wife's spirit – what she represents to him as a pure, spiritual ideal – but fails to appreciate her dynamic physicality – her rampant neuroses, psychological needs, and ever-present mortality. It isn't until the moment when the artist most needs the complex personality of his wife that he arrives to find her dead – wasted and used up during one of his reveries. Both men understand only too late that what we value most is that which is rarest and most finite: life, shared love, mutual affection and experiences – an ideal can live forever, and a portrait may outlive generations, but a life lost is a treasure destroyed.*

ABUSES *of power and privilege dominate the Victorian ghost story. Gender, class, parentage, age, race, wealth, education, and nationality all factored into a person's ability to defend themselves from those with greater power and opportunity. When Shakespeare chose to critique the flaws in English society, he chose the distance of time and country to allow his commentary to shock and offend and sink in without warranting the dismissal of patriots or the censorship of government (hence the times and settings of* Macbeth, Romeo and Juliet, *and* The Tempest). *Le Fanu chose the Golden Age of Netherlandish culture and civilization as the setting for this, one of his most acidic critiques of human nature, greed, and sexism. It is both erotic and macabre, tender and cold. Throughout the plot juxtapositions clash and clang – beauty and repugnance, love and selfishness, purity and corruption. It is perhaps fitting that the protagonist – Le Fanu's favorite artist – was renowned for his paintings which mixed swathes barren darkness with patches of pregnant light, and interspersed coquettishness with suspicion, clarity with concealment, and romance with mystery. That is why we open on a portrait of a woman whose dominating feature is a twisted smile: one which simultaneously suggests playful affability, erotic ideation, and sinister machinations.*

---

A STRANGE EVENT IN THE LIFE OF
SCHALKEN THE PAINTER
{1839, 1880[1]}
*J. Sheridan Le Fanu*

*"For he is not a man as I am that we should come together; neither is there any that might lay his hand upon us both. Let him, therefore, take his rod away from me, and let not his fear terrify me."*[2]

---

[1] First published in 1839 in a Dublin University magazine, then posthumously released in a newly edited format for *The Purcell Papers* (1880)

[2] Job 9:32. This reference introduces us to a critical theme in "Schalken" – the impropriety of the natural intermingling with the supernatural. The two

THERE EXISTS, AT THIS MOMENT, IN GOOD preservation a remarkable work of Schalken's[1]. The curious management of its lights constitutes, as usual in his pieces, the chief apparent merit of the picture. I say *apparent*, for in its subject, and not in its handling, however exquisite, consists its real value. The picture represents the interior of what might be a chamber in some

antique religious building; and its foreground is occupied by a female figure, in a species of white robe, part of which is arranged so as to form a veil. The dress, however, is not that of any religious order. In her hand the figure bears a lamp, by which alone her figure and face are illuminated; and her features wear such an arch[2] smile, as well becomes a pretty woman when practising some prankish roguery[3]; in the background, and, excepting where the dim red light of an expiring fire serves to define the form, in total shadow, stands the figure of a man dressed in the old Flemish[4] fashion, in an attitude of alarm, his hand being placed upon the hilt of his sword, which he appears to be in the act of drawing.

---

were not made to merge, and the results of such a union would be *grotesque*

[1] Godfried Schalcken (*sholl*-KEN) (1643 – 1706) was Dutch painter who studied under Dou, a student of Rembrandt's. His stormy, unsociable behavior – noted during a five year stint in England – and his suggestive paintings clouded the historical man with an aura of mystique and intrigue. His most famous paintings are chiaroscuro (pictures employing great darkness juxtaposed with bright highlights – such as the illustrations in this volume) studies of candlelight, fire, and faces or fabrics being illuminated by flame

[2] Mischievous, coquettish, flirtatious, even sexually suggestive: a crooked smile. According to a biography: "many of [his] images featured young girls smiling engagingly, somewhat coquettishly and mysteriously out within the pictures, illuminated by a candle or coal lamp. Not only sensual by virtue of Schalcken's bathing light over a figure, these images are often forthrightly erotic in their subject matter"

[3] A trick or prank

[4] In this case, Dutch (Flemish refers to the Netherlands, Belgium, Luxembourg, and French Flanders)

There are some pictures, which impress one, I know not how, with a conviction that they represent not the mere ideal shapes and combinations which have floated through the imagination of the artist, but scenes, faces, and situations which have actually existed[1]. There is in that strange picture, something that stamps it as the representation of a reality.

And such in truth it is, for it faithfully records a remarkable and mysterious occurrence, and perpetuates, in the face of the female figure, which occupies the most prominent place in the design, an accurate portrait of Rose Velderkaust, the niece of Gerard Douw[2], the first, and, I believe, the only love of Godfrey Schalken. My great grandfather knew the painter well; and from Schalken himself he learned the fearful story of the painting, and from him too he ultimately received the picture itself as a bequest[3]. The story and the picture have become heir-looms in my family, and having described the latter, I shall, if you please, attempt to relate the tradition which has descended with the canvas.

There are few forms on which the mantle of romance[4] hangs more ungracefully than upon that of the uncouth Schalken—the boorish[5] but most cunning worker in oils, whose pieces delight the critics of our day almost as much as his manners disgusted the refined of his own; and yet this man, so rude, so dogged, so slovenly, in the midst of his celebrity, had in his obscure, but happier days, played the hero

---

[1] We can with near certainty suppose that LeFanu – a great fan of Schalcken's moody studies with their weird figures and gloomy scenery – had seen a similar piece ("Lady Holding a Candle" and "Girl with a Candle" are both contenders; "Salome with the Head of John the Baptist," and "Man Offering a Gold Chain and Coins to a Girl" also evoke the themes described here) which caused him to wonder just such a thought

[2] Gerrit Dou (*dow*) (1613 – 1675) was one of Rembrandt's best students, well known for his studies of candlelight (like Schalcken) and for his optical illusions (such as a painting made to look like a man is hanging out of the frame)

[3] In Shalcken's will

[4] His rude and grumpy personality caused him to become a figure cloaked in thrilling intrigue

[5] Rude, offensive

in a wild romance[1] of mystery and passion.

When Schalken studied under the immortal Gerard Douw, he was a very young man; and in spite of his phlegmatic[2] temperament, he at once fell over head and ears in love with the beautiful niece of his wealthy master. Rose Velderkaust was still younger than he, having not yet attained her seventeenth year, and, if tradition speaks truth, possessed all the soft and dimpling charms of the fair, light-haired Flemish maidens. The young painter loved honestly and fervently. His frank adoration was rewarded. He declared his love, and extracted a faltering confession in return. He was the happiest and proudest painter in all Christendom[3]. But there was somewhat to dash his elation; he was poor and undistinguished. He dared not ask old Gerard for the hand of his sweet ward. He must first win a reputation and a competence[4].

There were, therefore, many dread uncertainties and cold days before him; he had to fight his way against sore odds. But he had won the heart of dear Rose Velderkaust, and that was half the battle. It is needless to say his exertions were redoubled, and his lasting celebrity proves that his industry was not unrewarded by success.

These ardent labours, and worse still, the hopes that elevated and beguiled them, were however, destined to experience a sudden interruption—of a character so strange and mysterious as to baffle all inquiry and to throw over the events themselves a shadow of preternatural[5] horror.

$\wp$

Schalken had one evening outstayed all his fellow-pupils, and still pursued his work in the deserted room. As the daylight was fast falling, he laid aside his colours, and applied himself to the completion of a sketch on which he had expressed extraordinary pains. It was a religious composition, and represented the temptations of a pot-

---

[1] A story of adventure, intrigue, mystery, and (erotic) romance
[2] Calm, unemotional
[3] The Western World (namely, Europe)
[4] Demonstration of skill
[5] Supernatural

bellied Saint Anthony[1]. The young artist, however destitute of elevation, had, nevertheless, discernment enough to be dissatisfied with his own work, and many were the patient erasures and improvements which saint and devil underwent, yet all in vain. The large, old-fashioned room was silent, and, with the exception of himself, quite emptied of its usual inmates. An hour had thus passed away, nearly two, without any improved result.

Daylight had already declined, and twilight was deepening into the darkness of night. The patience of the young painter was exhausted, and he stood before his unfinished production, angry and mortified, one hand buried in the folds of his long hair, and the other holding the piece of charcoal which had so ill-performed its office, and which he now rubbed, without much regard to the sable[2] streaks it produced, with irritable pressure upon his ample Flemish inexpressibles[3]. "Curse the subject!" said the young man aloud; "curse the picture, the devils, the saint—"

At this moment a short, sudden sniff[4] uttered close beside him made the artist turn sharply round, and he now, for the first time, became aware that his labours had been overlooked by a stranger. Within about a yard and half, and rather behind him, there stood the figure of an elderly man in a cloak and broad-brimmed, conical hat; in his hand, which was protected with a heavy gauntlet-shaped glove, he carried a long ebony walking-stick, surmounted with what appeared, as it glittered dimly in the twilight, to be a massive head of gold, and upon his breast, through the folds of the cloak, there shone the links of a rich

---

[1] St. Anthony the Great (ca. 250 – 350) was an Egyptian monk who was famously said to have been beset by a wild and nearly psychedelic series of supernatural temptations. The weird tale has generated a great amount of interest from artists, and famous depictions of his encounters with devils, demons, and imps has been painted by Bosch, Cezanne, Craesbeeck, Dali, Ernst, Huys and Grunewald. It follows Le Fanu's theme of unnatural encounters between the living and the undead

[2] Black

[3] Curses, profanity

[4] This intake of air will eventually be very telling – the moment Vanderhausen took a breath occurred simultaneously with Schalken's profane curse of both the holy and the damned

chain of the same metal. The room was so obscure that nothing further of the appearance of the figure could be ascertained, and his hat threw his features into profound shadow. It would not have been easy to conjecture the age of the intruder; but a quantity of dark hair escaping from beneath this sombre hat, as well as his firm and upright carriage served to indicate that his years could not yet exceed threescore[1], or thereabouts. There was an air of gravity and importance about the garb of the person, and something indescribably odd, I might say awful, in the perfect, stone-like stillness of the figure, that effectually checked the testy comment[2] which had at once risen to the lips of the irritated artist. He, therefore, as soon as he had sufficiently recovered his surprise, asked the stranger, civilly, to be seated, and desired to know if he had any message to leave for his master.

"Tell Gerard Douw," said the unknown, without altering his attitude in the smallest degree, "that Minheer Vanderhausen[3], of Rotterdam[4], desires to
speak with him on tomorrow evening at this hour, and if he please, in this room, upon matters of weight; that is all."

The stranger, having finished this message, turned abruptly, and, with a quick, but silent step quitted the room, before Schalken had time to say a word in reply. The young man felt a curiosity to see in what direction the burgher[5] of Rotterdam would turn, on quitting the studio, and for that purpose he went directly to the window which commanded the door. A lobby of considerable extent intervened between the inner door of the painter's room and the street entrance,

---

[1] Sixty

[2] Vanderhausen's weirdness drives the curses from Schalcken's mind – previously consumed with "the subject" of St. Anthony's dalliance with the supernatural, Schalcken is now stunned by – what time will show to be – his own

[3] Mynheer (muh-*neer*) is the Dutch for mister or milord. Vanderhausen is faux Dutch (actually a crude mixture of Dutch and German) for *"of the House"*

[4] Enormous shipping, commercial, cultural, and diplomatic center on Holland's southern shore

[5] Bourgeoisie – a gentleman

so that Schalken occupied the post of observation before the old man could possibly have reached the street. He watched in vain, however. There was no other mode of exit. Had the queer old man vanished, or was he lurking about the recesses of the lobby for some sinister purpose[1]? This last suggestion filled the mind of Schalken with a vague uneasiness, which was so unaccountably intense as to make him alike afraid to remain in the room alone, and reluctant to pass through the lobby[2]. However, with an effort which appeared very disproportioned to the occasion[3], he summoned resolution to leave the room, and, having locked the door and thrust the key in his pocket, without looking to the right or left, he traversed the passage which had so recently, perhaps still, contained the person of his mysterious visitant, scarcely venturing to breathe till he had arrived in the open street.

ℰↄ

"Minheer Vanderhausen!" said Gerard Douw within himself, as the appointed hour approached, "Minheer Vanderhausen, of Rotterdam! I never heard of the man till yesterday. What can he want of me? A portrait, perhaps, to be painted; or a poor relation to be apprenticed; or a collection to be valued; or—pshaw! There's no one in Rotterdam to leave me a legacy. Well, whatever the business may be, we shall soon know it all."

It was now the close of day, and again every easel, except that of Schalken, was deserted. Gerard Douw was pacing the apartment with the restless step of impatient expectation, sometimes pausing to glance over the work of one of his absent pupils, but more frequently placing himself at the window, from whence he might observe the passengers who threaded the obscure by-street in which his studio was placed.

---

[1] Without any particular cause, Schalcken already suspects Vanderhausen of being a sinister character – something about him is simply not quite right and off-putting

[2] Excellent piece of fear-psychology on Le Fanu's part

[3] There is simply no genuine reason to account for his fear; it is a weird anxiety

"Said you not, Godfrey," exclaimed Douw, after a long and fruitful gaze from his post of observation, and turning to Schalken, "that the hour he appointed was about seven by the clock of the Stadhouse[1]?"

"It had just told seven when I first saw him, sir," answered the student.

"The hour is close at hand, then," said the master, consulting a horologe[2] as large and as round as an orange. "Minheer Vanderhausen from Rotterdam—is it not so?"

"Such was the name."

"And an elderly man, richly clad?" pursued Douw, musingly.

"As well as I might see," replied his pupil; "he could not be young, nor yet very old, neither; and his dress was rich and grave, as might become a citizen of wealth and consideration."

At this moment the sonorous boom of the Stadhouse clock told, stroke after stroke, the hour of seven; the eyes of both master and student were directed to the door; and it was not until the last peal of the bell had ceased to vibrate, that Douw exclaimed—

"So, so; we shall have his worship[3] presently, that is, if he means to keep his hour; if not, you may wait for him, Godfrey, if you court his acquaintance. But what, after all, if it should prove but a mummery got up by Vankarp, or some such wag[4]? I wish you had run all risks, and cudgelled the old burgomaster soundly. I'd wager a dozen of Rhenish[5], his worship would have unmasked, and pleaded old acquaintance in a trice[6]."

"Here he comes, sir," said Schalken, in a low monitory tone; and instantly, upon turning towards the door, Gerard Douw observed the same figure which had, on the day before, so unexpectedly greeted his pupil Schalken.

There was something in the air of the figure which at once satisfied the painter that there was no masquerading in the case, and that he

---

[1] City hall

[2] A timepiece

[3] Dou's attitude is condescending and self-important – much like the later Schalcken

[4] Dou suspects that a rival (and fictitious) artist is playing a prank on him

[5] German white wine from the Rheinland

[6] Mere moment

380

really stood in the presence of a man of worship; and so, without hesitation, he doffed his cap, and courteously saluting the stranger, requested him to be seated. The visitor waved his hand slightly, as if in acknowledgment of the courtesy, but remained standing.

"I have the honour to see Minheer Vanderhausen of Rotterdam?" said Gerard Douw.

"The same," was the laconic[1] reply of his visitor.

"I understand your worship desires to speak with me," continued Douw, "and I am here by appointment to wait your commands."

"Is that a man of trust?" said Vanderhausen, turning towards Schalken, who stood at a little distance behind his master.

"Certainly," replied Gerard.

"Then let him take this box, and get the nearest jeweller or goldsmith to value its contents, and let him return hither with a certificate of the valuation[2]."

At the same time, he placed a small case about nine inches square in the hands of Gerard Douw, who was as much amazed at its weight as at the strange abruptness with which it was handed to him. In accordance with the wishes of the stranger, he delivered it into the hands of Schalken, and repeating his direction, despatched him upon the mission.

Schalken disposed his precious charge securely beneath the folds of his cloak, and rapidly traversing two or three narrow streets, he stopped at a corner house, the lower part of which was then occupied by the shop of a Jewish goldsmith. He entered the shop, and calling the little Hebrew into the obscurity of its back recesses, he proceeded to lay before him Vanderhausen's casket. On being examined by the light of a lamp, it appeared entirely cased with lead, the outer surface of which was much scraped and soiled, and nearly white with age[3]. This having been partially removed, there appeared beneath a box of some hard wood; which also they forced open and after the removal of two or three folds of linen, they discovered its contents to be a mass of golden

---

[1] Brief, choppy

[2] Document verifying worth

[3] Features that would indicate it having been buried underground – perhaps in a grave

ingots[1], closely packed, and, as the Jew declared, of the most perfect quality. Every ingot underwent the scrutiny of the little Jew, who seemed to feel an epicurean[2] delight in touching and testing these morsels of the glorious metal; and each one of them was replaced in its berth with the exclamation: "*Mein Gott[3]*, how very perfect! not one grain of alloy[4]—beautiful, beautiful!" The task was at length finished, and the Jew certified under his hand the value of the ingots submitted to his examination, to amount to many thousand rix-dollars[5]. With the desired document in his pocket, and the rich box of gold carefully pressed under his arm, and concealed by his cloak, he retraced his way, and entering the studio, found his master and the stranger in close conference. Schalken had no sooner left the room, in order to execute the commission he had taken in charge, than Vanderhausen addressed Gerard Douw in the following terms:

"I cannot tarry with you to-night more than a few minutes, and so I shall shortly tell you the matter upon which I come. You visited the town of Rotterdam some four months ago, and then I saw in the church of St.
Lawrence[6] your niece, Rose Velderkaust. I desire to marry her; and if I satisfy you that I am wealthier than any husband you can dream of for her, I expect that you will forward my suit with your authority. If you approve my proposal, you must close with it here and now, for I cannot wait for calculations and delays."

Gerard Douw was hugely astonished by the nature of Minheer Vanderhausen's communication, but he did not venture to express surprise; for besides the motives supplied by prudence and politeness, the painter experienced a kind of chill and oppression like that which is said to intervene when one is placed in unconscious proximity with the object of a natural antipathy[7]—an undefined but overpowering

---

[1] Bars of gold

[2] Pleasure-seeking lifestyle – giddy euphoria

[3] German: "My God!"

[4] Mineral imperfections

[5] Dutch national currency (*rijksdaalder* – the "national dollar")

[6] *Grote of Sint-Laurenskerk*, a Protestant church built in 1449 - 1525

[7] That is, when one unknowingly crosses paths with a person or thing which is destined to be an enemy

sensation, while standing in the presence of the eccentric stranger, which made him very unwilling to say anything which might reasonably offend him.

"I have no doubt," said Gerard, after two or three prefatory hems[1], "that the alliance which you propose would prove alike advantageous and honourable to my niece; but you must be aware that she has a will of her own, and may not acquiesce in what *we* may design for her advantage[2]."

"Do not seek to deceive me, sir painter," said Vanderhausen; "you are her guardian—she is your ward—she is mine if *you* like to make her so."

The man of Rotterdam moved forward a little as he spoke, and Gerard Douw, he scarce knew why, inwardly prayed for the speedy return of Schalken.

"I desire," said the mysterious gentleman, "to place in your hands at once an evidence of my wealth, and a security for my liberal dealing with your niece. The lad will return in a minute or two with a sum in value five times the fortune which she has a right to expect from her husband. This shall lie in your hands, together with her dowry[3], and you may apply the united sum as suits her interest best[4]; it shall be all exclusively hers while she lives: is that liberal[5]?"

Douw assented, and inwardly acknowledged that fortune had been extraordinarily kind to his niece; the stranger, he thought, must be both wealthy and generous, and such an offer was not to be despised, though made by a humourist, and one of no very prepossessing presence. Rose had no very high pretensions for she had but a modest

---

[1] Clearing his throat as an introduction

[2] Le Fanu's stories often follow the sin of abuse-of-the-will – making decisions for another which are not in their best interests. There is also a very interesting element of patriarchy here that would be well served by a feminist critical approach

[3] A sum paid to the groom (either the family or the man himself) by the bride's family

[4] Her interests, surely, would be best suited by allowing her to choose whom to marry

[5] Generous

dowry, which she owed entirely to the generosity of her uncle; neither had she any right to raise exceptions on the score of birth, for her own origin was far from splendid, and as the other objections, Gerald resolved, and indeed, by the usages of the time, was warranted in resolving, not to listen to them for a moment.

"Sir" said he, addressing the stranger, "your offer is liberal, and whatever hesitation I may feel in closing with it immediately, arises solely from my not having the honour of knowing anything of your family or station[1]. Upon these points you can, of course, satisfy me without difficulty?'

"As to my respectability," said the stranger, drily, "you must take that for granted at present; pester me with no inquiries; you can discover nothing more about me than I choose to make known[2]. You shall have sufficient security for my respectability—my word, if you are honourable: if you are sordid[3], my gold."

"A testy old gentleman," thought Douw, "he must have his own way; but, all things considered, I am not justified to declining his offer[4]. I will not pledge myself unnecessarily, however."

---

[1] Rich or not, even in republican, capitalist Holland, a man's station – his social origins and caste – was a critical element of his eligibility

[2] Make no mistake, this is a *tremendously* cheeky and insulting attitude for a suitor to display towards the guardian of his suit – regardless of social rank or wealth, such a bombast and disrespectful proposal would have likely been turned down without further discussion by any self-respecting gentleman

[3] Disrespectable, low-born. Vanderhausen disarms Dou's very realistic and fair hesitations by implying that his caution indicates a lower-class crudeness – a direct attack on Dou's honor, which puts the painter on the defensive when, in actuality, he has every right to demand verification of the suitor's good reputation. Le Fanu is playing to the character's vanity and social insecurities; when his true concern should be his niece's welfare, he is distracted by self-image and the token opinions of others

[4] Yes he is; by the standards of gentlemanly intercourse and 17th century chivalry, he has every right to decline such a sudden and disreputable offer; Dou is vain and insecure in the presence of Vanderhausen's unmistakable and unquestionable wealth

"You will not pledge yourself unnecessarily," said Vanderhausen, strangely uttering the very words which had just floated through the mind of his companion; "but you will do so if it is necessary, I presume; and I will show you that I consider it indispensable. If the gold I mean to leave in your hands satisfy you, and if you don't wish my proposal to be at once withdrawn, you must, before I leave this room, write your name to this engagement[1]."

Having thus spoken, he placed a paper in the hands of the master, the contents of which expressed an engagement entered into by Gerard Douw, to give to Wilken Vanderhausen of Rotterdam, in marriage, Rose Velderkaust, and so forth, within one week of the date thereof. While the painter was employed in reading this covenant, by the light of a twinkling oil lamp in the far wall of the room[2], Schalken, as we have stated, entered the studio, and having delivered the box and the valuation of the Jew, into the hands of the stranger, he was about to retire, when Vanderhausen called to him to wait; and, presenting the case and the certificate to Gerard Douw, he paused in silence until he had satisfied himself, by an inspection of both, respecting the value of the pledge left in his hands. At length he said—

"Are you content?"

The painter said he would fain have another day to consider. "Not an hour," said the suitor, apathetically.

"Well then," said Douw, with a sore effort, "I am content, it is a bargain." "Then sign at once," said Vanderhausen, "for I am weary[3]." At the same time he produced a small case of writing materials, and Gerard signed the important document.

"Let this youth witness the covenant," said the old man; and

[1] Suggestive of a written agreement with the Devil (cf. Goethe's *Faust*)

[2] Suggestive of just the sort of lamp-lit scene that made Schalcken's paintings famous

[3] Vanderhausen consistently appears to have brief reserves of energy, constantly being in a hurry to return to Rotterdam, ostensibly because of limitations of time or physical energy. We may wonder why these restrictions seem to afflict him so regularly, and whether these are the natural burdens of a busy aristocrat, or of a more sinister (e.g. vampiric) nature

Godfrey Schalken unconsciously attested the instrument which for ever bereft him of his dear Rose Velderkaust.

The compact being thus completed, the strange visitor folded up the paper, and stowed it safely in an inner pocket.

"I will visit you to-morrow night at nine o'clock, at your own house, Gerard Douw, and will see the object of our contract[1];" and so saying Wilken Vanderhausen moved stiffly, but rapidly, out of the room.

Schalken, eager to resolve his doubts, had placed himself by the window, in order to watch the street entrance; but the experiment served only to support his suspicions, for the old man did not issue from the door. This was *very* strange, odd, nay fearful[2]. He and his master returned together, and talked but little on the way, for each had his own subjects of reflection, of anxiety, and of hope. Schalken, however, did not know the ruin which menaced his dearest projects.

Gerard Douw knew nothing of the attachment which had sprung up between his pupil and his niece; and even if he had, it is doubtful whether he would have regarded its existence as any serious obstruction to the wishes of Minheer Vanderhausen. Marriages were then and there matters of traffic[3] and calculation; and it would have appeared as absurd in the eyes of the guardian to make a mutual attachment an essential element in a contract of the sort, as it would

---

[1] Even in the parlance of 17th century matrimonial arrangements, this language smacks of sexist objectification and dehumanization that should trouble Dou

[2] Le Fanu does little to conceal Vanderhausen's supernatural nature – he disappears rather than walk out of the building's single exit – because it is not in his artistic interest to be coy or ambiguous; nay, it is far better for the plot that we know with certainty that something is terribly and unnaturally amiss with Rose's fiancée

[3] Commerce, or exchange of property. Le Fanu is, however, incorrect on this mark. Marriage in the Dutch Republic (as well as in the American colonies and some areas of Britain) during the late 17th century was far closer to a contemporary marriage of compatibility (of temperaments and social standing) than the arranged marriage that Rose suffers. In the Dutch Republic, women owned their property and were able to sue for divorce – an unheard of liberality

have been to draw up his bonds and receipts in the language of romance.

The painter, however, did not communicate to his niece the important step which he had taken in her behalf, a forbearance[1] caused not by any anticipated opposition on her part, but solely by a ludicrous consciousness that if she were to ask him for a description of her destined bridegroom, he would be forced to confess that he had not once seen his face, and if called upon, would find it absolutely impossible to identify him. Upon the next day, Gerard Douw, after dinner, called his niece to him and having scanned her person with an air of satisfaction[2], he took her hand, and looking upon her pretty innocent face with a smile of kindness, he said:

"Rose, my girl, that face of yours will make your fortune." Rose blushed and smiled. "Such faces and such tempers seldom go together, and when they do, the compound is a love charm, few heads or hearts can resist; trust me, you will soon be a bride, girl. But this is trifling, and I am pressed for time[3], so make ready the large room by eight o'clock to-night, and give directions for supper at nine. I expect a friend; and observe me, child, do you trick yourself out handsomely[4]. I will not have him think us poor or sluttish[5]."

With these words he left her, and took his way to the room in which his pupils worked.

℘

When the evening closed in, Gerard called Schalken, who was about

---

[1] Patience, self-control, restraint

[2] She is physically attractive; he notes this with an air of satisfaction because he knows that this is the cause of Vanderhausen's interest — her erotic appeal alone has solicited his courtship

[3] Dou is treating the future of his niece like a superficial business transaction. Trifling? Pressed for time? Her very welfare is on the block, and he treats it as a small, forgettable appointment. Like Vanderhausen, he is disrespectful, dehumanizing, and vainly pompous

[4] To adorn oneself with attractive ornaments, jewelry, and ribbons

[5] Messy, trashy (not yet conotated with loose sexuality)

to take his departure to his own obscure and comfortless lodgings[1], and asked him to come home and sup with Rose and Vanderhausen. The invitation was, of course, accepted and Gerard Douw and his pupil soon found themselves in the handsome and, even then, antique chamber, which had been prepared for the reception of the stranger. A cheerful wood fire blazed in the hearth, a little at one side of which an old-fashioned table, which shone in the fire-light like burnished gold[2], was awaiting the supper, for which preparations were going forward; and ranged with exact regularity, stood the tall-backed chairs, whose ungracefulness was more than compensated by their comfort. The little party, consisting of Rose, her uncle, and the artist, awaited the arrival of the expected visitor with considerable impatience.

Nine o'clock at length came, and with it a summons at the street door, which being speedily answered, was followed by a slow and emphatic tread upon the staircase; the steps moved heavily across the lobby, the door of the room in which the party we have described were assembled slowly opened, and there entered a figure which startled, almost appalled, the phlegmatic Dutchmen[3], and nearly made Rose scream with terror. It was the form, and arrayed in the garb of Minheer Vanderhausen; the air, the gait, the height were the same, but the features had never been seen by any of the party before. The stranger stopped at the door of the room, and displayed his form and face completely. He wore a dark-coloured cloth cloak, which was short and

---

[1] Wealth and social rank continue to feature loomingly in Le Fanu's prose: it dominates and dictates the lives of those who lack or possess it, robbing Schalcken of a happy marriage with his sweetheart, diminishing Rose to a sexual commodity, and rewarding the nefarious Vanderhausen with possession of Rose's body and soul

[2] Gold is the only source of vision, direction, or understanding (symbolized by light and fire) that the characters in this tale recognize (or are *allowed* to recognize)

[3] Shocked from his callous, unemotional attitude, Dou is alerted to the possibly horrifying nature of his business transaction

full, not falling quite to his knees[1]; his legs were cased in dark purple silk stockings, and his shoes were adorned with roses of the same colour. The opening of the cloak in front showed the under-suit to consist of some very dark, perhaps sable material[1], and his hands were enclosed in a pair of heavy leather gloves, which ran up considerably above the wrist, in the manner of a gauntlet. In one hand he carried his walking-stick and his hat, which he had removed, and the other hung heavily by his side[2]. A quantity of grizzled[3] hair descended in long tresses from his head, and rested upon the plaits of a stiff ruff, which effectually concealed his neck[4]. So far all was well; but the face!—all the flesh of the face was coloured with the bluish leaden hue, which is sometimes produced by metallic medicines,
administered in excessive quantities; the eyes showed an undue proportion of muddy white, and had a certain indefinable character of insanity; *the nose was well enough, but the mouth was writhed considerably to one side, where it opened in order to give egress[5] to two long, discolored fangs[6], which projected from the upper jaw far below the lower lip* [italics: a clause used in the 1880 version but not the 1839]; the hue of the lips bearing the usual relation to that of the face, was, consequently, nearly black; and the entire character of the face was

---

[1] A rouqelaure, a short, thick cloak often featured in the fiction of Poe, and often associated with intrigue and sinister characters ("Cask of Amontillado," "The Man of the Crowd")
[2] Le Fanu masterfully builds tension by describing everything but his face first
[3] Streaked with grey
[4] We may have reason to wonder if Le Fanu's word choices are intentional: though the ruff was a fixture of fashion, he goes out of his way to describe its affect on Vanderhausen's throat – is there anything he might want to hide with this ruff? A rope's mark – like that of a hanged criminal – perhaps?
[5] To expose, to make way for
[6] Considering Le Fanu's famous forays into vampiric literature (*Carmilla*), it is not unreasonable to wonder if this detail is meant to color Vanderhausen as a vampire, or merely to give him a monstrous, animalistic, predatory bearing. Either way, the sight is ghastly and suggests violence

sensual[1], malignant, and even satanic *to the last degree; and, indeed, such a combination of horror could hardly be accounted for, except by supposing the corpse of some atrocious malefactor[2], which had long hung blackening upon the gibbet[3], to have at length become the habitation of a demon—the frightful sport of Satanic possession[4]*[italics: 1880 version] .

It was remarkable that the worshipful stranger suffered as little as possible of his flesh to appear, and that during his visit he did not once remove his gloves. Having stood for some moments at the door, Gerard Douw at length found breath and collectedness to bid him welcome, and with a mute inclination of the head, the stranger stepped forward into the room. There was something indescribably odd, even horrible, about all his motions, something undefinable, that was unnatural, unhuman; it was as if the limbs were guided and directed by a spirit unused to the management of bodily machinery[5]. The stranger spoke hardly at all during his visit, which did not exceed half an hour; and the host himself could scarcely muster courage enough to utter the few necessary salutations and courtesies; and, indeed, such was the nervous terror which the presence of Vanderhausen inspired, that very little would have made all his entertainers fly in downright panic from the room. They had not so far lost all self-possession, however, as to fail to observe two strange peculiarities of their visitor. During his stay his

---

[1] Being a face that suggests carnality, eroticism, and the mastery of impulse over conscience

[2] Criminal, wrong-doer

[3] Gallows – Vanderhausen's face resembles that of a convict who has expired after hanging, being blackened and rigid

[4] Vanderhausen's face suggests that of a hanged convict whose corpse has become animated by a demonic possession. Whether Le Fanu supports this as an interpretation of plot or intends it merely as a literary illustration is unclear

[5] Le Fanu suggests that some weird, supernatural puppetry is responsible for the corpse's animation. Similar language (describing the odd, unnatural, awkwardly mechanical motions) has been used to describe veridical supernatural events, such as the men-in-black phenomena

eyelids did not once close, or, indeed, move in the slightest degree[1]; and farther, there was a deathlike stillness in his whole person, owing to the absence of the heaving motion of the chest, caused by the process of respiration. These two peculiarities, though when told they may appear trifling, produced a very striking and unpleasant effect when seen and observed. Vanderhausen at length relieved the painter of Leyden of his inauspicious presence; and with no trifling sense of relief the little party heard the street door close after him.

"Dear uncle," said Rose, "what a frightful man! I would not see him again for the wealth of the States[2]."
"Tush, foolish girl," said Douw, whose sensations were anything but comfortable. "A man may be as ugly as the devil, and yet, if his heart and actions are good[3], he is worth all the pretty-faced perfumed puppies that walk the Mall. Rose, my girl, it is very true he has not thy pretty face, but I know him to be wealthy and liberal; and were he ten times more ugly, these two virtues would be enough to counter balance all his deformity, and if not sufficient actually to alter the shape and hue of his features, at least enough to prevent one thinking them so much amiss."

"Do you know, uncle," said Rose, "when I saw him standing at the door, I could not get it out of my head that I saw the old painted wooden figure that used to frighten me so much in the Church of St. Laurence at Rotterdam[4]."

Gerard laughed, though he could not help inwardly acknowledging the justness of the comparison. He was resolved, however, as far as he could, to check his niece's disposition to dilate[5] upon the ugliness of

---

[1] As if they are fixed in death or – perhaps more gruesome – painted on or prosthetics
[2] The Republic of the Seven United Netherlands
[3] But are they!? He has absolutely no idea what Vanderhausen's character is, but his conduct has been anything but respectable
[4] This raises two particular possibilities: Vanderhausen could be an animated statue (Le Fanu's original version suggests this by describing his eyes as appearing painted), or the statue noticed in the church is a depiction of the man whose corpse has been possessed
[5] Muse over, ponder

391

her intended bridegroom, although he was not a little pleased, as well as puzzled, to observe that she appeared totally exempt from that mysterious dread of the stranger which, he could not disguise it from himself, considerably affected him, as also his pupil Godfrey Schalken.

80

Early on the next day there arrived, from various quarters of the town, rich presents of silks, velvets, jewelry, and so forth, for Rose; and also a packet directed to Gerard Douw, which on being opened, was found to contain a contract of marriage, formally drawn up, between Wilken Vanderhausen of the *Boom-quay*[1], in Rotterdam, and Rose Velderkaust of Leyden, niece to Gerard Douw, master in the art of painting, also of the same city; and containing engagements on the part of Vanderhausen to make settlements upon his bride, far more splendid than he had before led her guardian to believe likely, and which were to be secured to her use in the most unexceptionable manner possible—the money being placed in the hand of Gerard Douw himself.

I have no sentimental scenes to describe, no cruelty of guardians, no magnanimity of wards, no agonies, or transport of lovers[2]. The record I have to make is one of sordidness, levity, and heartlessness[3]. In less than a week after the first interview which we have just described, the contract of marriage was fulfilled, and Schalken saw the prize which he would have risked existence to secure[4], carried off in solemn pomp by his repulsive rival. For two or three days he absented himself from the

---

[1] A prestigious street in Rotterdam (literally, the Tree Quay)

[2] Tropes of sentimental and Gothic romances

[3] Indeed, Le Fanu's story is one which highlights human cruelty, callousness, and lack of feeling. It is a study in the moral frailty, emotional shallowness, and personal apathy

[4] And yet, as Le Fanu wishes us to note, he does not challenge the match, run away with Rose (who certainly would welcome an opportunity to escape), or take Dou into his confidence. While Dou is callous and insecure, Schalcken – who gives in to his master's schemes rather than risk his displeasure – is cowardly, uncommitted, and apathetic

school; he then returned and worked, if with less cheerfulness, with far more dogged resolution than before; the stimulus of love had given place to that of ambition. Months passed away, and, contrary to his expectation, and, indeed, to the direct promise of the parties, Gerard Douw heard nothing of his niece or her worshipful spouse. The interest of the money, which was to have been demanded in quarterly sums, lay unclaimed in his hands.

He began to grow extremely uneasy. Minheer Vanderhausen's direction in Rotterdam he was fully possessed of; after some irresolution he finally determined to journey thither—a trifling undertaking, and easily accomplished[1]—and thus to satisfy himself of the safety and comfort of his ward, for whom he entertained an honest and strong affection[2]. His search was in vain, however; no one in Rotterdam had ever heard of Minheer Vanderhausen. Gerard Douw left not a house in the *Boom-quay* untried, but all in vain. No one could give him any information whatever touching the object of his inquiry, and he was obliged to return to Leyden nothing wiser and far more anxious, than when he had left it.

On his arrival he hastened to the establishment from which Vanderhausen had hired the lumbering, though, considering the times, most luxurious vehicle, which the bridal party had employed to convey them to Rotterdam. From the driver of this machine he learned, that having proceeded by slow stages, they had late in the evening approached Rotterdam; but that before they entered the city, and while yet nearly a mile from it, a small party of men, soberly clad, and after the old fashion, with peaked beards and moustaches, standing in the centre of the road, obstructed the further progress of the carriage. The driver reined in his horses, much fearing, from the obscurity of the hour, and the loneliness, of the road, that some mischief was intended. His fears were, however, somewhat allayed by his observing that these strange men carried a large litter[3], of an antique shape, and which they

---

[1] A journey of less than 25 miles

[2] Le Fanu is not a complete cynic: he views humankind as complex – not entirely selfish or callous – but inclined towards shallowness and fear

[3] A light vehicle in the form of a couch carried by servants on and covered by a canopy of curtains

immediately set down upon the pavement, whereupon the bridegroom, having opened the coach-door from within, descended, and having assisted his bride to do likewise, led her, weeping bitterly, and wringing her hands, to the litter, which they both entered. It was then raised by the men who surrounded it, and speedily carried towards the city, and before it had proceeded very far, the darkness concealed it from the view of the Dutch coachman. In the inside of the vehicle he found a purse, whose contents more than thrice paid the hire of the carriage and man[1]. He saw and could tell nothing more of Minheer Vanderhausen and his beautiful lady.

This mystery was a source of profound anxiety and even grief to Gerard Douw. There was evidently fraud in the dealing of Vanderhausen with him, though for what purpose committed he could not imagine. He greatly doubted how far it was possible for a man possessing such a countenance to be anything but a villain, and every day that passed without his hearing from or of his niece, instead of inducing him to forget his fears, on the contrary tended more and more to aggravate them. The loss of her cheerful society tended also to depress his spirits; and in order to dispel the gloom,
which often crept upon his mind after his daily occupations were over, he was wont[2] frequently to ask Schalken to accompany him home, and share his otherwise solitary supper[3].

ᴇᴏ

One evening, the painter and his pupil were sitting by the fire, having accomplished a comfortable meal, and had yielded to the silent and delicious melancholy of digestion, when their ruminations[4] were

---

[1] Money once more features in Vanderhausen's encounters with people
[2] Had a tendency
[3] Rose left a considerable gap in Dou's life, a gap that was interpersonal, not material or financial; her absence created a vacuum that allowed loneliness and isolation to flood his formerly apathetic life, and even Schalcken's company is a mere distraction from incurable alienation. Le Fanu, despite his cynicism, recognizes the importance of human relationships and sincere affection
[4] Deep thoughts, ponderings

394

disturbed by a loud sound at the street door, as if occasioned by some person rushing and scrambling vehemently against it. A domestic[1] had run without delay to ascertain the cause of the disturbance, and they heard him twice or thrice interrogate the applicant for admission, but without eliciting any other answer but a sustained reiteration of the sounds. They heard him then open the hall-door, and immediately there followed a light and rapid tread on the staircase. Schalken advanced towards the door. It opened before he reached it, and Rose rushed into the room. She looked wild, fierce and haggard with terror and exhaustion, but her dress surprised them as much as even her unexpected appearance. It consisted of a kind of white woollen wrapper[2], made close about the neck, and descending to the very ground. It was much deranged and travel-soiled. The poor creature had hardly entered the chamber when she fell senseless on the floor. With some difficulty they succeeded in reviving her, and on recovering her senses, she instantly exclaimed, in a tone of terror rather than mere impatience:

"Wine! wine! quickly, or I'm lost[3]!"

Astonished and almost scared at the strange agitation in which the call was made, they at once administered to her wishes, and she drank some wine with a haste and eagerness which surprised them. She had hardly swallowed it, when she exclaimed, with the same urgency:

"Food, for God's sake, food, at once, or I perish."[4]

---

[1] Servant

[2] A very sinister garment: a plain shift or loose-fitting robe, wrappers were often used as burial garments. The description of this gown which covers her from throat to toe is that of a shroud

[3] Tangible sustenance. Associated with mirth and merry company, wine – so she supposes – will draw her back into the convivial society of humankind and away from her cursed alliance with Vanderhausen, who needs neither drink nor victuals to sustain his body and soul, as he is (as most interpretations of this story assert) a possessed corpse

[4] She continues to plead for material sustenance as if to feed her starved Self. Both body and spirit have been subjected to starvation of their essential elements: the body of nutrition and sustainment, and the spirit of

A considerable fragment of a roast joint was upon the table, and Schalken immediately began to cut some, but he was anticipated[1], for no sooner did she see it than she caught it, a more than mortal image of famine, and with her hands, and even with her teeth, she tore off the flesh, and swallowed it. When the paroxysm[2] of hunger had been a little appeased, she appeared on a sudden overcome with shame, or it may have been that other more agitating thoughts overpowered and scared her, for she began to weep bitterly and to wring her hands.

"Oh, send for a minister of God[3]," said she; "I am not safe till he comes; send for him speedily."

Gerard Douw despatched a messenger instantly, and prevailed on his niece to allow him to surrender his bed chamber to her use. He also persuaded her to retire to it at once to rest; her consent was extorted upon the condition that they would not leave her for a moment[4].

"Oh that the holy man were here," she said; "he can deliver me: the dead and the living can never be one: God has forbidden it[5]."
With these mysterious words she surrendered herself to their guidance, and they proceeded to the chamber which Gerard Douw had assigned to her use.

"Do not, do not leave me for a moment," said she; "I am lost for

---

society and fellowship, for – as she suggests – there can be no sanctioned fellowship between the dead and the living
[1] Intercepted, "beat to the chase"
[2] Violent outburst or fit
[3] The body – the vessel of the spirit which unites it in fellowship to the living – has been ministered to with meat and drink, but now she turns to her starved soul and pleads for sustenance in that respect, too: a minister who can hear her confessions and advise her in what course to take
[4] She craves fellowship and society, yes, but her desire for company is more than the yearning of an long-isolated soul, it is a means of sustaining her tenuous grip on the world of the living: to be in company is to be among the alive, to be alone is to be vulnerable to the dead
[5] Recalling the epigraph from Job (which warns against the terrors of uniting the natural with the supernatural), she mourns that she has entered into a holy marriage with an unsuitable mate – a member of the dead

ever if you do."

Gerard Douw's chamber was approached through a spacious apartment, which they were now about to enter. He and Schalken each carried a candle, so that a sufficiency of light was cast upon all surrounding objects[1]. They were now entering the large chamber, which as I have said, communicated with Douw's apartment, when Rose suddenly stopped, and, in a whisper which thrilled them both with horror, she said:

"Oh, God! He is here! He is here! See, see! There he goes!"

She pointed towards the door of the inner room, and Schalken thought he saw a shadowy and ill-defined form gliding into that apartment. He drew his sword[2], and, raising the candle so as to throw its light with increased distinctness upon the objects in the room, he entered the chamber into which the shadow had glided. No figure was there—nothing but the furniture which belonged to the room, and yet he could not be deceived as to the fact that something had moved before them into the chamber. A sickening dread came upon him, and the cold perspiration broke out in heavy drops upon his forehead; nor was he more composed, when he heard the increased urgency and agony of entreaty, with which Rose implored them not to leave her for a moment.

"I saw him," said she; "he's here. I cannot be deceived; I know him; he's by me; he is with me; he's in the room. Then, for God's sake, as you would save me, do not stir from beside me." They at length prevailed upon her to lie down upon the bed, where she continued to urge them to stay by her. She frequently uttered incoherent sentences, repeating, again and again, "*the dead and the living cannot be one: God has forbidden it.*" And then again, "*Rest to the wakeful—sleep to the sleep-walkers*[3]." These and such mysterious and broken sentences, she continued to utter until the

---

[1] Another Schalcken-esque scene. Additionally, the introduction of light is meant to signify the warmth, clarity, security, and truth (that is, the truth of Rose's mortal nature) that the two men provide her with their company and ministry

[2] He has, by now, earned a reputation: only gentlemen carried swords, and an established and respected painter could meet this description

[3] To those who wake from the sleep of death; to those who – most sinister of all – rise, walk, and act after falling into the sleep of death

clergyman arrived. Gerard Douw began to fear, naturally enough, that terror or ill-treatment, had unsettled the poor girl's intellect, and he half suspected, by the suddenness of her appearance, the unseasonableness of the hour, and above all, from the wildness and terror of her manner, that she had made her escape from some place of confinement for lunatics, and was in imminent fear of pursuit. He resolved to summon medical advice as soon as the mind of his niece had been in some measure set at rest by the offices of the clergyman whose attendance she had so earnestly desired; and until this object had been attained, he did not venture to put any questions to her, which might possibly, by reviving painful or horrible recollections, increase her agitation. The clergyman soon arrived—a man of ascetic countenance[1] and venerable age—one whom Gerard Douw respected very much, forasmuch as he was a veteran polemic[2], though one perhaps more dreaded as a combatant than beloved as a Christian[3]—of pure morality, subtle brain, and frozen heart. He entered the chamber which communicated with that in which Rose reclined and immediately on his arrival, she requested him to pray for her, as for one who lay in the hands of Satan, and who could hope for deliverance only from heaven.

That you may distinctly understand all the circumstances of the event which I am going to describe, it is necessary to state the relative position of the parties who were engaged in it. The old clergyman and Schalken were in the anteroom of which I have already spoken; Rose lay in the inner chamber, the door of which was open; and by the side of the bed, at her urgent desire, stood her guardian; a candle burned in the bedchamber, and three were lighted in the outer apartment. The old man now cleared his voice as if about to commence, but before he had time to begin, a sudden gust of air blew out the candle which served to illuminate the room in which the poor girl lay, and she, with hurried alarm, exclaimed:

---

[1] With a serious, pleasureless face

[2] Vicious debater; one prone to argument. Presumably, this man is a debater in theological matters, and therefore a tremendously pious – if not benevolently Christian – man

[3] Like Vanderhausen, he is respected more for what he can demonstrate to be (rich man : clergyman) than what his character is (evil man : brutal man)

"Godfrey, bring in another candle; the darkness is unsafe[1]."
Gerard Douw forgetting for the moment her repeated injunctions, in the immediate impulse, stepped from the bedchamber into the other, in order to supply what she desired.

"Oh God! do not go, dear uncle," shrieked the unhappy girl—and at the same time she sprung from the bed, and darted after him, in order, by her grasp, to detain him. But the warning came too late, for scarcely had he passed the threshold, and hardly had his niece had time to utter the startling exclamation, when the door which divided the two rooms closed violently after him, as if swung by a strong blast of wind. Schalken and he both rushed to the door, but their united and desperate efforts could not avail so much as to shake it. Shriek after shriek burst from the inner chamber, with all the piercing loudness of despairing terror. Schalken and Douw applied every nerve to force open the door; but all in vain. There was no sound of struggling from within, but the screams seemed to increase in loudness, and at the same time they heard the bolts of the latticed window withdrawn, and the window itself grated upon the sill as if thrown open. One *last* shriek, so long and piercing and agonized as to be scarcely human, swelled from the room, and suddenly there followed a death-like silence. A light step was heard crossing the floor, as if from the bed to the window; and almost at the same instant the door gave way, and, yielding to the pressure of the external applicants, nearly precipitated them into the room. It was empty. The window was open, and Schalken sprung to a chair and gazed out upon the street and canal below. He saw no form, but he saw, or thought he saw, the waters of the broad canal beneath settling ring after ring in heavy circles, as if a moment before disturbed by the submission of some ponderous body[2].

---

[1] It is in darkness – in the absence of emotional warmth, intellectual insight, and spiritual vision – that our spirits become vulnerable to existential assault and psychological terror

[2] Water can symbolize resurrection and purification... if a character emerges from it. Without emerging, Rose has symbolically been dragged to a world of death and damnation

~~~
ℭ
~~~

No trace of Rose was ever after found, nor was anything certain respecting her mysterious wooer discovered or even suspected—no clue whereby to trace the intricacies of the labyrinth and to arrive at its solution, presented itself. But an incident occurred, which, though it will not be received by our rational readers in lieu[1] of evidence, produced nevertheless a strong and a lasting impression upon the mind of Schalken. Many years after the events which we have detailed, Schalken, then residing far away[2] received an intimation of his father's death, and of his intended burial upon a fixed day in the church of Rotterdam. It was necessary that a very considerable journey should be performed by the funeral procession, which as it will be readily believed, was not very numerously attended. Schalken with difficulty arrived in Rotterdam late in the day upon which the funeral was appointed to take place. It had not then arrived. Evening closed in, and still it did not appear.

Schalken strolled down to the church; he found it open; notice of the arrival of the funeral had been given, and the vault in which the body was to be laid had been opened. The sexton[3], on seeing a well-dressed gentleman, whose object was to attend the expected obsequies, pacing the aisle of the church, hospitably invited him to share with him the comforts of a blazing fire, which, as was his custom in winter time upon such occasions, he had kindled in the hearth of a chamber in which he was accustomed to await the arrival of such grisly guests and which communicated, by a flight of steps, with the vault below. In this chamber, Schalken and his entertainer seated themselves; and the sexton, after some fruitless attempts to engage his guest in conversation, was obliged to apply himself to his

---

[1] In the place of

[2] In England, during the 1690s. At the time, Great Britain was the shared kingdom of King William and Queen. William was a Dutchman, and during his tenure on the throne, Dutch influence and culture cross-pollinated with that of England

[3] The janitor and caretaker of the church, its properties, and its graveyard

tobacco-pipe and can[1], to solace his solitude. In spite of his grief and cares, the fatigues of a rapid journey of nearly forty hours gradually overcame the mind and body of Godfrey Schalken, and he sank into a deep sleep, from which he awakened by someone's shaking him gently by the shoulder. He first thought that the old sexton had called him, but *he* was no longer in the room. He roused himself, and as soon as he could clearly see what was around him, he perceived a female form, clothed in a kind of light robe of white, part of which was so disposed as to form a veil, and in her hand she carried a lamp. She was moving rather away from him, in the direction of the flight of steps which conducted towards the vaults. Schalken felt a vague alarm at the sight of this figure and at the same time an irresistible impulse to follow its guidance. He followed it towards the vaults[2], but when it reached the head of the stairs, he paused; the figure paused also, and, turning gently round, displayed, by the light of the lamp it carried, the face and features of his first love, Rose Velderkaust. There was nothing horrible, or even sad, in the countenance. On the contrary, it wore the same arch smile[3] which used to enchant the artist long before in his happy days. A feeling of awe and interest, too intense to be resisted, prompted him to follow the spectre, if spectre it were. She descended the stairs—he followed—and turning to the left, through a narrow passage, she led him, to his infinite surprise, into what appeared to be an old-fashioned Dutch apartment, such as the pictures of Gerard Douw have served to immortalize. Abundance

---

[1] The Dutch were notorious pipe smokers; their long-stemmed, white, clay pipes became iconic

[2] These subterranean caverns were filled with the bones of the dead. Graveyards could only hold so many dead – especially in Europe's crowded urban centers – and every several hundred years, the old graves were exhumed, the long-forgotten bodies collected, and their ragged bones stacked in vaults beneath the church (still on holy ground)

[3] There is something truly awful about this playful and yet sinister facial expression. Coquettish, flirtatious, and even sexually suggestive in life, the twisted smile takes on a unnerving, even sinister mantle when creasing the face of this so obviously "spectr[al]" vision. She appears to be up to some sort of mischief – arranging a kittenish prank or a teasing trick

of costly antique furniture was disposed about the room, and in one corner stood a four-post bed, with heavy black cloth curtains around it; the figure frequently turned towards him with the same arch smile[1]; and when she came to the side of the bed, she drew the curtains, and, by the light of the lamp, which she held towards its contents, she disclosed to the horror-stricken painter, sitting bolt upright in the bed[2], the livid[3] and demoniac form of Vanderhausen. Schalken had hardly seen him, when he fell senseless upon the floor, where he lay until discovered, on the next morning, by persons employed in closing the passages into the vaults. He was lying in a cell of considerable size, which had not been disturbed for a long time, and he had fallen beside a large coffin, which was supported upon small pillars, a security against the attacks of vermin.[4]

To his dying day Schalken was satisfied of the reality of the vision which he had witnessed, and he has left behind him a curious evidence

---

[1] It is almost as though she is checking to make sure Schalcken is paying attention; she wants to be sure to witness his reaction to her little "trick"

[2] The imagery – especially for the 1830s, when the first version of "Schalken" appeared – is horrifically erotic. The readership understands what married persons do in bed, and without being too graphic, Le Fanu – famous for his subtle and unnerving employment of sexuality in horror – aggressively implies that the corpse has been (to use the only term appropriate to the gravity of the situation) molesting Rose in their macabre bedchamber. This is a sexual relationship, and sexuality – in the culture of Victorian Britain – was seen as an act of spiritual unification: to make love was to become one spirit, and when one makes love to a possessed corpse, one becomes part and parcel of a spirit that one may loathe and revile. In the 1979 film adaptation, *Schalcken the Painter*, the eroticism is explicitly depicted: Rose, upon unveiling the bedded Vanderhausen, pulls her wrapper over her head, exposing herself, climbs on top of a clearly naked Vanderhausen, and begins vigorously humping the unblinking cadaver

[3] Blackened, bluish-gray – the color of a decomposing corpse

[4] We may safely imagine that this is the coffin of a corpse which became Vanderhausen; whether the dead body was "Vanderhausen" or whether it was repurposed by a demon which called itself "Vanderhausen" remains unclear

of the impression which it wrought upon his fancy, in a painting executed shortly after the event I have narrated, and which is valuable as exhibiting not only the peculiarities which have made Schalken's pictures sought after, but even more so as presenting a portrait of his early love, Rose Velderkaust, whose mysterious fate must always remain matter of speculation.

---

*ROSE, like many of Le Fanu's fictional victims, is swept up by merciless forces that leech on the unsuspecting and torment the innocent. Vanderhausen – whom we may reasonably take for a reanimated corpse: either a lustful ghost or a convenient vessel for a prowling albeit incorporeal demon – represents more than a simple supernatural intruder: he is the embodiment of human want and insensitivity, a rapacious, consuming dominator whose obvious corruption and sinister mystique can be excused on account of his wealth. Virtue, Le Fanu suggests, has often been prostituted for the sake of material gain, and purity has been bartered without the guidance of conscience or love, even when the seller is an overall loving and compassionate person. Douw cared deeply for Rose – he was not an archetypal callous guardian, fixated on wealth and devoid of humanity – and that makes his bargain all the more loathsome and disturbing, and the moral message all the more ambiguous. Power can excuse wickedness and wealth can cause the most intangible and spiritual elements of our lives – love, purity, family – to become material commodities. Rose is objectified by Vanderhausen's offer, and is whored out without inquiry or objection. Le Fanu's atmospheric prose frequently mulls over clashing juxtapositions – wealth and poverty, virtue and vice, the sanctity of a church and the carnality of wedding bed – and it is ultimately Rose's marriage to Vanderhausen (between purity and corruption, life and death) that dominates the reader's memory. This binding ownership of goodness by evil, a paradox of love, is permitted by materialism and the confident respect which we often assign to wealth. Society's worship of power and wealth can lead us to stifle the objections of instinct and conscience, until our true treasures – character, truth, and virtue – are irrecoverably lost. Le Fanu leaves us with a candlelit phantom fading into shadow, and its disquietingly twisted smile – erotic and macabre, alluring and menacing – before the scene blackens and we are left in darkness.*

# About the Editor and Illustrator

Michael Grant Kellermeyer -- OTP's founder and chief editor -- is an English professor, bibliographer, illustrator, editor, critic, and author based in Fort Wayne, Indiana. He earned his Bachelor of Arts in English from Anderson University and his Master of Arts in Literature from Ball State University. He teaches college writing in Indiana where he enjoys playing violin, painting, hiking, and cooking.

Ever since watching Bing Crosby's *The Legend of Sleepy Hollow* as a three year old, Michael has been enraptured by the ghastly, ghoulish, and the unknown. Reading Great Illustrated Classics' abridged versions of classic horrors as a first grader, he quickly became enthralled with the horrific, and began accumulating a collection of unabridged classics; *Edgar Allan Poe's Forgotten Tales* and a copy of *The Legend of Sleepy Hollow* with an introduction by Charles L. Grant are among his most cherished  possessions. Frequenting the occult section of the Berne Public Library, he scoured through anthologies and compendiums on ghostly lore.

It was here that he found two books which would be more influential to his tastes than any other: Henry Mazzeo's *Hauntings* (illustrated by the unparalleled Edward Gorey), and Barry Moser's *Great Ghost Stories*. It was while reading through these two collections during the Hallowe'en season of 2012 that Michael was inspired to honor the writers, tales, and mythologies he revered the most.

Oldstyle Tales Press was the result of that impulse. Its first title, *The Best Victorian Ghost Stories*, was published in September 2013, followed shortly by editions of *Frankenstein* and *The Annotated and Illustrated Edgar Allan Poe*.

In his free time, Michael enjoys straight razors, briarwood pipes, Classical music, jazz standards from the '20s to '60s, sea shanties, lemon wedges in his water, the films of Vincent Price, Alfred Hitchcock, and Stanley Kubrick, sandalwood shaving cream, freshly-laundered sheets, gin tonics, and mint tea.

Made in United States
North Haven, CT
21 May 2023

36823697R00222